Black Feathers

Black Feathers

DARK AVIAN TALES:
AN ANTHOLOGY

EDITED BY
ELLEN DATLOW

PEGASUS CRIME

NEW YORK LONDON

BLACK FEATHERS

Pegasus Books Ltd.
148 W 37th Street, 13th Floor
New York, NY 10018

First Pegasus Books cloth edition February 2017

Interior design by Maria Fernandez

Library of Congress Cataloging-in-Publication Data is available.

ISBN: 978-1-68177-321-6

10 9 8 7 6 5 4 3 2 1

Printed in the United States of America
Distributed by W. W. Norton & Company

To Frankie and Johnny

Contents

Introduction

ELLEN DATLOW

Birds are usually loved for their beauty and their song. They symbolize freedom, eternal life, the soul. Owls denote wisdom. Blackbirds are good omens. Bluebirds can bring happiness. Crows are otherworldly and can be symbolic of ancestral souls. The dove symbolizes peace, purity, innocence. The pigeon (although a cousin to the dove) is given a bad rap. The hawk and falcon are hunters of weaker birds.

There's definitely a dark side to the avian, which is not surprising considering that they're currently believed to have evolved from dinosaurs. Birds of prey sometimes kill other birds (the shrike), destroy other birds' eggs (blue jays), and even have been known to kill small animals (the kea sometimes eats live lambs). And who isn't disgusted by birds that eat the dead—vultures awaiting their next meal as the lifeblood flows from the dying. One of our greatest fears is of being eaten by vultures before we're quite dead.

Is it any wonder that with so many interpretations of the avian, the contributors herein are eager to be transformed or influenced by them? Included in *Black Feathers* are those obsessed with birds of one type or another. Do they want to become birds or just take on some of the "power" of birds? The presence or absence of birds portends the future. A grieving widow takes comfort in her majestic winged neighbors, who enable her to cope with a predatory relative. An isolated society of women relies on a bird to tell their fortunes. A silent young girl and her pet bird might be the only hope a detective has of tracking down a serial killer in a tourist town. A chatty parrot makes illegal deals with the dying. A troubled man lives in isolation with only one friend for company—a jackdaw.

In each of these fictions, you will encounter the dark resonance between the human and the avian. You see in yourself the savagery of a predator, the shrewd stalking of a hunter, and you are lured by birds that speak human language, that make beautiful music, that cypher numbers, and that seem to have a moral center. You wade into this feathered nightmare and brave the horror of death, trading your safety and sanity for that which we all seek—the promise of flight.

O Terrible Bird

SANDRA KASTURI

Pass not beneath, O Caravan, or pass not singing. Have
  you heard
That silence where the birds are dead yet something
  pipeth like a bird?

—James Elroy Flecker,
"Gates of Damascus"

Have we met before, O Terrible Bird?
You, the child of a thousand pecks,
descendant of lizards, your wings
a flash of destruction against the sun.

I know you—your soul of black
feathers, each a caress of the razor.
The curve of your beak rending
the livers of poets and gods.

Tell me, O Terrible Bird,
when you and your brethren
swooped down in a thundercloud—
was it you that took them?

I imagine the dark *V*'s of your shadows
sailing over the grass, sailing
over my children's faces
as they looked up to squint at you.

Was it you? Are they limp in your claws?
Or worse: nestled smiling under
your terrible down, their small faces
tucked contented into your thieving breast?

O Terrible Bird! I heard the silence,
that stillness before the dark rush
from that sunny, traitorous sky,
heard the stifled cries. I heard.

I saw the deserted lawn, saw
that one small slipper still rolling
in the grass where it had fallen
from your awful clutch.

But you have mistaken me, O Bird.
Can you not hear? I am the silence
and the piping and I am coming.
And it is I—I who am terrible.

The Obscure Bird

NICHOLAS ROYLE

The obscure bird clamour'd the live-long night.
—William Shakespeare, *Macbeth*

It was late. Gwen spent ten minutes helping Andrew tidy up the kitchen and then put her arms out for a hug and said she was going up to bed.

"I won't be long," Andrew said as he released her with a kiss.

Gwen smiled.

"Of course not," she said.

It was a ritual. She knew it would be at least an hour, probably two, maybe more, before he joined her.

Outside, an owl hooted.

Andrew's eyes were dark behind the round lenses of his glasses, unfathomable.

He turned to the sink as she walked towards the door to the hall, where she stopped and looked back at him. With his hands resting on the edge of the basin he appeared to be staring out of the window into the garden, which was cloaked in darkness. She watched him for a moment before turning to go.

Gwen lay in bed thinking about Andrew, worrying. She remembered one night earlier in the week when she had got up to go to the bathroom. Andrew's side of the bed had been empty, cold. She had presumed him to be in his study, or downstairs, but when she had chanced to look out the bathroom window she had seen him standing in the middle of the lawn, his pale, round face upturned, staring at the mature trees at the end of the garden. As she lay in bed she remembered thinking that the right thing to do would be to go down and speak to him, perhaps gently guide him back into the house as you would a sleepwalker, but she had done neither. She had returned to bed instead and fallen back to sleep. When Gwen had woken in the morning, Andrew had been beside her as normal.

She heard him climbing the stairs and reached for the switch to turn off her bedside light. Lying in the darkness, she heard his carefully weighted footsteps approach their bedroom door, stop for a moment and then continue past. She heard him stop outside the baby's room, where he would be listening for the sound of Henry's breathing, and then continue on down the landing to his own study at the rear of the house. She heard the door click shut and imagined him sitting at his desk, raising the lid of the laptop and then staring alternately at the screen and out of the window. She had stood at his open door one night, watching him divert his attention from one to the other and back again, until he had caught sight of her reflection in the window and spun around on his chair, blushing. She had allowed her eyes to drop to his computer screen, but instead of the lurid insult of pornography she had seen nothing more unsavoury than the boxy iconography common to social networking sites.

"You know, you really should get more sleep," Gwen murmured in the morning as Andrew brought her a cup of tea.

"I know, but . . . you know," he said.

"What?"

"The professorship thing. I might not get it anyway, but I certainly won't if I don't get these papers done."

"Mmm."

In the bathroom, Duffy the cat lay on her back on the bath mat. Legs extended at either end of her glossy black body, she looked like a giant skate egg case. Gwen tickled her tummy and Duffy's head darted forward to nibble at her wrist.

Gwen checked in the baby's room and then went downstairs. A floorboard creaked as she entered the kitchen. Andrew had paused in the act of emptying the dishwasher and was staring out of the window at the garden. She went up behind him and threaded her arms under his and held him tightly around the chest, resting her chin on his shoulder.

"There's nothing we can do," Gwen said.

Andrew's head swivelled around on his neck.

"About Henry," she said, pulling back.

"Oh," he said. "No. I know."

They disengaged and Gwen watched Andrew's back as he continued to empty the dishwasher. His shoulders were tense, hunched up. When he had finished, he closed the door of the machine with a quiet snap.

"It's all going to go, you know. All that," he said, looking out of the window again. "Not our trees, obviously, but everything beyond, in the old railway cutting."

He turned to look at her. She didn't know what to say.

"I mean, I know it's a good thing," he continued, "extending the tram system, or at least I thought it would be, but now I'm not so sure. Not now that I think of the ecological cost. All those trees. Countless nesting sites."

She looked at him without speaking for a moment before saying, "I've got to go to work."

At the hospital, Gwen sat in the canteen with Angela.

"How's Henry?" asked Angela.

"We won't know for a while," Gwen answered. "Thanks for asking."

"Fingers crossed, love."

"Thanks."

"What about Andrew?" she asked.

"He's under pressure at work. Going for a professorship."

"Ooh, professor, eh?"

"Doesn't half make him sound *wise.*" Gwen thought for a moment. "Andrew's changing, though," she said. "Whether in response to Henry or what, I don't know."

"What do you mean?"

Gwen looked at the fine lines fanning out from the corners of Angela's eyes, which deepened as she smiled.

"I saw an exhibit in the Didsbury Arts Festival," Gwen said. "It was in that new food shop on Burton Road. There was a bamboo cage hanging from the ceiling with a tiny little screen in it playing a video of birds filmed in Beijing. Apparently, according to the artist's blurb—Daniel Staincliffe, his name was—old men meet up in the mornings to play chess all over Beijing and they take their songbirds with them in little cages. They hang the cages up in the branches of nearby trees and while the old men play chess the birds sing to one another."

"Aah."

"Yeah, cute, isn't it?" Gwen said. "But it made me think of Andrew. He's like one of those birds stuck in his cage tweeting to other lonely people trapped in their own cages."

"Tweeting?"

"You know, Twitter, Facebook."

"Waste of time."

"I know."

"Something's happening to him. He's changing. We hardly talk any more; we never have sex. I almost wish he'd raid the savings account and buy a sports car or have an affair."

Angela laughed.

Gwen looked at her watch.

"Better get on," she said.

Gwen was standing at the kitchen table checking through the post.

"Anything?" said a voice behind her.

"Christ!" She spun around. "You made me jump. You creep around so bloody quietly these days."

"Sorry."

Duffy joined them in the kitchen.

"She's got something," Andrew said, bending down.

Duffy opened her jaws and dropped a dead mouse on the wooden floor.

"Well done, Duffy," Gwen said. "That's a good girl." She knelt down to tickle her and stroke her.

"You make more of a fuss of the cat than you do of me—*these days*," Andrew said.

Gwen gave him a look and he smiled weakly.

"Sorry," he said.

"What do you want to eat?" she asked him.

"I don't know."

"Well, Duffy knows what she wants, don't you, Duffy?" she said, as if speaking to a baby.

The cat closed her nutcracker jaws around the mouse's head and bit down with a sustained audible crunch. They both watched as Duffy worked on the mouse, tearing at the skin and cracking its tiny bones. After a short while, the remains on the kitchen floor were no longer identifiable. Gwen wondered if Duffy would leave the guts and the legs and the tiny feet, but she swallowed every last shred, the bristly tail slipping down her throat last of all. Gwen realised she was grimacing; she felt a little sick. Previously when Duffy had brought in birds or mice, either Gwen or Andrew had taken them off her and, if they were still alive and not too badly damaged, freed them outside.

Knelt down next to her, Andrew turned his head through ninety degrees to look directly at Gwen. His black eyes were expressionless.

Gwen rose to her feet, knee joints popping. She went to the fridge and got out a plastic container of leftover homemade soup.

"We'll have this," she said, and pressed the button to open the door of the microwave. She gave a small cry and dropped the container of soup. It landed on its corner, dislodging the lid, and most of the soup splashed out on to her stockinged feet and on to the floor, quickly spreading.

"What the fuck is that?" she shouted, pointing inside the microwave.

"Ah, sorry," Andrew answered, grabbing a roll of kitchen paper and a couple of tea towels, and mopping ineffectually at Gwen's feet. "That's an owl pellet."

"What the fuck is an owl pellet and what is it doing in the microwave?" she yelled.

"Owls regurgitate the parts of their prey they can't eat. Bones and fur and stuff. It all comes out in a little bundle, all carefully wrapped up like that. It's called an owl pellet." As he explained, Andrew wiped the floor. He filled a bowl with soapy water and started scrubbing.

"Why is it in the microwave?"

"Oh, because if you want to dissect one you should sterilise it first and the best way to do that is in the microwave. Otherwise the pellet can still be carrying rodent viruses or bacteria."

"Jesus!"

Gwen left the room.

Dinner that night was a strained affair. Afterwards they sat at opposite ends of the sofa watching something on television that neither of them wanted to watch. As soon as it was over, Gwen announced she was going to bed.

"It'll give you a chance to dissect your owl pellet," she said. "Where did you get it, anyway?"

"In the cutting. I climbed over our back wall and had a bit of a look around. It's amazing. It's completely overgrown. There must be so much wildlife there that will all be left homeless when they clear everything for the tram tracks."

"It was a railway line in the first place."

"I know, but that was forty or fifty years ago and an entire ecology has grown up there since, and now that's going to be destroyed, for what? So that we can take the tram to Chorlton? No one's going to use it to go all the way into town. It's a long and roundabout route. It'll take forever and cost a fortune. They should have had the bottle to take it up Wilmslow Road and get rid of all those awful buses."

She looked at him and shrugged her general agreement with his argument.

"I found the owl pellet at the base of one of the trees. There must have been an owl roosting there."

"Right," she said, softening. "See you later. Will you look in on Henry?"

"Yes, of course. Goodnight."

Gwen fell asleep straight away. Some time in the night, she was aware of the duvet being lifted on Andrew's side and cold air wafting over her arm. Then the draught was shut off and she felt the warmth of his body next to hers. As she started to drift back to sleep, she heard him softly speak.

"It's because of the serrations on my remiges."

"What?" she said, confused, half-asleep.

"That's why I move so silently. From room to room."

"Go to sleep, Andrew. Please."

He fell silent.

Gwen woke again and felt anxiety's talons seize her immediately.

Andrew's side of the bed was cold, empty.

She got up and walked on to the landing. The darkness told her it was still night-time. She checked her watch; it was almost three A.M. She opened the door to Henry's room. She saw his blue-and-white-striped BabyGro stretched out in the cot. Andrew was not in the room. The door to Andrew's study was open; he was not inside. Slowly she descended the staircase and turned left at the bottom to stand in the kitchen doorway. Andrew was standing in front of the sink staring out of the window. She took a step forwards and one of the wooden boards creaked. Andrew's head started to turn.

And continued to turn. It turned through ninety degrees and kept turning.

She stood absolutely still, scarcely breathing.

Andrew had not turned his body from the sink, but his gaze was now directed towards the fridge just to her left. Another few seconds and he would have twisted his neck through a hundred and eighty degrees.

Gwen felt the hairs on her arms rise. She backed out of the room and walked quickly but quietly upstairs.

She lay in bed and did not hear any movement from downstairs. At some point she fell asleep.

In the morning, making the bed, she found a feather on the bottom sheet. She inspected the pillows and plumped them up.

Andrew was in the kitchen. They tiptoed around each other.

At work, Gwen logged out of the hospital intranet and on to the Internet. She looked up "remiges," trying various spellings until she found the right one.

"Tiny serrations on the leading edge of their remiges help owls to fly silently," she read.

She decided they needed to talk.

When Gwen arrived home, the kitchen was in darkness, but the light at the top of the stairs was on. She hung up her coat and stowed her bag. She wondered about making a drink and waiting in the kitchen. At some point, he would have to come down. And she would ask him to explain himself.

Instead, she found herself walking up the stairs. She was halfway up when she heard him cough. He coughed again, abnormally, as if he was trying to clear his throat. Then there was a series of choking sounds. Her brother had once choked on a piece of meat when they were small, and their mother had saved him by performing the Heimlich manoeuvre, sending a scrap of roast beef shooting out of his mouth, but it had been the choking sound that had stayed with Gwen. She was hearing it again now, a desperate, almost metallic squawking, mechanical and animalistic at the same time. She ran up the remaining stairs and stopped on the landing.

Andrew was standing in the middle of the bathroom, bent over at the waist. There was a small, indistinct bundle on the floor in front of him and a string of drool hanging from his mouth. The bundle—the pellet—was rounded, tapered at one end and bristly with hair. Under the brightness of the bathroom light, the whiteness of bone gleamed.

She turned away. On the floor outside the baby's room at the other end of the landing she saw something she thought she recognised. She took a step towards it.

Even in the half-light she could make out the blue and white stripes.

The Mathematical Inevitability of Corvids

SEANAN McGUIRE

Morning means chaos at the birdbath, the beating of wings and the opening of beaks, threat displays and warnings. The early bird may get the worm in someone else's garden, but here, it's the early bird that gets the best shot at the water. I put the food out when I finish my own morning tasks, and that includes counting out the birds at the bath, making sure everything is properly weighted for the day to come. The birds know that. They don't check the feeder before the door opens anymore, or sit outside my window and scream. We've come to an agreement, them and me.

The big Steller's jay is in the middle of the bath again, throwing water over his feathers and fluffing them out like he thinks he's impressing someone. I dutifully note him down. The count always begins from the center out, and today he's the first bird, the sorrow bird, the bird that brings down the sky. My chest is tight when I look at the bath again—a tightness that fades as I spot the two northwestern crows behind him, grooming each other with careful strokes of their beaks. The joy bird and the girl bird, in one swoop. *Joy, girl, joy*, whispers the voice of my grandmother, who taught me the crow-count when I was little and lost and needed something to hold on to.

One's for sorrow, two's for joy, three's a girl, and there's four, for a boy: the little black-billed magpie who's been coming around, shy as anything, holding back when the others mob the feeder. She's getting enough to eat, but she's not going to find a mate if she stays around here. We don't have many black-billed magpies in this area. She's the first I've seen in years. She's the only one that's stayed. And then there are three. My little murder, sitting on the rim of the bath and watching the window with clever crow-eyes, waiting for me to move away from my binoculars. They'll be at the feeder by the time I open the front door, ready for their due.

I note them down, one after the other. Five's for silver. Six for gold. Seven's for a secret, never to be told.

I am very good with secrets.

There are other birds at the birdbath, little brown hopping things with inquisitive voices and skinny orange feet that never move separately but always together, like the birds themselves are spring-loaded. None of them matter for my count. Perhaps somewhere there is someone who keeps their time by sparrows, or marks the passage of the starlings, but that is not me. That is not my job. I put my binoculars aside, slip my notebook into the pocket of my coat, and rise.

It is time to feed the birds.

My name is Brenda. It means "raven." I did not choose it for myself. My mother says it was the name of my great-grandmother, who died before I was born. I would ask my grandmother, who one assumes would remember her own mother, but my grandmother died as well, three years ago, after a week where I never counted more than a single corvid in a single day. *Sorrow, sorrow, sorrow*, said the birds, and sorrow was what I got: sorrow, and a long polished box, and shoes that pinched, and a mother who cried for days before she dried her eyes and started looking at me critically, quizzically, like somehow my strangeness had been invisible before my grandmother had to go.

My name is Brenda. I am fifteen years old. I learned to count when I was two, marking things off on my fingers, looking for the answers. If I counted one of something, it was mine: one crib, one bear, one mommy, who still stroked my hair and smoothed my brow and called me her beautiful girl back then, before things got complicated. I learned to count higher numbers when I was four, when my mother came home from the hospital with a small, red-faced thing that squawked and squalled and smelled of sour milk and talcum powder. His name was David. His name is still David now, eleven years later, and he still lives with us, although he doesn't smell of sour milk as often anymore. His father still lives with us too, tall and cold and unforgiving toward me, cuckoo child hatched from another man's egg but still living in his nest.

I do not count cuckoos. Cuckoos are not part of my numbers. I think cuckoos could be counted with owls, maybe, measured in those columns, but I do not know the rhyme, and I am happy with my corvids—my ravens and crows and jays. They know me and I know them, and I no longer need the bird books that sit in stacks around my bed to pick their familiar profiles out of the throng. There are crows I've never seen before, Jamaican and palm and Cuban, here in North America, and a hundred more scattered around the world, in Australia and Asia and Europe, but here, all the corvids are familiar. They are known. They can be counted. I would be a fool to change my numbers now, when I am fifteen, when I am so close to understanding their equations.

"Brenda!" Mother's voice is thin as she calls me from the kitchen window. I have been on the porch too long, watching my birds attack their breakfast of dry dog food and chopped-up eggs, waiting to see if any more will appear. I would like to count eight before my day moves on, or better still, ten. I would like to be secure.

I turn. "Yes?"

"School," she says wearily. "You need to come in and eat something before the bus gets here."

"Yes, Mother," I agree. If eight comes, I will not see it, nor nine. Some numbers are invisible, seen only in retrospect, when the day does not align with my count. Those days are the bad ones. Those days are the ones where I have to sit in my bed for hours, matching numbers to likely birds, tracing migration routes, apologizing, apologizing, always apologizing for getting the math wrong.

The day my grandmother died, my count said "joy," but when I got home, it was sorrow waiting on the phone, sorrow waiting in the deep lines of my mother's face. One's for sorrow, yes, but eight's for Heaven. If I had counted that high, I would have known that my grandmother was at peace. Nine's for Hell. If I had counted *that*, I would have scoured the whole city, if that was what it took, to bring the count higher, to find her a better ending. Ten's for the Devil. I don't believe in him, not really. Eleven's for penance. Twelve's for sin.

There are as many numbers as there are corvids, and someday I will catalog them all, and then nothing will ever slip by me again.

Mother is watching me with loving exasperation on her face. She never looks at David like that. He is only eleven, but he is already the good child, the normal child, the child who concerns himself with things that she can understand and does not focus on things she can't. David understands me better than she does, I think, because he's never lived in a world where I was expected to be normal; he's only ever lived in a world where I was his beloved older sister, strange as an out-of-season Steller's jay. I count on my crows. He counts on me.

Today, I will tell him the corvids have said a secret, and he will smile his small and shining smile, and we will be happy together, he and I.

I sit at the table and eat my cereal. David sits across from me. He enjoys Lucky Charms, the welter of shapes and colors and flavors pleasing to his tongue. I can't abide the idea of so many unlike things touching inside my mouth. When I have Lucky Charms, I have to separate all the pieces out, one from another, putting them into different bowls before I can eat them. That makes it a bad cereal for me on school days. I would be late, if I had Lucky Charms. I have Frosted Flakes. Sometimes they can be different sizes. I don't like that. I eat them anyway. I have to make an effort to accommodate the rest of the world, even as the rest of the world is making an effort to accommodate me.

"Eat up," says David's father. His name is Carl. He is looking at me. I try to hunch my shoulders, to pretend that I don't see, but it's too late; he knows I can hear him. "I'm dropping you off, and I'm not going to be late because of you."

He never wants to be anything because of me. Didn't want to be a father because of me; waited until he had a child of his own to marry my mother. Didn't want to go to family counseling because of me, even when my therapist said that it would help us all, even when my mother begged him. No matter how you sliced it, I wasn't his fault, he argued, and argues, and will always argue, even when the sky goes black with crows: I am the way I am because the genes I got from my father and the genes I got from my mother counted themselves out and decided on a girl who saw patterns everywhere, who saw the sky falling when they weren't followed exactly as they ought to be. I am not his fault at all.

This may be the only area where Carl and I have ever agreed. I am not his fault. I am nothing of his. David is his, by half, and I think, sometimes, that all that is good in Carl went into the making of my brother, who is the best thing in the world, and the only thing I do not need to count. He is a constant. There is gravity, and there is oxygen, and there is David.

We finish our cereal. We climb into Carl's car, me in the back, David in the front, where he can shyly answer his father's questions about homework and sports and girls—all the things Carl has already decided will be important to his son. I say nothing, even though I know that David would rather talk about art class, and the way sunlight slants through flower petals, and the boy who sits next to him in band, the one who plays the cello with his quick and clever fingers. I keep my eyes on the window all the way to school, watching for the flash of familiar wings against the charcoal sky.

I count two more corvids before we reach the parking lot. Nine's for Hell.

This will not be a good day.

I am a genius, according to the people who take and review the tests, measuring minds in columns of numbers and vocabulary words. I am in the top 2 percent nationally, not just for my age range, but for high school students as a whole. Sometimes I wish they had drawn a different conclusion from my scores. With my intelligence, they argue, mainstreaming is not only the appropriate course of action, it is the only course of action. Our Special Education program is underfunded and understaffed, and its resources are better spent on those who truly need them, while those like me, who can keep up with the classwork and excel at the material, are pushed out into the "real world" to fend for ourselves.

My mother attempted to contest the mainstreaming once, citing my absence seizures and my tendency to see catastrophe in the movement of the air as reasons that I needed more support. Carl put a stop to her objections. "She's going to have to deal with the real world in three years," he'd said, voice cold as ever. "She can't stay here after she turns eighteen. I'm not going to be a nursemaid to your little mistake for my entire life."

When Carl speaks, my mother stops. That is how it has been for as long as he's been a part of our lives, for as long as David can remember, for there has never been a time when there was David and no Carl. They are part of the same equation, one for sorrow and two for joy, and to have the one I must accept the other. I would prefer David with no Carl, but as that is not, is not, is not to be, I am willing to have what I have. And what I have is classes with peers who will never belong to me, for their math is too different from my own.

Some of them are kind to me. Some of them are cruel. The lines do not follow the patterns that the television tells me they should; the math does not align. The ones in fancy clothes and letter jackets, with makeup done just so and eyes rimed in colors bright as birds, they are usually gentle; they remember my name, ask me about my birds, and do not mock me. The ones with tattered paperbacks in their hands and mockery ringing in their own ears, who have been kicked often enough to yearn to do the kicking, they are all too often cold; I am a target that cannot turn on them, I am vulnerable, I am a bird without a flock to come to my defense.

I sit quiet. I do my work, when I can, and I sit and stare silent at my desk when I can't, my fingers tapping out the memory of birds against the wood. One for sorrow, two for joy, three's a girl, four's a boy. This is a nine-bird day, and I am on edge from the beginning. Something is going to happen.

Midway through first period, I cannot take it anymore. I put up my hand. I wait. The teacher ignores me as long as she can, but eventually, she must acknowledge my palm, pale and starfish-patient as I turn it toward the ceiling. She sighs, looking to me, and asks, "Yes, Brenda?"

"I need to go outside," I say. "I need to go out into the field."

Her exasperation grows. She likes my mainstreaming less than my mother does; to her, I am a trial, sent to test her, when she already has too many students to keep track of. I would apologize, if I could, but when I have tried, she has never understood what I was struggling to say. Sometimes I think I should bring David to class and have him translate me for her. He always knows what I am trying to say. "Why do you need to go outside, Brenda?"

"I counted nine corvids this morning. The math is bad. Nine means something will happen. I don't want anything to happen. Please, can I go outside? I need to find more birds. I need to raise the count."

For a moment, my teacher looks like she wants to put down her head and cry. I am more complex than she is paid to handle. She has the certifications, and she knew when she took the job that she might be teaching mainstreamed students. She did not expect me, did not expect obsessions and compulsions and the never-ending mathematics of a complicated, shifting sky. I am more trouble than I am worth.

She looks around the class. The other students are watching her, some with patience, others with irritation. None of them look as if they will object to her releasing me.

"You may be excused, Brenda," she says finally. "Please come back quickly."

"Yes, thank you, I will," I say, and stand, and leave the classroom without look back. None of these people are birds. None of them are here to be counted.

(I have seen people who should be counted, ravens in human skins, crows with girl-faces who peek, shy and silent, from beneath the fringes of their blackened bangs. My psychiatrist says that these delusions are secretly good things, are proof that my mind is trying to translate what it needs and knows into what the world around me requires. When I can cast all people as birds in human guise, can see the feathers underneath their skins, I will be able to *relate*. I will be able to *empathize*. My psychiatrist is wrong. David is not a bird, is not something to count or configure, and I relate to him. I empathize with him. I am not impossible to reach. I simply do not care about reaching people who do not reach for me.)

The halls are empty, the students prisoned in their individual classrooms. I do not care for high school. Last year, David and I attended classes on the same campus. I always knew that he was near, that if I needed him, I could go to him; that he would pause in his own education to clarify the complications with mine. Carl said that it was unfair for me to lean so heavily upon my little brother, but David swore he didn't mind, and if I must believe one of them over the other, I will always believe David, who has never lied to me, or threatened to be rid of me. David only ever needs to love me.

Outside the school, the air still smells like morning. Seagulls and pigeons clog the field, beaks stabbing at the sprinkler-softened ground, searching for meals of worms and beetles and burrowing things. I walk past them, scanning the trees, searching the sky, looking for flashes of black against the bright and blinding world. Nine is no good. Eight would have been fine, would have been a day cast in heavenly brightness, but nine? No. I cannot abide a day defined by nines. I need ten, eleven, something I can trust not to betray me.

One of the school's security guards sees me across the lawn, offers me a nod, and minds his own business. We have an accord, the security and I. I don't bother them with things they don't care about, and they don't bother me when I'm walking the school grounds, looking for birds. A few students have grumbled in my hearing about how I get "special treatment," but they've all stopped when I offered to trade them. They can have the constant count, the looming catastrophe, the knowledge that if they relax, even for a moment, they might be responsible for the end of the world. I'll have their well-thumbed paperbacks and their easy smiles, their constant conviction that the world is not doing them ill somehow when they're not looking.

It wouldn't be a fair exchange and I wouldn't know how to make it if one of them said yes, but I would try if they told me to. It would be worth it to smile at David and see no shadows lurking overhead.

I search the grounds until the bell rings in the building behind me. I count no corvids, catch no crows. This day is still defined by nines, and I am afraid. I am so very, very afraid.

My second-period teacher is less exhausted and, consequentially, less forgiving. He will not let me go. Neither will my third-period teacher, and by fourth period, the morning has bled away, leaving us marooned well in the body of the day, which is digesting us all one minute at a time. I glance anxiously at the windows as I move through the halls alongside my schoolmates, trying to mask my unhappiness. My psychiatrist says that when I am nervous, others around me are nervous, because I am so bad at concealing it. She says this puts an undue psychological burden on the people who have to interact with me.

When I ask her what to tell them about the undue psychological burden they put on me by asking me to be silent and still and not tell them when I see the shadows, she has nothing to say. There is a lesson in that, as much as in her requests for quiet. The world is a lesson, if you know how to look for it.

I am allowed to have my phone during the school day. I am a high school student now, and more, I am "special needs," even with the mainstreaming, even with the teachers who frown and don't know what to make of me. I could make a call. But David isn't allowed to have his phone during the day, and his breaks aren't the same as mine, and I have no one else to call. My mother doesn't want me to contact her while I'm at school unless it's an emergency. Her definition of the word is not the same as mine. Her definition is not the same as mine at all. So I run my fingers over the screen, feeling how comfortingly smooth it is, knowing that the ghosts of numbers whisper past my skin, pressed flat in digital display and waiting to be needed. I carry the mathematical world with me everywhere I go.

Lunch comes. I go to my usual bench and look at pictures of crows and ravens and jays on my little screen, trying to take comfort in the shape of their beaks, the subtle patterns of the feathers on their heads. Not all the pictures are mine. Some are downloaded from the Internet, carefully curated to soothe the parts of my soul that know, all the way to the bone, how essential it is to count the corvids accurately and chart the pattern of the day. But a few, a precious few, are pictures I took myself. They show familiar birds, birds whose voices I know, and I allow them to calm me.

I am calm when I return to class after the lunch bell rings again. I am calm as I sit in my desk next to the window and listen to the teacher droning on about material I will not understand until I see it written down. My assessments say that I am a visual learner, not an auditory learner, but somehow the accommodations intended to make me equal to my classmates never seem to come with handouts to read while the lecture goes on. I am expected to listen. I am not expected to retain.

I am calm when the classroom door opens and my principal steps inside. She is a lovely woman, aesthetically speaking. Her hair is always perfect, and her suits are always tailored just so, fitting the curves of her body without emphasizing them. She is a creature well-suited to her natural habitat, and I can't imagine what she looks like outside the boundaries of the school.

My teacher stops mid-lecture, moving to the doorway, where she speaks with the principal in a low, hushed voice. I can't hear what they're saying, but I know they're talking about me. They glance in my direction several times, and this was a day defined by nines, even though I tried to make it better. Something bad was preordained.

By the time they're ready to turn and beckon me forward, I have already gathered my things. I am serene. I am prepared for anything.

The principal's voice is gentle. "Brenda," she says. "There's been an accident."

I am not prepared for this.

Carl went to collect David from school, early. Too early. Why? There is no knowing. Carl is in the hospital, Carl is blood and bandages and uncharacteristic silence. Maybe he wanted to take David for some father-son time. Maybe he was finally making good on his threat to leave my mother and take his son away from her, away from me, the damaged sister who might damage him in turn. Maybe he just felt like it. There is no knowing, and there will never be any knowing. I could ask Carl over and over again forever, count the crows in his wake, divide by the rare and hesitant ravens pecking at the highway median, and still never find the answers I need.

He won't tell me. Even if he wakes up, even if he recovers completely, a father with no son to call his own, he won't tell me. He hated me when I was a shadow in his home, taking up space that he could have occupied, using up resources that he could have taken for his own child. Now that David is gone, Carl will hate me even more. The numbers support the conclusion.

Carl went to collect David from school without telling anyone, took his car and drove it to the school I used to attend. I can see it if I close my eyes, his little red sedan easing its way into the parking lot. Carl in the office, speaking in contemptuous tones to Miss Engleton, the front desk secretary, whose job it was to keep students in class whenever possible. Carl leading David to the car, insisting he sit in the front seat, even though all automotive safety recommendations said that David should sit in back, should be safer, should be farther from the probable point of impact.

I should have stopped counting at seven. I should have closed my eyes and stumbled blindly through my day, rather than risk a nine. Rather than risk everything.

Carl put David in the front seat and he drove away from the school. And maybe he was driving too fast, or maybe he wasn't paying attention, and maybe maybe maybe doesn't matter, because all the maybe in the world won't change anything. Carl drove. Carl entered an intersection. Carl slammed headlong into a truck heading in the opposite direction.

Carl sustained injuries to his head and spinal column, and David was killed on impact, David never even made it out of the car, never even made it to the hospital, *never had a chance*, and now there is Carl and no David, just like when I was a child. But time does not rewind. Time does not reset. Just because we have returned to a world without David, that doesn't mean we have returned to a world *before* David. David wasn't; David was; David is no longer.

My brother is dead.

I sit in the hospital hallway, clutching my knees, fighting the urge to rock back and forth, to whip my head from side to side and feel the reassuring brush of my hair against my ears. It upsets people when I do that, even though it isn't hurting them, even though they have their own little calming rituals. My psychiatrist says I mustn't upset people, no matter how harmless it seems, says that when I indulge my strangeness, the people around me see me less as one of them and more as something to be avoided and feared.

It isn't fair. They have their cigarettes and their chewing gum and their bitten nails, and all those things are normal, because some quiet council to which I was not invited deemed it so. I have my flapping hands and my shifting hips, and those things are strange, because they do not share them with me.

David never thought that I was strange. David only loved me.

The urge to move flees as abruptly as it came, replaced by a frail and frigid stillness. I'm thinking of my brother in the past tense. There is no present tense for David, not any longer, and it burns. It burns so badly that when my mother comes down the hall, pale ghost of a woman with one child broken and the other gone—one's for sorrow, two's for more sorrow still—I don't say anything, don't ask if I can go out and search the parking lot for corvids, don't tell her that I'm hungry or that I need to use the bathroom. I follow her without saying a word, into a world that doesn't have David in it anymore.

I count three crows on the sidewalk during the drive home, one two three's a girl. I am a girl, I am a three of crows, and I am alone in the world.

The house is empty, filled with shadows. My mother and I rattle through the rooms like peas in a glass, rebounding off things that should be familiar, would be familiar, were it not for the feeling of absence that wreathes everything in smoke and silence. David is not here. I should still be at school, should be there for another hour, but David should be home, sitting at the kitchen table, going over his homework as he waits for me to come and help him with his math.

Doing math with David is one of my favorite things in the world. The thought that I will never have it again is ashes on my tongue. I have to stop what I'm doing and count the shadows on the wall before I feel like I can continue. My mother is still a ghost, haunting the front room now, a photo album open in her lap. The sound of her weeping is steady, unrelenting. She can't understand how her world has changed so utterly, so unforgivingly.

I have more experience than she does with living in a world set against you, a world that will not forgive your flaws or take back its cruelties. For a moment, I want to go to her, to sit down beside her and take her hand and try to explain. I don't. I can't. The wall between us is too high, and I don't know how to climb it. She built it one brick at a time, and Carl was always there to help her build it higher, and only David ever cared about me enough to help her tear pieces of it down. We are strangers to each other, she and I, even though she's my mother and I'm her little girl.

Listless, unsure of what else I have to do, I go outside.

The birdbath is surrounded. In a flash, I add six, seven, eight corvids to my count. If I add them to the three I saw on the way home, I have eleven, eleven, eleven is for the gates of Heaven. If I add them to the nine I lived with all day, the nine that took David away from me forever, I have twenty. The rhymes are unclear past thirteen; I have had to find the definitions myself, teasing them out of the world through trial and error.

Eleven is for the gates of Heaven; twelve's for the man who lets you in.

Thirteen is for a broken promise; fourteen's the feathers underneath your skin.

Fifteen is for the things we carry; sixteen's for when we put them down.

Seventeen's all the lies and shadows; eighteen's the waters where we drown.

Nineteen has always been unclear to me. Odd numbers are usually less forgiving than even numbers, but ten's for the Devil his own self, and after that, the evens turn a little kinder. I don't know, I don't know. I think nineteen is for an unasked question, which would make twenty for an answer you won't want. It fits together. It feeds itself. A good rhyme—a good equation—should feed itself. But if I'm wrong about nineteen, I'll be wrong about twenty, and if I'm wrong about twenty, there's no saving the math. I'll have to start again.

Starting again won't bring David back. I stare at the crows around my birdbath, glossy and black and unaware that my heart is broken, my heart is breaking, my heart is an eggshell with nothing left inside, and for the first time, I hate them. I hate what they are to me, what my mind makes them into. I hate that they have seen David every day of their short and feathered lives, have watched him through the window while I prepared their food, and still they don't care. He's gone, and they don't *care*.

Screaming, I run at the birdbath with my arms up, making a monster of myself when they have only ever known me for a mathematician. The crows look at me in avian bewilderment until I get so close, and then they fly! Fly! Black wings beating against the air, black feathers sheeting down to litter the lawn like accusations, and I have nothing left to count, and I am alone. Here, and always, I am alone.

There are twenty feathers. Twenty corvids, twenty feathers: twenty is the answer, but the answer's still unclear.

I fall asleep sitting in the grass at the base of the birdbath and don't wake until morning, when the dew is sticky on my skin and the croaking of the crows who watch me, wary, from the fence filters into my consciousness. I sit up. They look at me accusingly.

"I'm sorry," I say. There are seven of them, a secret to start the day, lined up and watching me.

My mother is already gone, off to the hospital to be with Carl. I do not want to stay here alone, in this house where David isn't, and never will be again. I wash. I gather my things. I walk to the bus stop. I wait.

Two more corvids appear, a Steller's jay and a big, glossy raven. Nine. Again, nine. I consider turning around and going back inside, where I may be alone but at least I won't be out in the world. I am still considering when the bus pulls up, when the door hisses open, and my feet carry me onboard as much out of habit as anything else. The bus goes, and I go with it, bound for school. I watch the windows as we go. There are no more corvids to be counted.

First period has already begun when I arrive on campus. I consider going to the office to tell them I'm here, and dismiss it as a bad idea. The rules say that if I'm going to be late, my mother needs to contact the school and excuse me. I am sure she hasn't contacted the school, not when she didn't notice me sleeping in the yard, not when she has a son to mourn and a husband to fret over. With no call, there will be no waiting slip to explain my tardiness. Better go straight to class, to let my teacher decide what to do with me. I ghost through the halls, and no one stops me; no one sees me go. I might as well not be here at all.

My teacher is at the front of the room when I open the door. She turns toward the sound and stops, going very still, like a bird confronted with a cat. It's odd to think of myself as a predator, as something that consumes.

"Brenda," she says finally. "I didn't think you were going to be joining us today. Do you have a note from the office?"

"No," I say. "To have a note, your parent or guardian must contact the school to explain your reasons for tardiness or absence. My parent or guardian did not contact the school. May I sit?"

She sighs, pinches the bridge of her nose like I have pained her. "Brenda, you know I can't let you join late if you're unexcused. Can you call your mother and ask her for a note?"

"No."

She lowers her hand and frowns at me. A giggle runs though the class. "Why not?"

I am told that my tendency toward brevity when asked direct questions is troubling. I can see it now, in my teacher's face. "She's at the hospital with my stepfather," I explain politely.

My teacher's eyes flare with sudden alarm. "Is everything all right?" She probably isn't supposed to ask that. Even as a student, I'm meant to have privacy.

I don't mind. Privacy is for people with something to hide. I've never had anything to hide. I'll tell anyone who asks what I've counted. "No," I say. "My stepfather had an accident. My little brother was in the car with him. David died. Carl didn't. Please, may I sit down?"

The class isn't giggling anymore. The class is staring at me in wide-eyed horror, their looks of sympathy and dismay mirroring the teacher's. Belatedly, I realize that this may have been a bad decision, that they may see my presence on campus as proof that I have no real feelings. They already whisper that about me. It hurts. My feelings may not look like theirs do, but that doesn't make them any less real.

"I'm sorry," I say, before my teacher can answer me. "This was an error. I'm sorry."

Then I turn and walk out of the classroom, back across the campus, out to the street. There's no bus this time; it will be at least a half hour before the next bus comes. I don't want to wait here, visible from the school windows as I stand at the bus stop, while the students whisper and point. I set my feet to the sidewalk. I start walking.

My house is three miles from campus. On a good day, that can be a pleasant walk, almost enjoyable in its predictability. I know the route well enough that I don't need to watch where I'm going; instead, I can keep my eyes turned upward.

Ten and eleven are waiting for me on the corner, big black birds that take off when they see me coming. Twelve, thirteen, and fourteen are pecking at the gravel of the median when I turn. Fifteen caws at me from a power line. Sixteen and seventeen peek down from a rooftop. Eighteen flies back, dark wings across the horizon, and then nineteen is looking at me, standing in the middle of the sidewalk, fearless. It does not care that I am bigger than it is. It does not care that I am a human being.

I stop walking. The crow remains.

"Nineteen," I say. The crow remains.

Nineteen has always been unclear to me. I look at the crow, and the crow looks at me, and nineteen is not for an unasked question; this far into the rhyme, the questions have all been asked. The questions are clear.

"Nineteen is for the one who wronged you," I whisper, and the rest of the rhyme comes clear. It was only ever missing that single piece, that revelation around which everything else turned.

Nineteen is for the one who wronged you, and I'm running, I'm running; the crow takes off in a flurry of feathers and still I'm running as hard as I can toward home.

The twentieth crow flies by and *twenty is for a place to stand*, and still I'm running.

The twenty-first is a jay in a hedge, and *twenty-one's all you have to offer*, and still I'm running.

The twenty-second is another crow, this one perched on the edge of my birdbath, the birdbath where I counted most of my way to nine. It caws and takes off at the sight of me, black wings beating like a disembodied heart, and I'm home. I'm home. I don't need to run anymore, and I know what the twenty-second crow means. I understand everything. I close the door behind myself and head for the kitchen. Everything I need is there.

Hours pass before the front door opens. I've been sitting on the stairs the whole time, waiting. I hear my mother's voice. She's talking to someone, speaking softly, struggling to offer a comfort that shouldn't be asked of her, not yet, not with my brother's death so fresh that it still burns when I try to think about it. She should be free to mourn, not tethered to someone who doesn't understand that her pain matters as much, if not more, than his.

Carl's voice is under hers, a low rumble of discontent. I stay where I am, waiting for the moment when they come around the bend in the hall and see me there. Carl, face still bruised beneath his bandages, scowls immediately.

"What are you doing?" he demands. "Shouldn't you be in school?"

"David should have been in school," I say. He winces, looking ashamed.

My mother just looks sad. "Let us by, please, Brenda," she says. "Carl needs to rest."

I don't argue. I simply stand and walk back up to the landing, where I watch as she leads him up the stairs, supporting him every step of the way. He glares at me when they reach the top. I look impassively back.

"Creepy-ass kid," he says, and I say nothing, and my mother says nothing, and the crows have already been counted. They vanish into the bedroom that they share.

My mother comes back out alone a few minutes later. She pauses, looking at me, and for a moment—only a moment—I see the light that used to be there, when I was younger, when she didn't have Carl to tell her that I was broken. I am grateful for the existence of Carl; without him, there would have been no David, and everything has been worth it, I think, to live in a world with David in it, even if it was only for a little while.

My mother says nothing. My mother walks on. I watch her go before walking down the hall to the closed door of their bedroom. It's never locked. I turn the knob and let myself inside.

Carl is in their bed. He isn't asleep, not yet, and he turns toward the sound of my footsteps, his eyes widening at the sight of me. "What are you doing in here?" he demands.

"One's for sorrow," I tell him. "You were one."

"I swear to God, you crazy bitch—"

"Two's for joy," I say. "David was two." I'm not crazy—I've never been crazy—but that's a fight I've had and lost with him a hundred times already. I'm not here to have it again. "When you joined our family I was three, a girl, and he was four, a boy, and we were perfect. We were sixes and sevens, we were *everything*. But you tried to make me into a secret, never to be told, and I learned the rest of the rhyme because I had to. Don't you understand? This is all your fault. I might have learned to live inside the ordinary numbers, if you'd let me."

"*Joyce!*" he screams.

It takes me a moment to realize that Joyce is my mother's name. She's never been anything but Mother to me, the pale woman haunting the edges of the world, never brave enough to save me, never strong enough to let me go. I hear footsteps on the stairs. I turn my head and the door is open, and she's watching me from the hall. My back is to her. She has to see the knife. I'm not making any effort to hide it.

She looks at it. She looks at me. She looks at Carl, lying still and halfway helpless in his bed. She knows what I am here to do.

She closes the door, and Carl and I are alone.

"Eight's for Heaven," I say, turning back to him. "Nine's for Hell. I counted nine when David died. When you took him, because you were ten. Ten's for the Devil his own self."

"You need to get out of here."

I show him the knife. His face goes white as whey.

"Eleven is for the gates of Heaven," I tell him. "Sometimes it's for penance, and twelve's for sin, but when it's for the gates of Heaven, twelve's for the man who lets you in. I want that for David. Don't you?"

He doesn't answer me.

"Thirteen is for a broken promise," I say, and the distance between us is nothing; I am flying, I am flying, and the knife is in my hand. "Fourteen's the feathers underneath your skin."

Carl screams when the knife comes down. I stab and I stab, and I count the punctures one by one, until I reach nineteen, nineteen, nineteen is for the one who wronged you. Twenty is for a place to stand. Twenty-one's all you have to offer. Twenty-two's the knife bare in your hand.

The count is done. I pull away from him, a red girl in a red room, and the knife falls from my fingers: I don't need it anymore. I have counted off my corvids. The math is done. My mother will call the police eventually, if she hasn't already, and that's right, too; that was where this equation had to lead us. This is the mathematical inevitability to which I have been building all my life. I can feel the feathers under my skin, aching to be free.

My fingers leave red smears on the window when I pry it open. I know I can only fly for a moment.

I know that it will be enough.

Something About Birds

PAUL TREMBLAY

THE NEW DARK REVIEW PRESENTS
"SOMETHING ABOUT WILLIAM WHEATLEY": AN INTERVIEW
WITH WILLIAM WHEATLEY BY BENJAMIN D. PIOTROSKWI

William Wheatley's *The Artist Starve* is a collection of five loosely interconnected novelettes and novellas published in 1971 by University of Massachusetts Press (the book having won its Juniper Prize for Fiction). In an era that certainly predated usage of YA as a marketing category, his stories were from the POV of young adults, ranging from the fourteen-year-old Maggie Holtz who runs away from home (taking her six-year-old brother Thomas into the local woods) during the twelve days of the Cuban Missile Crisis, to the last story, a near-future extrapolation of the Vietnam War having continued into the year 1980, the draft age dropped to sixteen, and an exhausted and radiation-sick platoon of teenagers conspiring to kill the increasingly unhinged Sergeant Thomas Holtz. *The Artist Starve* was a prescient and visceral (if not too earnest) book embracing chaotic social and global politics of the early 1970s. An unexpected critical and commercial smash, particularly on college campuses, *The Artist Starve* was one of three books forwarded to the Pulitzer Prize Board, who ultimately decided no award for the year

1971. That *The Artist Starve* is largely forgotten, whereas the last short story he ever wrote, "Something About Birds," oft-reprinted and first published in a DIY zine called *Steam* in 1977 continues to stir debate and win admirers within the horror/weird fiction community, is an irony that is not lost upon the avuncular, seventy-five-year-old Wheatley.

BP: Thank you for agreeing to this interview, Mr. Wheatley.

WW: The pleasure is all mine, Benjamin.

BP: Before we discuss "Something About Birds," which is my all-time favorite short story, by the way—

WW: You're too kind. Thank you.

BP: I wanted to ask if *The Artist Starve* is going to be reprinted. I've heard rumors.

WW: You have? Well, that would be news to me. While I suppose it would be nice to have your work rediscovered by a new generation, I'm not holding my breath, nor am I actively seeking to get the book back in print. It already served its purpose. It was an important book when it came out, I think, but it is a book very much of its time. So much so I'm afraid it wouldn't translate very well to the now.

BP: There was a considerable gap, six years, between *The Artist Starve* and "Something About Birds." In the interim, were you working on other writing projects or projects that didn't involve writing?

WW: When you get to my age—oh that sounds terribly cliché, doesn't it? Let me rephrase: When you get to my perspective, six years doesn't seem as considerable. Point taken, however. I'll try to be brief. I will admit to some churlish, petulant behavior, as given the overwhelming response to my first book I expected the publishing industry to then roll out the red carpet to whatever it was I might've scribbled on a napkin. And maybe that would've

happened had I won the Pulitzer, yes? Instead, I took the *no award* des-
ignation as a terrible, final judgment on my work. Silly I know, but at the
risk of sounding paranoid, the no award announcement all but shut down
further notice for the book. I spent a year or so nursing my battered ego
and speaking at colleges and universities before even considering writing
another story. I then spent more than two years researching the burgeoning
fuel crisis and overpopulation fears. I travelled quite a bit as well: Ecuador,
Peru, Japan, India, South Africa. While traveling I started bird watching,
of course. Total novice, and I remain one. Anyway, I'd planned to turn my
research into a novel of some sort. That book never materialized. I never
even wrote an opening paragraph. I'm not a novelist. I never was. To make
a long, not all that exciting story short, upon returning home and very much
travel weary, I became interested in antiquities and bought the very same
antiques shop that is below us now in 1976. I wrote "Something About
Birds" shortly after opening the shop, thinking it might be the first story in
another cycle, all stories involving birds in some way. The story itself was
unlike anything I'd ever written; oblique, yes, bizarre to many, I'm sure, but
somehow, it hits closer to an ineffable truth than anything else I've written.
To my great disappointment, the story was summarily rejected by all the
glossy magazines and I was ignorant of the genre fiction market so I decided
to allow a friend who was in a local punk band to publish it in her zine. I
remain grateful and pleased that the story has had many other lives since.

BP: Speaking for all the readers who adore "Something About Birds," let
me say that we'd kill for a short story cycle built around it.

WW: Oh, I've given up on writing. "Something About Birds" is a fitting
conclusion to my little writing career as that story continues to do its job,
Benjamin.

⌐

Mr. Wheatley says, "That went well, didn't it?"

Wheatley is shorter than Ben but not short, broad in the chest and
shoulders, a wrestler's build. His skin is pallid and his dark brown eyes

31

focused, attentive, and determined. His hair has thinned but he still has most of it, and most of it is dark, almost black. He wears a tweed sports coat, gray wool pants, a plum-colored sweater vest, a white shirt, a slate bow tie that presses against his throat tightly as though it were gauze being applied to a wound. He smiled throughout the interview. He is smiling now.

"You were great, Mr. Wheatley. I cannot thank you enough for the opportunity to talk to you about my favorite story."

"You are too kind." Wheatley drums his fingers on the dining room table at which they are sitting and narrows his eyes at Ben, as though trying to bring him into better focus. "Before you leave, Benjamin, I have something for you."

Ben swirls the last of his room-temperature Earl Grey tea around the bottom of his cup and decides against finishing it. Ben stands as Wheatley stands, and he checks his pocket for his phone and his recorder. "Oh, please, Mr. Wheatley, you've been more than gracious—"

"Nonsense. You are doing me a great service with the interview. It won't be but a moment. I will not take no for an answer." Wheatley continues to talk as he disappears into one of the three other rooms with closed doors that spoke out from the wheel of the impeccable and brightly lit living/dining room. The oval dining room table is the centerpiece of the space and is made of a darkly stained wood and has a single post as thick as a telephone pole. The wall adjacent to the kitchen houses a built-in bookcase, the shelves filled to capacity, the tops perched with vases and brass candelabras. On the far wall rectangular, monolithic windows, their blue drapes pulled wide open, vault toward the height of the cathedral ceiling, their advance halted by the crown molding. The third-floor view overlooks Dunham Street, and when Ben stands in front of a window he can see the red awning of Wheatley's antiques shop below. The room is beautiful, smartly decorated, surely full of antiques that Ben is unable to identify; his furniture and décor experience doesn't extend beyond IKEA and his almost pathological inability to put anything together more complex than a nightstand.

Wheatley reemerges from behind a closed door. He has an envelope in one hand and something small and strikingly red cupped in the palm of the other.

"I hope you're willing to indulge an old man's eccentricity." He pauses and looks around the room. "I thought I brought up a stash of small white paper bags. I guess I didn't. Benjamin, forgive the Swiss-cheese memory. We can get a bag on our way out if you prefer. Anyway, I'd like you to have this. Hold out your hands, please."

"What is it?"

Wheatley gently places a bird head into Ben's hands. The head is small; the size of a half-dollar coin. Its shock of red feathers is so bright, a red he's never seen, only something living could be that vivid, and for a moment Ben is not sure if he should pat the bird head and coo soothingly or spastically flip the thing out of his hands before it nips him. The head has a prominent, brown-yellow beak, proportionally thick, and as long as the length of the head from the top to its base. The beak is outlined in shorter black feathers that curl around the eyes as well. The bird's pitch-black pupils float in a sea of a more subdued red.

"Thank you, Mr. Wheatley. I don't know what to say. Is it? Is it real?"

"This is a red-headed barbet from northern South America. Lovely creature. Its bill is described as horn-colored. It looks like a horn, doesn't it? It feeds on fruit but it also eats insects as well. Fierce little bird, one befitting your personality, I think, Benjamin."

"Wow. Thank you. I can't accept this. This is too much—"

"Nonsense. I insist." He then gives Ben an envelope. "An invitation to an all-too-infrequent social gathering I host here. There will be six of us, you and I included. It's in—oh my—three days. Short notice, I know. The date, time, and instructions are inside the envelope. You must bring the red-headed barbet with you, Benjamin, it is your ticket to admittance, or you will not be allowed entrance." Wheatley chuckles softly and Ben does not know whether or not he is serious.

⌒

BP: There's so much wonderful ambiguity and potential for different meanings. Let's start in the beginning, with the strange funeral procession of "Something About Birds." An adult, Mr. H_____ is presumably the father of one of the children, who slips up and calls him "Dad."

WW: Yes, of course. "It's too hot for costumes, Dad."

BP: That line is buried in a pages-long stream-of-consciousness paragraph with the children excitedly describing the beautiful day and the desiccated, insect-ridden body of the dead bird they take turns carrying. It's an effective juxtaposition and wonderfully disorienting use of omniscient POV, and I have to admit, when I first read the story, I didn't see the word "Dad" there. I was surprised to find it on the second read. Many readers report having had the same experience. Did you anticipate that happening?

WW: I like when stories drop important clues in a nonchalant or non-dramatic way. That he is the father of one, possibly more of the children, and that he is simply staging this funeral, or celebration, for a bird, a beloved family pet, and all the potential strangeness and darkness is the result of the imagination of the children is one possible read. Or maybe that is all pretend too, part of the game, and Mr. H_____ is someone else entirely. I'm sorry, I'm not going to give you definitive answers, and I will purposefully lead you astray if you let me.

BP: Duly noted. Mr. H_____ leads the children into the woods behind an old, abandoned schoolhouse—

WW: Or perhaps school is only out for the summer, Benjamin.

BP: Okay, wow. I'm going to include my "wow" in the interview, by the way. I'd like to discuss the children's names. Or the names they are given once they reach the clearing: the Admiral, the Crow, Copper, the Surveyor, and of course, poor Kittypants.

WW: Perhaps Kittypants isn't so poor after all, is he?

There is a loud knocking on Ben's apartment door at 12:35 A.M.

Ben lives alone in a small, one-bedroom apartment in the basement of a run-down brownstone, in a neighborhood that was supposed to be the next *it* neighborhood. The sparsely furnished apartment meets his needs, but he does wish there is more natural light. There are days, particularly in the winter, when he stands with his face pressed against the glass of his front window, a secret behind a set of black, wrought iron bars.

Whoever is knocking continues knocking. Ben awkwardly pulls on a pair of jeans, grabs a forearm-length metal pipe that leans against his nightstand (not that he would ever use it, not that he has been in a physical altercation since fifth grade) and stalks into the combined living area/kitchen. He's hesitant to turn on the light and debates whether he should ignore the knocking or call the police.

A voice calls out from behind the thick, wooden front door, "Benjamin Piotrowsky? Please, Mr. Piotrowsky. I know it's late but we need to talk."

Ben shuffles across the room and turns on the outside light above the entrance. He peeks out his front window. There's a woman standing on his front stoop, dressed in jeans and a black, hooded sweatshirt. He does not recognize her and he is unsure of what to do. He turns on the overhead light in the living area and shouts through the door, "Do I know you? Who are you?"

"My name is Marnie, I am a friend of Mr. Wheatley, and I'm here on his behalf. Please open the door."

Somehow her identification makes perfect sense, that she is who she says she is and yes, of course, she is here because of Mr. Wheatley, yet Ben has never been more fearful for his safety. He unlocks and opens the door against his better judgment.

Marnie walks inside, shuts the door, and says, "Don't worry, I won't be long." Her movements are easy and athletic and she rests her hands on her hips. She is taller than Ben, perhaps only an inch or two under six feet. She has dark, shoulder-length hair, and eyes that aren't quite symmetrical, with her left smaller and slightly lower than her right. Her age is indeterminate, anywhere from late twenties to early forties. As someone who is self-conscious about his own youthful, childlike appearance (ruddy complexion, inability to grow even a shadow of facial hair), Ben suspects that she's older than she looks.

Ben asks, "Would you like a glass of water, or something, uh, Marnie, right?"

"No, thank you. Doing some late-night plumbing?"

"What? Oh." Ben hides the pipe behind his back. "No. It's, um, my little piece of security, I guess. I, um, I thought someone might be breaking in."

"Knocking on your door equates to a break-in, does it?" Marnie smiles, but it's a bully's smile, a politician's smile. "I'm sorry to have woken you and I will get right to the point. Mr. Wheatley doesn't appreciate you posting a picture of your admission ticket on Facebook."

Ben blinks madly, as though he was a captured spy put under a bright lamp. "I'm sorry?"

"You posted a picture of the admission ticket at 9:46 this evening. It currently has three hundred and ten likes, eighty-two comments, and thirteen shares."

The bird head. Between bouts of transcribing the interview and ignoring calls from the restaurant (that asshole Shea was calling to swap shifts, again), Ben obsessed over the bird head. He marveled at how simultaneously light and heavy it was in his palm. He spent more than an hour staging photographs of the head, intending to use one with the publication of the interview. Ben placed the bird head in the spine of an open notebook, the notebook in which he'd written notes from the interview. The head was slightly turned so that the length of the beak could be admired. The picture was too obvious and not strange enough. The rest of his photographs were studies in incongruity; the bird head in the middle of a white plate, resting in the bowl of a large spoon, entangled in the blue laces of his Chuck Taylors, perched on top of his refrigerator, and on the windowsill framed by the black bars. He settled for a close-up of the bird head on the cracked hardwood floor so its black eye, red feathers, and the horn-colored beak filled the shot. For the viewer, the bird head's size would be difficult to determine due to the lack of foreground or scale within the photograph. That was the shot. He posted it along with the text "Coming soon to The New Dark Review: Something About William Wheatley" (which he thought was endlessly clever). Of course many of his friends (were they friends, really? did the pixilated collection of pictures, avatars, and opinions never met in person even qualify as acquaintances?)

within the online horror writing and fan community enthusiastically commented upon the photo. Ben sat in front of his laptop, watching the likes, comments, and shares piling up. He engaged with each comment and post share and couldn't help but imagine the traffic this picture would bring to his *The New Dark Review.* He was aware enough to feel silly for thinking it, but he couldn't remember feeling more successful or happy.

Ben says, "Oh, right. The picture of the bird head. Jeez, I'm sorry. I didn't know I wasn't supposed to, I mean, I didn't realize—"

Marnie: "We understand your enthusiasm for Mr. Wheatley and his work, but you didn't honestly give a second thought to sharing publicly a picture of an admission ticket to a private gathering, one hosted by someone who clearly values his privacy?"

"No, I guess I didn't. I never mentioned anything about the party, I swear, but now I feel stupid and awful." He is telling the truth; he does feel stupid and awful, but mostly because he understands that Marnie is here to ask him to take down his most popular Facebook post. "I'm so sorry for that."

"Do you always react this way when someone shares an invitation to a private party? When they share such a personal gift?"

"No. God, no. It wasn't like that. I posted it to, you know, drum up some pre-interest, um, buzz, for the interview that I'm going to publish tomorrow. A teaser, right? That's all. I don't think Mr. Wheatley realizes how much people in the horror community love 'Something About Birds' and how much they want to know about him and hear from him."

"Are there going to be further problems?"

"Problems?"

"Issues."

"No. I don't think so."

"You don't think so?"

"No. No problems or issues. I promise." Ben backs away unconsciously and bumps into the small island in his kitchen. He drops the pipe and it clatters to the floor.

"You will not post any more pictures on social media nor will you include the picture or any mention of the invitation and the gathering itself when you publish the interview."

"I won't. I swear."

"We'd like you to take down the photo, please."

Everything in him screams no and wants to argue that they don't understand how much the picture will help bring eyeballs and readers to the interview, how it will help everyone involved. Instead, Ben says, "Yes, of course."

"Now, please. Take it down, and I'd like to watch you take it down."

"Yeah, okay." He pulls his phone from out of his pocket and walks toward Marnie. She watches his finger and thumb strokes as he deletes the post.

Marnie says, "Thank you. I am sorry to have disrupted your evening, Benjamin." She walks to the front door. She pauses, turns, and says, "Are you sure about accepting the invitation, Benjamin?"

"What do you mean?"

"You can give back the admission ticket to me if you don't think you can handle the responsibility. Mr. Wheatley would understand."

The thought of giving her the bird head never once crosses his mind as a possibility. "No, that's okay. I'm keeping it. I'd like to keep it, please, I mean. I understand why he's upset and I won't betray his trust again. I promise."

Marnie starts to talk, and much of the rest of the strangely personal conversation passes like a dream.

—

WW: I'm well aware of the role of birds within pagan lore and that they are linked with the concept of freedom, of the ability to transcend the mundane, to leave it behind.

BP: Sounds like an apt description of weird fiction to me, Mr. Wheatley. I want you talk a little about the odd character names of the children. Sometimes I'm of the mind that the children are filling the roles of familiars to Mr. H_____. They are his companions, of course, and are assisting him in some task . . . a healing, perhaps, as Mr. H_____ is described as having a painful limp in the beginning of the story, a limp that doesn't seem to be there when later he follows the children into the woods.

WW: (laughs) I do love hearing all the different theories about the story.

BP: Are you laughing because I'm way off?

WW: No, not at all. I tried to build in as many interpretations as possible, and in doing so, I've been pleased to find many more interpretations that I didn't realize were there. Or I didn't consciously realize, if that makes sense. In the spirit of fair play, I will admit, for the first time, publicly, Benjamin, from where I got the children's names. They are named after songs from my friend Liz's obscure little punk band. I hope that's not a disappointment.

BP: Not at all. I think it's amazingly cool.

WW: An inside joke, yes, but the seemingly random names have taken on meaning too. At least they have for me.

BP: Let me hit you with one more allegorical reading: I've read a fellow critic who argues there's a classical story going on among all the weirdness. She argues that the Admiral, the Crow, and Kittypants specifically are playing out a syncretic version of the Horus, Osiris, and Set myth of Egypt, with Mr. H_____ representing Huitzilopochtli, the bird-headed Mexican god of war. Is she on to something?

WW: The references to those cultural myths involving gods with human bodies and bird heads were not conscious on my part. But that doesn't mean they're not there. I grew up reading those stories of ancient gods and mythologies and they are a part of me as they are a part of us all, even if we don't realize it. That's the true power of story. That it can find the secrets both the writer and reader didn't know they had within themselves.

~

Ben doesn't wake until after one P.M. His dreams were replays of his protracted late-night conversation with Marnie. They stood in the living area. Neither sat or made themselves more comfortable. He remembers part of their conversation going like this:

"When did you first read 'Something About Birds'?" "Five years ago, I think." "When did you move to the city?" "Three years ago, I think?" "You think?" "I'm sorry, it was two years ago, last September. It seems like I've been here longer. I don't know why I was confused by that question." "As an adult, have you always lived alone?" "Yes." "How many miles away do you currently live from your mother?" "I'm not sure of the exact mileage but she's in another time zone from me." "Tell me why you hate your job at the restaurant." "It's having to fake pleasantness that makes me feel both worthless and lonely." "Have you had many lovers?" "Only two. Both relationships lasted less than two months. And it's been a while, unfortunately." "What has been a while?" "Since I've had a lover, as you put it." "Have you ever held a live bird cupped in your hands and felt its fragility or had a large one perch on your arm or shoulder and felt its barely contained strength?" "No. Neither." "Would you prefer talons or beak?" "I would prefer wings." "You can't choose wings, Benjamin. Talons or beak?" "Neither? Both?" And so on.

Ben does not go into work and he doesn't call in. His phone vibrates with the agitated where-are-yous and are-you-coming-ins. He hopes that asshole Shea is being called in to cover for him. He says at his ringing phone, *The New Dark Review* will be my job." He decides severing his already fraying economic safety line is the motive necessary to truly make a go at the career he now wants. He says, "Sink or swim," then playfully chides himself for not having a proper bird analogy instead. Isn't there a bird species that lays eggs on cliffs in or near Ireland, and the mothers push the hatchlings out of the nest and as they tumble down the side of the craggy rock they learn to fly or perish? Ben resolves to turn his zine devoted to essays about obscure and contemporary horror and weird fiction into a career. He's not so clueless as to believe the zine will ever be able to sustain him financially, but perhaps it could elevate his name and stature within the field and parlay that into something more. He could pitch/sell ad space to publishers and research paying eBook subscription-based models. Despite himself, he fantasizes *The New Dark Review* winning publishing industry awards. With its success he could then helm an anthology of stories dedicated to Wheatley, a cycle of stories by other famous writers centered around "Something About Birds." If only he wasn't told to take down the bird head photo from his various social media platforms. He fears a real opportunity has been lost, and the messages and emails asking why he took down the photo aren't helping.

Instead of following up on his revenue generating and promotional ideas for *The New Dark Review*, Ben Googles the Irish-cliff-birds and finds the guillemot chicks. They aren't kicked out of the nest. They are encouraged by calls from their father below the cliffs. And they don't fly. The chicks plummet and bounce off the rocks and if they manage to survive, they swim out to sea with their parents.

Ben transcribes the rest of the interview and publishes it. He shares the link over various platforms but the interview does not engender the same enthusiastic response the bird head photo received. He resolves to crafting a long-term campaign to promote the interview, give it a long life, one with a tail (a publishing/marketing term, of course). He'll follow up the interview with a long-form critical essay of Wheatley's work. He reads "Something About Birds" eight more times. He tacks a poster board to a wall in the living area. He creates timelines and a psychical map of the story's setting, stages the characters and creates dossiers, uses lengths of string and thread to make connections. He tacks notecards with quotes from Wheatley. He draws bird heads, too.

That night there is a repeat of the knocking on his front door. Only Ben isn't sure if the knocking is real or if he's only dreaming. The knocking is lighter this time; a tapping more than a knock. He might've welcomed another visit from Marnie earlier while he was working on his new essay, but now he pulls the bedcovers over his head. The tapping stops eventually.

Later there is a great wind outside, and rain, and his apartment sings with all manner of noises not unlike the beating of hundreds of wings.

WW: Well, that's the question, isn't it? It's the question the title of the story all but asks. I've always been fascinated by birds and prior to writing the story, I'd never been able to fully articulate why. Yes, the story is strange, playful, perhaps macabre, and yet it really is about my love, for lack of a better term, of birds. I'm flailing around for an answer, I'm sorry. Let me try again: Our fascination with birds is more than some dime-store, new-age, spiritual longing, more than the worst of us believing these magnificent animals serve as an avatar for our black-hearted, near-sighted souls, if we've ever had such a thing as a soul. There's this otherness about birds, isn't there? Thank goodness for that. It's as though they're in possession of knowledge totally alien to us. I don't think I'm explaining this very well, and that's why I wrote the story. The story gets at what I'm trying to say about birds better than I can now. I've always felt, as a humble observer, that the proper emotion within a bird's presence is awe. Awe is as fearsome and terrible as it is ecstatic.

—

Ben wakes up to his phone vibrating with more calls from the restaurant. His bedroom is dark. As far as he can tell from his cave-like confines, it is dark outside as well. Ben fumbles to turn on his nightstand lamp, and the light makes everything worse. Across from the foot of his bed is his dresser. It's his dresser from childhood, and the wood is scarred with careless gouges and pocked with white, tattered remnants of what were once Pokémon stickers. On top of the dresser is a bird head, and it's as large as his own head. Bigger, actually. Its coloring is the same as the red-headed barbet. The red feathers, at this size, are shockingly red, as though red never existed before this grotesquely beautiful plumage. He understands the color is communication. It's a warning. A threat. So too the brown-yellow beak, which is as thick and prominent as a rhino's horn, stabbing out menacingly into his bedroom. The bird's eyes are bigger than his fists, and the black pupils are ringed in more red.

He scrambles for his length of metal pipe and squeezes it tightly in both hands, holding it like a comically stubby and ineffective baseball bat. He shouts, "Who's there?" repeatedly, as though if he shouts it enough times, there will be an unequivocal answer to the query. No answer comes. He runs into the living room shouting, "Marnie?" and opens his bathroom and closet doors and finds no one. He checks the front door. It is unlocked. Did he leave it unlocked last night? He opens it with a deep sense of regret and steps out onto his empty front stoop. Outside his apartment is a different world, one crowded with brick buildings, ceaseless traffic, cars parked end-to-end for as far as he can see, and the sidewalks as rivers of pedestrians who don't know or care who he is or what has happened. Going outside is a terrible mistake and Ben goes back into his apartment and again shouts, "Who's there?"

Ben eventually stops shouting and returns to his bedroom. He circles around to the front of the dresser so as to view the bird head straight on and not in profile. Ben takes a picture with his phone and sends a private group message (photo attached) to a selection of acquaintances within the horror/weird fiction community. He tells them this new photo is not for public consumption. Within thirty minutes he receives responses ranging from "Jealous!" to "Yeah, saw yesterday's pic, but cool" to "I liked yesterday's picture better. Can you send that to me?" Not one of them commented on the head's impossible size, which has to be clear in the photo as it takes up so much of the dresser's top. Did they assume some sort of photo trickery? Did they assume the bird head in yesterday's photo (the close-up of the head on the hardwood floor) was the same size? Did seeing the second photo re-calibrate the size of the bird head in their minds? He types in response, "The head wasn't this big yesterday," but deletes it instead of sending. Ben considers posting the head-on-the-dresser photo to his various social media platforms so that Marnie would return and admonish him again, and then he could ask why she broke into his apartment and left this monstrous bird head behind. This had to be her doing.

After a lengthy inner dialogue, Ben summons the courage to pick up the head. He's careful, initially, to not touch the beak. To touch that first would be wrong, disrespectful. Dangerous. He girds himself to lift a great weight, even bending his knees, but the head is surprisingly light. That's not to say the head feels fragile. He imagines its lightness is by design so that the great bird, despite its size, would be able to fly and strike its prey quickly. With the head in his hands, he scans the dresser's top for any sign of the small head Mr. Wheatley initially gave him. He cannot find it. He assumes Marnie swapped the smaller head for this one, but he also irrationally fears that the head simply grew to this size overnight.

The feathers have a slight oily feel to them and he is careful to not inadvertently get any stuck between his fingers as he manipulates the head and turns it over, upside down. He cannot see inside the head, although it is clearly hollow. A thick forest of red feathers obscure the neck's opening and when he attempts to pull feathers back or push them aside other feathers dutifully move in to block the view. There are tantalizing glimpses of darkness between the feathers, as though the depth contained within is boundless.

He sends his right hand inside the head expecting to feel plaster, or plastic, or wire mesh perhaps, the inner workings of an intricate mask, or maybe even, impossibly, the hard bone of skull. His fingers gently explore the hidden interior perimeter, and he feels warm, moist, pliant clay, or putty, or flesh. He pulls his hand out and rubs his fingers together, and he watches his fingers, expecting to see evidence of dampness. He's talking to himself now, asking if one can see dampness, and he wipes his hand on his shorts. He's nauseous (but pleasantly so), as he imagines his fingers were moments ago exploring the insides of a wound. More boldly, he returns his hand inside the bird head. He presses against the interior walls, and those walls yield to his fingers like they're made of the weakening skin of overripe fruit and vegetables. Fingertips sink deeper into the flesh of the head, and his arm shakes and wrist aches with exertion.

There's a wet sucking sound as Ben pulls his hand out. He roughly flips the head over, momentarily forgetting about the size of the great beak and its barbed tip scratches a red furrow into his forearm. He wraps his hand around the beak near its base and his fingers are too small to enclose its circumference. He attempts to separate the two halves of beak, a halfassed lion tamer prying open fearsome jaws, but they are fixed in place, closed tightly, like gritted teeth.

Ben takes the head out into the living area and gently places it on the floor. He lies down beside it and runs his fingers through its feathers, careful to not touch the beak again. If he stares hard enough, long enough, he sees himself in miniature, curled up like a field mouse, reflected in the black pools of the bird's eyes.

―

BP: A quick summary of the ending. Please stop me if I say anything that's inaccurate or misleading. The children, led by the Crow and the Admiral, reappear out of the woods that Mr. H_____ had forbidden them to go into, and you describe the Admiral's fugue wonderfully: "his new self passing over his old self, as though he were an eclipse." When asked—we don't know who the speaker is, do we?—where Kittypants is, the Crow says Kittypants didn't fly away and is still in the woods, waiting to be found and retrieved. Someone (again, the speaker not identified) giggles and says his wings are broken. The other children are eager to go to Kittypants and erupt into mocking chant and song. The dead bird that they had brought with them is forgotten. I love how it isn't clear if the kids have finally donned their bird masks or if they've had them on the whole time. Or perhaps they have no masks on at all. Mr. H_____ says they may leave him only after they've finished digging a hole big enough for the little one to fit inside and not ruffle any feathers. The reader is unsure if Mr. H_____ is referring to the dead bird or, in retrospect, if it's a sinister reference to Kittypants, the smallest of their party. The kids leave right away and it's not clear if they have finished digging the hole or not. Perhaps they're just going home, the funeral or celebration over, the game over. Mr. H_____ goes into the woods after them and finds his gaggle in a clearing, the setting sun throwing everything into shadow, "a living bas relief." They are leaping high into the air, arms spread out as wide as the world, and then crashing down into what is described from a distance as a pile of leaves no bigger than a curled-up, sleeping child. It's a magnificent image, Mr. Wheatley, one that simultaneously brings to mind the joyous, chaotic, physical play of children and, at the same time, resembles a gathering of carrion birds picking apart a carcass in a frenzy. I have to ask, is the leaf pile just a leaf pile, or is Kittypants inside?

WW: I love that you saw the buzzard imagery in that scene, Benjamin. But, oh, I wouldn't dream of ever answering your final question directly. But I'll play along a little. Let me ask you this: Do you prefer that Kittypants be under the pile of leaves? If so, why?

—

Tucked inside the envelope he received from Mr. Wheatley is a typed set of instructions. Benjamin wears black socks, an oxford shirt, and dark pants that were once partners with a double-breasted jacket. He walks twenty-three blocks northwest. He enters the darkened antiques store through a back door, and from there he navigates past narrow shelving and various furniture and taxidermy staging to the stairwell that leads to the second-floor apartment. He does not call out or say anyone's name. All in accordance with the instructions.

The front door to Mr. Wheatley's apartment is closed. Ben places an ear against the door, listening for other people, for their sounds, as varied as they can be. He doesn't hear anything. He cradles the bird head in his left arm and has it pressed gently against his side, the beak supported by his ribs. The head is wrapped tightly in a white sheet. The hooked beak tip threatens to rend the cloth.

Ben opens the door, steps inside the apartment, and closes the door gently behind him, and thus ends the brief set of instructions from the envelope. Benjamin removes the white cloth and holds the bird head in front of his chest like a shield.

There is no one in the living room. The curtains are drawn and three walls sconces peppered between the windows and their single bulbs give off a weak, almost sepia light. The doors to the other rooms are all closed. He walks to the circular dining room table, the one at which he sat with Mr. Wheatley only three days ago.

Ben is unsure of what he's supposed to do next. His lips and throat are dry, and he's afraid that he'll throw up if he opens his mouth to speak. Finally, he calls out: "Hello, Mr. Wheatley? It's Ben Piotrowsky."

There's no response or even a sense of movement from elsewhere inside the apartment.

"Our interview went live online already. I'm not sure if you've seen it yet, but I hope you like it. The response has been very positive so far."

Ben shuffles into the center of the room, and it suddenly occurs to him that he could document everything he's experienced (including what he will experience later this evening) and add it to the interview as a bizarre, playful afterword. It's a brilliant idea and something that would only enhance his and Mr. Wheatley's reputation within the weird fiction community. Yes, he would most certainly do this, and Ben imagines the online response as being more rabid than the reaction to the picture of the bird head. There will be argument and discussion as to whether the mysterious afterword is fictional or not, and if fictional, had it been written by William Wheatley himself. The interview with afterword will be a perfect extension or companion to "Something About Birds." Perhaps Ben can even convince Mr. Wheatley to co-write the afterword with him. Or, instead, pitch this idea to Mr. Wheatley not as an afterword but as a wraparound story, or framing device, within the interview itself. Yes, not only could this be a new story, but the beginning of a new story cycle, and Ben will be a part of it.

Ben says, "This bird head is lovely, by the way. I mean that. I assume you made it. I'm no expert, but it appears to be masterful work. I'm sure there's a fascinating story behind it that we could discuss further." In the silence that follows, Ben adds, "Perhaps your friend Marnie brought it to my apartment. We talked the other night, of course."

Ben's spark of new-story-cycle inspiration and surety fades in the continued silence of the apartment. Has he arrived before everyone else, or is this some sort of game where the party does not begin until he chooses a door to open, and then—then what? Is this a hazing ritual? Is he to become part of their secret little group? Ben certainly hopes for the latter. Which door of the three will he open first?

Ben asks, "Am I to put the bird head on, Mr. Wheatley? Is that it?"

The very idea of being enclosed within the darkness of the bird head, his cheeks and lips and eyelids pressing against the whatever-it-is on the inside, is a horror. Yet he also wants nothing more than to put the bird head over his own, to have that great beak spill out before his eyes, a baton with which to conduct the will of others. He won't put it on, not until he's sure that is what he's supposed to do.

"What am I supposed to do now, Mr. Wheatley?"

The door to Ben's left opens, and four people—two men and two women—wearing bird masks walk out. They are naked, and their bodies are hairless. In the dim lighting their ages are near impossible to determine. There is a crow with feathers so black its beak appears to spring forth from nothingness, an owl with feathers the color of copper and yellow eyes large enough to swallow the room, a sleek falcon with a beak partially open in an avian grin, and the fourth bird head is a cross between a peacock and a parrot. Its garish blue, yellow, and green feathers loom high above its eyes like ancient, forbidding towers.

They walk toward Ben without speaking and without ceremony. The soles of their bare feet gently slap on the hardwood floor. The man in the brightest colored bird mask must be Mr. Wheatley (and/or Mr. H_____) as there are liver spots, wrinkles, and other evidence of age on his skin, but the muscles beneath are surprisingly taut, defined.

Mr. Wheatley takes the bird head out of Ben's hands and forces it over his head. Ben breathes rapidly, as though prepping for a dive into deep water, and the feathers flitter past his eyes, an all-encompassing darkness, and a warmth in the darkness, one that both suffocates and caresses, and then he can see, although not like he could see before. While the surrounding environment of the apartment dims, viewed through an ultraviolet, film-negative spectrum, the bird feathers become spectacular firework displays of colors; secret colors that he was blind to only a moment ago, colors beyond description. That Ben might never see those colors again is a sudden and great sadness. As beautiful as the bird heads are, their owners' naked human bodies, with their jiggling and swaying body parts, are ugly, weak, flawed, ill-designed, and Ben can't help but think of how he could snatch their tender bits in the vise of his beak.

The two men and two women quickly remove Ben's clothes. The Crow says, "Kittypants is waiting to be found and retrieved. He didn't fly away," and they lead him across the living room and to the door from which they'd emerged. Ben is terrified that she's talking about him. He is not sure who he is, who he is supposed to be.

Through the door is a bedroom with a king-size mattress claiming most of the space. There is no bedframe or box spring, only the mattress on the floor. The mattress has not been made up; there are no bedcovers. There is a pile of dried leaves in the middle. Ben watches the pile closely and he believes there is a contour of a shape, of something underneath.

Ben stands at the foot of the mattress while the others move to flank the opposite sides. The lighting is different in the bedroom. Everything is darker but somehow relayed in more detail. Their masks don't look like masks. There are no clear lines of demarcation between head and body, between feather and skin. Is he in fact in the presence of gods? The feather colors have darkened as well, as though they aren't feathers at all but the skin of chameleons. Ben's relief at not being the character in the leaf pile is offset with the fear that he won't ever be able to remove his own bird head.

The others whisper, titter, and twitch, as though they sense his weakness, or lack of commitment. The Crow asks, "Would you prefer talons or beak?" Her beak is mostly black, but a rough, scratchy brown shows through at the beak edges and its tip, as though the black coloring has been worn away from usage.

Ben says, "I would still prefer wings."

Something moves on the bed. Something rustles.

The voice of Mr. Wheatley says, "You cannot choose wings."

Great Blue Heron

JOYCE CAROL OATES

That cry! Hoarse, not-human, fading almost at once. But in an instant she has been wakened.

The cry came from the lake, she supposes. Waterfowl on the lake—loons, geese, mallards. Through the night in her uneasy sleep she hears their beautiful forlorn cries, that are usually muted like human voices heard at a distance. Sometimes there is an agitation on the water, what sounds like a frantic flapping of wings—she listens acutely hoping not to hear cries of distress.

Too early for her to wake. Too early to be *conscious*.

She has been exhausted lately, sleep is precious to her.

Her nightgown is unpleasantly damp from perspiration. The bedclothes are damp. She is breathing quickly, thinly. The cry from the lake has unnerved her—it did not sound human yet it is familiar to her.

She whispers her husband's name. She doesn't want to wake him but she is feeling anxious, lonely.

The bed is larger than she recalls. Almost, she isn't sure if her husband is there, at the farther (left) edge of the bed.

But he is there, seemingly asleep. His broad naked back to her.

Gently she eases against him, craving the touch of another. The protective arms of another.

Her husband appears to be sleeping undisturbed. Whatever the cry from the lake, he has not been wakened.

He has thrown off most of the covers, his shoulders and upper back are cool to the touch. Without opening his eyes he turns sleepily to her, to close his arms around her.

Strong and protective the husband's arms. And his deep slow breathing a kind of protection as well. She lays her head beside his, on a corner of his pillow. In his sleep the husband does strange, sculptural things with pillows: bends them in two, sets them beneath his head vertically, merges two pillows into one, lies at an uncomfortable angle with his head crooked. Yet he sleeps soundly, the nocturnal birds rarely wake him.

Husband and wife are very comfortable together. Without needing to speak they communicate perfectly in their bed in the dark. The wife will claim that she is a light sleeper yet often she falls asleep close to the husband in this way, sharing just the edge of his pillow.

It is the purest sleep, sharing the edge of the husband's pillow.

Close about the roof of the house are smaller birds. Cardinals are the first to wake at dawn. Their familiar, sweet calls are tentative, like questions. They are asking *What is this? Where are we? What will be expected of us?* It must be terrifying to be a bird, she thinks. You must forage for food every minute, you must never rest or your small heart will cease beating.

You must fly, you must exert your wings. Frail bones, that can be snapped so easily. Yet these bones are strong enough to lift you into the air and to buoy you aloft through your life.

These are the birds of day—birds whose songs are familiar to the ear. On the lake and in the marshy land bordering the lake are larger birds, mysterious birds, that cry, call, hoot, moan, shriek, murmur, and make quavering noises, harsh manic laughter through the night.

The screech owl, a singular shuddering cry.

The great blue heron, a hoarse croak of a cry.

Take my hand. And take care.

Hand in hand they are walking along the edge of the lake. The earth underfoot is soft, spongy. It is a chill May morning. Color is bleached from the earth as from the sky. Tall grasses at the water's shore appear to be broken, trampled. There is a smell of wet rotted leaves. Though the season is spring it is a twilit time and all that she sees appears to be neither wholly alive nor wholly dead.

She is gripping her husband's hand just slightly tighter than usual. Perhaps the husband is limping—just slightly. It is natural for the wife to weave her fingers through the husband's fingers. He is the stronger of the two, she defers to him even in the matter of walking together. Soon after they'd met they began holding hands in this way and that was many years ago but in this twilight hour at the lake the wife is unable to calculate how long. A strange silence has come upon her like a veil tied tight against her mouth.

Come here! Look.

Carefully the husband leads the wife. Nearly hidden among tall grasses and cattails at the shore is what appears to be a little colony of nesting ducks—mallards.

These are the most common local ducks. The wife recognizes the sleek dark-green head of the male, the plain brown feathers of the female.

A light rain is falling, causing the surface of the lake to shiver like the skin of a living creature. The sun doesn't seem to be rising in the east so much as materializing behind banks of cloud—pale, without color, sheer light.

She is gripping her husband's hand. She thinks—*We have never been so happy.*

Has he brought her here, to tell her this? *Why* has he brought her here?

The lake at this hour appears different than it appears by day. It seems larger, lacking boundaries. Columns of mist rise, like exhaled breaths. By day you can see individual trees but in this dusk all is shadow like a smear of thick paint. And the surface of the lake reflecting only a dull metallic sheen.

A sun so hazy-pale, it might be the moon. (*Is* that the moon?) Obscured by clouds that appear to be unmoving, fixed in place.

There is something melancholy, the wife thinks, in such beauty. For the lake is beautiful, even drained of color. It is one of the beautiful places of her life, it has become precious to her. Though it is not a large lake in the mountains, only a semi-rural, semi-suburban lake of less than two miles in circumference, at its deepest no more than fifteen feet and much of the water near shore shallow, clotted with cattails.

It is difficult to walk along the lake, there is no single trail amid dense underbrush. Especially dense are stretches of *Rosa acicularis,* thorny wild rose that catch in clothing and raise bleeding scratches on unprotected skin.

Hand in hand walking along the shore. They have come to the end of their property and are making their way along a faint trail in the marsh. The wife is shivering, her feet are getting wet, she would like to turn back but the husband presses forward, he has something to show her. Through their long marriage it is the husband who has had much to show the wife.

Above the lake are flashes of lightning, soundless.

On the steel-colored lake are shadow-figures: a flotilla of Canada geese. The husband and wife stand very still observing the large handsome gray-feathered geese as they float on the surface of the water, heads tucked beneath their wings like illustrations in a children's storybook.

All is serene, near-motionless as in a dream.

Then, seemingly out of nowhere, about twenty feet away, there appears a curious long-legged creature making its way along the shore, in the direction of the mallard nests.

The wife stares, appalled. It is a great blue heron, a predator bird, very thin, with a long snaky neck and scaly legs, a long sharp beak. Eerie and unsettling that the thing, the creature, makes no attempt to use its wings to fly but simply walks awkwardly, yet rapidly, like a human being in some way handicapped or disfigured.

Before any of the mallards sights the predator it attacks the nearest nest. Its beak stabs pitilessly, with robotic precision. There is a violent struggle, there are shrieks, a frenzied flapping of mallard wings as the heron stabs at the nest, piercing eggs with its bill; within seconds it has gobbled down mallard eggs, brazen and indifferent to the smaller water-fowl hissing and flapping their wings in protest.

At another nest the heron discovers tiny unfledged ducklings. The affrighted mallard parents are unable to interfere as the tall snaky-necked bird lifts ducklings one by one in its bill, swiftly, and swallows them whole.

By now all the mallards are protesting, shrieking. There must be two dozen mallards aroused to alarm. Some are on land, at the shore; others are flailing about in the water. Their cries are *cwak-cwak-cwak*, emitted in fury and despair. But the cries come too late. The alarm is ineffectual. The great blue heron remains unmoved, indifferent. Within a minute it has eaten its fill and now lifts its wide gray-feathered wings, extends its leathery-looking neck, and flies away across the lake with a horrible sort of composure.

Only now does the predator emit a cry—harsh, hoarse, croaking—triumphant-sounding, grating to the ear.

Oh God!—she is waking now.

Now, her eyes are open, stark and blind. So surprised, she can't see at first.

For long minutes unable to move as her heart pounds. Stunned as if her body, in the region of her heart, has been pierced by the predator bird's long sharp beak.

She wills herself to wake fully. It is a conscious, moral decision, she thinks—to *wake fully.*

Throws aside the bedclothes that are stifling to her, removes her nightgown, damp with sweat, and tosses it onto the floor like a disgraced thing.

The bed beside her is empty. Of course, the bed is empty.

It is three weeks and two days since her husband's death.

He has left. He has gone. He will not be returning.

These words she tells herself a dozen times a day. These words that are the flattest recitation of horror yet somehow cannot be wholly comprehended. Thus, she must repeat.

He has left. He has gone. He will not be returning.

A jangling at the front door. There is no keeping the intruder out.

Not a predator bird but a scavenger bird. Hunched shoulders like deformed wings, rapacious bright eyes that move over the widow like hunger.

"You will want to sell this property. Of course."

No. I do not want to sell this property.

Gravely the brother-in-law speaks. Though she has told the brother-in-law that it is too soon after the husband's death to think of such matters.

". . . always said, the property is really too much for just two people. And now . . ."

He'd stood on the front stoop ringing the bell. Calling *Claudia! Claudia! It's me.*

And who, she wonders, is *me*?

What has she to do with this *me*?

She could not keep the brother-in-law out of the house. She could not run away to hide upstairs for he would have called 911 to report a desperate woman in (possible) danger of harming herself or worse yet he'd have broken into the house to find her, in triumph.

Saying then—*Poor Claudia! I may have saved her life.*

It is all beyond her control. What people say about her now that her husband has died.

It is astonishing: the (uninvited, unwanted) brother-in-law is sitting in the living room of this house in which he has not (ever) been a guest without the presence of his brother.

The first time (ever) that the brother-in-law has been alone with his brother's wife who has long been wary of him—his glistening eyes, too-genial smile.

The brother-in-law has even helped himself to a drink—amber-colored whiskey splashed into a glass, from a bottle kept in a cabinet with a very few other, select bottles of liquor. The brother-in-law has asked if the widow will join him in a drink and the widow has declined with a nervous smile. How strange, to be asked to join an unwanted intruder in a drink, and to murmur *No thank you* in your own house.

A numbed sense of horror is rising in the widow, of all that she has relinquished and lost.

In his earnest salesman's voice the brother-in-law is speaking of planning for the future, the widow's future. She is the executrix of the husband's estate which involves a good deal of responsibility, and "expertise"—which the widow does not have, understandably.

"I can help you, Claudia. Of course . . ."

How strange, her name on this man's lips—*Claudia*. Worse, he sometimes calls her *Claudie*. As if there were a special intimacy between them.

The brother-in-law speaks of "finances"—"taxes"—"lakeside property"—as if he is being forced to utter painful truths. As if this visit is not his choice (not at all!) but his responsibility as the (younger) brother of the deceased husband, the (concerned, caring) brother-in-law of the widow.

Politely, stiffly the widow is listening.

In truth, the widow is not listening.

Only dimly does the widow hear the brother-in-law speak for there is a roaring in her ears as of a distant waterfall. Only vaguely is she aware of the mouth moving. A kind of hinge to the mouth, like that of a scavenger bird.

Why is he here? Why is he here *with her*? This person in all of the world whom she has never trusted. This person who she believes borrowed money from her husband with the tacit understanding on both sides that the money would (probably) not be returned.

The brother-in-law who has expressed an awkward, unwished-for interest in her as if there were a kind of complicity between them. *You know—that I know—you will never tell Jim.*

Jim! But the husband was called *James*.

Except at times by the younger brother. With a smirking smile—*Jim*. Worse yet, *Jimmy*.

But this is so: she'd never told her husband how his younger brother has had a habit of standing uncomfortably close to her, looming his bulky body over her; he leans his face into hers, hugging her too tightly in greeting or in farewell, so that she is made to feel the unpleasant solidity and heat of his (male) body. How he addresses her in an undertone with a suggestive smile—*H'lo Claudie. Been missing you.*

Often, at family gatherings, the brother-in-law's breath smells of whiskey. Warm, gaseous. And his heavy hand falling on her arm as if accidentally.

She has never told her husband. She would have been embarrassed and ashamed to tell her husband. Rather she would keep a disagreeable secret to herself than share it and disturb others.

Her love for her husband had been a protective love, which she did not want to jeopardize. She did not want to be the bearer of upsetting news to her kindly, sweet-natured and trusting husband and had kept many things from him in the long years of their marriage.

She would keep from him now, if she could, the rawness of her grief. She would not want the (deceased) husband to know how she misses him.

She would not want the (deceased) husband to know how she distrusts, dislikes, fears his brother.

In any case (she has told herself) nothing is likely to happen between her and the brother-in-law because she would not allow it to happen.

"You're looking very pale, Claudia. We all hope you're getting enough sleep."

At this she smiles ironically. *Enough sleep!* There could be only *enough sleep* if she shut her eyes forever.

"Sure I can't fix you a drink? I think I'll have another—just a little . . ."

The brother-in-law is in his mid-fifties, several years younger than the (deceased) husband and of the widow's approximate age. He has made a show of being a devoted family man but his life has been carefully arranged so that he spends as little time with his family as possible. Solid-bodied, big-armed, despite his slightly hunched shoulders he has a ruddy golfer's face and the manner of one eager to *take charge* with his very hands if necessary.

The widow can see the hands *getting a grip*—on her.

As if she were a golf club. An instrument to be deftly deployed by one who will *take charge.*

"The real estate market isn't great at the present time—I acknowledge that. Mortgage rates are high. But with careful marketing, and sound investments after the sale of the property . . ."

The brother-in-law's eyes are damp, inquisitive. Moving over the widow's body like swarming ants as he pours himself another drink, and drinks.

". . . of course, it has been a terrible shock. You have had a *trauma.* Which is why . . ."

The brother-in-law is confident that he will win over the widow. Her silence is a goad to his ingenuity. Her politeness, her courtesy, her habit of deference are a goad to his loquacity. It isn't clear to him—it isn't clear that it much matters—whether the widow is near-catatonic with grief or is simply stiff-backed with female stubbornness in opposition to him precisely because he has the very best advice to give to her.

That is how women are—perverse!

In his professional life the brother-in-law has been an investment banker. He is not an investment banker now—(the widow isn't sure if he "has his own business" or is "between jobs")—but he retains the skills, the information, the experience of investment banking or at least the insider vocabulary, and he is after all the widow's brother-in-law, to whom the widow might naturally turn in this time of distress.

(Indeed the widow has been behaving strangely since the husband's death: keeping to herself, avoiding even her family, her closest relatives and friends. Avoiding *him*.)

"You know, Jim would want you to confide in me. He'd want you to bring me any questions you have about the estate, finances, death taxes, IRS taxes, putting the house on the market . . ."

But I do not want to put the house on the market.

He will be happy to take on the responsibility of acting as the executor of her husband's estate, the brother-in-law says. If she wishes. Naming him executor in her place would require just a consultation with her lawyer. Such an arrangement is "very commonly done"—"a very good idea"—when a widow is inexperienced in "money-matters" and has had a bad shock.

"Shall we make a date? An appointment? I can call your lawyer, we can set up a meeting early next week . . ."

The widow scarcely seems to hear. It is true that she is very pale, waxy-pale, her skin exudes a kind of luminescence that makes her appear younger than her age, as her loose, somewhat disheveled hair, streaked with gray, silver, white hairs and falling to her shoulders, gives her a look somewhere between despair and wild elation.

"I said, I'll call your lawyer and set up a meeting for us . . ."

The widow is staring out a window, at the rear of the house; a short distance away, down a slight incline, the wind-rippled lake reflects the light of late afternoon.

"Claudia? Are you all right? You've been listening, I hope . . ."

The brother-in-law's voice is edged with annoyance. The brother-in-law is not a man to be slighted. He is wearing an open-necked shirt of some fine, expensive material—Egyptian cotton perhaps. The shirt is a pale lavender as his cord trousers are a dark lavender. His shoes are canvas deck shoes. He makes it a point to be well-dressed though his clothes are usually tight and he looks crammed inside them, like an ill-shaped sausage.

The widow recalls how, only a few days before her husband was stricken and hospitalized, the brother-in-law, at a family gathering, had approached her when she was alone and stood uncomfortably close to her, as if daring her to acknowledge his sexual interest and push past him.

Been missin you, Claudie. You're looking terrific.

Always, insultingly, the brother-in-law has felt obliged to comment on his brother's wife's appearance. As if there were some competition between the brothers' wives, of which the wives themselves were not aware.

Since the brother-in-law has gained access to the house, and has been sitting in the living room, repeating his rehearsed words to the widow, the widow has been observing the movement of waterfowl on the lake—ducks, geese. Predators have not gobbled down all of this season's ducklings and goslings. There are even several cygnets, for there is a pair of resident swans on the lake. Dazzling-white swans of surpassing beauty and calm.

When she is feeling very sad, very lonely and distraught, the widow escapes the house in which the telephone is likely to ring, and walks along the lake shore counting ducklings, goslings. Cygnets.

She has sometimes seen the great blue heron, a solitary hunter. By day, the heron does not seem quite so terrifying as it has seemed by night.

"Oh, there!"—the widow speaks excitedly seeing a large rail-thin bird lift its wings suddenly and rise into the air, with initial awkwardness, alone over the lake.

"What are you looking at, Claudia? What's out there that is so damned interesting?"—the brother-in-law turns to look over his shoulder, his chin creasing fatly.

The great blue heron is a prehistoric creature, of a strange and unsettling beauty. The widow stares entranced as slowly and with dignity the heron flies out of sight. But the brother-in-law doesn't seem to have seen.

"Well, that's quite a view. You're lucky, to have such a lakefront property. Jim had the right idea, this property is quite an investment . . ."

The widow objects, more sharply than she'd intended: "James didn't think of it as an 'investment.' It was—it is—our home."

"Well, sure! I didn't mean . . ."

"We chose the house together. James and me. I think you know that. It wasn't the decision of just one of us."

"Right! No need to get upset, Claudia."

"I think—I think now that you should leave. I have many things to do . . ."

It is maddening, the widow hears her apologetic voice. Though trembling with dislike of the intruder yet she feels she must speak to him in a tone of apology.

The brother-in-law smiles, half-jeering. "'Many things to do!' Exactly, Claudia. Things you should certainly be doing, that I could help you with."

"No. I don't think so . . ."

"What d'you mean, 'I don't think so.' Jim would be concerned about you, Claudia."

The widow is stung by the casual way in which the brother-in-law has been uttering her husband's name as if it were an ordinary name to be batted about as in a Ping-pong game.

"No. I said—*no.*"

The brother-in-law blinks at her, and raises his eyebrows, in a pretense of mild surprise. She is in danger of speaking shrilly. She is in danger of betraying emotion. She knows how closely the brother-in-law is observing her, how he will report to others. *Claudia is looking awful. Obviously she hasn't been sleeping. Hope she isn't drinking—secretly. Can't imagine what Jim was thinking of, naming that poor woman executrix of his estate!*

The visit is over. But the brother-in-law is slow to leave.

He has set down his whiskey glass, which he seems to have drained. His face is flushed and ruddy, the little ant-eyes gleam with a malicious sort of satisfaction, yet aggression. For the brother-in-law is one to want more, more.

On their way to the door the brother-in-law continues to speak. The widow is aware of his hands gesturing—always, the man's gestures are florid, exaggerated. He is a TV sort of person—he could be a TV salesman, or a politician. The widow takes care not to be too close to him. For (she knows) the brother-in-law is considering whether he should lay his hand on her arm, or slide his arm across her shoulder. He is considering whether he should grip her hard, in an unmistakable embrace, or simply squeeze her hand, brush his lips against her cheek . . . The widow is distracted by how, though her backbone seems to have been broken and splintered, she is managing to walk upright, and to disguise the discomfort she feels.

The widow sees with a little thrill of horror that the front door has been left ajar . . .

The beginning. Just the beginning. Out of my control.

She will make sure that the door is closed securely behind the brother-in-law. She will lock it.

In a jovial voice the brother-in-law says: "Well, Claudia! I'll call you later tonight. Maybe drop by tomorrow. Will you be home around four P.M.?"

Quickly she tells him *no*. She will not be home.

"What about later? Early evening?"

How aggressive the brother-in-law is! How uncomfortably close to her he is standing, breathing his warm whiskey-breath into her face as if daring her to push him away.

"Goodbye! I'm sorry, I can't talk any longer right now . . ."

The widow would close the door after her unwanted visitor but with a malicious little grin the brother-in-law turns to grip her shoulders and pull her to him and press his fleshy lips against her tight-pursed lips—so quickly she can't push him away.

"No! Stop."

"For Christ's sake, Claudia! Get hold of yourself. You aren't the first person ever to have lost a 'loved one.'"

The brother-in-law speaks sneeringly. The damp close-set eyes flash with rage.

The brother-in-law shuts the front door behind him, hard. He is very angry, the widow knows. She can't resist the impulse to wipe at her mouth with the edge of her hand, in loathing.

From a window the widow watches the brother-in-law drive away from the house, erratically it seems. As if he would like to press his foot down hard on the gas pedal of his vehicle but is retraining himself. She thinks—*But he will return. How can I keep him away!*

She is feeling shaky, nauseated. She has neglected to eat since early morning. The remainder of the day—late afternoon, early evening, night—stretches before her like a devastated landscape.

When she returns to the living room she discovers the empty whiskey glass set carelessly on a mahogany coffee table. The rim is smudged from the brother-in-law's mouth. Somehow, the amber liquid must have splashed over the side of the glass for there is a faint ring on the beautiful wood table-top, an irremediable stain.

She is living alone since James's death.

It is maddening to be asked, as the brother-in-law has asked, Will you sell the house?

With subtle insinuation, Will you sell this large house?

Yet worse, have you considered getting a dog?

Well-intentioned friends, relatives, neighbors. Colleagues from the private school in which she teaches. Often she is unable to answer. Her throat closes up, her face flushes with pinpoints of heat. She sees these good people glancing at one another, concerned for her. A little frisson passes among them like a darting flame, their concern for the widow that links them as in an exciting conspiracy.

She has a fit of coughing. A thorn in her throat, she's unable to swallow. A thorn in a cookie brought to her by one of the well-intentioned, she had not wanted to bite into, but had bitten into that she might prove how recovered from shock she is, how normal she is, how normally she is eating, unwisely she'd bitten into the cookie accursed as a fairy tale cookie for she has no choice, such cookies must be bitten into. And she begins to choke for she can neither swallow the thorn nor cough it up.

"Claudia? Are you all right? Would you like a glass of water?"—the cries come fast and furious like bees.

Quickly she shakes her head *No no—no thank you.* Of course she is all right.

It is the widow's task to assure others, these many others, eager-eyed, greedy to be good at her expense, of course she is *all right.*

Her husband was a well-liked person, indeed well-loved. There is an unexpected burden in being the widow of a well-loved man. Your obligation is to assuage the grief of others. Your obligation is to be kind, thoughtful, generous, sympathetic at all times when all you want is to run away from the kindly prying eyes and find a darkened place in which to sleep, sleep, sleep and never again wake.

Children are brought to the widow's somber house. Staring-eyed children for whom death is a novelty that threatens to turn boring after just a few minutes.

Adults for whom the death of their dear friend James will provide some sort of instruction or educational interlude for their children.

A brash child who says *My mommy says your husband die-ed.*

The widow sees looks of shock, disapproval in the adult faces. Embarrassment in *Mommy*'s face. The widow wants to hide her own face, that the brash child will not see how his crude words have made her cry.

The widow stammers an excuse. Retreats to the kitchen.

The widow will not hear her visitors murmuring in the other room for they have pitched their voices low, and she would rather draw a sharp-edged butcher knife across her forearm than overhear what they are saying.

Has the widow become an object of fear? An object of terror?

Has she become *ugly?*

Has she become *old?*

She thinks of witches. Women without men to protect them. Women whose husbands have died. Women whose property might be annexed by rapacious neighbors. Fortunately, the widow does not live in barbarous times.

This widow is protected by the law. The husband left a detailed and fully executed will leaving her his entire property, his estate.

When the widow returns to the other room her guests smile at her nervously, worriedly. They have prepared something to tell her and it is the widow's oldest friend who rises to embrace her speaking of how James had "seen the best in everyone"—"brought out the best selves of everyone"— and the widow stands very still in the embrace, her arms limp at her sides, arms that are not wings, arms that lack the muscular power of wings to

unfold, to lift the widow out of this embrace and to fly, fly away for her
obligation is to submit to the commiseration of others and not scream at
them *Go away all of you! For God's sake go away and leave me alone.*

⌒

"James! Darling, come look."

She has begun to sight the great blue heron more frequently, at unpre-
dictable hours of the day.

She believes that there is just one great blue heron at the lake. At least,
she has never seen more than one at a time.

The large predator bird is fascinating to her. There is something very
beautiful about it—there is something very ugly about it.

On her walks the widow has discovered the solitary heron hunting
for fish in a creek that empties into the lake, that bounds the edge of her
property—standing in the slow-moving water very still, poised to strike.

For long minutes the heron remains unmoving. You might think that
it isn't a living creature but something heraldic wrought of pewter, an
ancient likeness. Then as an unwitting fish swims into view the heron is
galvanized into action instantaneously, stabbing its beak into the water,
thrashing its wings to keep its balance, emerging in triumph with a
squirming fish in its bill.

It is a shocking sight! It is thrilling.

No sooner does the widow catch a glimpse of the fish caught in the
heron's bill than the fish has disappeared, in a single swallow into the
predator's gullet. The rapacity of nature is stunning. Here is raw, primitive
hunger. Here is pure instinct, that bypasses consciousness.

Sometimes, if the fish is too large to be swallowed by the heron in a
single gulp, or if the heron has been distracted by something close by, the
heron will fly away with the live fish gleaming and squirming in its bill.

There is a particular horror in this. The widow stares transfixed. It is
not so difficult to imagine a gigantic heron swooping at her, seizing her
in its bill and bearing her away to—where?

The heron invariably flies to the farther side of the lake, and disappears into the marshland there. Its flight seems awkward, ungainly like a

pelican's flight—the enormous slate-gray wings like an umbrella opening, legs dangling down. Almost, if you don't understand what a killing machine the heron is, and how precise its movements, there is something comical about it.

Except this isn't so, of course. The heron is as much a master of the air as other, seemingly more compact and graceful birds.

The widow is appalled, yet riveted: that reptilian fixedness to the heron's eyes. Obviously, the heron's eye must be sharp as an eagle's eye, to discern the movement of prey in a dense and often shadowed element like water.

The long thin stick-like legs, that dangle below as the bird flies flapping the great wings. The long S-curved neck, the long lethal beak of the hue of old, stained ivory.

Difficult to get very close to the vigilant bird but the widow has seen that it has a white-feathered face. Dark gray plumes run from its eyes to the back of its head, like a mask. There is a curious rather rakish dark-feathered quill of several inches jutting out at the back of the heron's head—this feature (she will discover) is found only in the male. Its wide wings are slate-colored with a faint tincture of blue most clearly sighted from below, as the heron flies overhead.

Yet it is strange, the bird is called a *great blue heron*. Most of its feathers are gray or a dusty red-brown: thighs, neck, chest.

She has heard the heron's cry many times now: a hoarse, harsh croak like a bark. Impossible not to imagine that there is something derisive and triumphant in this cry.

"James, listen! We'd been hearing the great blue heron for years without realizing what it was . . ."

The harsh cry is a mockery of the musical cries and calls of the songbirds that cluster close about the house, drawn to bird feeders. (She and James had always maintained bird feeders. Among her dearest memories are of James biting his lower lip in concentration as he poured seed into the transparent plastic feeders on the deck at the rear of the house in even the bitterest cold of winter.)

In books on her husband's shelves the widow has researched the great blue heron—*Ardea herodias*. Indeed the heron is a primitive creature, descended from dinosaurs: a flying carnivore.

Its prey is fish, frogs, small rodents, eggs of other birds, nestlings and small birds. Eagles, the heron's natural predators, are not native to this part of the northeast.

Considering its size the heron is surprisingly light—the heaviest herons weigh just eight pounds. Its wingspan is thirty-six inches to fifty-four inches and its height is forty-five to fifty-five inches. It is described as a *wading bird* and its habitat is general in North America, primarily in wetlands.

She and James had favored the familiar songbirds—cardinals, titmice, chickadees, house wrens and sparrows of many species—and had less interest in the waterfowl, that often made a commotion on the lake; now, she is less interested in the small, tamer birds and is drawn more to the lake and the wetlands surrounding it.

In the night, the blood-chilling cry of the screech owl wakes her, but also comforts her. She keeps her window open, even on cold nights, not wanting to be spared.

She has come to recall the heron attacking the mallards' nests as an actual incident, shared with her husband. Vague in its context it is vivid in details and has come to seem the last time she and James had walked together along the lake shore, hand in hand.

Now I want only to do good. I want to be good.

If I am good the terrible thing that has happened will be reversed.

The cemetery is just ten minutes from the house. Very easy to drive there. No matter the weather.

It is not the cemetery favored by her husband's family, which is in the affluent community of Fair Hills fifteen miles away. It is not the cemetery the widow was expected to have chosen in which to bury her husband—that is, her husband's "remains." Instead this is an old Presbyterian cemetery in a nearby village, dating to the 1770s. It is small, it is not so very well tended. It is no longer exclusively for members of the church but has become a municipal cemetery. The earliest grave markers, close behind the dour stone church, are a uniform dull gray whose chiseled letters are worn smooth with time and have become indecipherable. The markers themselves are thin as playing cards, nearly; tilted at odd, jaunty angles in the mossy earth.

More recent grave stones are substantial, stolid. Death appears to be weightier now. Words, dates are decipherable. *Dearest Mother. Beloved Husband. Dearest Daughter 1 Week Old.*

Each day in the late afternoon the widow visits the husband's grave which is still the most recent, the *freshest* of graves in the cemetery.

The grave stone the widow purchased for the husband is made of beautiful smooth-faced granite of the hue of ice, with a roughened edge. Not very large, for James would not have wished anything conspicuous or showy or unnecessarily expensive.

In the earth, in a surprisingly heavy urn, the (deceased) husband's ashes.

No grass has (yet) appeared in the grave-soil though the widow has scattered grass seed there.

(Are birds eating the seeds? She thinks so!)

It is consoling to the widow that so little seems to change in the cemetery from day to day, week to week. The tall grasses are mowed haphazardly. Most other visitors come earlier than she does and are gone by late afternoon. If there is any activity in the church it is limited to mornings. Rarely does the widow encounter another mourner and so she has (naively) come to feel safe here in this quiet place where no one knows her . . .

"Excuse me, lady. What the hell are you doing?"

Today there has appeared in this usually deserted place a woman with a truculent pug-face. Like a cartoon character this scowling person even stands with her hands on her hips.

Claudia is astonished! Her face flushes with embarrassment.

In the cemetery at the gravesite of a stranger buried near her husband she has been discovered on her knees energetically trimming weeds.

"That's my husband's grave, ma'am."

The voice is rude and jarring and the staring eyes suggest no amusement at Claudia's expense, no merriment. There is a subtle, just-perceptible emphasis on *my*.

Guiltily Claudia stammers that she comes often to the cemetery and thought she might just "pull a few weeds" where she saw them . . . It is not possible to explain to this unfriendly person that untidiness makes her nervous and that she has become obsessed with a compulsion to *do good, be good.*

It is her life as a widow, wayward and adrift and yet compulsive, fated. After James's abrupt death it was suggested to her by the headmistress of her school that she take a leave of absence from teaching, and so she'd agreed while doubting that it was a good idea.

A five-month *leave of absence* it was. Seeming to the widow at the outset something like a death sentence.

She has busied herself bringing fresh flowers to James's grave, and clearing away old flowers. She has kept the grasses trimmed neatly by James's grave though (she knows) it is an empty ritual, a gesture of futility, observed by no one except herself.

There is not much to tend at James's neat, new grave. Out of a dread of doing nothing, as well as a wish to do something the widow has begun clearing away debris and weeds from adjoining graves.

Why do you need to keep busy, Claudia? All our busyness comes to the same end.

She knows! The widow knows this.

All the more reason to *keep busy.*

In the neglected cemetery the widow has been feeling sorry for those individuals, strangers to her and James, who have been buried here and (seemingly) forgotten by their families. James's nearest neighbor is *Beloved Husband and Father Todd A. Abernathy 1966–2011* whose pebbled stone marker is surrounded by unsightly tall grasses, thistles and dandelions.

Scattered in the grass are broken clay pots, desiccated geraniums and pansies. Even the artificial sunflowers are frayed and faded as mere trash.

Claudia has begun bringing small gardening tools and gloves to the cemetery. She has not consciously decided to *do good,* it seems to have happened without her volition.

The only sincere way of *doing good* is to be anonymous. She has thought.

But now she has been discovered. Her behavior, reflected in a stranger's scowling face, does not seem so *good* after all.

Quickly she rises to her feet, brushes at her knees. She is feeling unpleasantly warm inside her dark tasteful clothes.

She hears her voice faltering and unconvincing: "I'm sorry! I didn't mean to surprise or upset you. I just like—I guess—to use my hands . . . I come to the cemetery so often . . ."

"Well. That's real kind of you."

Just barely the woman relents. Though the woman doesn't seem to be speaking ironically or meanly it is clear that she doesn't think much of Claudia's charity, that has cast an unflattering reflection upon her as a slipshod caretaker of the *Abernathy* grave.

Unlike Claudia who is always well-dressed—(she is too insecure to dress otherwise)—the scowling woman wears rumpled clothing, soiled jeans and flip-flops on her pudgy feet. Her streaked-blond hair looks uncombed, her face is doughy-pale. She too is a widow whose loss has made her resentful and resigned like one standing out in the rain without an umbrella.

Claudia hears herself say impulsively that her husband is buried here also.

"He just—it was back in April—died . . ."

It is unlike the widow so speak so openly. In fact it is unlike the widow to speak of her personal life at all to a stranger.

Claudia has no idea what she is saying or why she feels compelled to speak to this stranger who is not encouraging her, whose expression has turned sour. Her brain is flooded as with a barrage of lights. How have you continued to live as a widow? *How did you forgive yourself? Why will you not smile at me? Why will you not even look at me?*

"O.K. But in the future maybe mind your own business, ma'am? Like the rest of us mind ours."

Rudely the woman turns her back on Claudia. Or maybe she has not meant to be rude, only just decisive.

Claudia returns to James's grave but she is very distracted, her hands are trembling. Why is the woman so hostile to her? Was it such a terrible thing, to have dared to pull out weeds on a neighboring grave?

Forget her. It's over. None of this matters—of course.

It is ironic, Claudia manages to elude friends, family, relatives who express concern for her, and worry that she is in a precarious mental state still; yet here in the cemetery, where Claudia would speak to another mourner, she has been rebuffed.

At James's gravesite she stands uncertain. She is grateful that in some way (her brain is dazzled, she is not thinking clearly) her deceased husband has been spared this embarrassing exchange. She is still wearing gardening gloves, and carrying her hand trowel. Her leather hand bag is lying in the grass as if she'd flung it down carelessly. Why is she so upset, over a trifle? A stranger's rudeness? Or is she right to feel guilty, has she been intrusive and condescending? A quiet woman, one of the softer-spoken teachers at her school, Claudia has occasionally been criticized as aloof, indifferent to both students and colleagues. She winces to think how unfair this judgment is.

She doesn't want to leave the cemetery too soon for the woman will notice and sneer at her departing back. On the other hand, she doesn't want to linger in this place that feels inhospitable to her. She dreads someone else coming to join the scowling woman, and the scowling woman will tell her what she'd discovered Claudia doing at Todd Abernathy's grave, and what Claudia had done will be misinterpreted, misconstrued as a kind of vandalism.

High overhead is a solitary, circling bird. Claudia has been aware of this bird for some minutes but has not glanced up since she supposes it must be a hawk, hawks are common in this area, and not a great blue heron for there isn't a lake or wetlands nearby . . .

She wants to think that it is a great blue heron. Her heart is stirred as a shadow with enormous outflung wings and trailing spindly legs glides past her on the ground and vanishes.

"Ma'am?"—the scowling woman is speaking to her.

"Yes?"

"There were potted geraniums on my husband's grave. Did you take them?"

"Potted geraniums? No . . ."

"Yes! There were potted geraniums here. What did you do with them?"

Hesitantly Claudia tells the woman that she might have seen some broken clay pots in the grass, but not geranium plants; that is, not living plants. She might have seen dead plants . . .

"And some artificial flowers? In a pot here?"

"N-No . . . I don't think so."

"Ma'am, I think you are lying. I think you've been stealing things from graves. I'm going to report you . . ."

Claudia protests she has not been stealing anything. She has cleared away debris and dried flowers, and pulled weeds . . . Everything she has cleared away is in a trash heap at the edge of the cemetery . . . But the scowling woman is speaking harshly, angrily; she has worked herself up into a peevish temper, and seems about to start shouting. Claudia is quite frightened. She wonders if she has blundered into a place of madness.

Is that what comes next, after grief? Is there no hope?

Abjectly Claudia apologizes again. In a flash of inspiration—in which she sees the jeering face of her brother-in-law—she offers to pay for the "missing" geranium plants.

"Here. Please. I'm truly sorry for the misunderstanding."

Out of her wallet she removes several ten-dollar bills. Her hands are shaking. (She sees the woman greedily staring at her wallet, and at her dark leather bag.) The bills she hands to the woman who accepts them with a look of disdain as if she is doing Claudia a favor by taking a bribe, and not reporting her.

With sour satisfaction the woman says: "O.K., ma'am. Thanks. And like I say, next time mind your own damn business."

At her vehicle Claudia fumbles with the ignition key. She is conscious that her car is a handsome black BMW; the only other vehicle in the parking lot, a battered Chevrolet station wagon, must belong to the scowling woman. More evidence that Claudia is contemptible in some way, in the woman's derisive eyes.

She is very upset. She must escape. The cemetery, that has been a place of refuge for her, has become contaminated.

A shadow, or shadows, glides across the gleaming-black hood of the BMW. Her brain feels blinded as if a shutter had been thrown open to the sun. She feels a powerful urge to run back to the scowling woman bent over her husband's grave in a pretense of clearing away weeds. She would grip the woman's shoulders and shake, shake, shake—she would stab at the sour scowling face with something like a sharp beak . . . .

Of course the widow does nothing of the sort. In the gleaming-black BMW she drives back to the (empty) house on Aubergine Lake.

"Claudie? I'd like to drop by this afternoon, I have a proposal to make to you . . ."

"No. I don't think so."

"I've been talking to a terrific agent at Sotheby's, you know they're only interested in exceptional properties . . ."

"I said *no*. I won't be home, this isn't a good time."

"Tomorrow, then? Let's say four-thirty p.m.?"

"I—I won't be home then. I'll be at the cemetery."

"Fine! Great! I'll swing around to the house and pick you up at about quarter to? How's that sound? I've been wanting to visit Jimmy's grave but have been crazy-busy for weeks and this is—the—ideal—opportunity for us to go together. *Thank you, Claudie.*"

Claudia tries to protest but the connection has been broken.

Your husband has left. Your husband has gone. Your husband will not be returning.

Calmly, cruelly the voice stalks her. Especially she is vulnerable when she is alone in the house.

Not her own voice but the voice of another speaking through her mouth numbed as with Novacaine.

Your husband has left. Your husband has gone . . .

Shaking out sleeping pills into the palm of her hand. Precious pills! One, two, three . . .

But the phone will ring if she tries to sleep. Even if there is no one to hear, the phone will ring. New messages will be left amid a succession of unanswered messages like eggs jammed into a nest and beginning to rot—*Claudia? Please call. We are concerned. We will come over if we don't hear from you . . . .*

The doorbell will ring. *He*, the rapacious brother-in-law, will be at the door.

"I will not. I've told you—*no*."

Hastily she pulls on rubber boots, an old L.L. Bean jacket of her husband's with a hood. She has found a pair of binoculars in one of James's closets and wears it around her neck tramping in the wetlands around the lake.

Here, the widow is not so vulnerable to the voice in her head. No telephone calls to harass her, no doorbell.

Rain is not a deterrent, she discovers. Waterfowl on the lake pay not the slightest heed even to pelting rain, it is their element and they thrive in it.

A sudden croaking cry, and she turns to see the great blue heron flying overhead. The enormous unfurled wings!—she stares after the bird in amazement.

Belatedly raising the binoculars to watch the heron fly across the lake. Slow pumping of the great wings, that bear the bird aloft with so little seeming effort.

Flying above the lake. Rain-rippled slate-colored lake. Chill gusty air, mists lifting from the water. Yet the heron's eyesight is so acute, the minute darting of a fish in the lake, glittery sheen of fish-skin thirty feet below the heron in flight, is enough to alter the trajectory of the heron's flight in an instant as the heron abruptly changes course, plummets to the surface of the lake, seizes the (living, thrashing) fish in its bill—and continues its flight across the lake.

That stabbing beak! There has been nothing like this in the widow's life until now.

She is determined, she will be *a good person.*

James would want her to continue her life as she'd lived her life of more than fifty years essentially as *a good person.*

This catastrophe of her life, a deep wound invisible to others' eyes, she believes might be healed, or numbed. *If she is good.*

She forces herself to reply to emails. (So many! The line from *The Wasteland* seeps into her brain: *I had not thought that death had undone so many.*) She forces herself to reply to phone messages by (shrewdly, she thinks) calling friends, relatives, neighbors at times when she is reasonably sure no one will answer the phone.

Hi! It's Claudia. Sorry to have been so slow about returning your call—calls . . .

I'm really sorry! I hope you weren't worried . . .

You know, I think there is something wrong with my voice mail . . .
Of course—I am fine . . .
Of course—I am sleeping all right now . . .
Of course—it's a busy time for a—a widow . . .
Thanks for the invitation but—right now, I am a little preoccupied . . .
Thanks for the offer—you're very kind—but—
Yes I will hope to see you soon. Sometime soon . . .
No I just can't. I wish that I could . . .
Thank you but . . .
I'm so sorry. I've been selfish, I haven't thought of you.

The phone drops from her hand. She is trembling with rage.

Still the widow is determined to *do good, be good.*

She will establish a scholarship in her husband's name at the university from which he'd graduated with such distinction.

She will arrange for a memorial service for her husband, in some vague future time—"Before Thanksgiving, I think."

She will donate most of his clothes to worthy charities including those beautiful woolen sweaters she'd given him, those many neckties and those suits and sport coats she'd helped him select, how many shirts, how many shoes, how many socks she cannot bear to think, she cannot bear to remove the husband's beautiful clothing from closets, she will not even remove the husband's socks and underwear from drawers, she has changed her mind and will not donate most of his clothes, indeed any of his clothes to worthy charities. *She will not.*

That hoarse, harsh cry!—it has been ripped from her throat.

Flying, ascending. The misty air above the lake is revealed to be textured like fabric. It is not thin, invisible, of no discernible substance but rather this air is thick enough for the great pumping wings to fasten onto that she might climb, climb, climb with little effort.

She has become a winged being climbing the gusty air like steps. Elation fills her heart. She has never been so happy. Every pulse in her being rings, pounds, beats, shudders with joy. The tough muscle in her bony chest fast-beating like a metronome.

Low over the lake she flies. Through ascending columns of mist she flies. The great blue heron is the first of the predator-birds to wake each morning in the chill twilight before dawn. It is an almost unbearable happiness, pumping the great gray-feathered wings that are so much larger than the slender body they might wrap the body inside them, and hide it.

Into the marshy woods, flying low. Her sharp eyes fixed on the ground. Small rodents are her prey. Small unwitting birds are her prey.

She will wade in the shallow water moving slowly forward on her spindly legs, or standing very still. She is very patient. Her beak strikes, she swallows her prey whole, and alive—thrashing and squealing in terror.

The hoarse, croaking cry—a proclamation of pure joy.

Yet she is happiest when flying. When she is rising with the air currents, soaring and floating on gusts of wind. When her eye detects motion below, a flash of color, fish-color, and her slender body instantaneously becomes a sleek missile, aimed downward, propelled sharply downward, to kill.

Through the air she plunges and her sharp beak is precise and pitiless spearing a small fish which in a single reflex she swallows alive, still squirming as it passes down her throat, into her gullet.

She hunts without ceasing for she is always hungry. It is hunger that drives all motion, like waves that never come to an end but are renewed, refreshed.

Again the triumphant cry which you hear in your sleep. *I am alive, I am here, I am myself and I am hungry.*

Each morning it has been happening. The widow wakes with a sudden violence as if she has been yanked into consciousness.

A hoarse croaking cry from the lake.

A blinding light flooding the brain.

She is furious with the (deceased) husband. She has told no one.

Why did you go away when you did? Why did you not take better care of yourself? Why were you careless of both our lives?

How can I forgive you . . .

Why had he died, why when he might not have died. As he'd lived quietly, unobtrusively. Always *a good person.*

Always *kind. Considerate of others.*

He'd had chest pains, a spell of breathlessness and light-headedness but he had not wanted to tell her. He'd promised he would pick up his sister's son at Newark Airport and drive him to relatives in Stamford, Connecticut; no reason the nineteen-year-old couldn't take a bus or a taxi but James had insisted, no trouble, really no trouble, in fact it is a good deal of trouble, it is a trip of hours, and some of these in heavy traffic. Already as he was preparing to leave she'd seen something in his face, a sudden small wince, a startled concentration, with wifely concern asking, Is something wrong? and quickly he'd said No, it's nothing, of course James would quickly say *It's nothing* for that is the kind of man James was. And that is why (the widow thinks bitterly) James is not that man any longer, he is not is, he is *was.* And she might have known this. She might have perceived this. Asking, But are you in pain?—and he'd denied pain as a wrongdoer would deny having done wrong for that is how he was.

She was saying, there was pettishness in her voice (she knows), why don't we hire a car service for your nephew, explain that the drive is just too much for you, and then you have to turn around and return and we would pay for it ourselves of course, but James said certainly not, no, he'd promised to pick up his nephew and drive him to Stamford, it would be an opportunity for him and Andy to talk together, for they so rarely saw each other in recent years. And he said my sister and brother-in-law wouldn't allow us to pay for a car service which seemed beside the point to Claudia who said exasperated, Then they should pay for the car! *Why are we quarreling, what is this about?*

Well, she knew. She knew what it was about: James's feelings of obligation to his family. James's habit of being *good.* His compulsion to *do the right thing* even when the right thing is meaningless.

Even when the *right thing* will cost him his life.

The husband's compulsion to be generous, to be kind, to be considerate of others because *that is his nature.*

And the pains had not subsided but increased as James drove along the Turnpike and in a nightmare of interstate traffic his vehicle swerved off the highway just before the exit for Newark Airport. And he was taken by ambulance to an ER in Newark where he would survive for ninety-six minutes—until just before the terrified wife arrives.

Exhausted insomniac hours at her husband's death going through accounts, bank statements, paying bills.

Not death, *desk*. She'd meant.

The brother-in-law has left a glossy Sotheby's brochure.

The brother-in-law has left a glossy brochure for a "genetic modification" research institute in Hudson Park, New Jersey across which he has scrawled *Terrific opportunities for investment here but it's "time sensitive"—before the stock takes off into the stratosphere.*

The brother-in-law has left a snide phone message—*Claudie? You must know that I am your friend & (you must know) you have not so many friends now that Jim is gone.*

She is not unhappy! She has grown to love rain-lashed days, days when there is no sun, mud-days, when she can tramp in the wetlands in rubber boots. In an old L.L. Bean jacket of her husband's with wonderful zippered pockets and flaps into which she can shove tissues, gloves, even a cell phone.

She will not usually answer the cell phone if it rings. But she feels an obligation to see who might wish to speak with her. Whom she might call back.

Not the brother-in-law. Not *him*.

She is returning to the house when she sees his vehicle in the driveway— a brass-colored Land Rover. She knows that he is ringing the doorbell, rapping his knuckles smartly on the door. She sees him peering through a window, shading his small bright eyes. *Claudie? Claudie it's me—are you in there?*

Amid dripping trees at the corner of the house the widow waits, in hiding.

She will say *It is very quiet at the lake. It is lonely at the lake.*
Most days.

"Stop! Stop that . . ."

Cupping her hands to her mouth, shouting at the boys throwing rocks out onto the lake at the waterfowl.

It is amazing to the widow—she is *shouting*.

Not for years, not in memory has she *shouted*. The effort is stunning, her throat feels scraped as with a rough-edged blade.

"Stop! Stop . . ."

Most of the rocks thrown by the boys fall short. Only a few of the youngest, most vulnerable birds have been struck—ducklings, goslings. The boys, who appear to be between the ages of ten and thirteen, are not wading in the water—(it's as if they are too lazy, too negligent to hunt their prey with much energy)—but run along the lake shore hooting and yelling. The adult mallards, geese, swans have escaped toward the center of the lake, flapping their wings in distress, squawking, shrieking. The boys laugh uproariously—the birds' terror is hilarious to them. Claudia is furious, disgusted.

"Stop! I'll call the police . . ."

Boldly Claudia approaches the boys hoping to frighten them off. She is panting, her heart is pounding with adrenaline. She seems oblivious to the possibility that the boys might turn to throw rocks at *her*.

Their crude cruel faces are distorted with glee. They seem scarcely human to her. They glare at her, leer at her, trying to determine (she guesses) if she is someone who might recognize them and tell their parents; if she is someone whose authority they should respect.

"Don't you hear me? I said *stop!* It's against the law, 'cruelty to animals'—I will report you to the sheriff's office . . ."

The words *sheriff's office* seems to make an impression on the older boys who begin to back off. Claudia hears them muttering

Go to hell lady, fuck you lady amid derisive laughter but they have turned away and are tramping back through the marsh to the road.

Six boys in all. It is disconcerting to see how unrepentant they are, and how young.

Claudia supposes the boys live nearby. Not on the lake but near.

Their laughter wafts across the marsh. She is shaken by their cruelty, and the stupidity of their cruelty. What would James have done!

On the lake the terrified birds continue their protests, *craw-craw-craw*. They are swimming in frantic circles. They can't comprehend what has happened to their young, what devastation has rained down upon them. The widow is terribly upset and can't come closer to the carnage. A number of the young birds must have been killed in the barrage of rocks. Others must have been injured. She does not want to see the living, injured creatures floating in the lake. She does not want to see their writhing little wings, she does not want to see the distress of the elder birds, this has been enough, this has been more than enough, she does not want to feel anything further, not at this time.

And yet: pursuing the boys from the air. Beating her great wings, that are powerful with muscle. Glancing up they see her bearing upon them, their faces are rapt with astonishment, shock, terror. It would seem to them (perhaps) that the creatures they had tormented had taken a single, singular shape to pursue them. It would seem to them (perhaps) that a primitive justice is being enacted. The creature that swoops upon them is not a large predator, not an eagle. But her slate-colored outspread wings are as large as the wings of an eagle. Her beak is longer than the beak of an eagle, and it is sharper. The screams of the cruel boys will not deter her—nothing will deter her.

The boys run, stumble, fall to their knees before reaching the road. They try to shield their faces with their uplifted arms. She is fierce in her assault, she attacks them with both her wings as an aroused swan would attack, beating them down, knocking them to the ground. And once they are on the ground they are helpless to escape the talon-claws that grip them tight as with her pitiless beak she stabs, stabs, stabs at heads, scalps, faces, eyes.

The boys' cries are piteous, pleading. Blood oozes from a dozen wounds and darkens the marsh grasses beneath them.

~

Her dreams have become agitated, she is afraid to sleep.

Especially, she is afraid to sleep in the large bedroom at the upstairs, rear of the house overlooking the lake.

She moves to another, smaller room, a guest room overlooking the front lawn of the house. This room has pale yellow chintz walls, organdy curtains. She keeps the windows shut at night. She is determined, she will regain her soul.

She will *make amends.*

"Why, Claudia! Hello."

"Claudia! What a surprise . . ."

Greetings are warm at the private girls' school to which she returns for a visit. It has been too long, she says: four months, two weeks, six days! She has missed them all.

Unable not to see how, irresistibly, uncannily, every colleague she meets, everyone who shakes or grips her hand, embraces her, exclaims how much she has been missed, glances at the third finger of her left hand: the rings the widow (of course) continues to wear.

Do you expect to see nothing there? But of course I am still married.

In the seminar room she meets with her honors students.

These are bright lovely girls who have missed their favorite instructor very much. They all know that her husband has died and are shy in her presence. Several girls had written to her, halting little letters she'd read with tears in her eyes, and had set aside, meaning to answer some time in the future as she means to answer all of the letters she has received some time in the future.

The girls do not glance at the widow's rings, however. They are too young, they have no idea.

(But—what is wrong? Is something wrong? In the midst of an earnest discussion of that poem by Emily Dickinson that begins *After great pain, a formal feeling comes* the widow begins to feel faint, light-headed.)

Perhaps it is too soon for the widow to return to the school where she'd once been so happy, as she'd been younger. Too soon to be talking animatedly with bright young girl-students as if she were as untouched as they, stretching her wound of a mouth into a smile.

Later, speaking with colleagues in the faculty lounge she feels an overwhelming urge to flee, to run away and hide. Her arms ache at the shoulders, badly she wants to spread the enormous muscled wings and fly, fly away where no one knows her.

She excuses herself, stumbling into a restroom. All her colleagues are women, their voices are pitched low in concern she wishes avidly not to hear—*Poor Claudia! She looks as if she hasn't been sleeping in weeks.*

Jangling at the front door. The widow would run away to hide but she cannot for she is powerless to keep the intruder out of her home.

Claudie he calls her in his mock-chiding voice laying his heavy hand on her arm as if he has the right.

Has she made a decision about the house?—the brother-in-law inquires with a frown.

Listing the property with Sotheby's as he has urged. Exceptional private homes, estates. The brother-in-law has contacted a realtor who can come to meet with them within the hour if he is summoned.

No she has told him. *No no no.*

And the pharmaceutical research company? It is "urgent" to invest before another day passes, the brother-in-law has tried to explain.

The brother-in-law is bemused by her—is he? Or is the brother-in-law exasperated, annoyed?

Badly he wants to be the executor of his deceased brother's estate for (of course) the grieving widow is not capable of being the executrix.

I will help you, Claudie. You know Jim would want you to trust me.

She sees how he is eyeing her, the small bright eyes running over her like ants. He is very close to her, looming over her about to seize her by the shoulders to press his wet fleshy mouth against her mouth but she is too quick for him, she has pushed away from him, breathless, excited.

Claudie! What the hell d'you think you are doing . . .

He is flush-faced and panting. He would grab her, to hurt her. But she eludes him, her arms lengthening into wings, her slender body becoming even thinner, pure muscle. Her neck lengthens, curved like a snake.

And there is the beak: long, sharp, lethal.

The brother-in-law is dazed and confounded. In quicksilver ripples the change has come over her, it is the most exquisite sensation, indescribable.

She is above the enemy, plunging at him with her sharp long beak. So swiftly it has happened, the enemy has no way of protecting himself. The great blue heron is swooping at him, he is terrified trying with his arms to shield his head, face, eyes as the beak stabs at him—left cheek, left eye, moaning mouth, throat—blood spurts onto the beautiful slate-gray feathers of the heron's breast as the enemy screams in terror and pain.

Afterward she will wonder whether some of the terror lay in the brother-in-law's recognition of *her*—his brother's widow Claudia.

The exhilaration of the hunt! The heron is pitiless, unerring.

Once your prey has fallen it will not rise to its feet again. It will not escape your furious stabbing beak, there is no haste in the kill.

Once, two, three . . . The widow shakes out sleeping pills into the palm of her hand.

Badly she wants to sleep! To sleep, and not to wake.

On the cream-colored woolen carpet of the guest room with chintz walls, organdy curtains, just visible inside the doorway is the faintest smear of something liquid and dark the widow has not (yet) noticed.

"My God. What terrible news . . . ."

Yet it is perplexing news. That the brother-in-law has been killed in so strange a way, stabbed to death with something like an ice pick, or attacked by a large bird—his skull pierced, both his eyes lacerated, multiple stab wounds in his chest, torso.

The brother-in-law was discovered in his vehicle, slumped over in the passenger's seat, several miles from his home.

(But closer to his home than to the widow's home on Aubergine Lake.)

He'd been missing overnight. No one in his family knew where he'd gone. In the brass-colored Land Rover, at the side of a country road, the brother-in-law had died of blood loss from his many wounds.

It was clear that the brother-in-law had died elsewhere, not in the vehicle in which there was not much blood.

Hearing this astonishing news the widow is stunned. How is it possible, the brother-in-law is—*dead?* It doesn't seem believable that anyone she knows can have been murdered, the victim of a "vicious" attack.

A man with "no known enemies"—it is being said.

Local police are describing the attack as "personal"—"a kind of execution." Not likely a random or opportunistic attack for the victim's wallet was not missing, his expensive new-model vehicle had not been stolen.

There are no suspects so far. There seem to have been no witnesses on the country road.

The murder of the brother-in-law has followed soon after the assault of six local boys by what two survivors of the assault described as "a big bird like an eagle" that flew at them "out of the sky with a stabbing beak"—injuries to the boys' heads, faces, eyes, torsos that closely resemble the injuries of the brother-in-law.

Four boys killed in the savage attack, two boys surviving in "critical condition." They'd been attacked in a marshy area near Lake Aubergine where there are no eagles, no large hawks, no predator-birds of any species capable of attacking human beings, or with any history of attacking human beings.

Yet the survivors insist they'd been attacked by a *big bird out of the sky with a stabbing beak.*

Like the brother-in-law, each of the boys was blinded in the attack.

Their eyes badly wounded, past repair. Stabbed many times.

Trembling, the widow hangs up the phone.

She has heard about the boys—the deaths, the terrible injuries. She has not wanted to think that something so awful could take place so close to her own home and when police officers have come to ask her if she'd seen or heard anything, if she knew any of the boys or their families she'd said only that they were not neighbors of hers and her husband's, they lived miles away and she knew nothing of them.

I'm afraid that I have seen nothing, and I have heard nothing. It's very quiet here at the lake.

More astonishing to her is the news of her brother-in-law—dying so soon after her husband James.

How devastated their family is! She is no longer the most recent widow among the relatives.

The phone will continue to ring but the widow will not hear it for she has stepped outside the house. Her lungs crave fresh air, it has become difficult to breathe inside the house.

Outside, the lawn has become overgrown. She has terminated the contract with the lawn service for she prefers tall grasses, thistles, wild flowers of all kinds—these are beautiful to her, thrilling.

A shadow gliding in the grasses at her feet.

She looks up, shading her eyes. She is prepared to see the great blue heron in its solitary flight but sees to her surprise that there are two herons flying side by side, their great slate-gray wings outstretched as they soar, the wing tips virtually touching.

From below she can see the faint tinge of azure in the gray feathers. Such beautiful birds, flying in tandem! She has never seen such a sight, she is sure.

Transfixed the widow watches the herons fly together across the lake and out of sight.

That cry! Hoarse, not-human, fading almost at once. But in an instant she has been awakened.

Cries of nocturnal birds on the lake. Loons, owls, geese. In the marshy woods, screech owls. Herons.

Sleepily she moves into her husband's arms. She is very content in his arms, she doesn't want to wake fully, nor does she want her husband to wake. Consciousness is too painful a razor's edge drawn against an eye—never are you prepared for what you might see.

The Season of the Raptors

RICHARD BOWES

1

One recent summer, Greenwich Village fell in love with carnivorous fledglings. Beloved birds of prey in the heart of New York seemed ironic. I pointed it out to friends as a suitable metaphor for a town with a sentimental side and a savage side.

Then on a morning early in June, a red-tailed hawk alighted on a ledge outside the back windows of my apartment, and things started to get personal. Behind my building is a forgotten New York: a tangle of alleys, second-story patios, and tough survivor trees. All was silence out back and I was sure the pigeons, the sparrows, the pair of mourning doves who nested there had either fled or were as still as stones.

The hawk looked over the side of the ledge. Sparrows were too small to interest him and I didn't care if he made off with a pigeon. But I worried that he might find the doves. Their forlorn cooing was like something out of another time and place. And I would miss that sound in the mornings.

I knew the visiting red-tail was male because of the color of his plumage. And I believed that he was the mate of the hawk, which famously nested over on Washington Square.

There wasn't a camera handy. As I studied him, he studied me: first with his right eye, then with both eyes. He moved his head to get a few more views of my face—like a photographer looking for the perfect shot.

He swiveled his head 180 degrees; gave me one last look and took off. The visit evoked memories I'd managed to forget.

He and his mate raised their young on the very ample windowsill of the president of New York University. The president himself had more than a touch of the raptor about him and he welcomed the red-tails like they were relatives. A camera called "The Hawk Cam" was set up on the window ledge twelve stories above the trees and fountain of Washington Square Park.

Any time you wanted to know what the hawk kids were up to you could watch them. Often you saw nothing but still forms, downy or feathered. Other times you might see the mother, with her fierce beak and murderous eyes, shove bits of fresh rat down her children's gullets.

2

I worked at an information desk in the university library. Greenwich Village with its old buildings, underground streams, and centuries as a port for ships from around the world, has a lively rat population. We always got questions about the rats of New York. The hawks and the camera meant we began to get questions about birds eating rodents.

One patron, scruffy and middle aged, wanted to know how the hawks caught live rats in the middle of the day when humans so rarely saw them by daylight. I'd wondered the same thing and trotted out what information we had. But none of it was what he was looking for. Then, as bothersome patrons so often do, he revealed what was actually on his mind. "It's fresh meat. Nothing from factories! Right here in the city," he said, seeming almost dreamy.

I showed him a list of rat-borne diseases and found he didn't want to know. The next day he appeared with a newspaper article. It seemed that fans of the nestling hawks had persuaded City Pest Control to stop putting down rat poison in the park. They feared the eyas, as baby hawks are called, would die from eating poison.

The guy went away with a look of what seemed to me an unhealthy satisfaction. I found myself thinking about the public's fascination with the lives of birds of prey.

Even before the nestlings, hawks had been around Washington Square Park off and on for quite a while. One sunny afternoon a couple of years before, I was walking through the park on my way back from lunch when I saw a crowd. It was maybe two hundred people, lots of them tourists, but plenty of students and local residents. They stared up silently and watched a hawk in the branches of an old tree tear into a squirrel with its claws and beak.

That hawk and others seemed to like an audience. I had once seen one stand on the back of a park bench as she stared with unblinking eyes at a terrified squirrel just barely hidden behind a small bush. She did this with people not that far behind her, like she knew we all had her back.

3

Things like that were on my mind early one morning a week or two after the hawk's first appearance at my window. I went to my desk and there he was on the ledge outside the window. I was sure it was the same one. He was utterly motionless and staring at something farther down the back alley.

My camera was on the desk and I picked it up. Maybe I was too sudden. The bird swiveled his eyes and beak in my direction, looked me in the face, spread his wings, rose up, and disappeared before I could take a shot.

I was surprised by my own regret at a missed photo opportunity and how I was becoming engrossed with hawks.

But the full shock of recognition came when I decided to put on the mask. It was on one of my bookshelves, the souvenir of an interactive play I'd attended. In one scene we in the audience put on carnival masks and cavorted in a noir Renaissance Venice.

This one wasn't a full-face, *Phantom of the Opera* model. But it was larger and far more ornate than a mere Lone Ranger–type mask. I donned it and found myself looking from the mirror to the window through slots set in a black and silver feathered face.

It was like I expected the hawk to come back and be taken by the mere sight of me. That didn't happen. But I did snap photos of myself in the mask and put them up on Facebook. For a day or two, it amused online friends who were bored by their jobs.

A couple of old acquaintances sent me joking, "Are you all right?" emails. I assured them that I was.

What bothered me a bit was that beneath the joke, I was actually disappointed that I couldn't entice the hawk back; let him know he was among friends. This was not an eccentricity I wanted to think about.

In late summer on the Hawk Cam, the red-tail fledglings sat on their windowsill and stared at the nooks and crannies in the neighboring buildings and at tourists feeding pigeons and squirrels amid the trees and flower beds across the street in Washington Square Park.

They began to make short gliding hops to other windowsills and to the branches of trees. When that happened, the parents stopped feeding them.

One day, the older one flew off, a few days later the younger did the same. The parents were no longer around the windowsill. When, after a week or two, none of them had reappeared, the Hawk Cam was turned off and that episode of the raptors in Washington Square seemed to be over.

Right around then I had a jumbled dream of childhood, which featured the Atlantic Ocean, large birds that talked to me, and cousins of mine about whom I hadn't thought in years.

Waking up, I remembered snatches of the dream and matched them to my memory of a train trip from Boston out to Cape Cod that my parents and I had taken when I was six years old.

This was where my father's family came from. I remember an aunt and uncle greeting us. My two boy cousins, Neil and Frankie, eleven and eight, in faded jeans and nothing more, stared at me in shirt and tie and shorts and shoes like they couldn't believe it.

They were bigger and older. Neil seemed halfway to adulthood and was fascinating and scary.

Maybe the second day of the visit I was out with my cousins in their tiny sailboat, which had a mast but no sails. The sun was mostly behind clouds; the light was silver with a touch of gold.

We all wore swimming trunks and paddled with oars.

Looking around I saw we were beyond sight of land. I'd heard their father tell them not to do that. I was uneasy and noticed both of them but especially Neil, smiling like they'd gotten away with something. I wanted to go back but didn't dare to say anything. Neil looked at me like he knew just what was going on in my head and was amused.

As we paddled, out of nowhere, a gull alighted on the mast. Neil nodded and said, "That's our guide. They always look toward land."

The gull's eyes were sharp. They reminded me of the pirate parrot's eyes in the movie *Treasure Island.* I looked away and the bird suddenly screeched. Turning, I saw it trying to fly away from where it had roosted. A huge bird, an eagle as I found out, was on the gull with talons planted in its back. The gull, screaming, tried to wrench free.

The eagle tore off the head, ripped apart the flapping wings, and flew off with the twitching remains. I cried and almost pissed myself. My cousins were wide-eyed. But Neil said, "He'll lead us home." We followed the eagle with the dead gull in its claws and in a few minutes I saw land.

They laughed at my tears. Neil looked down at me and said, "You got to raise your right hand and promise before God not to tell anyone how far out we went. Break your word and you go to hell!"

And because he wasn't bothered by the birds and the blood and because I was terrified, I raised my hand and promised.

"And you don't tell anyone," he said, "about what happened to the gull. Or the same thing will happen to you." I nodded, and at that moment he was a big and scary as the eagle.

The adults were all in a bad mood when we showed up. I think my parents and I left the next day. I never saw any of that family again. Except maybe Neil some years later.

4

"I forgot about the seagull and the eagle until years after it happened," I said. I'd just described the boat trip to my best friend Lois. We go way back to college. She was in New York on a short visit and I amazed her by talking about birds of prey.

"The first time I thought about those birds again was when I was in my teens in Boston," I told her. "There was this guy who dealt meth and who liked to go after kids. So he was called Super Chicken Hawk.

"He had his lair in this old apartment building over near the Charles River. It had large windows looking out on the water. And stuck right inside the apartment nailed onto one of the window frames was this big old iron birdcage. It had a little, narrow entrance drilled in the windowsill, so small birds could get in from the outside but not large ones. He had finches building nests and singing in his living room, which was nice but creepy.

"The trick with this guy was getting him to sell you the speed without letting him get into your pants. He was weird enough that after a couple of visits I stayed away for maybe a year. When I went back there were some older guys, even a woman, people in their twenties, maybe thirties, standing around, looking whacked out and amused.

"There was a much different birdcage, large enough to hold a crouching person, and there was a bare-ass kid inside it. He had to scrunch down because of these big wings he was wearing. He kept his face turned away so I couldn't really see him. But what he reminded me of, the way he held himself, was my cousin Neil, who I hadn't seen since the boat trip. The chilling coincidence was that a gull was hanging in the air outside, looking in at us.

"When I tried to get a closer look, Neil, if that's who it was, raised his shoulders so that the wings covered his face. He didn't want me to see that but didn't seem to care other if people in the room looked. That made me double down on the idea he knew me and I knew him.

"The dealer/hawk was all over me. Sold me the speed but said, 'Next time I want you in the cage,' and the people liked that.

"It was a long time before I went back and when I did, it was all gone. The downstairs door was wide open and I could hear drilling and hammering somewhere in the building. Then I found the door of Super Chicken Hawk's apartment hanging on its hinges. It was empty. The window that had the cage was broken. The only trace of anything that had once gone on there was some feathers on the floor."

5

Lois shook her head. "With you I never know what's real. I mean, I *like* the feathers left on the floor and the weird and twisted underground in Boston circa 1960. But the dangerous bird motif and your long-lost cousin locked in a cage? I have trouble with those items."

"I know I can be a chore."

"I met you a couple of years after that in college," she said. "And at one point in our extended adolescences, I got to see you interact with a bird and it wasn't nearly as scary and a lot more hilarious than the story you told me."

At first, I didn't know what she was talking about. Then she asked, "Remember the Educated Chicken?" For a moment I didn't. "Down in Chinatown fifty years ago, on Mott Street and Pell, there was this sleazy arcade. We used to come into the city from school on weekends. And you'd always insist on going there."

It all came back to me. I even saw it through a drunken teenage haze just like the first time. A gray hen strutted across a tic-tac-toe board and hit the center square with its beak. The Educated Chicken always went first. I'd put an X on another square but already I'd be at a disadvantage. Before I knew it the bird had filled in a row of X's and I'd lost.

My college friends, kids at least as drunk as I was, were hooting, yelling, "You going to take that from a chicken?"

My answer was that no bird would ever make a fool of me. Everything I hadn't spent on beer and grass, I lost playing tic-tac-toe.

It became a weekend ritual. I can remember shoving one quarter after another in the slot. I'd beg or borrow it from Lois if I was broke. And the chicken would come strutting out and hit the center square, leaving me as badly off as ever.

"We'd have to drag you back to the car when the arcade closed for the night," Lois said. "One time you stood on the sidewalk of Mott Street and Pell, shaking your fist at the arcade and saying you were coming back as a eagle to kill every chicken in the place.

"Even the people hanging around that corner at three A.M., who you have to figure had seen a lot, were impressed."

We both laughed, and this memory of the chicken ran through my head like a cartoon. But the idea of me long ago threatening to come back as a great bird caught me.

6

Lois had departed and the Village was all autumn leaves and early dusk as I walked through Washington Square a week or two later. A crowd had gathered and was looking up—not at a hawk but at something even more remarkable.

The guy, who I remembered for his questions at the information desk about fresh rat meat, stood naked on a tree limb. He was making a weird kind of cawing sound and crying, "Feed me! Bring me my food!"

Some people in the crowd laughed. I felt that I kind of understood what he was going through and wanted to get close, maybe talk him down. But as I headed that way, park workers with ladders appeared and first a cop car, then an ambulance arrived with sirens blaring.

They wrapped him in blankets and he was bundled into the ambulance. The guy was more than a little disturbing.

7

I was walking home in the early-morning hours from a party on the night before Halloween. All Hallows the next evening is beyond a doubt the biggest date of the year in the Village. But on this night the neighborhood was quiet.

The street where I live abounds in all manner of bars and restaurants and a few remnants of the glory days of Greenwich Village. But there's one store that really only stands out very late at night. CIGARS, HOOKAHS, TOBACCO reads the sign that blazes over the door, an oasis for certain wanderers. The silver light in the front window reaches onto the dark sidewalk.

On the almost empty street, I passed that shop and something inside hooked my eyes. I'd caught a glimpse of a young guy bent down and looking away from me. I thought he was somehow familiar even before I saw the wings on him.

This was the kid in the birdcage but now in another city and another century. And no, I don't drink much or get stoned much these days. I walked back, looked in the door and saw him again but only in profile. He was wearing tights, a pair of wings and shoes that looked like bird feet. Another guy was adjusting the wings for him. I understood this was practice for the Halloween parade.

He did look like Neil, or looked the way my cousin might have looked if he'd become a dancer and stayed eighteen forever. In reality, Neil died of a heart attack some years ago. Maybe he never got much of anywhere. But right now he seemed a lot more alive than I was.

By afternoon the next day my street was full of drunken vampires, male witches, female princes, and scandal-plagued celebrities in multiple sizes and shapes. In tribute to last summer's fad, a couple of human-size hawks came out of a bar on Bleecker Street. They were tacky—not even close to what I was looking for.

That night I went to a party at the house of a friend of a friend whose front windows overlooked Sixth Avenue and the passing parade. We nibbled hash brownies and I dutifully applauded the float loads of musicians and the many-legged dragons, monstrous cartoons, and singing mermaids who shimmied, strutted, and marched up the avenue.

I waited impatiently. But when the Raptors appeared they were entirely worth the wait. They swooped from one side of Sixth Avenue to the other with bloody beaks, glistening wings, mad, staring eyes that flickered, then stared again. The Neil I'd seen the night before was all shimmering feathers and savage glances as he swept forward.

People yelled and applauded. This was Raptor worship and I was impressed. The kid, whoever he was, showed artistry. It seemed that his wings, not his legs, carried him.

Even knowing it was all performance, I still expected him to rise off the street and fly. When he remained earthbound and the Raptor cult passed on up the Avenue, I was disappointed.

But like a retort aimed at my doubt, a form flew out of the dark sky and hovered motionless above the marchers. Everyone at the party told one another this was a trick and tried to explain it. When the hawk rose into the sky and disappeared they lost interest. But I was hooked all over again.

I wanted to fly out the window and follow the man who'd been followed by a hawk. Instead I ran down the stairs, kind of wobbly from age and the brownies. The building was only a couple of blocks from the parade's end.

By the time I got there, the Raptor contingent was lost somewhere in the chaos at the finish line. I caught glimpses of them through the crowd but couldn't get close.

8

An eagle stood at a podium and spoke in savage cries to a roomful of birds of prey and to human devotees of birds of prey with feathers pasted on their bare skins. All of them screeched at each thing he said.

I stood in a dark hall in that old building and looked into the lighted room. The bird at the podium swiveled his head my way and looked me over.

"Another featherless one, frightened and fascinated by our ways," he said quite clearly, and I found myself moving toward him while birds and humans stared and cried out. All of this seemed familiar, like I'd done it before but couldn't remember when.

Suddenly there was no one in the room beside me. Despite that, the crowd noise continued. Then another bird stood at the podium: the Educated Chicken. "Come here often, sucker?" she asked. I realized I was naked and thought of the man in the tree.

I awoke in my bed and still heard the cries. I looked around my bedroom for the birds and realized my dream had ended, but the Halloween party that was this neighborhood continued out on the street.

I dozed but didn't get a lot of sleep. Early the next morning, in the full glory of All Saints' Day, I staggered into my front room. The hawk sat outside my window. He glanced my way, as he tore into a small bloody carcass.

Wanting to make him feel at home, I put on my feathered mask and sat close to the window. We exchanged stares. I was being summoned to worship. I wouldn't have Neil's immortality. And I might end up as a lunatic in a tree. I was fascinated but terrified.

The hawk flicked a small bloody clump from the carcass it held. It fell on my windowsill. He waited to see what I'd do.

The Orphan Bird

ALISON LITTLEWOOD

The lake was silent. Its surface was utterly unmoving and the deepest grey in hue, except where the light made it shine the no-colour that Arnold saw in this place and this place alone. The only thing stirring the surface was his own head, a slick, dark mound in the hood of his wetsuit, as he turned to look at the bitterns. There was no other way to see them. No one else knew they were there. The only way that Arnold knew was the sound of their booming, which he had heard one day ringing emptily across the lake like a call from beyond the world. For a time, he had almost believed that it wasn't a real thing; then he had seen the source and had been astonished, despite all his knowledge, that such a sound could come from so ordinary a creature.

The bitterns had nested in the swampiest part of the shore, if it could be truly called a shore at all. It was a nowhere place, belonging to neither lake nor land, covered by treacherous reeds that would not support the weight of a man.

Arnold lifted his camera, bulky in its waterproof housing, to the surface of the lake, tilting it to let the greyish water run off the transparent plastic without making any dripping sounds. He'd zoomed in before he'd set off that day; he didn't want the low whirring of the mechanism to alert the birds to his presence. Now he waited for one of them to raise its head from the mud before he pressed the shutter release, barely hearing the *click*. The birds didn't hear it either. They were among the rarest creatures to be found in these parts; indeed, they had never before nested by the lake until this year. It felt like a kind of portent. They were red-listed, and yet they looked like nothing. Shorter than a heron, more thick-set and with brown feathers, they were nondescript, like him. Arnold smiled. They passed through the world with secrecy and silence, despite their ability to roar. Sometimes it was good to do that, to be able to avoid being noticed.

He watched them a little longer, already knowing how he would paint them. The male would be side-on, his head raised, watching something that could not be seen beyond the edge of the page. The female's head would be lowered, her beak ready to dart into the water to catch some fish or insect, and yet her eyes would be fixed upon whomever looked at the picture.

Arnold relaxed into the water, lifting his feet from the soft mud and floating. He rolled over onto his back, resting the camera on his chest, seeing only the grey lid of the clouds folding over the grey lake. He knew that no one was watching him. No one ever came here. The lake was too far from any decent road for coaches to come and disgorge their cargo of old ladies; too muddy for hikers with their noisy dogs; too far from anything, even the mountains he could just see rising in the distance. This part of Cumbria wasn't an attraction. Here were no neat shores, nowhere to sunbathe, no shops selling sandwiches or gift-wrapped gingerbread or mint-cake.

He thought of all the depth of cold, dark water beneath him, of all the life that was in and around and within it, seen and unseen. A slow smile spread across his features as he allowed himself to drift. In his mind he was already mixing the paints; selecting the brush; making the first bold mark on a fresh white sheet of paper.

Later, the image he had visualised so clearly began to appear in front of him. It was never the same as the golden perfection he had built in his mind, not quite, but that wasn't the point. The process, for him, was as important as the result.

As he worked, adding streaks and bars to a bird's wing, he meditated on the creature. His knowledge of it, the depth of his research, was invisible, and yet he felt it gave him an understanding and a connection with his subject that no one else had. The bittern was known as *hæferblæte* in Old English. Its current name came from Old French: *butor*, which in turn derived from Gallo-Roman *butitaurus*, a compound of Latin *būtiō* and *taurus*. Taurus was a reference to the bittern's incredibly deep cry: it was a bird with the cry of a bull. Bitterns were a member of the heron family, the *botaurinae*. Arnold wondered what the other herons, the tall, grey, stately creatures, would think of their ugly little brother.

He narrowed his eyes, forcing himself to concentrate more deeply. He would render the creature to perfection, capture it on the page. He would study it and describe it in the only way he knew how and finally file it, in his cabinets, along with all the information he had found. He sold his pictures, mainly to publishers of ornithological texts, but that wasn't the point either. He had so many birds in his cabinets, along with some insects and plants; one little piece of the world after the next, catalogued and understood. Made safe. One day, perhaps all of it would be in there. Then nothing would surprise him, not any longer. Nothing would have the strength to hurt; their power over him would be altogether lost.

He realised he was staring into space, or rather, out of the window of the tiny cabin he owned near the lake, but seeing nothing that was in front of him. He didn't realise how he was torturing the brush with his free hand, flexing and forcing it, until it gave with a sudden sharp snap, sending droplets of burnt umber across his painting.

He let out a breath with a hiss, dabbing at the paper with a tissue, but it was too late. The picture was ruined. He picked up the end of the brush with the bristles attached and realised something worse. It was his favourite, the smallest he possessed: size 000, perfect for fine work. Now it was useless. He would have to go into town before he could hope to paint the birds again.

Arnold got ready, changing his worn and paint-spattered T-shirt for a clean one, his filthy trousers for faded blue jeans. He looked at himself in the mirror before he went out. The effect, he knew, was not good. His eyes were watery and bloodshot. His hair was never anything but lank, looking almost black where it was slicked down over his forehead. His skin was pale and yellowish, and his eyes were a little too small.

He took a deep breath and picked up the keys to his dirty Land Rover. The nearest art shop was in Windermere, a good thirty minutes away, if the little roads weren't clogged with tourist traffic. He pulled a face at himself in the mirror before he set off, twisting his florid red lips.

The sun had come out after all, sparkling off the wide blue expanse of Windermere Lake, and it had brought with it large numbers of people. The rowing boat hire, in a little inlet at the roadside, was busy. Stick-thin boys and girls lined up on the pebbly shore with their mothers and fathers and there was noise, lots of it: the hollow wooden sound of oars in rowlocks, the endlessly passing cars, a motor boat chugging somewhere out on the water. And always, there was the talk: chirping and clucking and squawking.

Arnold parked opposite. He had been lucky that someone was just leaving, so that he could nudge into the narrow space they'd left behind. As he closed the door he turned to see a small child—a girl, long hair, snub nose, blue eyes, freckles, frock—licking at an ice cream as she watched him. She gave a sly smirk before her mother said something sharp and she turned away, forgetting him instantly.

He edged around a couple of bare-chested young lads, their shoulders burnt to cadmium red, smelling of beer. He ignored the slurred cry of "Hey, mate . . ."

Across the road, a family was waiting to cross: boy, girl, mum, dad, flowery shirts, beach bag, sunglasses. He felt the father's stare through his lamp-black lenses as Arnold walked rapidly past them and towards the shops. He kept his stride sure. He knew that was the only way. He couldn't let them see how his heart was beating so rapidly. He had to quell the instinct to turn and run, to throw himself into the clear blue water, to swim and swim until no one could see him any longer; until no one could scrutinise him and find him wanting.

Hey, mate . . .

Look at his hair!

He's got no mum! No wonder he's . . .

Oi, Spotty! What you looking at, Spotty?

He paused on the corner, breathing hard, leaning against an old slate wall. The voices around him had changed. He couldn't see the speakers' faces, but he knew who they were. The first had been Batty Briggs, the lad with sticky-out ears. People called him Batty and it was not his name, but they did it in a way that made everybody laugh. It was different to the way they called Arnold Spotty, or worse.

He hated Batty Briggs. He always had, ever since the first day when Arnold had been shown into class and introduced and the boy had burst out laughing, as if the teacher had just told a fine joke.

Batty's friends were Scott Williams and Dale Carter. They always laughed when Batty did, though never quite as loud. Scott and Dale always noticed every little thing that was wrong with Arnold's clothes. They would laugh, now, at his T-shirt. He hadn't seen any of them for ten years, not since he'd been in school, but he could hear them all the same.

"Watch out . . ."

Arnold pressed himself back against the wall as an arm brushed against his. He looked up. It was not Batty or Scott or Dale. A couple had come around the corner, a man he didn't know with a beer belly and a woman with harshly bleached hair, brown at the roots. Her strappy top revealed a tattoo of a cobalt and rose madder butterfly just above her right breast.

Arnold's mouth opened and closed as they went by. He couldn't seem to pull the air into his lungs. He felt as if he was drowning, and he knew that in a way, he was. It had always been like that: out of place, out of step. Out of his element. He longed, suddenly and deeply, for the grey lake where nobody came. That was where he belonged, in the water, content with the dark and the slime and the mud, with all the creatures that slithered and flapped and did not speak.

He forced himself to start walking, more quickly than before. This medium was strange to him—he could not flourish here, did not know how to be—but it would not kill him. The sooner he had finished, the sooner he could escape.

He reached the art shop without catching anyone's eye. He made his purchase, throwing in some extra tubes of paint so that he would not have to visit again too soon. The shopkeeper tried to make conversation, telling him about some new papers that had just come in, and he simply nodded and took his change. Then he hurried away, his head bowed, his legs moving rapidly, like a sanderling rushing along the shore.

When he got home and closed the door behind him, Arnold took out one of the books he had illustrated. It was his favourite. Although the pictures were rather small, they were printed neatly in little boxes, each with the bird's classification and habitat and geographical spread marked next to it. He began to breathe more deeply as he looked at it. He didn't take in any words in particular—he had seen them all already—but the images, along with the little charts and maps, comforted him. The pages didn't turn easily because of the photographs that were thrust between them, the thicker paper impeding the flow of the book. Arnold wasn't ready to look at them but after a while he was, and he let one fall, randomly, into his lap. He had seen it before but he studied it anyway. It showed a son and his father in a rubber dinghy, wearing blue trunks and identical grins, plastic oars clutched in their fists.

He put the photograph back. The next one chosen by the book showed a whole crowd of people standing on the shore at Windermere. It had been a hot day then too. It had sapped the strength from the flock: faces were red, every bench was occupied, and some of them had flopped to the ground until it was coated in shorts, hats, swimming costumes in harsh primary colours. He made out a brother and sister, her sitting cross-legged, his arms slung casually about her shoulders. A group of children wearing tabards and school caps walked in a line towards the dock.

None of them was looking at the camera.

After a while, Arnold slipped the photographs back into the book and returned it to the shelf, lining up its spine with the others. It was all right again; he was calmer. He was ready to go to work.

Arnold drifted down through the layers, feeling the coldness seep under his wetsuit. His arms were outstretched, loose, and he stared up at the sky as he sank, the sun a diminishing white hole. Everything else was the deep green of rotting things, of liquid that was rich in nutrients, the soup of life. It was as dark as the water in the jar he used to rinse his brushes.

He was close to the farthest banking of the lake, where twisted trees bent their limbs down towards the water. The muddy drop beneath the surface was full of fallen and waterlogged branches where black grubs squirmed and wriggled. He thought of the drenched wood as *loak*, though he did not know why. It was not a word, at least not until he had named it. He gazed at it all through his mask without blinking. He did not flinch at the quick, silver dart of a fish. It was natural, and he was part of it. He turned lazily in the water as a stickleback swam by, and he ran his fingers through a gelatinous clump of frogspawn. A kick of his legs took him in towards the banking. Below the trees' roots and the fallen wood were outcroppings of rock, greened with slimy weed. Among them was a dark, blank opening.

Arnold went toward it. The water held him, suspended; it accepted him. He stared into the hole. That was where the chicks were, he knew that. He came often to check on their progress. They were enveloped by the shade, where they liked it best, but he could just make out the suggestion of a form here and there: darkness that hinted at empty sockets, twined shapes not quite like branches, interlaced so that nothing could separate them.

The fish had found them. There were more of them here, twitching and circling in excitement. Arnold watched without touching them. He only needed to see.

After a time he let the water carry him away into the deeper cold. Then he began to kick back towards the day, savouring the moment of lightness. Soon his body would take on weight again. It would feel all the more leaden, knowing what he had lost.

"Bring him over here."

Arnold leaned more closely over the paper. Usually, when he worked, he thought of nothing else. There were only the facts he had learned and the photographs and the paint. A new bittern was taking shape under his hands: the bird with the cry of a bull.

"Hold him down."

He shook his head, the forms in front of him blurring as if seen through dark water. What was *wrong* with him?

"Give it here. There's something *wrong* with you."

He let the brush slip from his fingers and rubbed his eyes. It was like yesterday. *Batty*, he thought. *Batty and Scott and Dale.* He should have left them alone. He should always have left them alone. That was what people like him did.

He closed his eyes and remembered. He had been walking through the middle of the town he'd been sent to and had reached the river. Cars idled to a stop and roared away, their drivers irritated by the hump-backed bridge they had to cross in single file. Someone had told him this was where the trolls lived, but there were no trolls now. There were only Batty and Scott and Dale.

He must have been walking back to the home from school, because he could remember the weight of his backpack, and it must have been summer because wherever the backpack clung to him was running with sweat. He hadn't intended to stop; he hadn't wanted to see anything. But there they were, the three of them, playing with a kitten.

He knew at once that it wasn't a nice game. He could tell from their voices, which were bright and sharp and cut through the air. "Give it here!"

He looked over the bridge. They were on the riverbank, clustered together. Batty broke away for a moment to take something from his schoolbag: a magnifying glass. Scott was holding the kitten. It was small and it only took one hand, wrapped tightly around its ginger fur to hold it still.

Batty held up the magnifying glass before focusing the sun's heat on the kitten's left eye.

The three boys closed around it. Arnold could not see it squirm but he heard a single plaintive *mew*. He did not think but climbed the stile set into one side of the bridge and he slithered down the banking towards them. He did not shout; he didn't need to. The boys swivelled their heads towards him, as if drawn by his presence.

"Or what, dickhead?" Batty said, as if Arnold had spoken; as if he ever spoke. At least he had lowered the magnifying glass. Scott clutched the kitten tighter and Arnold stared at it. Too late, he realised that Batty had nodded a signal at Dale. The lad ran towards him. Arnold froze, like prey. He knew there was no use in running. The taller boy would only take him down. Instead Dale stopped when he reached him then just stood there, as if he didn't know what to do.

"Bring him over here."

Dale reached out, tentatively, then grabbed Arnold's shoulder and dragged him over to Batty.

"Hold him down."

Scott reached out one-handed, grabbing Arnold's hair and together they tugged on him. It wasn't quick. It wasn't like fighting in films.

"Not like that." Batty sighed as if they were idiots and he stood and kicked Arnold in the back of the knee while shoving his chest. Arnold went down flat, his backpack digging into his spine. He wriggled. He was pinned; he was an ant.

Batty's lip twisted as he aimed the magnifying glass once more, focusing the light on Arnold's wrist. He tried to pull away, but Dale held onto him. He was not strong enough; he could not get free. He couldn't even see what was happening, but the heat was a liquid weight on his white skin.

"You'll get done," Scott said. "He'll go crying to his mum."

"I'll not. He hasn't got a mum."

"He hasn't got a mum?"

"Course he hasn't."

Arnold squirmed. He kicked at their legs experimentally, then harder as the pain bit.

"Hold him *steady*."

The look on their faces hadn't changed. There was interest in their eyes; there was curiosity.

The pain grew worse. In another minute Arnold couldn't think of anything else, and then it intensified and he began to scream, not just one single sound but again and again.

"Shit! Make him be quiet."

"Shut it, dickhead!"

"Fuck this. Come on."

Just like that they left him, their shadows fleeting, the sunlight subsiding to its usual life-giving glow. There was a livid pink patch on Arnold's wrist. He looked at it for a while, half expecting to see smoke rising from the skin, and then he raised his head and saw something in the grass.

He forgot his wrist and crawled over to the kitten. It wasn't moving and he scooped it up; it did not struggle. He cradled it in his arms, lifting its head with a finger. It wasn't breathing. They had broken it between them; they had ended it.

He slipped his arm from the strap of his backpack, then stopped himself. He lay the little creature on a flat grey stone by the riverbank and stroked it once. Then he walked away.

He knew he couldn't take the kitten back to the home. No matter what they said, he wasn't that stupid.

Of all the treatises and encyclopaedias and guidebooks and catalogues, Arnold liked medieval bestiaries the most. They didn't just describe animals within their pages but told mankind how to deal with them, what cunning could be expected of them. They told of the essential nature of the beast that lay beyond the reality. Sometimes they amused him with their fanciful descriptions, but mostly they felt like armour: plates of steel, each overlapping the next. Their truths were not to be found anywhere else.

From Bartholomaeus Anglicus, he discovered that the eagle will slay any of its offspring that cannot stare unflinchingly into the sun. He learned that the swan sings its sweetest song before it dies. He found out from Pliny the Elder that cranes take turns to watch for enemies through the night, holding a stone aloft in one claw; if they should fall asleep, the stone will drop and wake them. Many of the bestiaries contained similar information, but there was only one that told of the Orphan Bird.

The Orphan Bird had the body of a crane and the beak of an eagle. Its feet were a swan's, its chest and neck those of peacock, and its wings had feathers of black and red and white. The Orphan Bird lays its eggs in the water and the chick grows almost at once. The good eggs float and are hatched beneath its mother's wings; she then leads the good chicks, with great rejoicing, back to their father.

The bad eggs—the bad chicks—sink to the bottom. There they hatch, beneath the water, and there they are condemned to live and die in darkness and in grief.

Red and white and black, Arnold thought. He had woken late in the night, as he often did. *Red and white and black. Blood. Skin. Hair.*

This bestiary was written by a man called Pierre de Beauvais at some lost time, though it was known to date from before 1218. His was the only known mention of the Orphan Bird, though the author referred to himself as "the translator." Arnold understood that. He was a translator too: birds into diagrams, feathers into shades in a painter's palette; life into terms he could understand. *Skin. Hair. Blood.* Not messy but neat and ordered, everything in its right place.

The scar on his wrist itched and he rubbed at it. He was not a child any more. The child had long since passed away; now only the man remained.

The girl was watching the swans at the edge of the car park. They were big and bold and hissy, and would stick their heads through people's car windows to grab sandwiches or crisps, dripping lake-weed over the glass and painted metal. They were as tall as she was, but she wasn't afraid. Arnold knew that her parents must be somewhere near, hiring a boat perhaps, or queueing for ice creams.

He went over to her, bending to pick up a single long white feather. After a while, he realised she was looking at him.

"A wing feather." His voice was dry from lack of use. "See how the outer edge is curved? It's so the swan can fly."

Her eyes opened wide as if he'd told her some great secret; and perhaps he had. He smiled, started to set it down, then noticed the others, scattered all around. More white ones, some muddied to brown, but there were other kinds too. He caught his breath as he saw the brilliant emerald neck feather of a mallard.

"Do you know what they all are?" she asked.

He turned to her, feeling what he thought was a smile break out on his features. "Yes," he said, "I do."

The boys at school had laughed at him, but they had never known how to hurt him, not really. They had never known what he was. They said he had no mother, but that wasn't true. Arnold had had a mother once, although she had given him up. He often imagined her doing it, a woman without a face handing him over like an unwanted parcel, her other hand still clutching tightly onto another hand . . .

He could not remember his sister. He only remembered her existence, like a fact written in one of his books and nothing more. She was the good chick his mother had kept. He was the bad chick she had given away.

He didn't feel anything about it, not really, not now. It simply was.

He stared down at the feathers on the shore, the leavings of all the good chicks who had been nurtured and who had grown and eventually flown. The sky was the same as always: grey and flat and featureless. Under it, birds sang and hissed and clicked. He could hear them but he couldn't see them in their hiding places among the reeds.

The one in his hand pulled and spat and made an almost eerie wailing that rang out across the water. He had covered her mouth and thrown her into the back of the Land Rover, knocked out by chloroform. Arnold had obtained it long before on the grounds of subduing samples for his art but it still worked. She had woken on the way back and she had cried then too, but it hadn't taken long. Now he was by his own quiet lake, wearing his wetsuit, sleek and dark. He turned to her and smiled. He knew she could see everything in that smile, if she looked properly.

She had fought and kicked and screamed. *Bad chick.*

He waded into the water. His feet were bare and mud oozed and slid beneath his toes. Her cry grew louder but he didn't stop, just took her with him, and her teeth began to click with the cold of it. He steadied himself against a low branch and went deeper still.

Beneath the surface, in the cold, the others were waiting. He could feel them. When he attained the right depth, a mass of bubbles spewing from her lips, he went in closer than he had before. He could see where their eyes had been. No trace of them remained but they stared anyway and he remembered the glutinous globes, round and ripe. The fish must have taken them first.

Now, not even their clothing looked the same. The water had claimed everything; they were stained and dark. Particles drifted before his eyes, blurring everything but not hiding it.

He pushed the chick into the hole with the others, in among the stones and rot and slimy things; in among the loak. She still clutched and grasped, but she was weak and he pushed her in deeper. He seized a pale arm, wrapping it around her for company—the skin was torn and nibbled, mottled with fish eggs—and he shifted a branch to cover them both. He held it in place for a while, not really looking at anything, and then he drifted into the darkness and the grief.

He could feel them watching him still, watching without eyes. He knew that they knew him for what he was; what he had always been. He was one of them, the bad chicks. This was his home. Now it was their home too.

All the bright children with their bright stares, bold and mocking and *knowing*. It was surely only their parents who could ever mistake them for good chicks, surely only their parents who would ever call them that. It did not matter. A bad chick could never be made good, could not be made to feel at home in the air and in the light; he knew that. But a good chick could most certainly be made bad, and he had made them, again and again.

At least she was with her sisters and brothers. She need never be alone, not like him.

Later, he finished off his painting of the bittern. This time there were no smudges and no smears, nothing at all to mar the perfect surface.

Arnold had gone back only because he had been curious about the kitten. He climbed the stone stile and went down to the riverbank. The kitten was still there. Its skin had been opened like a bag that had been unzipped. What was in there was like white worms, bloodied and mauled. The clean ginger fur was bloodied too. It no longer had any eyes.

Arnold was leaving soon, transferring to a home somewhere else, somewhere he might fit in. He already knew that he would not. There was never any use in flying away; he would still be the bad chick, the one who wasn't wanted.

As he thought it, a fist bashed him around the ear. "Fight," a voice shouted, in the way that boys did when there was a fight.

Arnold whirled to see Batty's face up close. "Fight, fight," Scott and Dale chanted as Batty grinned and lashed out, catching him under the chin. Arnold's teeth clicked together painfully.

Batty hit out again and Arnold stumbled, driven back farther and farther, until his leg slipped from beneath him and he took another step to regain his balance and found there was nothing there. He went over, flailing, and suddenly he was in the water.

The boys laughed, leaning with their hands on their knees, slapping and jeering. Arnold couldn't make out the words. He pushed himself up, his hands clutching at the slippery stones. The water no longer felt cold; it was warming against his skin, running down his face and into his eyes. His fist had closed around a smooth rock; it was shaped a little like an egg. He pushed himself up and climbed out of the water. The boys didn't move. They didn't see the rock until he reached Batty and hefted it and brought it down on the taller lad's skull.

There was a sharp, loud *crack*, and Batty stopped laughing. He stopped doing anything at all. He fell to his knees on the grass. His mouth hung open, a dribble of spit suspended from his lip.

Arnold raised the stone to strike again. Batty didn't move. The only thing that did was a line of blood that emerged from the cut on his scalp and trickled slowly onto his forehead. His eyes swivelled up to the rock—the egg—in Arnold's hand.

Arnold looked at it too. Then he let it fall to the ground. He walked past them, not looking at them; he did not even glance over his shoulder. Batty wasn't at school the next morning, although he did go back. The three friends never told on Arnold for what he'd done that day; perhaps it would have been better if they had.

It didn't matter. It wasn't as if it was something he could ever know. The black and the white of it would never be printed in any book. It was better not to think of it; better not to wonder.

It wasn't bad, at the bottom of the lake. It was dark but the chicks didn't mind that. They didn't cry and they didn't go hungry and they didn't thirst.

In a way, Arnold's mother had done only what was best for him. She must have known he would prefer it where he was. He didn't like being out in the world. That was where the foxes were, things that were ready to rend and bite and stare with their unblinking eyes.

He turned in the water and rose to the surface. Water bubbled from his ears and sound returned: the hooping call of a curlew somewhere on the riverbank, perhaps searching for a mate. The harsher grating of a crow, looking for carrion. The frantic cheeping of hungry chicks, hidden within the reeds.

Arnold knew that the Orphan Bird didn't exist, at least not in the way that Pierre de Beauvais might have imagined. But then, who would know? Historians had been able to discover nothing about the man's life. They said he had intended the bird as an allegory for good and bad souls and what became of them, but Arnold didn't think it was an allegory for anything. Things were as they were, as they had to be.

He felt that certainty again, the moment he saw the boy.

His parents had their backs turned, tending to his sister, because his sister was screaming. She was in a rowing boat and would not get out. Arnold could not hear her cries because of the summer crowds, everyone gabbling, gabbling, like a flock of geese; but he could *see* the sound. Her mouth was stretched wide open, screwing her eyes into slits.

He glanced around. Police had been watching the place for weeks, but most assumed the girl had drowned and there was only one officer there now, standing by the jetty, wiping sweat from beneath his hat and looking bored.

It was the boy who chose Arnold. It usually happened that way. He just walked straight up and said, "What's that?"

The boy was portly with sun-reddened cheeks, his hands thrust into his jeans pockets. He had orange hair and a T-shirt with the name of a band Arnold didn't recognise.

Arnold looked down at the object in his hands. It was a brass compass, its shell marked with an intricately etched design representing the heavens and the earth, all laid out in neat geometry. He still didn't know why he'd bought it. He'd seen it in the window of an antiques shop and had loved it at once, enough to overcome his reluctance to go inside. All he'd been able to think about was de Beauvais, the shadow of a man nobody knew anything about, except that he'd also written some lives of saints and a mappemonde, a work of geography and cosmology. Perhaps he would have been able to read the lines, to explain what they meant.

Arnold held it out, not wanting to speak. He hadn't planned this, hadn't wanted the contact with the surly shopkeeper, didn't want the contact now. But the child drew in close, his eyes widening. He reached out, stretching his index finger to touch the dial, and Arnold snatched it back.

"Can I see?" The boy's voice was breathy. He didn't look around at his parents, didn't seem to care about his sister. He had forgotten them just like that, and Arnold found himself wondering how he'd done it.

He turned away, starting to walk towards his car, leaving it up to the boy. The boy made his decision: he chose to follow.

He didn't scream, not like the others. His face creased in anger as Arnold clamped a chloroformed rag over his lips, and he struggled, though he couldn't make a sound. Arnold threw him into the back of the Land Rover. As he drove away, he saw the policeman watching him, his eyes narrowed. Had Arnold exposed himself somehow—should he have looked about more, smiled more? He didn't know; then the policeman rubbed his eyes, and Arnold realised he had only been dazzled by the sun.

He drove straight to the lake. He didn't have his wetsuit, but he would have to do without it, just this once. It wouldn't matter. He belonged to the water and the boy had come to him, and that showed it was meant to be. The boy was a bad chick, like the others. He needed to be with his brothers and sisters.

Arnold kicked off his shoes, shrugged his shirt over his head, and removed his trousers. He folded the clothing and placed it carefully on the passenger seat before taking off his socks and putting the left one in the left shoe, the other in the right. Then he stepped over the gritty surface, flexing his toes, and unlocked and opened the back door.

The boy glared, blinking as if he had just awoken. Arnold got him out of the gap behind the seats, pulling on his legs, then twisting him and grasping his flailing arms. He was solid but light, as all of them were. He glanced around but he knew the only eyes watching him were those of birds and insects, the things that belonged in this place. The sky was the drained white of a new sheet of paper.

He waded into the shallows, clamping his arms tightly around the boy, sinking into the mud. The chill was familiar, but he had no wetsuit to capture his own warmth and insulate his skin. He took another step, sinking more deeply until the water was above his knees. Another, and he started to shiver. He pushed forward anyway, until he was floating, the boy frozen in his arms.

The chick's eyes were closed. His eyelids were almost transparent and Arnold could see the veins within them. It was fascinating. He thought for a moment of painting him, then pushed the idea aside, remembering the policeman's look. He reminded himself that he never had been that stupid.

Arnold swam towards the place where the trees reached down into the water. Then he drew in a deep breath and ducked under, shocked by the cold. The boy accepted it. He struggled briefly and then he stopped. Arnold hooked his toe under a loop of branch he knew was there and used it to pull them both down.

The overhang was waiting, its dark hole a mouth waiting to be filled. He pushed the boy inside. The cold was everywhere, enveloping him, and he shivered as he quickly shoved in a heavy branch after him and turned, pushing himself away, thrusting himself back towards the surface.

He hurried back to the car, heavy and earthbound once more. He was shuddering. His clothes stuck to his skin as he pulled them on, fighting him. He was still shaking as he drove away, turning on the heat as high as it would go.

Back in the cabin, all was quiet. Arnold placed the brass compass on his desk and stared at it for a long time. It was only lines, he thought, not the world, nothing real, and he did not know why, and he did not like the silence in the house and did not know why that was either; only that it was a lifeless, dry, dead sound. It wasn't like the silence in the lake.

He showered, turning up the water as hot as he could bear. Then he dried himself and put on fresh clothes. He went downstairs and looked at his desk. His brushes were ready, beside the compass, but he knew he would not be able to settle to his work.

He sighed and put on his coat. He had to do something. If he had done with the bitterns, he could research the next painting; he would stand among the birds and build a new image in his mind.

It felt better, being outside, though he still wasn't warm and it wasn't a warm day. The sky was as white as dead eyes, but that was all right too. It wasn't long until he approached the lake, the grass whisking past his legs in loud whispers. The water was grey, just like always, and he stared at it. Something had changed, but he did not know what it was. It was something he could feel but not see until he turned and looked at the trees.

There, just above the waterline, stood a small boy with hair that had once been orange and was now plastered to his skull. He stared straight at Arnold. His eyes were small but brilliant, like drops of water; like a bird's.

Arnold looked at the boy and the boy looked back. He could no longer read the words that were written on his T-shirt. Everything was dark and clinging and covered in filth and dripping with water, and it was only when the boy tried to climb up through the branches that Arnold realised he was not a ghost.

His heart beat painfully. He did not know what he was supposed to do. He started to walk towards the boy, who didn't scream and didn't run away. He only stood there and opened his mouth. Arnold half expected to hear the cry of a bird but there was no sound at all.

He went to the trees and reached down through the branches, his face pressed into the slimy moss. Cold fingers clasped his own.

He pulled the boy up through the rustle and snap of twigs and deposited him on the banking. The boy sank to the ground and looked at Arnold from the dark hollows of his eyes.

"You took me under there."

Arnold nodded.

"Why?"

"I had to."

When the boy spoke again he whispered, and Arnold strained to hear the words. "Am I going back in the water?"

Arnold did not answer. He did not know what the answer was. Then he said, "You can't. It wouldn't keep you."

The boy began to sniffle, all air and water. Arnold didn't say anything else and he didn't try to comfort him. All he could think was, *The good chicks float.* He did not know how the boy had done it. He must have woken beneath the water, but how had he held his breath when Arnold had taken him down? Now the water had given him back.

The good chicks floated and hatched beneath the mother's wings. Then she led the chick, with great rejoicing, back to its father.

He looked across the lake again, making sure they were alone. But they were never alone, were they? Pond skaters made minuscule ripples across the surface. Leaves stirred as an unseen bird darted away. Somewhere, a bittern was raising its chicks.

He looked at the boy, whose face was blurry with tears. "You need to go home," he said.

They walked side by side, the boy occasionally stumbling. Arnold put out a hand to steady him, feeling the small, round bone in his shoulder. As he went, something lifted inside him. He was doing the right thing. The good chick floated; it would be raised in the light. He would never shout at other boys and he wouldn't bully them and his hands would be gentle. When Arnold thought of the child being that way, in the world, where he was supposed to be, he felt something he hadn't experienced in a long time; it was more than contentment, lighter than peace.

At the cabin, he brought the boy a towel and rubbed it vigorously against his scalp. The feathers were clumped and he could see white skin between them, naked and vulnerable. He brought him food and watched him gulp it down, his throat bobbing.

"Am I going back to my mum now?" the boy said.

Arnold frowned. "You have a sister, don't you?"

The boy nodded. Arnold remembered the girl's scrunched-up face, her mewling mouth. It seemed this time the bad chick had escaped. He went to his desk and picked up the brass compass and passed it to the boy, who turned it in his hands. He was getting fingerprints all over it, but that didn't matter, either.

"My mum's called Sandra," the boy said. "I have her number. Or if you called the police, they'd know what to do." He spoke casually, as if he was saying something that wasn't really important. "My name's Todd."

Arnold stared at him. Slowly, he shook his head.

"My sister's Sophie and Dad's called John."

Arnold shook his head again. "You don't have a name."

The boy pouted. "I do so."

"You don't need a name. There are only two of us." It didn't matter about his name. Birds didn't have names, but they knew each other anyway. They knew who and what they were, and they knew what they were supposed to do. They knew their place in the world; no one needed to tell them what it was, except, perhaps, this boy. But that was what the parent did, isn't it?

"You have no name now," he said again, and the boy stared at him. Some kind of understanding began to dawn on his face and his lip trembled. The lesson was already being learned, Arnold realised. Some lessons were hard, but they were necessary. Soon he would learn a new language too, the only one he needed; the language of fish and trees and beasts and birds. He would learn how to be; he would learn how to fly.

The Orphan Bird never had been an orphan, not really. It's just that it didn't have anyone who was prepared to nurture it. The good birds raised only the good chicks, who went on to raise more good chicks. The other ones, the bad ones—they weren't supposed to have chicks of their own, were they? And yet it seemed they could.

Condemned to live and die in darkness and in grief, he thought. But maybe it didn't have to be that way.

A tear slipped from the boy's eye and ran down his cheek. Then he screwed up his face and he suddenly looked like the other, like his sister. "Don't do that," Arnold said sharply. The boy began to cry harder and so he grasped his puny shoulders and pushed him ahead of him, up the stairs. He pulled open the door to the store cupboard. It was dark in there and there wasn't much room, but the boy fit easily. He shoved the door closed after him, pressing his hands against it. Inside, the boy fluttered, banging against the sides, throwing himself against the walls.

Arnold leaned his cheek against the door. Parents had to show the way, didn't they? And he found he knew how. It was all instinct, after all. He would keep him quiet and keep him safe. Eventually, the chick would learn.

He reached out and turned the key in the lock. The first lesson was silence. When he had learned that, he could come out; and silence would keep him safe. It would keep them both safe.

He walked away down the hall, ready to resume his work at last. New energy was coursing through him. It was good to have responsibility, to take care of something other than himself. Above him, the door rattled. He smiled. He knew that he had patience, and patience, above all things, is what he would need. All young birds needed a nest; and this one would not be ready to fledge for a long, long time.

The Murmurations of Vienna Von Drome

JEFFREY FORD

Pellegran's Knot, in spring and summer, appeared an idyllic city. There was the shore, a vast park with hiking trails and, in the center of its enormous lawn, a working carousel. There were excellent restaurants, an historic district with a Pre-Empire cathedral (Saint Ifritia's) and secret tunnels, an observatory, museums, a modern street car, and reasonable lodgings city-wide. The place was off the beaten track in the best of ways. As I noted above, *the Knot*, as we called it, "appeared" idyllic. There were, though, two very glaring aspects that disrupted its claim to quaint tranquility. One was disturbing in a kind of wonderful way, the other in a decidedly horrible way, and the truth was they were inextricably intertwined.

There was, in the Knot, a history of murder. Once every few years a body was found, always in the winter months, always after a fresh snow, the face shredded as if by claws, the abdominal cavity split open in a crude fashion and the spleen removed. Remnants of the partially devoured spleen were usually found near the victims but sometimes as far away as a half mile. My predecessors in the constabulary had determined that all these brutal killings had been carried out by the same person. The scenarios were identical. There were clues—long white hairs found upon and in the vicinity of the bodies. Strange dental marks in whatever remaining piece of spleen might have been recovered.

I came on the scene at the age of fifty, after having spent twenty years as an officer of the constabulary. It was a surprise promotion—head investigator for the third of the brutal murders. There was no way to sugar coat it: we had a serial killer living in our midst, someone all us citizens no doubt passed at one point or another on the street. Eventually, the newspaper dubbed our malefactor, *the Beast*. We locals discussed the existence of the maniac only among ourselves, keeping the tourists out of it. Everyone knew to keep mum in spring and summer. The newspaper never dared print a word about it each year until the leaves had turned orange. Even the killer acquiesced and killed well after the last of the bathers, sightseers, gourmands, had left for home.

A question you might ask is, "Was there never a witness to any of these crimes?" In fact, I met the young Vienna Von Drome through the treacheries of the Beast. Its third victim was Professor Clifford Von Drome, a naturalist and physician who taught at the local Lyceum. He was slain in his rooms overlooking the park—face torn to shreds and his spleen missing. The room the murder took place in, the parlor of his spacious apartment, was spattered and soaked in blood as if a blood tornado had cut through the center of the place. The only thing different about this incident as opposed to the Beast's other attacks is that there was a witness. We were fairly certain that Von Drome's thirteen-year-old daughter and her pet were present during the entire macabre act. Why she wasn't killed as well, we had no idea.

Of course, I questioned her. She wore a student uniform, plaid skirt, white blouse, dark blazer—a pretty young girl with long hair, lighter than blond, clear blue eyes, and pale skin the color of cream. Her stillness and silence put me in mind of a ghost. She sat across from me in my office, and I asked her what happened. Not a word. The city doctor said she was in shock from seeing her father butchered. I asked her to write down whatever she could, but she just sat there and stared at me without blinking.

I sent Vienna home and had one of my officers go in a horse and carriage to pick up the professor's. The woman, like myself, was a native of the Answer Islands, a colonial holding of the Empire. I knew her. Priscilla Goggin. Her aunt came from my old village. We got on very well, and she told me what I needed to know about the girl, her father, and her dead mother.

It was from her that I learned about Mortimer. Supposedly, the girl's father was out in the local woods one day and discovered an abandoned chick. He brought it back to his home and gave the tiny bird to his daughter. "It's a starling," he said and handed her a small wire cage. My guess is he wanted her to have some responsibility to take her mind off her mother, who'd passed away only a couple of years earlier. The girl managed to raise the creature, which was no easy thing. By the time Vienna witnessed her father's killing, the bird went everywhere with her, either flying close behind or sitting on her red beret. The starling knew hand signals and a few verbal commands, but he also could speak in a girl's voice—a wide variety of sayings. You know, of course, that birds like the starling, the crow, the magpie, the mockingbird, can all be taught to speak like parrots. Here was my question, though. Priscilla told me that the girl's silence and inability to communicate had come upon her quickly, sometime between when her mother and father had died. So if the girl wasn't talking, who taught the bird how to speak?

I watched her for half a year before I started to believe that her affliction was real. It was about this time that it became clear to me that the only way an Answer Islander could ascend to Inspector was if it was a job that no one else wanted. Chasing the Beast frightened my colleagues. They were more than willing to sacrifice one citizen every few years to stay as far afield of it as possible. I was the one upon whom the scorn was to be directed when it killed. I'd have quit if I hadn't promised Priscilla that I'd avenge her employer.

At the end of the first year following the murder of Vienna's father, I ordered the girl and the bird to be brought in for questioning. We sat on the balcony on the southern side of the station house. I made us a pot of blue nerve tea. The weather was beautiful. We sipped in relative silence. The girl said nothing. "We're all at sea. All at sea," said the bird. I realized it was just nonsense, but I wondered if its voice was that of Vienna Von Drome. I'd asked Priscilla about that, and she said she didn't know as she had come to be employed by Clifford Von Drome after the girl had lost her ability to communicate.

Vienna seemed touched. Her wealthy relatives, Clifford's brother and sister, who lived mid-empire in the city of Totenveit, paid to keep her at a distance, with Priscilla as her guardian. Still, she was all I had to go on, and once she recovered enough to leave her apartment, I tailed her. She walked far and wide, the bird, of course, accompanying her—on her shoulder, her hat, flying from branch to branch along her path. She led me through the city gardens where she often rested on a bench beneath the ancient yew, led me along Philo's colonnade, across the square in front of City Hall, along the twisting cobble stone streets of the old part of town, and sometimes out to the shore to ramble in and out among the dunes. On the days I followed her, I'd return to my apartment exhausted.

Then, in October, of the second year after her father's murder, precisely on the fifteenth, I, along with my assistant, Jallico, another Answer Islander, newly hired by me to help in the investigation (I had to threaten to quit to get him a job), followed her to a bench just outside the carousel at the center of the park. There were maybe two or three people traipsing across the enormous lawn. The temperature had dropped and the wind was fairly high. Dead leaves blew out of the trees at the boundary of the field and rolled in waves across the expanse. From where Jallico and I sat, about a hundred yards away, pretending to have a conversation, we saw the bird, Mortimer, lift off her hat and fly into the treetops. That's when I noticed that the branches were teeming with dark birds. When the wind momentarily let up, you could hear the din of their squawks and warbles.

I was taken by surprise, and Jallico jumped out of his seat, when the birds—starlings, I know now—burst forth from the branches at the edge of the field and flew in a swarm, rising and falling, twisting and turning. It was remarkable how they moved as if with one mind. They made shifting, fluid shapes in mid-air. But just as the energy of the flock was about to dissipate, and they were to fly apart and back to their branches, they made one more turn and what happened next I wasn't quite sure I believed. When the amazing display was over, I saw Mortimer fly back to perch on Vienna's shoulder. She got up and walked directly toward us. I took the newspaper from my pocket and brought it up to cover my face.

Jallico, without a newspaper, improvised with the lame ruse of having fallen asleep. After she had passed, I turned to my assistant and said, "Did you see it there at the end?"

"The Fountain?" he said.

"Precisely." In an instant the conglomeration of dark birds—as if the strokes of an ink pen upon blue paper—transformed into the image of a fountain. Starlings in the form of water, sprayed at the top and fell into the catch basin. The entire thing lasted no more than ten seconds but I distinctly saw it.

"If I'm not mistaken, Inspector," said Jallico, "that was not just any fountain, but the fountain over by the cathedral."

I realized he was right. "So it was," I said, and patted the young man on the shoulder.

On the first anniversary of the murder of Clifford Von Drome, Jallico and I lurked in corners where we'd not be seen. From mine, the fountain was due west, and straight through the front doors of the cathedral. The wind blew through in gusts, leaves and stray paper, but not a soul. Later we walked the twisting cobble stone streets back into the ancient neighborhood. As day slid toward night, it began to snow. We got lost finding our way back to the cathedral where, when we finally arrived, we huddled for warmth before trying to make it to the streetcar. Jallico had a nasty habit of cigarette smoking, but I tolerated it because it helped him think. We sat in the front pew before the altar and beneath the empty echoing dome. We could hear the wind outside.

"He's not coming, is he?" asked my assistant.

"What do you mean?"

"I mean he's not coming out this year to kill. I think I can feel it."

"You're delusional, brother," I told him. "The first time you think that, he will assuredly strike."

As it turned out, Jallico was right, but that didn't spare us the angst of the months between the end of autumn and spring. News of a body seemed always waiting just around the corner until late March.

It was three years before the Beast returned. Jallico and I stayed on the case, trading off days during which one of us either tailed Vienna Von

Drome or wandered the streets around the cathedral. We witnessed the girl grow into a young woman. As she got older, it seemed that she became more aware of the existence of other people. She noticed, watched, winced, and nearly smiled once, or at least that's what I thought. Mortimer stayed by her side. She never left the apartment without him. Almost every day, a long walk all around the Knot. And yes, on October 15 of each of the three years, Jallico and I witnessed, in the empty park, the murmurations of Vienna Von Drome. Each year the swarm left us with another clue: a cat, a triangle with a circle above and one below, and a giant starling. Although my assistant and I never disagreed about the images, there was always the slight sense that they were no more than a figment of the imagination. In other words, there was doubt.

The hissing cat head was a thousand starlings or more. The creature pounced into the air and burst apart. In the moment it was airborne, its hair was depicted as sharp angles and its eyes were enormous. The same thing with the giant starling made of starlings. A conundrum but it too was impressive. Once you'd seen these images born of the bird's unified flight, there was no forgetting them. I wondered how much Vienna's pet, Mortimer, had to do with it. "What if the bird's running the show?" I said to Jallico.

He shivered slightly. "If that were the case," he said. "I'd quit on the spot, but what if the Von Drome girl is the one who killed her father?"

"Vienna the Beast?" I said. "I suppose it's possible, but she'd have had to have been ten when the first of the murders took place."

We learned from the Commissioner of the constabulary that our office and our budget line would be stricken from existence if the Beast didn't kill in the fourth year since its last slaughter. Our good fortune depended upon someone's murder. That October there was no murmuration. Vienna and Mortimer showed up on the bench beside the carousel, but the bird never left her shoulder.

Something was up. She'd met a young man on the patio of the Coffee Exchange in late August. I watched the entire affair transpire from a distance. I'm not even sure you could call it an affair. They sat at a metal table, each drinking coffee, watching the horse-drawn carriages ferrying citizens off to their appointments. She didn't speak to him. He carried on a conversation for the two of them. The few times I drew close enough to catch the topic of his monologue, he was going on about love and the cosmos. Jallico pegged him as having a loose screw. Still, Vienna, who cast no eye his way or gave any indication that she was listening to him, came every afternoon for two weeks in August to sit and drink coffee. That was it. Of course, the bird was with her. And old Mortimer wasn't that pleased with the fellow. He'd fly high above them and shit on the young man's hat. We did a background check on the guy, Kemton Lair, a pretentious lout living off his wealthy mother's money. My assistant and I took him aside and warned him that there should not be any improprieties with the young woman. We told him we were watching. Then Jallico punched him in the gut as hard as he could. Definitive punctuation to an important message. One of the good reasons to have a younger assistant.

We kept an eye on Vienna's meetings with Lair. Once winter set in and the weather grew very cold as it does in the Knot, they moved their rendezvous inside the Coffee Exchange. The surveillance seemed pointless. Nothing was happening. Still, one of us usually followed her. One day in January when it was Jallico's turn (I was over in the old town skulking around the cathedral), he saw, from a bench across the street from the Exchange and through its plate-glass window, Lair surreptitiously pull a knife on Vienna and grab her arm. He forced her to stand and he led her out the back door of the place. My assistant took off, bolting through the coffeehouse and out the back. The two had a head start on him but they made slow progress. Mortimer, who'd been riding his mistress's shoulder all morning, now flew wildly around the young man's head pecking at his eyes and pulling his hair and ears with sharp talons. As they came into view, Jallico drew his pistol, took a bead on the assailant's forehead, and yelled for him to stop. Kemton Lair pushed Vienna to the ground and fled.

My assistant helped Vienna to her feet, made sure she was fine, and gave chase. As luck would have it the suspect ran into the old town, and I saw Lair pass at the cross street I was approaching. A moment later Jallico ran by in the same direction. I called out to let my assistant know I was also in pursuit. Kemton ducked into the municipal entrance of the historic underground, a confusing warren of paths and dimly lit passageways that ran beneath the entire old neighborhood. Jallico asked if we should split up. "He has a knife," he said as we bounded down the stairs to the first level of tunnels. "We stay together," I told him. I drew my weapon, and we started slowly ahead through the shadows. We got lost for hours, never seeing a soul and never finding a flight of stairs up to the street. "Good lord," I said, "by this time he could have eaten a half dozen spleens."

"You think this white worm is the Beast?" said Jallico. "I don't think he could cut bread with that knife."

"I'm not sure what to think," I said.

As it turned out, my assistant was right. Kemton Lair was not the Beast. In fact, we found him in our 3rd and a half hour of looking for a way up and out. He was slumped against the wall in a particularly dark passage, only one torch to light the entire length of it. Jallico retrieved the torch from off the wall and brought it up close for us to see. Lair had been raggedly cut from larynx to navel. His face was shredded so badly it was like a mop head of skin ribbons rinsed in blood. I knew before we even heard back from the coroner that his spleen was missing.

"I made a mistake," Jallico told me. "I should have followed them a little longer to see what was going on."

"You did right. He had a knife on her," I said.

The monetary line for our unit remained intact. I kept my job as Inspector and Jallico remained my assistant. The Commissioner called me in one afternoon and told me that there were those in the constabulary who posited that Jallico and I did away with Lair, making it look like a Beast attack, to keep our unit together. I was sitting across from him. I stood up and leaned over his desk. "You know, we found a note from the Beast," I whispered. "He wrote that this year he is hunting you." Of course, a lie. The very thought of the Beast actually writing a note seemed amusing to me.

My superior trembled slightly and yelled, "That's not true."

I backed away, smiling and nodded.

"Well, catch the damn thing, will you?"

"Will do, sir," I said.

Winter gave way to spring and, in the intervening months, Jallico and I looked more thoroughly into the background of Kemton Lair, the way we should have to begin with. Apparently the old woman he was often seen in the company of was not his mother. It was an assumption of those who knew him from the Coffee Exchange and the wine bar around the corner from the cathedral. As one woman put it, "I swore it was his mother by the way she yelled at him in a whisper, but when I referred to her as his mother, he shook his head. 'She's my fiancé,' he said. Well that struck me because she looked saggy and old with that crazy white hair. He was so young and handsome and she was a mess."

We asked after the woman, but nobody knew her nor where she lived, except that she seemed to be local, a resident of the old town. We couldn't find Lair's address either. We set that information aside for a while, since it was going nowhere, and went back to shadowing Vienna. It was difficult to tell whether she acknowledged that Lair was missing from their rendezvous. I watched her from a considerable distance through a spy glass as Jallico watched her from a bench ten feet away. She peeked in the Coffee Exchange window, hesitated a moment, and then fled in her inimitable style—like a sleep walker.

All spring and into late summer, I played the voyeur, setting myself in some vantage point in town from where I could spy on Vienna's progress as she circumnavigated Pellegran's Knot. I told my assistant to follow her every day. I tracked them as they made their way. Why? What did I have to prove? Nothing. I was waiting for Vienna's next murmuration, for the Beast to strike again. Waiting and watching. In addition, we accomplished one other thing. We tested the white hairs we found on the body of Lair and a few of the other victims, seeing as that the old woman was said to have a shaggy head of white hair. We found in all cases, though, with the exception of one, that the hairs were not human—believed to be those of a cat. In the one exception, the victim's own hair was white and that is what was believed to have been found.

We were reminded of the murmuration of the image of the cat, but it turned out to be as fruitless as the image of the fountain or of the starling itself. That summer was balmy, slow and still. Pellegran's Knot had never seen so many tourists, but they were a subdued lot. I admittedly dozed through most of the spring and summer when I wasn't spying on Vienna and Jallico. Then in late August I noticed that Vienna's daily constitutional shifted course and the walk now took her, every day, out of sight, behind the giant sand dune east of the harbor known as the Eruption. For a good five minutes she and Jallico were blocked from my view. When the young woman finally appeared on the other side of the Eruption, she was walking in her usual somnambulant gait, and Jallico followed a surreptitious distance behind.

Vienna's autumn murmuration that year told the tale. As clear as day, all made of birds flapping and soaring, she and Jallico embraced and kissed for distinctive seconds and then shattered into individual starlings dispersing.

Jallico and I sat side by side, across the field from Vienna, who was, as always, on the bench beside the carousel.

"Was that you?" I asked him.

He turned lightning quickly to face me. "Are you serious?" he said. "It's not me."

"Behind the Eruption perhaps?" I said.

"Never," he said. "That bird is trying to frame me. I'm almost positive it knows I am following her."

"Very well," I said. "I trust you would tell me everything. But I do have to ask. You understand."

"Of course."

Still I was mightily suspicious. It could have been Lair in the murmuration, but the way the long hair hung in the back was the picture of Jallico, and his height. Lair was much taller. "Who do you think it is?" I asked him.

"It could be anybody. It could be her imagination," he said.

After that day, I took Jallico off the duty of tailing Vienna and put him on a detail of searching through the old town for the woman with white hair. I followed Vienna with my spy glass from the bell tower of the cathedral, and I noticed that once Jallico was no longer pursuing her, she no longer passed behind the Eruption on a daily basis. In fact, she never did again. As the cold weather came on, her walking route stayed clear of the shore, and passed through the most pedestrian parts of town—the field with the carousel, the city square, Saint Philo's colonnade, etc. One place she was making new visits to, though, was the Lyceum where her father had been a professor.

It was three weeks after we'd witnessed the starlings' depiction of Vienna sharing a kiss with a young man—a cold and dreary Friday that made me feel my age. The old women who gathered on the benches in the city square were predicting a snow storm the likes of which hadn't been seen in the Knot in years. That was the word from Jallico as he arrived at our offices at the constabulary just after the rolls and coffee had been delivered.

"You know what that means?" he said. "The snow?"

"I could smell it in the air," I told him. "While I was waiting for you, I cleaned my pistol and made sure it was loaded."

"Do you feel the Beast will strike today?"

"I'd like to put an end to this bloody case and retire."

Before setting out—Jallico for the old town and me for the Lyceum, we decided to use a runner. We needed some way to keep in touch throughout the day, and so we put in with the Commissioner to procure a child messenger, willing to run word between us as the day progressed. The girl, Meralee, I was told was quite fast and could be trusted with any assignment. She was very attentive, her face like an axe-head pointing forward, ready to cut into the day. Long red hair and freckles; a lively child. Even as fed up with life as the Beast had made me, she brought a smile to my face. I would give her a handsome tip well past what the constabulary would pay her. Jallico and I decided that he should take her first as there was a greater chance that he might run into our quarry. The Beast had already struck a few times in the area around the cathedral and fountain.

"Send the girl off before you engage in anything the slightest bit dangerous," I said. "And if you pick up the trail of the Beast, contact me and wait till I arrive."

It had already begun to snow, and so I took a coach and four to the Lyceum. It was a hulking, somber old place built of granite shipped in from the majestic cliffs of Answer Island—even the least of my homeland's attributes were appropriated by the empire. Of course, academics rarely work a full week, and the place was like a ghost town. I showed the secretary of the zoology lab my badge and asked to see Clifford Von Drome's offices and effects. The fellow looked to be a science experiment himself, a shambling wreck in a moth-eaten sweater, a bent primate with long arms and short legs. Stokes was his name, and though he was certainly not much to look at, he knew where everything was.

An hour after I arrived at the empty school, I found myself knee deep in cartons of paper in a dimly lit room. Sifting through the professor's work, I slowly came to realize he was a serious scientist. His specialty appeared to be centered on the nexus between human and animal disease. He seemed to be looking for human cures in the animal world. Most of the work dealt with immunology. There were papers on certain failings of human health and animals' natural protection against those diseases—the slow loris, ghost lemurs, certain members of the cat family, civets, raccoons. There was a series of daguerreotypes I uncovered of individuals half naked and beset by strange growths and postures, odd manifestations of the face, like one old fellow with pointed ears and long incisors.

After a while I took a break and went out into the hallway to escape the stuffy room. Stokes came by and inquired if I needed anything. I asked him why all these boxes and notes were kept. He told me that Von Drome was a brilliant researcher and some of his investigations into the Natural world had resulted in cures and products that brought the Lyceum and the city quite a bit of money. I asked him to stay still for a moment and went back into the room to fetch the browning daguerreotypes of the patients. I'd hoped that he might be able to identify one or two of them even though time had moved on. I handed him the lot and said, "Do you know who any of these people are?"

"I'd seen them in here years ago," he said. I remember these poor souls but their names are long gone. He came to the last of the pictures and held it up. "This one is Tessa," he said.

"Tessa?"

"Von Drome, Clifford's wife. If you ask me, it was the reason he undertook the study of these diseases and the search for cures. When they'd first married, she'd contracted something strange up in the forests of Lindrethool where they'd gone on their honeymoon. The symptoms of the disease showed themselves years later."

I took the picture from him and beheld a lovely young woman whose upper body, stomach to breasts to neck was covered with a fine white down. Her pupils were pure black.

"It finally killed her some years back when that poor daughter of theirs reached her teen years. A damn shame. Not to mention her father being murdered just a couple of years later."

"She's been coming here lately, hasn't she, Vienna Von Drome?"

"Yes, I let her in to look at her father's things. Why not, what could it hurt? I've known her since she was a girl."

"Does she speak to you?" I asked.

Stokes smiled and shook his head. "Not a word."

A half hour later, I was sitting in the Lyceum café, sipping a cup of chocolate, and studying the daguerreotype of Vienna's mother. The place was empty, and I could see through the floor-to-ceiling windows that the snow was angling down. I heard the wind howling. The next thing I knew, there was a small mittened hand upon my jacket sleeve. I looked up. It was Meralee. She leaned over, out of breath, and dug into her coat pocket. A moment later she was flattening a piece of paper on the table. I lifted the cup of chocolate and handed it to her and told her to sit down and rest. I picked up the paper and read it. Jallico had scribbled me a note. At the top there was a drawing of the triangle with a circle above it and a circle below it, precisely the image we'd seen created by the flock of starlings during one of the murmurations. Beneath that was an address—62 Marfal Street, old town.

"Can you show me where it is?" I asked the girl.

She nodded, threw back the rest of the chocolate, and we were off. I flagged down a coach outside the Lyceum, and we hopped aboard. It was a relief to be out of the stinging snow. I offered the driver a tip if he could hurry but he told me that the cobblestones were slippery and therefore treacherous. He told me he'd go as fast as he could but the cobblestones were slippery and therefore treacherous. The red-haired girl was good to her word and brought us to a small side street in the old town. I had the driver pull up a few yards away as to retain the element of surprise. The buildings were close together in that area, and the streets were like narrow canyons that cut through them, hardly enough room for two small coaches to pass side by side. I got out and paid the driver. Then I paid Meralee and told her to stay in the coach, head back to the center of the city. She asked if I might need her later, disappointed that she was no longer part of the investigation. It was obviously too dangerous for me to allow her to remain. I saw her off down the street and then pulled my pistol and approached the house.

It leaned slightly forward out over the street. Its shutters were chipped and splintered as was the door. Green paint was faded or curling. On a wooden plaque screwed into the face of the house next to the letter box there was a figure, rendered in fading chalk—a triangle with a circle above it and one below. I didn't knock but tried the knob. It wouldn't budge. I kicked it in with little resistance from the flimsy lock. I peered into the dark, and my heart started to pound. "This is all wrong," I remember thinking. I'd given orders for him to wait for me if he came upon something. The snow came down harder, the sound of the wind confused me. All I could manage to think was, "It's the season for killing." I stepped into the darkness.

I stood with my gun raised, waiting for my eyes to adjust, relieved, at least, to be out of the storm. A minute passed and then I heard something knock against the floor upstairs just above me. Slowly, I groped around and by lighting a match I was able to find the stairs. Retaining the element of surprise in an effort that involved climbing stairs was difficult. I breathed shallowly and tiptoed one step at a time. Although I'd just come out of the frozen afternoon, I was already sweating. The worn steps cracked and popped like an old man's spine. The tension built to a breaking point and to relieve it, as I reached the top step, I called out for Jallico. A loud groan emanated from behind a closed door at the left end of a hallway. I suddenly had a purpose and moved without a second thought.

I kicked that door in as well. It swung back, and I stepped into a large room lined with bookshelves. Straight ahead, I saw no one, but as I turned the corner into the room, I went into shock. My training and my experience should have directed me to pull the trigger, but instead the hand holding the gun fell limp at my side. Jallico was slumped against the wall, his face in bloody shreds. His shirt and coat were ripped away and his torso was cut from top to bottom, a gaping cavity of gore. I saw rib bones and intestines. Leaning over him was someone, no, something, with a large serrated blade in one hand and a raw piece of dark bloody meat in the other. It ripped off a piece of the spleen with its sharp teeth, the blood smearing all over the long white hair on its body and head. I needed to stop seeing what was before me. I lifted the gun to obliterate the sight and saw Jallico's eyes move and his mouth open. Instead of firing on the Beast, I shot my assistant in order to spare him. The creature shrieked and leaped at me like a cat, swiped the gun from my hand by raking the flesh off my wrist. I was slammed against the wall with such force that I momentarily lost consciousness.

I came around a minute or so later to the sensation of someone lightly stroking my forehead. I knew immediately I couldn't move. Opening my eyes, I saw a blurry figure leaning over me. I was almost positive it was Vienna. There was blood on her lips and she made a soft trilling noise. That's all I remember before falling again into total blackness. When I came to, it was also to the sensation of someone lightly stroking my forehead. Again I opened my eyes, and saw it was the red-haired messenger girl, Meralee. "Get help," I managed to grunt. I saw her nod and she was off. In the hour it took for the constables to get there with an ambulance, I tried to hold on to that vision of Vienna I'd had, tried to determine if it was real or a dream. Eventually, I saw it all as a murmuration, a swarm of birds that became the world and then flew me into night.

Two years later, and the Beast hadn't returned. I had been fired from the constabulary for being implicated in the death of my partner. It was my bullet they found in his forehead. I'd tried to explain but had no energy for it and let them railroad me out of the department. I wasn't even sure why they felt they needed to get rid of me. I suppose they had some other hapless Answer Islander on the case. My reputation and name were derided in the newspapers as if it was all my fault that my partner and the other victims of the creature had died. Incompetence, a lack of professionalism, an implied lack of intelligence were my résumé by the time the affair had settled down. I never even made it to Jallico's funeral. I was in the hospital for six months with two broken legs, broken ribs, a dislocated shoulder, and headaches like a sudden axe attack.

Eventually, I wound up back at my empty apartment. I'd never married, as the work demanded too much of my time and self. The commissioner got me a small pension to live on, knowing what the truth was behind my service. It was good to know that not everyone in the Pellegran's Knot hierarchy was a complete scoundrel. I stayed away from people. Lived for myself. Walked everyday through my loneliness. I tried not to think about the case, but it came back to me, springing out of the dark like a cat. I couldn't help but see the headlines in the racks outside the stores I passed on my daily constitutionals. I skipped the park on October 15 the first year after my dismissal from work. There was a killing that winter. Stokes, the secretary at the Lyceum in charge of Clifford Von Drome's old papers and experiments. The fact that he was connected to the Von Dromes was another maddening detail. I pushed it out of my mind and waited for the warmer weather when the bustle of tourists seemed to drive the nightmare from the mind of the city.

As the temperature became more accommodating, I took to ending my walk each day in the lemon tree orchard on the west side of town, near the observatory. There was a small café there, and it was a place even the tourists usually weren't aware of. Sitting quietly, daydreaming—in other words setting my imagination against the images of my past—I drank lemon gin until night came on and covered my drunken retreat home. One evening while sitting there I was approached by a very young woman, wearing a boy's shirt and trousers. She didn't wait to be invited but pulled the empty seat at my table out and sat down. At first, she said nothing but stared at me. Then I recognized her red hair and her eager face. It was Meralee, the messenger who worked for the constabulary.

"Do you know me?" she finally asked.

I nodded. "Thank you for saving my life," I said.

She took a slip of paper out of her pants pocket and slid it along the tabletop toward me. "When Stokes was killed this past winter, I was on the scene at the Lyceum when the constables found him. In his office, where I was poking around, I uncovered this beneath the blotter on his desk. It's a note made out to you. You might find it interesting. I've shown it to no one else."

"I don't know that I want it," I said, but reached into my pocket and brought out a few bills as a tip for the messenger.

"No, no, Inspector. It's for nothing. I recognize you're a good person. My father was from the Answer Islands. I'm young but I see everything."

She got up and walked away down the row of lemon trees and disappeared amid the white blossoms. I sat for another hour, had two more drinks. When I paid, I decided to leave Meralee's note behind. "I can't," I told myself. I got twenty yards toward home and then stumbled back and grabbed the slip of paper before the waiter cleared it away with the trash. I waited till the next morning to read it, when I was sober.

After a night of troubling dreams, slightly hungover and standing in my kitchen, reading by the sunlight streaming through the window, I learned that Tessa and Vienna both were born with a rare disease that attacked the immune system. Stokes wrote, "Forgive me for lying to you about the fact that Tessa contracted her disease in Lindrethool. I was trying to put you off the truth." Elite physicians of the empire who were aware of it called the congenital disease Pedlep's Coronation, a condition where the body's immune system stripped off layers of brain matter, eating away toward the reptilian center of consciousness and revealing different evolutionary stages of awareness as it went. It was Clifford's desire to cure his wife and daughter. Instead, his chemicals and techniques, elixirs and minor electrocutions, had made them more or less than human, depending on how you saw it. Stokes revealed in the note that he knew Tessa wasn't dead but instead escaped from her coffin with the help of her husband and now roamed the underground of the old town and other secret spots until she needed the platelets produced by the spleen to heal the ravages of the mutation Dr. Von Drome had initiated. I didn't know whether to believe it. I thought maybe Meralee was sent by the other constables to torment me with this farfetched story, but how farfetched *was* this really in relation to what I'd already witnessed?

After that morning in my kitchen, I did three things—stopped drinking, bought a gun, and waited for October. At the end of the summer, I contacted Priscilla by mail and asked that she retrieve a daguerreotype of Tessa Von Drome from the apartment for me. She met me one day at the Coffee Exchange with an envelope and the picture I'd requested.

"I'd read that you were responsible for Jallico's death," she said.

I didn't try to explain. All I responded was, "You can't believe everything you hear."

"His wife and children have returned to Answer Island, and she is certain you are a murderer. She'll defame you in your village."

I nodded and sighed. My hands were clasped on the tabletop and she covered them with her own. "I trust you," she said.

"Tell me about the girl."

"She's hardly a girl anymore," said Priscilla. "A young woman is more like it. She is somewhat more cognizant. I can get her attention and speak to her and she seems to understand, but . . ."

There was a pause. "But what . . . ?"

"She's changing. There's something about her. Her nose is becoming pointed and she's become thinner, lighter, and always anxious. Meanwhile her shoulders appear more powerful. I never see her not bundled up in heavy shirts. The nails on her toes grow long and sharp. I find indigo feathers about the apartment that I know are not Mortimer's. She must be keeping another pet a secret from me."

I lifted the daguerreotype of Tessa Von Drome and compared it to my fleeting memory of the Beast as it lunged across the room at me in the house on Marfal Street. At one moment I could see her face amid the wild white hair of the creature, and in another it didn't seem possible that this lovely woman could be the same animal/person. No matter how many times I looked, I just couldn't decide. I gave the picture back to Priscilla and asked her to return it. After that we sat for a while and talked about the old days back home. She mentioned my little brother, who died of the fever when he was very young. "I thought of him just the other day," she said. "He was such a mischievous little scamp."

I nodded and smiled. "Jallico reminded me of him," I said.

We both wiped tears from our eyes; so far away from home.

On October 15, I awoke early, made my way to the park, and took a seat on the bench that offered a view of the front of the carousel. I waited for hours, but then I caught sight of someone shuffling out of the woods. I'd not seen her in quite a while but was able to spot her due to Mortimer riding on her shoulder. Vienna had changed a great deal, as Priscilla had suggested. She sat down on her bench, and I eased back on mine. Some time passed but throughout it I was in a state of alertness. I relaxed finally when I saw Mortimer take off into the treetops of orange leaves alive with the chatter and whistle of starlings. When the murmuration began, I had tears in my eyes. The flock made beautiful designs in the air, as if they were making it special because it would be the last I'd see. At the end they created an image of the cathedral—the whole weighty edifice moving through the sky for several seconds before dispersing.

Mortimer returned to Vienna's shoulder and she rose and started across the field in my direction. I didn't move, and I didn't pretend to be asleep. She passed and stared directly into my eyes. Her look was hypnotic at first, but when I heard that low trilling sound, I had to turn away. When I looked back she had passed on. I got up to return home and on my way found a beautiful indigo feather in my path. I picked it up and slipped it in my pocket.

It was a little early for snow, and the old women in the city square didn't foresee it, but I paid no attention to them. Instead, I prepared my pistol and headed for the old town. It was still early in the day when I arrived. Mass was under way, so I sat in the back pew in the corner and watched the proceedings with a kind of dull awareness. When the prelate had droned his last invocation and the sacraments had been divvied out, the assembled rose and headed for the doors. As the great oaken panels swung open, a stiff wind blew up the aisle of the cathedral carrying with it a dusting of snow. The place cleared out quickly, and all that were left was myself and the two volunteers who cleaned out the pews. One of these, a girl caught my eye. She had red hair, and it only took me a minute to discern that it was Meralee. I didn't bother her in her duties but stayed still. I don't think either she or the young man who assisted her saw me there in the back corner.

I watched the two sweep and polish, and move up and down the aisles. Every now and then I looked to the three clear panels in the giant stained-glass window behind the altar and checked the increasing severity of the snowfall. It was still coming down, more rapidly now than before. It struck me then that I never got a grasp on why these killings only happened when it snowed. "Something to do with body temperature?" I wondered. It was beyond me. That and why Tessa might have killed her husband. Perhaps it was for what he'd turned her into. I closed my eyes and dozed.

I don't know how long it was later, not more than an hour, that I was awoken by a scream. Groggy and off-kilter, I rose and stepped out into the main aisle between the sections of pews. I scanned the altar and the seats but saw no one. Lifting the gun, I bent as low as I could, ridiculously trying to conceal my presence, and moved toward the front of the area of worship. As I drew closer to the altar I saw out of the corner of my eye, Meralee, a white, clawed hand covering her mouth, being dragged by the Beast down a side hallway toward a door. She saw me and managed to free her mouth and cry out again. I leveled the gun, but the creature held her tightly as a shield. I wasn't a good enough shot to guarantee I wouldn't kill the girl. As the Beast dragged her and itself through the doorway, I saw that old, rusted serrated blade in its other hand. An instant later, the door slammed shut and they were gone.

I shoved the door open with my shoulder, the gun directly up in front of my face. Instead of being met by the fierceness of the Beast on the other side of the door, I was confronted by a spiral stairway that led up and up. I took the stairs as quickly as I could for an old man, huffing and wheezing as I climbed, leaping two steps at a time when my knees would allow. There were flimsy banisters to either side, something of a comfort as heights frightened me. The creature was strong and had no difficulty on the ascent, but it was dragging Meralee, which slowed it down just enough that with my best effort, I was able to catch up. They were two turns ahead of me and at times I could clearly see them. At other points the construction of the steps obscured them. I surmised that we were heading to the bell tower, and I was unsure if I was trapping the Beast or she was drawing me in. As I came around another twist of the stairs, I saw an open shot at the flank of the creature and was fairly assured I had little chance of hitting the girl. I took it.

Just before the thing darted around another turn, I saw a burst of red against the white hair. I heard an animal screech and then the screech of Meralee. The Beast had dropped her and she came sliding down the stairs. I lunged ahead and caught her by the calf just before she slipped out beneath the bannister and fell to the stone floor below. I laid the gun on the next step and used two hands to pull her out of harm's way and set her upright. She was breathing heavily and in shock. I made her sit and leaned her back against the step. Lifting my pistol, I told her, "Wait till you can breathe and your head is clear and then run to the station house."

She nodded. I started up the stairs again. She tried to hold me back by wrapping her arms around my leg, but I disengaged myself and continued.

There was a doorway at the top of the steps that I guessed led into the belfry. I was terrified, but I so badly wanted to squeeze off the rest of the pistol rounds into the damnable creature that I charged in. As soon as the door opened, I realized the area I'd just entered was open to the weather. It was freezing and the floor was slippery with snow due to the two wide-open sides to the left and right. There were no railings. I lost my footing and went down, sliding toward one of the open sides till my head and shoulders were leaning out into the air above the courtyard. I'd managed to hold onto the gun, though, expecting an attack from the Beast. The white hair appeared above me. I fired and heard the bullet ricochet off the bell. In the next instant the serrated blade lacerated my hand with a deft slice and the pistol went flying out over the side and to the roof of the cathedral's dome. A set of claws came down from above and ripped through my face on one side. I screamed as the agony nearly made me pass out. Warm blood seeped everywhere.

Through the blur of red on that bad side and my one clear eye, I saw the Beast rise up above me, lifting the knife to plunge into my chest and cut through my stomach. It was Tessa Van Drome. I could make her out behind the deformities and the catlike monstrosity she'd become. The look of fierce desire on her face shocked me, and I couldn't move. At first I thought it was that the wind had increased and the snowflakes had grown enormous and black. They came with such rushing force that they pushed the Beast back away from me. As I watched the dark storm pound against the white monster, I realized it wasn't the weather. It was a swarm of starlings. Their familiar chirps and warbles and high-pitched chatter became clear to me. Tessa was forced backward to the opening on the other side of the belfry and then the murmuration became a hand that gave her a fateful push into nothing. I heard her hiss and wail as she descended through the snow.

The birds as quickly disappeared, and I heard the tramping of footsteps ascending the spiral staircase. Meralee was to rescue me again. Still, when they were only halfway to me, I noticed something quietly move out of the shadows in the corner. It was thin and frail and the same color as the heart of the night. Vienna Von Drome covered in indigo feathers, with a nose and mouth that had become a beak and feet like talons. Her wings lifted in the back. She leaned over and gently touched my forehead. Then with one graceful move she stepped out into thin air, flapped her wings, and climbed toward the clouds. She moved with such grace, it soothed the mess that had been made of the side of my face. When Meralee and the constables finally reached the belfry, Vienna could still barely be seen, disappearing into the falling snow, followed by Mortimer. I said nothing and did nothing to point her out. The killer had been stopped, and the city that did not want me had lost something wonderful.

Blyth's Secret

MIKE O'DRISCOLL

I n the winter of 1995, six weeks after I turned nine, I discovered the
partially devoured body of my mother in Glasfynydd Forest. She'd
vanished one month after my birthday. Three days passed before my
father, Wyn Blevins, reported her missing. It wasn't her first disappearance, but after three days, it was the longest she'd been gone without
contacting us. Father said she'd been suffering one of her "episodes" and
had probably gone to spend some time with her sister. I didn't understand
the nature of these episodes, other than that they induced in my mother
periods of frantic industry or of prolonged silence when she could scarcely
bring herself to step foot outside the house.

I have only a vague memory of the days between her disappearance and
my discovery. Police came and spoke to my father. He mentioned words
like *depression* and *bipolar*, strange words then, and all too familiar
now. A policewoman spoke to Sara and me, asking what kind of woman
mother was and if we'd noticed anything different in her behavior. Aunt
Mary came to stay. We went to school and in the evenings I played with
the pair of red canaries Mother had given me for my birthday. I'd named
them Mickey and Icarus and taught them to leave their cage and alight
on my fingers, where I'd feed them little tidbits. Over dinner Father would
do his best to distract us, asking about our day and how was school, all

the time seeming more distracted than either Sara or me. Some evenings, he'd sit me in his lap and ask me to read to him. While I read he'd stare at nothing at all. If the phone rang I'd feel his body stiffen. He'd wait for Aunt Mary to answer it. While she listened, I'd feel his heart beating like a canary's, loud and fast. And only after she'd let him know there was no news would I feel the agitation flow from his body.

The police searched the house and the brick garage from which Father ran his car repair business. They searched the open country to the south and the woods to the north and after a week they stopped. They said she must have left of her own volition. There was no evidence to the contrary, and so little more they could do other than to keep her listed as a missing person.

I don't recall much of what I felt at that time. I thought perhaps it was a game and that she'd turn up any day and laugh at what a big fuss we'd all made about nothing. Or maybe that she'd scold us for not making more of an effort to find her. One afternoon, shortly after the search was called off, I managed to escape the fretful concern of Aunt Mary and set off into the forest. I knew parts of Glasfynydd well from frequent explorations with my sister and had no fear of getting lost. I headed west with the ground rising steadily, until I came to the crest of a steep, wooded gulley. Dusk was in the air and I was about to turn for home when I heard a squabbling in the dense pines below. I scrambled down the slope, struck by a strong, sickly smell. Covering my mouth and nose I pushed through the undergrowth and saw a dozen or more large crows fighting over what I took to be an animal carcass. Moving closer I saw the familiar blue dress, all torn and dirty. And yet, I still didn't fully understand what I was seeing, not until I stepped closer again and saw the open chest and pale, shredded ruin of my mother's eyeless face.

Time contracts and expands without regard for reason. The events of childhood seem more recent than things that happened a few short weeks ago. I was busy defleshing a crow when a tapping at the window disturbed me. Looking up I saw Blyth perched on the sill. He ruffled his black feathers and called out kaaaarr, alerting me to the presence of a car driving toward the house. Though a somewhat unpleasant task, I found the removal of the organs and the sectioning of the body a welcome distraction from the more rigorous demands of my real research. I set the bird aside, washed my hands, and went out in time to see the police car turn in through the open gate. A policeman of medium height and stocky build got out. He was jacketless, with his shirt sleeves rolled to his elbows. "Wil Blevins?"

"Yes?"

"PC Carroll," he said. "David Carroll."

"So?"

He took off his cap and wiped perspiration from his forehead. "You don't remember me, do you? We were in the same school."

"No."

"No matter," he said good-naturedly. He looked past me, his gaze taking in the brick workshop and the stand of rowan and sycamore beyond. "You escaped, didn't you?"

"What?"

"Made it out of Cray. One of the lucky ones, went off to university. Biochemistry, wasn't it?"

"Zoology," I corrected him. "How do you know all this?"

"Your sister. We were in the same year. She told me you were home. You've been back . . . two years?"

"Three. Is there something . . ."

"Sorry. I don't know if you've heard. About a boy gone missing."

"No."

He scratched the side of his face. "Seven-year-old named Jon Walters. Disappeared yesterday afternoon, in Glasfynydd Forest."

"He was alone?"

"No. Three families on holiday. Spent the day at Usk reservoir. Kids went off exploring in the forest. When they got back to the lake, they noticed the boy was missing."

"That's terrible."

"You know the forest well?"

"I guess."

He took a photograph from his shirt pocket. A young, fair-haired boy with a red baseball cap worn backwards. "That's him."

I stared at the picture. "Poor kid."

"Any chance you were in Glasfynydd yesterday?"

I shook my head.

"When were you last there?"

"I don't know—a few days ago."

"Doing what?"

"Watching birds."

"Birds, yes. Sara used to talk about it."

"Talk about what?"

He gave me an odd look, then smiled. "Just that you always had this fascination with birds. You study them, right?"

"She talked to you about me?"

"We went out together, for a short while. We were eighteen. Then she went off to university, and I went off to work."

"I didn't know that."

"We stayed in touch." He gestured in the direction of the house. "You don't mind living out here now, on your own, I mean?"

"I wouldn't be here if I did," I said, resenting the implication. "I've been managing for three years."

"Well, it's good you're back. How's your dad? Haven't seen him in—"

I flinched. "I have nothing to do with him."

He seemed surprised. "I'm sorry to hear that."

"Don't be."

He showed me the photo again. "You're sure you don't recognise him?"

"I'm good at faces," I said.

"I guess you have to be. Well, thanks anyway." He stuck out his hand and we shook.

As he got in the car, I said, "What you said, about escaping—did you ever leave?"

He stood there, half in, half out of the car. "As a kid I used to dream about leaving Cray. Making a new life in Cardiff or London. I did for a while. Never thought I'd come back but, I guess this place, the Black Mountain, it gets a hold on you, calls you back."

I nodded. "I had that same dream."

"Don't feel bad about it." He got in the car and drove away.

It's been three years since I returned to Cray. After my discharge from Redlands, I lived with my sister in Cardiff for six months. Sara was three years older than me, married with two children. It was a new experience, spending time with Molly and Rhodri, my young niece and nephew. Being around them helped me rediscover the curiosity and drive I thought I'd lost. As time passed I began to feel a need to reconnect with my own childhood and the place that shaped who I had become.

In the years since my father had left Cray to shack up with a woman half his age in Llandovery, the house had fallen into some disrepair. While I continued my recovery, Sara organised a local contractor to carry out the necessary remedial work. By the time it was completed, I was excited about going back home. Yet, when the day came and we drove north through Powys, I felt a sudden apprehension about returning to the place I'd spent most of my youth trying to escape. It rained that morning, but as the road wound up into the higher country the sky cleared and sunlight sparkled off the hills and trees. After she'd helped me unpack and we were stood in the yard saying our good-byes, a black Land Rover turned in from the lane. A man I didn't know got out.

Sara waved. "Edward," she said. "This is my brother, Wil."

The man came to us and shook my hand. He wore a blue baseball cap over shoulder-length brown hair. His eyes were blue and his grip was strong. "How do, Wil," he said. "I've heard a lot about you."

Sara said, "This is Edward. He did the work on the house."

"I hope it's up to scratch," he said.

"I'm grateful to you," I said.

"I save my best work for your sister." He gave her a grin. "I've come to fetch my ladders." He walked off around the side of the garage.

"You don't remember him, do you?" Sara said.

I shrugged.

"Edward Owens. He was in my class in school. We went out for a bit. He lives over in Llanddeusant now." She kissed me on the cheek and got into her Volvo. She spoke through the open window. "He said you can call him if you need anything doing. I've left his number in the kitchen."

"I'll be okay."

Sara reached through the window and squeezed my hand. "Listen, Wil—he could be a friend to you."

The man came back into sight carrying an aluminum extension ladder on one shoulder. He hoisted it up on the roof rack of his vehicle and tied it down. I watched as Sara drove out of the yard. A minute later, the man got in the Land Rover. As he pulled away he turned and raised a hand, giving me a thumbs-up.

It took time to get used to being home, in the shadow of the Black Mountain. I was twenty-four and hadn't lived in the house for nearly six years. Leaving for university I was sure I'd never return. I'd stayed on in York at the end of each academic year taking whatever work I could find. After my masters' I'd applied and failed to obtain funding for a PhD. It was this that had, in part, precipitated my breakdown. That, and my landlord's discovery that eight crows shared the flat with me. I tried to explain that they were essential for my research. He found it unacceptable, and when I refused to remove the birds, he called the police. Consequently, I was sectioned for the third time and spent four months in Redlands.

I'd had episodes of mental instability before. At seventeen, Wyn Blevins accused me of trying to murder him in his bed. I don't recall what happened, though I believe that if I had harmed him, there must have been some provocation on his part. I argued my case when they came for me, but, as a consequence of previous episodes, when it came down to his word or mine, his lies won the day. The first incident occurred when I was fourteen and had attacked a classmate I'd witness kill a magpie with an air rifle. In the ensuing fight I'd bitten off half his right ear. I spent three weeks in the children's wing of a mental hospital for observation and assessment.

Every one of the clinicians and therapists I have spoken to over the years has assumed that my episodes of mental fragility stem from the discovery of my mother's body. This was a reasonable assumption but it wasn't right. Though saddened at the loss of my mother, it would be a lie to say I was greatly stricken or traumatised. Following her suicide, I had to endure months of counselling that served only to keep the sight of her body fresh in my mind. The sessions continued until it dawned on me that what was needed were expressions of sorrow and pain. After acting out these emotions over two or three sessions, I was deemed to have finally processed my grief.

The thing I never talked about in those sessions was what had happened the night after Mother's funeral. Disturbed by some noise, I'd crept downstairs, bleary-eyed and half-conscious, and walked into the living room where Wyn Blevins, drunk as hell, sat on the floor with Mickey in one fist and Icarus in the other. Their eyes were black with fear. I tried to speak but my tongue was paralysed. He told me he knew what they'd done to her. Said there'd be no more birds in his house. I stood and heard the crack of bones as he crushed the life out of my canaries.

I confess I wasn't entirely truthful with that policeman. I had in fact been in Glasfynydd Forest the day the boy went missing. Blyth and I had gone seeking fresh specimens for our research. He knew the trails that sectioned the forest as well as I ever did, and he had a good nose for the dead. After an hour I had a young crow and a tawny owl in my rucksack. About a mile or so southwest of the dam the trail curved to the right. I heard voices and then saw eight or nine children loping along the trail towards me, caught up in some game of war. As they drew near, one young boy saw me, pointed his wooden stick, and told me to drop the rucksack and stick my hands up. I did as he said while the others came closer. The boy, brown-haired and lightly freckled, asked what was in the rucksack. I undid the straps and tipped the dead birds out on the ground. "Did you kill 'em?" he asked, and when I told him no, he said, "What you got 'em for?"

The others crowded around, staring at the birds. "Are they really dead, mister?" a red-haired girl asked. When I nodded, she asked if she could touch them.

I picked up the crow, a young adult about eighteen inches from head to tail. Moving his head as though addressing them, I said, in a harsh, cawing voice, "How'd you like it if I touched you?"

She jumped back, startled. The others laughed.

"So, it's a laughing matter, is it?" I cawed.

One boy, taller than the others, wanted to know what I was going to do with them. I put the crow down, picked up the owl, and made a hooting noise. "Don't you mean what are we going to do with him?"

The boy stared at the owl. "Are you going to eat them?"

I shook the owl's head. "We might eat him."

The boy grinned. In my own voice I asked them if they wanted to meet a friend of mine. I made a clicking sound and Blyth dropped out of the canopy and settled on the ground a few feet away. *Chyak-chyak*, he cried, marching forward a few steps, then back, as though performing some avian waltz.

"That's a crow," said a young boy from beneath his red baseball cap.

I told them he was Jackdaw. "Say hello, Blyth." He lowered his front, dipped his head, then raised it to the sky, crying *Chyak-chyak*.

They were smitten. He obliged with a few simple tricks and I told them the story about the king of birds, only I changed it so a jackdaw came out on top. Each took turns in touching the dead birds, and though they were keen to pet Blyth, he skipped away whenever they approached. The kids told me they staying at a campsite north of Trecastle. They were at the lake for the day with their parents. After a while the tall boy said it was time they headed back. They talked about it and seemed to disagree on which way to go. I pointed out the trail and told them not to get lost.

Alone again, I returned the birds to the rucksack. Blyth, who had a temperamental streak, suddenly cried out, *kaaarr, kaaarr!* I recognized his alarm call and watched as he took off after the kids, then veered sharply off to the left. Near the spot where he vanished into the trees, I saw movement, a glimpse of blue and a face that, just for a moment, I half-recognised. Then Blyth was silent and who, or whatever, I had seen, was gone.

I should tell you about Blyth. One morning, three months after my return, I decided to make a start on converting Wyn Blevins's garage into a work-shop. Carrying wheel rims out behind the building, I saw what I took for a crow atop an old Austin Cambridge, one of the half dozen eviscerated vehicles that had become homes to a variety of birds. I remembered the car. It had been two-tone blue with blue leather seats and round wing-mounted mirrors. It had served as a plane, a tank, and a spaceship, yet now it stood wheeless on concrete blocks at the rear of the yard, bereft of colour, oxidised by time and rain into something other than a car. The tangled undergrowth encroached from the rear and outlier weeds grew up out of the coverless boot. The wing mirrors were long since gone.

When the bird saw me it hopped from one foot to the other. It leaned forward, flattening its body and thrusting its purple-sheened head in my direction. *Chyak-chyak*, it called. As I approached it ruffled its feathers and raised its wings. I'd always been fascinated with birds. Unlike Wyn Blevins I didn't hold them responsible for my mother's death. On the contrary, in the following years I had increasingly associated them with curiosity and playfulness. The bird lowered its wings and stood, head tilted to the sky. The yard seemed unnaturally quiet. A dozen or more black-eyed rooks watched from the trees. I reached out to the bird, seeing something almost disdainful in the silver white eyes that marked it as a jackdaw. For a moment it held my gaze, then took off.

Intrigued, I opened the car door and looked inside. On the cracked leather seat was a nest constructed from twigs and scraps of card. Something shiny caught my eye. I reached in and picked up a coin. As it came out of the nest I saw that it was a number of coins threaded onto a piece of nylon line. I held it up to the afternoon light, seeing the peacocks, penguins, eagles, and other birds whose names I'd forgotten, depicted on the coins. Memories overwhelmed me. I'd made the chain of coins after my mother's death. It was a talisman I'd kept hidden in a yellow cardboard box beneath my bed. Fifteen years had passed since I'd last seen it.

I got out of the car, the chain in one hand. The bird mobbed me feet first, scratching at my head until I managed to beat it away. It flew and tumbled around the yard, shrieking madly. Finally, it settled again on the roof of the car. *Chyak-chyak*, it cried, head bobbing downwards. After a moment or two I understood. It watched as I returned the chain to the nest. If what had once been mine was now his, then I figured that signalled a connection between us. In honour of his standing out from his fellow corvids, I named him Blyth after an eccentric ornithologist in whose discredited work on natural selection I had once taken an interest.

The boy's disappearance troubled me. Inevitably, it called to mind the fate of my mother. As then, police were out searching Glasfynydd and the wild country to the south, around the Black Mountain. His face was on the news and in the papers. When my sister called, she spoke about how awful it was. After four days, he hadn't been found. I thought about his parents and tried to imagine how they felt. I wondered if he'd been one of those I'd met in the forest. Had I spoken to him? After they'd gone, I remembered Blyth had alerted me to the presence of someone else in the woods.

I found him on the roof of the Austin. I asked him if he recalled the day we met the kids, how he had seen someone or something after they had left. *Chyak-chyak*, he cried. I asked him to tell me what it was. Blyth tilted forward, half-turning to show me his nape. He ruffled his head feathers, as though he wanted me to groom him. I pleaded with him to tell me what he knew.

He ignored me and began to preen.

Although it wasn't uncommon for him to behave that way, his diffidence angered me. It seemed deliberate, an affectation meant to provoke me. I decided not to rise to his bait. "All right, Blyth," I told him. "Have it your way."

I went to the workshop and began assembling the newly bleached bones of a raven. Since returning to Cray, I had taught myself the art of skeletal articulation. My knowledge of avian physiology helped, and the rudiments of maceration were not hard to grasp. The process was absorbing and helped take my mind off the theoretical aspects of my real work. While still an undergraduate, I had begun to focus on birds, particularly on avian intelligence. An investigation into the language of Corvids formed the basis of my masters thesis and would, so I had planned, go on to provide the platform for further research. Although those plans had stalled in York, I had come to see that the isolation of Cray and its abundant birdlife, offered an opportunity for a radical new approach. Blyth's friendship served only to increase my hopes of success.

I worked on the raven late into the evening, feeling an odd detachment from my surroundings. I was aware of the maceration vessels beneath the worktop and the half dozen bird skeletons I'd successfully articulated. Two rooks hung from the roof beam as though suspended in flight; a magpie and a crow were perched on separate shelves. They seemed to be watching, waiting for their fellow corvids to be reborn. My thoughts loosened, became abstract and indecipherable. I felt separated from my body, hovering in the air above, looking down on someone with whom I felt only a tenuous connection. Disoriented and vertiginous, I sought for something to hold onto, something around which my sense of being could coalesce. Abruptly, I became aware of another presence seeping into my consciousness, allowing me to see the world through different eyes. The night opened up and waves of electromagnetic energy streamed across the sky, through a body that was no longer earthbound. I tumbled and soared, riding currents of air. Around me, the sky teemed with a great clattering of rooks and crows, their calls echoing across the night. We flew over forests and mountains, over landscapes I had never seen, and I felt as though I could fly to the edge of the world.

I woke at dawn, in an old sycamore. The branches were heavy with birds cawing to greet the day. My head was fuzzy, my throat raw. I had no idea how I had got up there. Scraps of memory drifted through my mind, elusive as dreams. Had I spent the night roosting with these birds? It wouldn't be the first time. I looked for Blyth, struck by a sense of weightlessness, of having been outside myself. Leaning forward to ease the stiffness in my back, I lost my balance and nearly fell out of the tree. I grabbed the branch in time and hung on. After a while, I clambered down to the lowest branch and dropped to the ground.

I'd been having such dreams for two years. I'd come to believe that Blyth was the stimulus. I reasoned that just as migratory birds could detect magnetic fields and use them for navigation, Blyth drew on similar electromagnetic tools that allowed him to project his consciousness into my dreams. Thus I saw the world through his eyes, and as exhilarating and profound as that was, at the dream's end I was left only with nebulous impressions that could not be transcribed in the rational world of human consciousness. That failure ate at my soul.

I stumbled across the yard, searching for Blyth. I needed him to decode the dream for me. I staggered towards the Austin and pulled the door open. Inside I found a red baseball cap with a cartoon logo on the front such as a child might wear.

A week ago I watched a young kite die among the rocks in the pass below Fan Brycheiniog. We were hiking along Fan Hir when Blyth heard its cries. He took off over the ridge and disappeared from view. Minutes later he came back, sounding his alarm. I found the kite about halfway down the *bwlch*. One wing was badly broken, and her breast was torn and bleeding. I held her until she was dead. Afterwards, I put her in my rucksack and headed northwest along the ridge. The sky was clear and the sun shone bright on the Black Mountain. Though I regretted the kite's demise, I was pleased to have such a specimen to investigate.

Soon, we descended to Llyn y Fan Fach below the north face of the ridge. Children played and swam in the clear, blue water. I watched them awhile, Blyth circling overhead before settling at the water's edge. While he drank I took out the kite and began to wash the blood from her plumage. A boy who had been wading nearby came closer. He asked if the bird was dead. I told him it was. He asked what had happened to it.

"Got in a fight with another bird, I guess. Probably over carrion."

"What's carrion?" He was nine or ten, tall and skinny. His arms and legs were red from the sun.

"Dead animals. Rabbits, sheep, other birds."

"They eat dead animals?"

"Sure."

"Why?"

"They have to eat and something dead is food to them."

Blyth hopped closer and cried out, startling the boy who took a couple of steps back. "Don't mind Blyth," I said. "He's just curious."

The boy stared at Blyth. "How do you know that?"

"Blyth and I, we're friends."

A voice called out. Blyth flew off. A man waved to the boy from thirty yards away. "It's my dad," the boy said.

I nodded. "Okay." I watched as he walked towards his father. The man spoke to the boy. I stood up and put the kite into the rucksack. The man came over. He stared at me, his eyes squinting in the afternoon sun.

"That was my boy you were taking to," he said.

"Yes?"

"What business did you have with him?"

"We were just talking."

"About what?"

"Birds."

"Birds?" He stepped closer. "Well, how about you stay the fuck away from my boy? You think you could do that for me?"

I wondered how a corvid would react. How they perceived anger or fear. Did they understand what it was to be irrational? Did they even have a concept for reason? "I'm sorry," I said, after a while. "I meant no harm."

The man nodded and walked away.

Ten minutes later I reached the high ground east of the lake. I stopped to look back and saw the children playing in the water. Blyth flew above them. He banked to the right and dropped towards the ground north of the lake. Something caught my eye. I saw a man crouched behind a rock. He was looking out over the lake and when I followed his line of sight, I saw that he was watching the kids. When I looked back, he seemed to be staring right at the spot where I stood. A second later he had slipped out of sight behind the rock.

I examined the red baseball cap. It had a cartoon dinosaur on the front. The day I found it I'd almost burned it. Instead, I hid it in a drawer in my bedroom. It was a sign from Blyth, I believed. I'd asked for help and he'd given me this sign.

So it was that two weeks after the boy disappeared, I set out to cycle the six miles to Trecastle. I'd never learned to drive, much less owned a car. It never seemed necessary. The caravan park, I discovered after enquiring at the post office, was a mile northwest of the village.

Once there I was at a loss. I hadn't given much thought as to what I'd do or who I'd speak to. I bought a tea from the café in the reception building and took it outside to a bench. I watched cars come and go, families setting out for the reservoir or the Black Mountain. More people left on bikes or on foot. Two girls approached the bench. One of them, a red-haired girl, stood looking up at me. "You're the man with the bird," she said.

I recognized her as one of the kids I'd met in Glasfynydd. I looked around for her parents.

"Is the bird here?"

"I don't think you should talk to me."

"Why not?"

Her friend laughed and said, "I knew it. I knew you made it up."

"Made what up?" I asked.

The red-haired girl pointed at her friend. "She thinks I lied about the bird."

I sipped my tea. "You mean Blyth. He's around here somewhere. I expect he's minding his business."

"What business?" the other girl said.

"Bird business."

"Does he do tricks?"

"When he has a mind to."

"Call him," the red-haired girl said.

I was about to call Blyth when a woman came out of the building. "Come here now, Ellie. You too, Lizzie. Stop bothering the man."

I told her they weren't bothering me. "We're just talking."

"Well, they're not allowed to talk to strangers," she said, agitated. "Not after what happened to that boy."

"It's okay, we're not exactly strangers. Isn't that right?"

Before the girl could respond, a man approached. "What's going on?"

"He's got a bird does tricks," the girl said.

"Who are you?" the man said.

"He was talking to the girls," the woman said. She made it seem like an accusation. The man glared at me. Another couple emerged from the building and stood watching us. The woman said, "He says they're not strangers."

"We met before, her and some others, in the forest a while back. We talked, that was all."

"He had birds," the girl said. "Two were dead and another one danced and did tricks."

The other couple pressed forward. "What's that?" the second woman wanted to know.

"He makes birds do tricks for kids," the first man said.

"Are you staying at this site?" the second man said. "You know these kids?"

I shook my head and scratched my stomach. I felt tense and agitated, wondering if I should tell them about the red baseball cap.

"What are you doing here?" the first woman said. "Why're you speaking to my girl?"

More people came out of the reception building. A dozen or so rooks gathered in the trees at the park entrance. The tension in the air seemed palpable as a gathering storm. I stood up. "Look, I'm sorry. I shouldn't have come here."

"That's right, you shouldn't," said another man. "Not when that boy's still missing."

"You like to play with kids, do you?" the first man snarled in my face.

"Why don't you leave me alone?" I told him.

He grabbed the front of my shirt. "Why? What are you going to do?"

My hands flew up and clawed at his face. He fell and as I tried to move past him, another man got hold of my arm. I spun and we grappled, crashing over the bench. People surged around us as he punched me in the stomach. I caught his arm and bit him above the elbow, sinking my teeth through flesh until I heard him scream. The raucous cries of corvids suddenly filled the air, and I saw hundreds clamouring in the trees. The crowd screamed and shouted, oblivious to their presence.

"What's all this?" somebody called out, pushing through the fevered crowd. "What's going on?" It was Edward Owens, the man who had fixed up my house. "Stop all this," he said, waving his baseball cap at the crowd, motioning for them to back away.

I saw Blyth with the other birds and sensed they were preparing to mob my assailant. I shook my head and mouthed the word no. Owens looked at me and at the other man. "I know this man," he said. "He's Wil Blevins, lives down the road there, in Cray."

Somebody said, "He was enticing the kids."

"You're all concerned," Owens said. "There's a child missing, but Wil's not the one that took him. I promise you that."

I got up and stepped back from the man I'd fought with. He held his arm and examined the bleeding bite mark. He stared at me in disbelief. "Fucking lunatic bit me, for God's sake!"

A woman wiped the blood with a tissue. "What's he doing here?" she said. "Why don't you ask him that?"

Owens stared at her, then turned to the others. "I told you all—I know him. I know he meant no harm."

"Bastard paedo," a voice in the crowd called out.

Owens steered me away. "You all right?" he asked.

The birds had fallen silent though their eyes were fixed on me. "I'm not hurt."

"What'd you come here for, Wil? You have no business here."

I knew he was right. It had been a mistake. He led me to my bike. "I thought I could help. I think I saw the boy."

Owens shook his head. "You can't help, Wil. You'd best be off home."

"You think he's still alive?" I looked over his shoulder at Blyth.

"I think people are right to be afraid," Owens said.

I wheeled the bike out into road and set off for home.

Word gets around fast in small communities. I knew someone would come. I had been listening to a recording I'd made the night the boy had disappeared. Blyth had been roosting with a small parliament of rooks in the trees at the rear of the yard. I was listening for some correspondence between what was spoken then and his more recent utterings. But I found it difficult to concentrate in the light of what had happened at Trecastle.

The sound of the car turning into the yard came as a relief. I went out to meet him. The day was overcast and muggy. It had rained earlier and looked to do so again. It was the same policeman as before. He got out and surveyed the yard, his gaze slow and steady, as though searching for something in particular. Finally, his eyes found mine. "Wil. How are you keeping?"

"You didn't drive all the way up here to ask after my well-being."

"No. I didn't." He took out his notebook and opened it. "The last time we spoke, you said you hadn't been in Glasfynydd the day Jon Walters disappeared. Any chance you were wrong?"

"Why?"

"I think you know why. I spoke with a girl called Ellie Lewis this morning. She says she met you in the forest the same day Jon Walters disappeared."

I looked past him, to the rooks gathering in the old rowan, clots of darkness among the bright red berries. They seemed intent on us, like jurors weighing the truth of our testimony. "I spend a lot of time there," I said.

"You said."

"I lose track."

"So, did you speak to her and some other kids that same day?"

"Maybe. I don't recall the specific day."

He wrote something in his book. "You remember any of the other kids? Could Jon Walters have been one of them?" He showed me the same picture that he'd shown before. The boy with the red baseball cap.

"I don't think so."

"You never saw him?"

"I can't say—I don't recognize him."

"See, Wil. According to Ellie, and the parents, Jon Walters was with that group."

My fingers and toes tingled with pins and needles. My chest tightened and I felt something pressing against the inside of my skull, something cold and immense trying to burst out into the air. "There were a lot of kids. I spoke to one or two. That boy, he might've been there but I didn't see him."

"Did you see anything out of the ordinary? Anyone else around? See, we believe now that somebody took him. That he was abducted."

"Nothing," I said, trying to recall exactly what it was I'd seen among the trees after the kids had gone.

"What happened up at the caravan park yesterday? A man claims you assaulted him."

I stared at the ground and scratched my arm. "He attacked me. I was defending myself."

"Well, lucky for you there's a witness confirms that."

"Owens?"

"Edward Owens, yes. Said he fixed this place up before you moved back."

I told him that was the case, that my sister had arranged it. He nodded again and something I couldn't read crossed his face. "He said your sister had asked him to watch out for you."

"I don't know about that. I don't know him well."

"Why'd you go there, Wil? What business did you have there?"

"I don't know. I thought I could help."

"Are you holding something back, Wil?"

"The search," I said, in desperation. "I know the woods. I just wanted to help."

"So you spoke to Ellie Lewis."

"The girl, the one with the red hair? She recognised me. Asked after Blyth."

"That'd be the jackdaw, I'm guessing? You trained him?"

"Befriended."

"I never knew you could do that with ordinary birds. Parrots and budgies, but not them."

"He's not ordinary."

"You trap those dead birds you showed her, Wil?"

"I don't trap birds."

"What about that dead kite at Llyn y Fan Fach four days ago?"

"I didn't kill it," I said, seeing the trees black and heavy with birds. "It was still alive when I found it. I tried to help her but she was too far gone."

"What is it with dead birds? What is it you do with them?"

I felt light-headed and queasy. Sweat ran down my face. I doubted he'd understand. "I preserve them," I said. "Their bones."

I saw the puzzled look on his face. "Why would you do that?"

"It's like taxidermy. It's no big deal."

"Show me."

The air around us vibrated with the slow steady thrum of wings. He stared at me, waiting. I raised a hand to still the rooks and led him to the workshop. I switched on the light, told him to cover his mouth, and pointed out the articulated bones suspended from the roof beam, the skeletal magpie and crow perched on a shelf. He gagged and made no move to step inside. "That smell, Jesus," he managed to say.

"Rotting tissue," I said. "First you remove as much tissue and organs as you can. Then section the bird, suspend the pieces in a solution of water and biological washing powder heated to thirty five degrees. It's called maceration—accelerated decomposition. When the process is complete you're left with a complete set of bones. Then it's a matter of cleaning them, and assembling the skeleton."

He shook his head and turned away. "For what purpose?"

"You wouldn't understand."

"No, I probably wouldn't." He glanced back inside the workshop and shook his head. I followed him back to his car. "This is part of your research?"

"No," I admitted. "Not really. My work is trying to understand how birds communicate. Not with one another, but with us."

"They do that?"

"I believe so."

"Do you know what they think of us?"

"No. Not yet."

He got into his car and spoke through the open window. "Look, Wil. I know what you've been through and maybe you don't look at the world the way others do. But it's the others in charge. You have to abide by their rules. This stuff"—he gestured at the workshop—"it's not normal. You can't talk about rotting birds like you're talking rugby. It unsettles people. And you especially can't go talking to kids about it. It's best you don't talk to kids at all. You understand what I'm saying?"

I told him I did.

"Good." He started the car. "Just, for your own sake, try to stay out of trouble, okay?"

I didn't see Blyth until the next day. More and more he kept his distance from me, as though dissatisfied at something I'd done. If I had done anything to slight him I would gladly have made amends. I found him the next day in his usual place at the car. I sat on the rusted bonnet and showed him the red cap. He looked at it, ruffled his feathers, but made no comment.

"Did it belong to the boy?" I asked him. "Was that why you brought it here?" He leaned forward and gave a muted *kaaarrr*.

I asked if he knew what had happened, if he knew where the boy was. He turned and looked directly at me. I searched his eyes for some clue as to what he was trying to communicate. After a while I turned away. I had seen nothing there, nothing at all.

And yet, I knew there must be something. I had felt it before—an urgency, a need to get through, to communicate his perspective. It was just a matter of translation.

Later that evening my sister called. She'd heard from Owens. She was concerned. "Is everything okay?" she asked.

"I'm fine."

"Have you seen Joanne lately?"

Joanne was my social worker. "Yes," I lied.

"I spoke to her, Wil. She says you missed your last appointment."

"Please, Sara, I'm okay."

"Are you taking your meds?"

"For fuck's sake—you don't need to worry about me."

"I'd come up tomorrow if I could, bring the children. But this missing child. I mean, it's so awful. I'm scared to bring them."

"I don't expect you to come up," I assured her.

She didn't speak for a moment. I realized she was struggling to say what she wanted to say. "Wil, listen. David called me."

"Who?"

"David Carroll. The policeman up there in Sennybridge. He asked me what you've been up to. This thing with the bones. What is that, Wil? I don't understand."

"It's nothing," I said. "Just a distraction."

"Distraction from what?"

"Nothing—I told you." I couldn't keep the anger from my voice.

"Jesus Christ, Wil. You would tell me, right?"

"Tell you what?"

"If, if you were in trouble. If you weren't well."

"There's nothing to tell."

"Why were you speaking to those kids? You don't know them. What were you doing?"

"No reason. I swear to you."

"I don't know anymore. I don't know what you're capable of. I've thought about Molly and Rhodri, when we've been up to see you. Oh God, did you hurt that child, Wil? Did you take him?"

I hung up, unable to take anymore. I picked up the red cap and took it outside. I wanted to get rid of it, burn the damn thing. It had nothing to do with me. Instead, I took it to the Austin and left it there for Blyth.

I felt burdened with doubt and uncertainty. Since the incident at the caravan park, discord had come between Blyth and myself. I couldn't explain it. After three years, it was hard to take. I tried to walk off my anxiety but when I returned to the house, it was still there.

Entering the yard, I saw Joanne standing by her car. I could tell by her expression that my appearance concerned her. I suppose I looked somewhat unkempt and undernourished. I hadn't been eating regularly.

"Wil," she said. "You knew I was coming, right?"

I told her I didn't.

"I left a message this morning. I know it's short notice but, well, it's been a while."

"You shouldn't have come."

"Well, I'm here now. Okay?"

"I guess."

"Can we go inside?"

In the kitchen I made her a cup of tea and asked what was so important she had to come on an unscheduled visit. "Your sister called me yesterday," she said. "She's concerned about you. She thinks you're off your meds."

I got up and opened the wall cabinet above the fridge and took down the empty bottles labelled aripiprazole and lithium. Joanne frowned. "You flushed them? A month's supply?"

"I haven't taken any pills for months."

"We've talked before about what happens if you don't take them. How you become unstable."

"I'm stable."

"Sara doesn't think so. She mentioned an incident the other day. Said the police came to see you."

"Did she?"

"Are you eating properly? You've lost weight."

"I eat what I need."

She sighed. "You got into a fight with some guy."

"It was a misunderstanding."

"You've been talking to kids, putting disturbing ideas in their heads."

"Kids are inquisitive. They're more receptive than us."

"Receptive to what?"

"Things we don't see or that scare us."

"The police believe that boy was abducted."

I stared at her, trying to read what was in her head. "You think I have something to do with that?"

"No. But look how it seems. People who are well don't carry around dead birds or have crows as pets. They don't show them to young kids. When people are frightened, they look at strangers, at those who don't seem normal."

"Do I seem normal to you?"

She brushed the hair back from her forehead. "It doesn't matter what I think. It's what others think and right now they're saying things about you."

"Because I study birds?"

"Because of your behaviour."

"They stopped my funding, you know. My research."

"What has this got to do with—"

"The crow family are the smartest of all birds, smarter than most animals. I'm trying to find ways to communicate with them, learn their languages."

"Languages?" she said, bewildered. "Birds don't talk."

"Don't they? Let me show you something."

She followed me outside. I made a clicking sound, calling to Blyth. I repeated the sound, three, four times but he didn't come.

Joanne touched my arm. "What are you trying to do?"

"Blyth," I said, "A jackdaw with a secret. He's gone."

"A secret?"

"Something he's trying to tell me."

"The noises that birds make—it's not real communication."

"What is? Being told what you can and can't do? That how you act puts the shits up people? Is driving people crazy, locking them away—is that real communication?"

"Please, Wil."

"Putting our terrors into the minds of kids—is this what it's about?"

"No!"

"He understands how to live, how the system works. And he knows we're messing it all up."

"Stop!" she shouted. I could hear the nervousness in her voice. "I have to be honest with you: I've always tried to be straight with you. I don't think your behaviour is entirely rational."

"You think I'm acting irrationally. Come here."

I grabbed her and pulled her towards the workshop. She came willingly enough at first, but as I opened the door and the smell hit her, she blanched and struggled. I opened both doors wide to let in the light.

"Jesus, what's that smell?" She stood there, her free hand over her mouth, gazing into the interior. I flipped on the light. I watched as she took in the sight of skeletal corvids hanging from the roof beam. "What are they?" she whispered.

"Birds."

"Real?"

"They were."

"How? I mean, why?"

I pulled her inside and grabbed a cloth from the worktop. I told her to hold it over her mouth and nose. I lifted a plastic tub up onto the worktop. She watched while I prised off the lid. Inside, the ends of three nylon stockings—each containing a section of the dismembered kite—were suspended in the solution. She vomited. I reached out to help her but she panicked and stumbled, and as she fell she grabbed the vessel, dragging it down on top of her. She sat there, clothes covered in the stinking, fat-rich solution. She was silent for a moment, then started to scream. I tried to help her. She pushed me away, scrambled to her feet and ran from the workshop. "Wait," I called as she ran to her car. "Jo," I said. "It's not what you think. It's just birds."

The engine turned and failed, turned again and fired up. I walked to the car, my shirt splattered with kite tissue. Jo spun the car and gave me one last hollowed-out look before accelerating out of the yard.

I enter the house, knowing this won't be the end of it. Joanne will see to that. She'll return soon, very soon. And she won't be alone. Exhaustion eats into my bones. I haven't slept in three days, not since Trecastle. I shut my eyes. Soon, my thoughts become inchoate, I dream I'm searching for Blyth in the forest. I'm running and then I'm flying, gliding through the dark canopy. I search for what seems an eternity, always about to close in on something that is never quite in reach. A truth, the truth of what Blyth knows. I can smell it in the damp, viscid air. When the sky is at its blackest, my feathered body slows and hovers, and a sudden, powerful dread pushes me down. Sinking through the branches, the feeling of horror grows and my screams are smothered in the deep, unforgiving darkness.

I wake, heart racing. A tapping noise scatters the last remnants of the dream. I don't know what time it is, not until I paw at my eyes and glance at the window where Blyth stands framed in the late-afternoon light. We stare at each other for a moment and I try to fathom what it is he wants from me. He waits but doesn't speak. I climb the stairs and change into a black shirt and jeans. I go back downstairs and venture out into the evening. Blyth has disappeared again. Dusk is not far away. The rooks have gathered to greet me. They begin to cry out, screeching until a great clamour of approval fills the air.

Suddenly, they fall silent. Blyth has come. He looks at me from the roof of the Austin, lifts his head, and calls: *chyak, chyak*. He skips forward, dips his head, and lifts something in his black bill. Moving closer I recognise the chain of coins. He flaps his iridescent wings and rises. The rooks remain silent while he tumbles in the air then spirals off towards Glasfynydd. I follow him. In the forest, the ground begins to rise steeply. I struggle through the long, dew-covered grass, scanning the sky. At the single lane road that cuts north through the forest, I stand a moment to catch my breath. Up ahead, a steep bank rises above the road. I hear a scratching noise and see Blyth a few feet away. Then he is gone, leaving a coin on the tarmac. I pick it up and crawl up the bank, dragging my body through the gorse and ferns. After a while, the ground clears and I press on deeper into the forest. Soon, I cross a dirt track. There's no sign of Blyth. I drop to my knees and search the ground until I find another coin on the far side of the track.

I plunge into the trees ahead, the low branches and brambles tearing my arms and face. The ground continues to climb. My legs ache and my lungs seem about to burst. I grab branches to pull myself up the slope, feeling like I've been here before. This sense of déjà vu grows stronger as I emerge from the trees at the top of a ridge. The sun has disappeared behind the hill to the west, leaving only a darkening, bruise-coloured sky. The air is still and quiet.

I stare down into the dark, pine-crowded gulley. I'm oppressed by a sudden, immense dread. I look for Blyth in the preternatural quiet. "I'm here, Blyth. Now show me."

Kyow-kyow, comes from down in the gulley. My body trembles as I move over the edge, sliding through the scrub until I hit the base of a tree at the bottom. The ground is wet, and an acrid stench hangs in the thick, warm air. Through the undergrowth I see something red. I crawl forward, unable to make it out. A shadow moves across my line of sight and Blyth is there, skipping through the scrub to a mound of earth. I rub my eyes, open them, and see the small body curled in the dirt, a red cap over the head. Crawling over black feathers, I reach out and lift the cap. See the holes where eyes once were and the open wounds where the corvids have been feeding.

Chyak-chyak, says Blyth, hopping backwards up the slope.

"Is this why you brought me here? To show me this?" If Blyth is aware of my anger he doesn't let on. He stands there, inscrutable.

"I don't get it," I cry out. "What is it I should know?"

He gives a piercing shriek and disappears. As I look up a larger figure looms over me and a powerful pain explodes in my skull.

When I come to, my vision is blurred and pain pulsates in my head. Something presses on my chest and I can barely breathe. I try to lift one arm but it feels weak and lifeless. I lay still, aware of a weird falling sensation that I can't explain. After a while the pain eases a little and my eyes have adjusted to the darkness. I sense a more solid darkness a yard away. The dark mass moves, and in the moonlight I see a blue baseball hat, and then beneath it, the serene face of Edward Owens.

I try to speak but my lips won't move. I try to sit up but a terrible weakness is upon me. I turn to one side and see an arm outstretched, blood draining from a wound that runs from wrist to elbow. I panic and try to grab the arm to stanch the flow of blood. Then I realise my other arm has been similarly cut.

Edward Owens leans over me. He rolls his head as though to work out a knot of tension. I want to ask him something but the thought slips from my mind before I can turn it into words. He shows me a knife, puts it in my hand, and closes the fingers about the shaft. I want to resist, but all I can do is stare at the empty space where he stood just a moment ago. A space filled now only with night and the stars.

I am not entirely alone. Blyth is perched in a branch close by. After a while, a rook settles beside him. Soon, other corvids arrive in the gully. I watch Blyth, staring at his moon-silver eyes. I understand the nature of his secret. As I lie there dying, I recognise the cold truth of his disinterest, his corvid indifference to my fate, or to any human endeavour. First Blyth, then the rooks, move closer.

The Fortune of Sparrows

USMAN T. MALIK

The courtyard of the orphanage was haunted by birds.

Songbirds, sparrows, gray hornbills, yellow-footed green pigeons, starlings, crows—every species ever glimpsed in Lahore. Twice or thrice a week they came in doles and murders and murmurations, swooping down and carpeting the roof and the walls. To this day I've not figured out where they came from in such large numbers or why they gravitated to the orphanage at peculiar intervals. Unsatisfactory theories involving magnetism and satisfactory gossip about corpses buried beneath the old housing were flung about, but no one could explain why on arrival these birds were so quiet—why they would neither cheep nor caw; nor a warbler warble. Hushed, they clung to the courtyard trees, congregated on high wires running parallel to the enclosure walls from one electric pylon to another. It was a sight that gave many a twilight visitor pause when they first glimpsed these silent sentinels. At least until the muezzin called the maghrib prayer and, suddenly, the courtyard came alive with the sound of bird music, the notes of the melodies in harmony with bird colors. The warbler, the cuckoo, the bulbul, the mynah—how they would sing!

For a long time now I have been afraid of birds.

But, then, living in the orphanage with my sisters, playing Ice Water when it drizzled, listening to the gurgle of water sluicing off rain gutters into the courtyard's red earth, I was not. I liked them. All us girls did. We picked their feathers off the ground and made garlands out of them. We looked for bird nests in the courtyard trees and giggled when Mano stalked them, his mangled tail bristling, and, from hidden corners, sprang at the crows, parrots, and pigeons, making the creatures explode skyward in a flurry of black, blue, and green. The color specks circled the enclosure until night crept up from the horizon and took the birds with it.

Mano the wedding cat belonged to Bibi Soraiya, who managed the orphanage's affairs. Mano was old and two-colored. Neha used to say that was why prescience boiled in his blood, that he was a creature fleshed from opposites and could glimpse things we could not. Angels, jinns, and the ghosts of martyrs walk among us, and everyone knows spirits are fond of cats. Who knew what they whispered in his ear when they floated past him or brushed his fur?

And when Mano settled down by the orphanage gate, licking his fur and purring, we knew the Rishtay Wali Aunty was to come for us that day or night.

The wedding cat was never wrong about the matchmaker's arrival. That was why he was the wedding cat.

My sisters and I were fond of Mano—we fed him from our plate—but sometimes, when the wedding cat's eyes gleamed in the darkness and he slid across the courtyard, back arched, the sounds from his throat indistinguishable from the rumble of a motor engine outside the orphanage door or the passage of something large and ponderous high above the clouds, we weren't so fond of him.

Sometimes we wished Mano would run away and not come back.

The orphanage was a house of many doors.

A long time ago, during the British Raj, we were told, it was a hospital with two wings that flanked the courtyard. The east wing was the smaller building with limited rooms for dying or contagious patients, as if they were the same. It had a long corridor that ran parallel to the courtyard and formed a semicircle connecting it with the west wing, where the rest of the patients were housed.

These rooms were ours now and we loved playing in them. Most of us had mirrors above the washbasin and we pretended that people from the past still stayed within our rooms, that the change of morning and afternoon light in the mirrors meant they were stirring and moving about and such cohabitation made us all a big family. The lives of our family spanned centuries.

I remember one afternoon when we were playing Ice Water. Barefoot, we rushed at the fleeing team, trying to touch their arms or torsos, to pretend-petrify them into captivity. The escapees would circle back and try to tap the captives "awake." Half of my sisters were already statues frozen by the chasing team, but Neha cheated by hiding, which wasn't allowed.

It had rained the night before. The ground was marked with footprints. The trees whispered in the courtyard and the mirrors in our rooms rippled when we ran past the open doors, and I thought I heard Neha giggle and dive into one of the rooms at the end of the east corridor. I sprinted across the courtyard, shouting her name. She giggled again and waved a spindly arm from the doorway. I reached the corridor and went in after her.

No one was in the room. A large wet crow with a broken wing perched on the edge of the skylight. It watched me with red beady eyes and shook raindrops off its feathers.

I whirled, taking in each corner. I remember feeling a sense of loss. Daylight was waning, and when I turned again it wasn't the room I'd entered. Instead of the sparse wooden charpoy there was a finely made bed with pillows and brocaded quilts, a sandalwood footstool placed at its end. A body-length mirror gleamed beside the bed. The walls were hung with canted paintings whose beauty, strangely, could not be admired: the moment I leaned in for a closer look, the pictures blurred.

I turned to look at the mirror. It was a fabulous piece of workmanship, its edges carved in mahogany with sparrows in flight. The girl in the mirror looked back at me with wide, black eyes. She couldn't have been more than my age. Her eyelids were swollen, her lips red, shaped like leaves felled by autumn rain. A bruise flowered from the root of her left ear, all the way up her scalp. She looked neither happy nor unhappy. A passing ghost, I thought, gone forever the moment I departed from this strange new room.

As I watched, the girl in the mirror leaned back, pointed at me, and began to laugh. The sound filled the room, a cacophony of maddened bird-song. She laughed and laughed and the air heated with her laughter and the skylight darkened with night. A whoosh of blistering air, my nostrils filling up with a bitter smell like charred flesh or feathers, and the girl in the mirror was smoking. Coils of gray-black rose from her hair like braids. Smoke ringed her eyes, now orange-blue. She flapped her skinny, crinkling arms, and I cried out and turned, knocking over the footstool, and fled from the room.

Later, after I was calmed by Sangeeta Apa and Bibi Soraiya with hot tea and a thin slice of buttered bread, I told them about the room and its fiery inhabitant. Sangeeta Apa and Bibi glanced at each other.

"Was there a stove in the room?" Bibi Soraiya asked.

"I didn't see one," I said.

She nodded. "Go to your room, *bachey*. Shut the door and get some sleep. I'll tell your sisters not to bother you."

Neha came to my bed that night. We were roommates, three of us, but our third was sick and they'd put her up in the east wing. "What happened?" Neha asked, draping an arm across my body.

I told her. When I got to the part about following her into the room, her eyes widened, like the girl-in-the-mirror's had and she began to breathe irregularly—an exacerbation of her asthma. We had to rush her to Mayo Hospital where the doctors made her spend that night and the night after.

To this day she insists that girl with the spindly arm wasn't her. Neha was hiding atop one of the courtyard trees and showed me fresh scratches from the branches on her left arm. I believed her. I have always believed her.

That was the first time I saw a ghost in the orphanage. There were two more instances.

Both on the night before Sangeeta Apa's wedding dinner.

In story hour on a Friday, Sangeeta Apa told us the tale of the mythical bird Huma. Persian legend holds, she said, that the Huma never rests. It circles ceaselessly high above the earth forever, invisible to prisoners of earthly time; impervious.

Furthermore, they say (said Sangeeta Apa):

It eats bones. The female lays her eggs in the air. As the egg drops, the hatchling squirms out and escapes before the shell hits the earth. It is a bridge between the heavens and earth. It's a bird of fortune. The shadow of the Huma falling on a man bequeaths royalty on his person. The Huma once declined to travel to the far ends of the earth, for wherever its shadow fell the masses would become kings and the Huma is very particular. Like the phoenix, it is old and deathless. In an alternate form, it has seen the destruction of the world three times over

and

it cannot be taken alive. Whosoever captures it will die in forty days. It is a story I have thought about many times since.

We were all in love with the bird man. Who wouldn't be?

Every evening he came cycling down Multan Road, trilling the bell on his bicycle, which was laden with birdcages and wicker baskets. The baskets brimmed with candles, lice combs, fans, attar bottles, incense, and other household items. The bird man was a short, thin man, and very clumsy—I can't tell you how many times we helped him pick up dropped merchandise, cages, even his turban. His turban was large and sequined with a starched turra at the top. Many times we saw him in clothes with holes in them—once he even circled the neighborhood barefoot—but we never saw that turra unstarched, even if his awkwardness meant we frequently glimpsed his long, beautiful, well-oiled hair, which would have suited our own heads so well, we thought.

The bird man would stop under a peepal tree near the entrance of the orphanage. Grinning, he'd get off the bicycle and spread a wool shawl on the ground. He'd set his cages down and begin twittering. He could whistle, warble, chirrup, cheep, and caw as well as any bird he carried, startling new customers and delighting old.

He followed this musical prologue with a show displaying his birds' impeccable training in divination.

The bird man sold all manner of bird: parrots, pigeons, bank mynahs, Australian lovebirds (his hottest item), but there were two he wouldn't part with—a pair of green rose-necked parakeets. These parakeets had mastered the art of soothsaying. They fluttered impatiently in a painted blue wooden cage, while the bird man fanned out a stack of white envelopes on the shawl. The envelopes had gilded borders, and soaring birds, dulled by time and use, were embossed in the corners.

Curious customers, many of them prematurely aged women, would come up and look. Shy at first, they would slowly gather courage, put out their hands for examination, and pose their questions:

Will I ever get married? Will my firstborn be a boy? Will that please my husband? My mother-in-law wants more dowry and loathes me. What should I do?

and

Should I stay away from the gas stove in the kitchen?

We girls would gather around the bird man as he frowned and took their hands. His fingernails were long and manicured, and softly they traced the lines on the women's palms. He had a comforting smell about him, like earth, or bird, or the way my hands smelled after rolling dough peras on the nights it was my turn to bake roti. He spoke gently to the women, whispering, calming their nerves.

Only then would he lift the door of the blue cage, letting one of the parakeets hop out.

The bird would pace back and forth across the envelopes. It nipped and pecked at them, its small head darting, until finally it gripped an envelope's edge. It would lift it in its beak and prop it against its emerald body. The bird man would take the envelope, extract the piece of paper inside, pop a tablet of sweet choori into the parakeet's beak, and read the prophecy to the wide-eyed customer.

He was never wrong, the women said. So many before him were charlatans, they said. Their eyes glowed when they said it and the bird man's admirers grew and grew.

My sisters and I were his admirers as well. Sangeeta Apa would watch him from the entrance, the end of her cotton dopatta caught between her teeth. He would laugh with us and tell us our fortunes for free. Sometimes he teased Apa, "Whoever you marry will become a king among men." Often he would give us gifts: bird-shaped candles he'd designed, vials of cheap attar, bottles of scented rubbing oil. He was a good man, we thought. Wise and ageless.

Sometimes after the Rishtay Wali Aunty had been by, we would ask him to tell us the would-be bride's future. Always he refused.

"Palm lines and the paths of heavenly bodies are malleable. Hard work, prayer, love—they can reshape them," he would say. "Take care of your families and all will be well."

We wanted to believe him and sometimes we did, but, even at that age, we knew better. The orphanage was our father and mother. Beyond its walls, who knew?

The walls of the orphanage were dun-colored.

I remember this even if I have forgotten other things—the face of the old pastor who came tottering down the courtyard on Sundays; the smell of trees that lined the courtyard (which trees? I remember orange and red mulberry, but which one at the courtyard's end by Sangeeta Apa's room that cast a long, shocked shadow); the color of the bird man's turban, the sequins of which flared red as he pedaled his bicycle down Multan Road at dusk. Strange how we drown in recollection at the least propitious of times but cannot pluck memories from the past's branches when we need them.

Sangeeta Apa.

No end or beginning to some tales, but middles are always there. She was the middle of all our stories, the center sitting still and somber when everyone around her rode, quickly or sluggishly, the tide of time in the orphanage. Days and weeks and months and years—the Rishtay Wali Aunty's arrival marked them and whittled them away. Thirty-six girls of all ages. So many marriages and migrations. So many of my sisters came and went, yet Sangeeta Apa remained, braiding our hair, peeling mangoes, husking peas and walnuts, dyeing Bibi Soraiya's hair with henna (the smell of that henna, rich and secret, like a sunset glimpsed from a crevice under the canal bridges); and as we giggled and ran around the courtyard, singing songs

> We are a flock of sparrows, Father
> One day we will fly away

Sangeeta Apa would shake her head and laugh, the sound ringing out loud and shrill and mysterious, until its final notes couldn't be told from the twilight birdsong.

It was a very long time before the Rishtay Wali Aunty came for her. By then Apa was in her forties, half her head silvered with age.

I remember the day well because Mano was sick, he had been puking all morning. Red and black feathers glistened in the wedding cat's vomit. Bibi Soraiya fretted over him and fetched him digestive sherbet from the animal doctor in the alley three streets down, but Mano wouldn't touch it. Nor would he eat anything else. He just crawled across the courtyard and lay next to the entrance, waiting.

The Rishtay Wali Aunty arrived in a green-backed rickshaw. We were in class in the north corridor and from the window I saw her dismount. A squat woman with one droopy eye and features hardened by time and sun, she waddled to the entrance and rang the bell. Bibi Soraiya appeared and opened the door. Together, they stepped over Mano, crossed the courtyard, and disappeared behind the thick line of trees in the direction of Bibi's quarters.

A good match had been found for Sangeeta Apa, we would discover.

"The boy is fifty-one and very pious," Bibi Soraiya told us the next day when we assembled in the courtyard to sing the national anthem. "He lives in Gujranwala and owns a dairy shop. Your Apa is really lucky. His dowry demands are so reasonable."

We whooped and cheered and congratulated Apa. She stood there, still as a lake, her gaze on the wedding cat, who was feeling better and kept walking between her legs, mewling. The hem of Apa's dopatta crept into her mouth and the din we made startled a host of sparrows that escaped, cheeping, into the sky.

That night I saw my second and third ghosts.

I was returning from the cigarette stall—Bibi Soraiya had a fondness for hookah and gave me a bar of Jubilee chocolate each time I fetched her tobacco. A clear night with a blue moon full as a houri's lips shining above the orphanage, and Mano was by the entrance, his tail twitching. I bent to scratch his chin. He slipped away, turned, and watched me, eyes glinting like coins in the dark beneath the trees.

"You hungry? Want some milk, Mano-billi?" I said, patting my pocket to make sure the roll of tobacco hadn't fallen out.

The wedding cat purred. He arched its back, twisted, and started for the east corridor. He circled a (maple?) trunk, stopped, looked back at me.

"What is it? Not feeling better?"

Mano gazed at me. Night dilated around us. The cat shivered and hissed, his tail puffing up, and lunged toward the trees. I would have left him to whatever mischief he was up to and gone my way, but Mano had been acting odd all day. I called, then dashed after him.

He was a blur in the blackness and sometimes he was a sound. I followed him to the edge of the east corridor where he waited, ears pinned back, pawing the ground before one of the rooms. He saw me and blinked.

The wedding cat went inside the room.

I glanced down the unlit corridor. Nothing moved through its length. No sounds. Not one rectangle of light stretching from open doorways, which seemed more numerous and narrower than I had ever seen.

I looked at the room Mano had entered. A peculiar effect of light and dark turned the framework of its door pale blue, as if a thin coating of paint had been applied to the wood. The doorway was wedged between Sangeeta Apa's room and another girl's whose name escapes me. Inside, silver light flickered. Shadows moved beyond a curtain of mist or smoke.

I mothed to the strange light and entered the room.

By this time I had been at the orphanage for a number of years and watched half a dozen of my sisters get married. Their ages ranged from thirteen to thirty. Out of the six, we escorted three to the train station and one to the bus. One disappeared, nobody knew where, and one was married to an elderly clerk in the local municipality office who was, happily, receptive to bribes from the needful. This man had thrived and could afford a lavish wedding in a real wedding hall—Lala's Shadi House near Data Darbar. My sisters and I, therefore, had occasion to put on our best dresses, and we danced and sang at the baaraat party to our heart's content. It remains one of my fondest memories.

The wedding hall I was in now made the other seem like a shanty.

It was the grandest room I had ever seen or would. Pentagonal in shape, flanked by pillared archways, it was strewn with rose petals at the entrance and the far end. Motia and bright feather wreaths decked the walls, as did colorful mosaics and tapestries (these blurred when I passed them so I could never make out the images). Persian rugs were arranged in geometric patterns on the floor and spiraling crystal chandeliers sparkled and glimmered overhead. Candelabras lined the walls and threw a chiaroscuro of light and shadow such that the rugs (so fine they felt like extensions of my skin) seemed to shift beneath my passage.

My memory of the room is perfect, so vivid that it still lives behind my eyelids. I can shut my eyes now and see everything in profuse detail.

At the far end of the room was a cage on a raised platform. A bridegroom and his bride sat cross-legged on an embellished takht inside it.

I walked forward. The groom wore a sherwani glittering with sequins, and garlands of red flowers and rupee notes around his neck. His face was covered with a veil of charred feathers. The woman wore a gold-red wedding dress and was laden with jewelry from head to toe. Wherever her skin was exposed it was painted with henna. She was breathtaking.

Now I noticed other cages secreted away in arched recesses on either side of me. Silent men and women in colorful shalwar kurtas and saris sat inside on wooden perches and swings. Their eyes followed me as I moved down the hall. Their lips were parted. From each mouth protruded what I first thought were albino tongues. A second look dismissed the idea. The objects were pale and card-shaped.

Soundless, the doors of all cages slid up. The inmates rose and stepped outside.

I was surrounded by the wedding procession now. My nostrils filled with a smell as organic as it was old.

In a flurry of blue and green and black we marched to the couple's cage. Their door swung open, revealing a three-step deck carpeted with red feathers and fall leaves. The crowd surged forward, elbow to elbow, carrying me on its breast. Their footfall was perfectly silent. I couldn't even hear their breathing.

We halted before the stage.

Two men in raven black swept across the hall, up the stair deck, into the cage. They held a bowl of milk. The bridegroom swung his veil of burnt feathers aside and sipped. The raven men presented the bowl to the bride. She dipped her head coyly (but not before I saw that her eyes were large and different-colored) and drank until the man gently removed the bowl from her lips and placed it on the step deck.

Mano the wedding cat appeared from behind the stage. He sauntered up the steps and began to lap up the remaining milk. Come to me, Mano, I tried to say, but the words wouldn't leave my lips. Satiated, Mano yawned, licked his haunches, and started circling the wedding cage.

A woman in all white with a birthmark beneath her left eye was beside me. She was built like a briefcase, short and squat and business-like. She gazed at me for a moment and pointed at the ceiling.

I looked up.

The hall's ceiling was covered in the fresco of a giant bird. The bird was perfectly captured in mid-flight, its golden-dark serrated wings scything a blue sky. It had a rainbow plumage, black horns, and a peacock tail. Glinting feathers, like embers, showered from its underbelly. In the flickering light, the painting appeared to cast a vast shadow over the proceedings.

I lowered my gaze and the woman was gone. In her place was one of the raven men. Gray sparrows sat on his shoulders and pecked at his hair. He held out an enamel basin in front of him. Liquid sloshed inside. Its vapors made my eyes water.

The raven man bowed and began walking to the wedding cage.

Now rose excited chittering as the guests removed the card-like objects from their mouths and showered the wedding couple with them. Prayers, cheers, shouts, and the wailing of women overcome by the prospect of a daughter's separation mounted, until you couldn't tell if the procession were celebrating or mourning.

Mubarak! Mubarak! Be blessed in your husband's house.

May you never have cause to leave that home. May you never be short of dowry.

May your firstborns be healthy baby boys.

May your mother-in-law never hate you.

May you never return to your parents. Should you return, come only as a dead body

and

may you stay safe from the stove, the stove, the stove!

Now burst the wedding songs from a hundred throats, ancient, powerful, entrancing, loving, imprisoning, humiliating; and yet the raven man walked, he walked toward the bride with the basin of slopping liquid that gave off fumes.

She sat in her cage, placid as a sea, ageless like a vow unfulfilled. Only when the man reached her and doused her in the vaporous liquid did she stir. Her jewels slid and chinked. The tapestries on the walls darkened. The groom's veil of charred feathers dropped from his head and the red of the bride's dress deepened until it turned a perfect black.

The procession rejoiced.

May you stay safe from the stove!

Mano was between my legs. The wedding cat flicked his tail and tripped me. I flailed my arms, stumbled, and when I looked up, the wedding hall was gone. The cages, the guests, the beautiful bride with her splendid mismatched eyes (which I have seen in dream many times since), the elegant ornamentation—all vanished.

Just an orphan's room, empty of poise and promise.

I was afraid. I wasn't afraid. I was crying. I went back to the courtyard and looked at the sky. So many stars that night, and the blue moon, it watched the world as it always had. A bulbous bird staked to the heavens, it spread its vast gaze over all our affairs. Its eye was filled with something deep and raw. Now when I close my eyes and imagine that moon, I think what I saw was mystery and memory and a longing so old it makes me shudder.

I went to deliver the tobacco (still in my pocket) and as I passed Sangeeta Apa's door, the sounds of hushed conversation came, as did soothing odors of incense, earth, and rubbing oil. When I returned from Bibi Soraiya's quarters, the door was ajar. Leaves rustled. I glanced up to see a figure, bulky, as if with a thick garment, clinging to the tree (which tree?) outside her room.

The moon fled behind a cloud. When it returned, the ghostly figure was gone.

The wedding dinner was short and sweet. There was biryani, sweet lassi, mangoes, and lychees (it was summer). Rumors of silver-papered firni-in-jotas from Gawal Mandi floated for a while before Bibi Soraiya dismissed them.

The groom was a looming, forbidding man who bowed his head again and again and made squeezing gestures with his fists when too many of my sisters crowded him. Sangeeta Apa and he wore matching wedding outfits. She wouldn't look at him but peeked from behind her ghoongat, smiling, when Neha and I tried to steal his brown leather shoes—Joota Chupai is an accepted custom. Bibi Soraiya yelled at us and we reluctantly returned them.

They left for Gujranwala the next day by train.

I have not seen nor heard of my Sangeeta Apa since. If she called or wrote letters, Bibi Soraiya didn't tell us, which was strange because my others sisters stayed in touch—for a few years, at least, before life overtook them. The unsettling shadow of Apa's absence grew, but even after I was all grown up, if I asked about her, Bibi's eyes would change. With age, Bibi developed a tremor in her face and limbs, and mere mention of Apa would send her shaking to bed.

It got so bad that I stopped asking.

In ensuing years, Neha and many of my other sisters were married off. Sorted out, arranged, and packed away. Bus stops with their tang of sweat and diesel on your tongue. Train stations odorous with dust and cheap perfume and the ashy smell of sparks from rail tracks. Young girls appeared and replaced my sisters—a ceaseless commotion of laughs and shouts and dopattas flying in the courtyard wind. I loved them all, but, bless my memory, I remember few. Sometimes when I peered at their faces, it seemed as if their features blurred and ran together and one familiar mask emerged, winter breath rising from its lips like smoke. When that happened, I would get up and walk to the entrance of the orphanage. I would stand there and watch the world beyond those walls, an unfettered landscape stretching away beyond the limits of my vision. Somewhere out there, I thought, you didn't need to be wedded to resignation or despair. There was stuff in between. Hearths instead of stoves. If you got too warm, you could step away. You could leave. You didn't have to leave. You didn't have to fear leaving, or falling, or ceaselessly circling and not ever coming to rest.

You could travel to the ends of the earth. You didn't have to fear remembering.

By then I was busy helping Bibi run the orphanage. I had to put such thoughts out of my head. Still, I sometimes dreamed. Of discomfiting things that became grainy, wispy echoes in the morning. Crossroads with signs askew pointing this way and that; graveyards planted next to wedding halls; windows that shuttered open and closed; doorways that seemed to lead to more doorways, their gaping mouths atremble with flickering light; and in the distance, always, the flutter of dark wings. I would wake from these dreams with my fists darkened by sweat and dust, the taste of smoke already fading from my tongue.

The bird man still visited. He crouched on his shawl and twittered and chirped and spread the gilded envelopes, waiting for his parakeets to tell his admirers' fortunes. Maybe I was getting older or he, but his bird music seemed duller to me, as if his voice had aged. Once he came inside the orphanage to talk to Bibi Soraiya about something and my sisters gathered around him. I sat and watched him play to the girls. He turned his head from side to side. His turban fell off. I picked it up and handed it to him.

"Thank you," he said, dusting it with his large earthy hand. "Sometimes I wonder if it's time to take this off for good."

"Why?"

"Vanity be damned, it's just an old turban, you know." He laughed, a loud, booming sound that startled me. "One can dream, but that won't change it to a crown." His eyes looked a little feverish. He said, "You know sparrows are a delicacy in Gujranwala. They trap dozens in nets and roast them slow on large stoves. My father used to go eat with friends once in a while, but my mother would get angry. She said the poor things had no meat on them at all and it was a sin to take so many tiny lives for nothing."

I must have frowned or my face lost color, for he changed the subject. Shortly after, he left.

The oddest thing I remember after Apa's departure?

Exactly forty days after Bibi took her to the train station, all the birds, the silent birds, the soaring, splendid birds that came to us from every corner of Lahore, stopped visiting. The courtyard trees grew heavy with unpecked fruit, the electric poles became forlorn. Long after they vanished, the courtyard remained filled with the rich, old smell of bird. (These days, the odor makes me break out in a sweat.)

And in our rooms the mirrors rippled and moonlight changed and people from the past walked restlessly back and forth between places of someone else's making.

Pigeon from Hell

STEPHEN GRAHAM JONES

I would have done CPR if there'd have been any chance of CPR working. I'm certified, I mean. You don't get to put your name up on the baby-sitting board at church unless you're certified.

For the whole month after what happened, that's what I kept wanting to tell Tad and Kim Rogers. That, if there would have been even the slightest chance, even the whisper of one, even the ghost of the ghost of a hope, then I would have straddled Ben's small body in the street, never mind my new skirt, or the toes of my new shoes, or getting blood all over me, never mind any of that. I would have sat right there on him in the middle of traffic and everything, and I would have breathed all the life I could into him, and then pressed on his sternum with the heel of my right hand, my left hand on top of it, heavy but not too heavy. What I wanted to tell them, to show them, was that I would have done that until the ambulance screeched up, and then the medics would have had to pull me off. But I would have been clawing at the asphalt, trying to get back, to pump his heart just one more time. To get one last breath into his chest.

Promise.

Really.

Kara could have done it too, if she'd been there, instead of crying into the phone about she didn't know where he was, that's why she was *calling*, goddamnit.

Who she was calling at that point, it was the cops.

Thing was, it could have been me on my knees by Tad and Kim Rogers's breakfast bar at six thirty on a Friday, their phone dragged down with me. Except it wasn't my turn.

We were trading babysitting jobs, Kara and me. She'd get one, then I'd get one. The idea was that, if we traded like that, our money would save at the same rate, so when we went shopping together right before our senior year, we'd have the same amount, could get the same halter tops and skirts we were planning to own the school with.

Ben was Kara's turn, though. I'd had him the week before, for the church's bingo night. What Kara had him for was Tad and Kim Rogers's fifth anniversary. It didn't hurt that she was kind of in love with Tad, either. Not in any bad kind of way, just—he was somewhere in his midtwenties, was a thousand years younger than our dads but so much more mature than her college-brother Samuel, and, importantly, he adored Kim, he doted on Kim. Kim could do no wrong, as far as he was concerned.

What girl doesn't want to live on a pedestal like that?

I thought Tad was all right too, but this is all before, of course.

Losing a child, it ages a person. It sounds like something you'd see needle-pointed onto a pillow, but we don't need to see it spelled out, anymore; we can just look at Tad. The time off from work hasn't helped him.

You're not supposed to judge, I know.

I try not to. It's sad, though. Hard to look away, I mean.

One night, maybe two weeks after that Friday, I'd decided to just tell them, to get it over with, but I lost my nerve a few houses down, had to pull over to cry. It wasn't fake, either. Puffy eyes and smeared makeup wasn't going to be any kind of disguise, any cheap tactic. That was really going to be me.

But when I looked up from the heels of my hands, there was Tad, on the sidewalk by their mailbox. He had Ben's stupid rehab pigeon balanced there in his palm.

I shouldn't call it that, I know, but Ben being gone doesn't make that pigeon smart, I don't think.

He'd found it flapping in the gutter with a broken wing the day of his preschool graduation, and cradled it all the way home. Kim told me she'd seen it first and tried to steer them away, but it must have been fate.

Some boys have puppies, or iguanas, or fish.

Ben had a dirty gray pigeon.

When I'd babysat for bingo, Ben had let it out of its cage (a converted raccoon trap), and it flap-walked all over the house, finally hid under Tad and Kim's bed—the room Kim had politely asked me not to go in if I didn't need to. Under their king bed, I found out why: the clear flat tub rolled under there was where Kim kept her lingerie. It made me study Tad in a new way. A better way.

When it was Kara's turn to babysit Ben, she had that tub open as soon as Ben was in the bath. I know because she called me, so she could do her thrilled whisper about all of it—crotchless? seriously?

Seriously, girl. Yes.

I dared her try to them on, and try not to think about Tad when she did.

This isn't where Ben drowns in the bathtub. He never drowns in the bathtub.

If only.

What Kara did then—I've known her since second grade—was stand fast and wheel away from the idea, playacting wide-eyed insult, like the choir girl had just been offered a joint.

But she was already unsnapping her jeans, I knew.

What she would tell me weeks later, like the worst secret ever, was that, when that stupid bird started screeching in its wire cage, she'd thought it meant Tad and Kim were home early, so she'd shimmied back into her jeans, stepped into her shoes at a dead run, dove over the back of the couch, because in movies like the one playing in her head, every step can get you caught.

It was the next morning before she realized she still had Kim's crotchless panties on.

I went with her to bury them in the woods.

She doesn't think I know, but she went back to dig them up, bury them somewhere different. It's mostly what she does with her nights now: rebury those panties.

You don't have to die to become a ghost.

But, Tad, with that stupid pigeon, the day I came to confess everything.

There he was by the mailbox, blubbering and crying in his ratty robe, everybody on the street pretending not to be watching through their mini-blinds. The pigeon just looking around like the pigeon-brain it was.

Kim said it had been hit by a car, probably. Meaning, even among pigeons, this one hadn't been exactly quick. Now here it was at the edge of the street again. Except now it stood for something. Now it was a promise, an offering. Was its wing going to be good enough to fly? If it did fly, would that mean Ben was coming back?

It had been seven weeks, then. Still, when Tad scooped that pigeon up into the air, my heart went with it.

"Go," I said into the bad taste of the cracked vinyl horn button of my steering wheel, and the pigeon reached out with its wings, cupped just enough air not to plummet headfirst into the asphalt, and then it remembered what it was.

It caught. It flew. It flapped into the sky.

Tad fell to his knees, his robe pooling around him, and Kim rushed out across the grass, hugged him from behind, and I tried to just stare right into the digits of my odometer.

I had to assume they were exactly sixty-six point six evil miles past where they'd been the night Ben went missing. The night Kara called me in a panic, crying so I could hardly understand her. The night I'd just spent half my babysitting money on a new skirt because there'd been only one left in mine and Kara's size.

The shoes were from my mom, a surprise.

What I gathered on the phone from Kara was that he'd been in the bath, Ben, he'd been in the bath, and *now he wasn't*!

They don't train you for this in babysitting certification.

Losing your charge—how does this even happen, when you're already attending to his every need, keeping him from every sharp corner, and enriching his mind and improving his eventual life in between?

It doesn't happen. But it had.

I didn't even check in with Mom that I was leaving—standard proce-dure when dusk was even *close* to dusking—I just breezed through the kitchen, got my keys from the hook without missing a step, and like that I was going to save my best friend's life, to clean up this mess before it pooled big enough to lap up around my new shoes.

The reason I was supposed to check in on the way out, it was that the grainy light of dusk, that's when accidents like to happen, according to my dad.

He was right.

For exactly one half of an instant, just past Pine, almost to Spruce—Tad and Kim Rogers live on Magnolia—for exactly one slice of inattention, one moment of looking behind *that* planter, behind *those* rosebushes, there was a blot in my headlights.

Then that blot was a sound. Then a bump.

How Ben had gotten nine houses down from his house is a complete mystery, even now. He had pants on too, which made even less sense. What four-year-old has shame enough to get dressed?

I should have stopped, I know. I know I know I know. Except I was screaming. Except my brain was just one white line of sound.

I whipped into the last turn before Magnolia—Evergreen Court—and I stopped down at the round curb at the edge of the culvert. Because the edge of the culvert was always crumbling away, there were no houses down there.

This whole thing would have gone a completely different way, had some lookyloo PTA watchdog been keeping vigil at a window.

I was alone, though. Alone with what I'd done, alone with what had just happened, with what was going to ruin my whole life if I let it. Finally I quit screaming and hammering my hands onto the dash.

In my mind, I was four hundred yards behind, on the street, admi-nistering CPR.

I still kind of am, I guess.

Except for the proof otherwise. The proof still stuck under the car, up in the wheel well.

Ben was that little, yeah.

I went cold all over. Cold and mechanical.

All I could see was my dad, looking up from his chair at the kitchen table, asking me what was wrong, dear?

"Everything," I would have told him, I know. *Everything.*

And that would be unacceptable.

So, with my cold, mechanical hands and arms, with my new shoe pushing against the fender, I hooked a finger through Ben Rogers's belt loop and extracted him from the front left wheel well of my handed-down Buick Regal.

He came out in one piece.

I dropped him into the culvert with all the open-lidded washing machines and sprung shopping baskets and sumac and general grossness.

Which I'm sorry for. So sorry. He deserved better. Anybody does.

Then, because my brain had gone cold and mechanical too, I did what I had to do: drove over to Elm.

Curtis Grant's rangy yellow lab was loping around like always, trying to race every car that dared its street.

I dared.

And at a certain point in the race, I jerked the wheel over to the left, sucked that big yellow dog up into the wheel well, then let it cycle a bit before screeching the brakes loud, to draw people out into the street, alibi me.

Ben Rogers, his hair had been blond.

Nobody suspected anything.

I can't say for sure—all I've got to go on's what's happening *now*—but here's what I figure happened.

A boy is walking home from his half-day preschool early in May. His mom's bopping along beside him in her cute way. Some days it's his dad, since the mom and dad both manage to work from home, and know they get only so many "hold my hand"-walks total. But today it's the mom, her hair in a messy bun on top of her head, a spring in her step because she's basically living the dream, here. One she's thankful for every day.

This boy, see—you have to understand what a walking-talking miracle he is.

It's been four years, so everybody in town has kind of got accustomed to him, but there was a time.

My mom explained it to me in hushed tones over the breakfast table one day. Evidently, you used to have to get blood tests before you got married. They told you it was to get the bride and groom clean bills of health—no gonorrhea here, sir, ma'am—but the whispery part of it, the reason my mom waited for my dad to be gone to say it, was that she'd heard the test was to make sure mixing blood with this other person wasn't going to create some sad monster.

"Eugenics?" I asked my mom, because I'm all A's *and* not a Nazi, and in reply she'd covered my hand with both of hers, heated her eyes up to match her the downturned lines of her mouth, and said it hadn't been a bad idea. Some people's blood just shouldn't touch, even in a petri dish. It was as easy and as obvious as that.

In the case of this boy, his mom and dad, as perfect as they were, they weren't the genetically compatible kind of perfect. The doctor figured it out about halfway through the pregnancy and had the necessary sit-down with the couple.

They understood what needed to be done. That didn't mean they could *do* that, however.

Instead, they brought it before the church, and it became this big test-of-faith thing, where the whole congregation got together in the main chapel and held hands and prayed together, with this mom-to-be—already showing, she's got such a small frame—with her in a middle pew, her head leaned into her husband's shoulder, both of them crying freely.

The end result was that, very much against medical advice *and* second-opinion medical advice, they let this doomed pregnancy keep happening. No medicine because there is no medicine, but a lot of prayer, which my *dad*, never one not to know a detail or object to a wrong one, explained to me.

What we call "prayer" these days, he said, well, a whole long time ago, it was considered spells.

"Like *witches?*" I asked.

This was a long time ago, he explained. But, before industrialization and technology and all the wonders of our modern world, people, they'd figured out a different way of engineering their world. With magic. My dad said it like a dare, like I *should* object here. Like he was all ready for me to. I told him to just tell me already, please. Not like he wasn't going to anyway. The power of spells, he went on with a shrug like this was the most obvious thing, it came from a group of like-minded people all like chanting and wishing for the same thing. The power of positive thinking, basically. That was my takeaway: happy thoughts don't just make you feel good. They can actually fix things, sometimes. Or change them, anyway.

But then witches got uncool—probably because of Halloween or *The Wizard of Oz*, I don't know—our religion took over the good part of the world, and now a spell is a prayer: a whole chapel of people holding hands in a circle, chanting under their breath, wishing hard for one, single, specific thing.

For one whole half of a pregnancy, that one specific thing was this boy.

And, lo and behold, it worked. This mom *became* a mom over thirty-eight sweaty hours, and what the nurse carried out to the now-dad, it was a bouncing baby boy, perfect in every way. It was a miracle. It proved the power of prayer. That year the new baby had a special role in the nativity play, even, so we all forgot he wasn't who everyone was pretending he was.

This is that boy, that mom.

And they're just walking along that early May day, preschool over at last, his tiny graduation robe flapping, the whole broad expanse of summer opening up before them.

But first there's this bird, the one the mom is trying to steer the boy away from.

It's probably crawling with bird-mites and avian flu and just basic germs. People don't call them rats of the sky for nothing.

The mom wouldn't be a mom if she told the boy to leave the poor bird there to die, though. Better that it die in a shoe box in the bathroom down the hall from the boy, right? It's the time-honored tradition. It's how the world works. There would be a funeral later in the week, and then, soon, the bird would be replaced with a healthy puppy the boy can grow up with.

Just as soon as this dirty bird dies.

Except it doesn't.

This is the important part, the part I've thought about and thought about.

The bird doesn't die, even though that's what hurt birds kids smuggle home have been doing since forever.

Why?

It's residue.

The boy, he's this big miracle. And he's still got some of that church juice. All the chanting that let him develop naturally in the womb, that kept him symmetrical, that lined his genetic ladder back up so he could climb it into this world, it infused him, I think. If he'd have been a four-year-old craps player, then the dice would have always rolled in his favor, I'm pretty sure. Not because he was telling them to, but because he wanted to win.

What I see when I look back to the rest of that May, it's the boy, creeping from his bed after lights out, making his way down to the bathroom to whisper love to this bird. Or what he thinks is love.

Really, it's the leftovers of the spell that kept him whole. The magic still cycling through him. And it's being wasted on a dirty, broken bird, yeah. But it works all the same.

The bird refuses to die. To the parents' consternation—*they* kind of want a puppy, just for the soft-focus postcards those photos will make: boy and dog, the endless summer.

But maybe this bird, maybe it's a lesson of sorts for them, right? Maybe they're supposed to learn from it that love and happiness comes in all kinds of packages. Sermons don't always come from the pulpit.

What really matters, it's how the boy dotes on the bird, they tell each other. Like talking themselves into it. And how long does a pigeon live, anyway? This will come to a natural end soon enough, one way or another.

Maybe they name the pigeon, maybe they don't, it doesn't matter. I'd guess that naming a bird is like naming a turtle, or a snake, or a fish. Or your second-favorite hairbrush.

What the boy called it the one time his eventual killer babysat him, it was "Mine." And I guess it was.

Only, it didn't stop there, I don't think.

I'm pretty sure that stupid bird, it's still his.

It's something, anyway.

So Kara and me, we've always been inseparable, right? Since grade school. You date one of us, you're dating both of us. You give one of us detention, the other's showing up too.

I guess Ben's disappearance is kind of where that stopped.

The investigation did come to my front door, of course. Tad and Kim Rogers's telephone records would have led the cops here anyway, but it didn't need to go that far. I volunteered that Kara had called me in a panic. While I said it I was holding Kara. She was crying so hard she couldn't breathe, and there was snot on her lips and she was hitting her fists into my shoulders, these weak little nothing hits, like she was trying to fight her way out of a plastic bag. I just pulled her tighter, closer.

I wouldn't tell her about Curtis Grant's dog until the end of the week. But I told the cops right away. They hadn't been called to Elm when I'd let my car roll up onto the sidewalk—there was no real damage, no call to respond to—but Animal Services had showed up to document.

My dad met me there, took over the scene like he always has to. I drove his car home, and he took mine to the carwash, fed quarters through the pressure-sprayer until all the evidence was gone, gone, gone.

All I could think about was Ben Rogers, down in the culvert with the trash.

I kept picturing him crawling into the open mouth of one of the washing machines. Using it like a cocoon, like a chrysalis.

I know from Mr. Simonson's psych course that what's really growing in the belly of that machine is my guilt, of course. I knew right away, I mean, the first time I thought it.

It doesn't help. Especially at night.

But I never went back. That's rule number one, pretty much: Do Not Return to the Scene of the Crime, Young Woman.

For all I knew, the cops had found Ben Rogers right away, that first night. They'd found him and were letting him decompose there now, shifts and shifts of them pulling overtime to sit in some close-by attic, their spotting scope set up behind the rose window up there. Waiting for me—no, waiting for whoever would be stupid enough to confess by showing back up.

Instead, I go find Kara for her parents, when they call. And they call a lot. They think she's still out there looking for Ben.

I tell them everything will be okay, it'll all be all right, I'm there for her.

It's not completely a lie.

The first few times, I did follow her flashlight out into the trees. But then I watched from those trees before moving in.

It was the panties. Those guilty crotchless panties.

I'm pretty sure what Kara was actually burying and reburying— what she was *literally* still carrying around like psychic baggage, Mr. Simonson—was the memory of her strutting around that bedroom, playacting like she was Kim Rogers, making steamy eyes at her husband.

Doing all that while her son was . . . *what*? Not drowning, not electrifying himself with a light socket, not falling into the sharp corner of the bed frame with the delicate bones of his still-growing head.

Not anything, really.

She tried to talk to me about it once or twice, what could have happened. To get me spitballing with her. What the police and neighborhood and the whole town was somehow missing. Had some demon-monster oiled up through the bathtub drain, spirited Ben Rogers back down to hell with it? That, really and truly, was Kara's best and most rational guess.

A demon-monster.

What it was, she explained to me out in the woods, crying, her shovel fallen over beside us, what it was was the world, calling in its marker. Ben Rogers wasn't supposed to have happened, he was a cheat, one the church had slipped past the guard gate. And so the world was reeling that life back in, to keep things balanced.

Translation: Ben Rogers died for all of us. He was still the star of that live-action nativity from four years ago.

Translation of *that*? Kara was the hero of this story, for letting that happen. For enabling it. For taking on the guilt of it.

It's what she wanted me to say.

Except—well.

She couldn't see it, but that demon-monster she was so sure of, it already had her in its embrace. It was patting her back, its chin on her shoulder, its dead eyes looking out into the darkness.

The darkness stared back, just as empty.

Fast-forward past the awkward parts now. Move past Kara, staking out Tad and Kim Rogers's house, waiting for Kim Rogers to step out. Don't watch her pathetic attempt to stand in (*lay* in) for Kim Rogers, there on the porch, Tad Rogers all the way up to jeans and sandals now, in the grief-cycle. She was trying to trade herself. She was trying to say she was sorry. She was fumbling at the buttons of his jeans. It was inappropriate, but I could hardly call it an attempt at seduction.

I know because I had that house staked out as well.

When you see the part where Kara slashes at her wrists in the bathroom later that day, just keep moving. She doesn't really mean it. She means something, definitely—she means that she hates that Tad Rogers had no choice but to call her parents, and then Preacher Dan. She hates that Kim Rogers knows what happened. She hates that she ever took a stupid babysitting certification course.

But mostly she's still just saying sorry.

Has she finally started wearing those surely rotten panties by now? I honestly don't know. In the Dark Ages, they had hairshirts, I understand. It was how you did penance. These are different Dark Ages, though. Maybe in these, you slither into your guilt both legs at once, lying on your back on your queen bed, and then you hide it under your hip-huggers.

Nobody would know, right?

I hope she is wearing them, really. Serves her right. She *should* have been watching Ben Rogers every single second, like that course had told us to. If she had, then none of this would have ever happened.

I wouldn't keep finding myself in the garage, I mean, staring at our washing machine. Waiting for the lid to crack open.

More important, that stupid pigeon would be dead by now. Instead of whatever it is.

Don't misunderstand—I'm not claiming to be able to tell one pigeon from another pigeon.

But I don't have to, either.

This pigeon, it can tell *me* from all the other people on the street.

I know because, maybe nine weeks into it, maybe ten—you lose track—there I am sitting in my Buick, no headlights, no parking light, no dome light. What I'm doing is kind of idly watching Kara's flashlight cut through the trees out there.

School started last week, but she's not going. Instead she's out in the night, like trying to find the doorway into another, better world. One in which little dead boys get to still be alive.

I'd guess Tad and Kim Rogers are looking for that same door.

I shouldn't smile, though. I'm sure I'd be destroyed, if I were Kim Rogers. And angry, too.

That little bitch who let my son die?

I'd take an eraser to her barely sketched-in life, you can count on that. Anybody would.

The punishment on me for even just *thinking* that the first time, it was an eyeball, splatting into my windshield. At first I didn't know what was happening—had I parked under a pear tree? do raccoons throw things? was somebody else out here with me?—but then I kicked my wiper on, and that single eyeball, stalk and all, it smeared across, like climbing the glass up to where it could see me better.

I dove from the car, crawled backwards away from this . . . this whatever the hell it was.

At which point something fell onto the fingers of my hand.

It was a small, pale finger. Smaller than my own. Pale from not having any blood under the skin.

And then a pair of small, smug wings flapped up there, left me alone to deal with this.

When I could breathe again, and think, I flicked the eyeball from my car and stepped on it until it was gone. I tried to do the same with the finger but it kept pointing at me, even when it was just bone.

I opened my hood just like my dad had taught me, and dropped that finger into the spinning fan.

Black rotted blood sprayed back up. Onto my face. Onto the underside of the hood.

I blew it all off at the car wash, and washed my face in the stinging mist, and left my left shoe in the trash there, after spraying it clean as well.

Only when my mom asked was she okay did I remember Kara. She was the reason I'd checked in on the way out.

"She has to work through it," I said in the most sulky way I could, and limped upstairs, hid my head under the pillow.

Now who I hated, it was the cops.

How could they not have found a rotting body barely even hidden in the culvert? Isn't the closest trash pile the first place you look when somebody goes missing? Haven't they ever watched a police show?

If they'd found him like it was their *job* to do, then Tad and Kim Rogers could have had a coffin that weighed almost what it should, right? They could have had a service to move on from. And Kara would have known, at least.

And—more important—there wouldn't be a little body out there in the weeds and the sumac, a decaying, putrid corpse a bird could find, settle down on. Pull parts from to bomb me with, give me away for anybody with eyes to see.

I fucking hate that bird.

Every sound I heard on the roof afterward, I knew it was more body parts. That our gutters were going to be clogged with Ben Rogers.

Finally, my parents sleeping off their pitchers of beer from bowling night, I did what I knew I shouldn't: unlimbered the long aluminum extension ladder from the garage, walked it out the side door because the actual big garage door would wake everyone. I tipped the ladder up against the roof as gently as I've ever done anything.

I was going to throw Ben Rogers back into the sky.

Up on the shingles, though, it felt like I was about to fall up into that blackness myself. It felt enough like that that I hunched down.

It was just the usual tree-trash I'd been hearing, too. Like I should have known. Leaves, twigs, something like an acorn that wasn't going to ripen, I don't know, I'm no tree-nerd.

I didn't know if I should be happy or pissed about this.

I sat down, hugged my knees, and tried to cry.

The rest of the town had no problem bringing forth the tears. They did it every time they even thought about Tad and Kim Rogers, and Ben.

Not me. Because I was carrying the burden for all of them. Because I knew what had happened.

I don't want to claim I'm the victim, but I don't want to make being me easy, either. The old me, she would never have thought that the ladder creaking behind her was because of the weight of a small body, settling onto it. The old me wouldn't have backed away, all the way to the edge, forty feet opening up behind me. The old me would have known to breathe, would have known not to watch that open space at the top of the ladder.

This was the now-me, though. The one already planning things out: how she was going to guide Kara out to the trash pile in the culvert—trash delta, more like, thank you, tenth-grade geography—how she was going to guide Kara out there, so either Ben Rogers could finally be *found*, or, when he pulled himself back together with the good and hopeful but terribly misguided wishes of the whole church, he could claw his way into her stomach, not mine.

I'm not the one who lost him, after all. But now I *am* the one who will be seeing more and more pieces of him raining down on me in my car. Some of them mixing with a secret leftover piece of Curtis Grant's yellow lab, so that, when this reconstituted little boy claws up onto my hood, he'll have a canine muzzle, and long downy blond hairs coating what's left of his decaying skin.

Is this how it always is when you accidentally kill someone?

"No," I say out loud, like to make it real up here alone on top of the house.

The old me wouldn't have been scared to walk right over to the top of the ladder and turn around, climb back down it.

I'm not either.

And it all goes fine, hand over hand, feet feeling down for each careful, certain rung. It all goes fine until I look up.

The pigeon, that stupid goddamn pigeon, it's up there on the right post of the ladder. I expect the evil eye from it, but it's too dark for that. It's just a shape up there—if it's even that.

What if I'm making it up, right? What if I'm dreaming it into place?

To prove I'm not, I shake the ladder once, risking the sound of aluminum rattling.

Instead of lifting off to become part of the sky again, like, you know, a bird, *this* pigeon, it falls straight down like the stupid dead weight it is, right through the rungs, not even dinging into one of them.

"Dead weight" is right, too. If there's a way to add "for weeks" in there.

I didn't just heart-attack this pigeon with my ladder-shake. It's been dead for weeks, it looks like. It's been dead long enough that it bursts a little bit when it lands, onto the side of one of my shoes that I'm still calling new, just because I haven't worn them to school yet.

I shriek on accident then clap my hand over my mouth, fall back into the sharp bushes my dad says are better than a fence.

The pigeon doesn't clump up onto its stick legs. It doesn't do anything. It's just and simply dead. Without Ben Rogers to whisper life in through its little beak, it's nothing but gross meat, dirty feathers.

When I can breathe normal again, I stand, drag the side of my shoe on the wet grass even though I know I'm never wearing it again.

I guess I'm crying now, finally. Snot on my lips, the whole package.

"I'm sorry!" I scream across to the pigeon, to the neighborhood, to the town. To Tad and Kim Rogers.

No lights go on in my house. None next door either.

This makes me think that maybe when I came down the ladder, it was into another place.

My heart slaps inside my chest but I shake my head no, you're being stupid, girl.

Because my dad will figure this all out if I leave the ladder up—he's got what he calls a devious mind—I edge close enough to lean it back my way, then I hand-over-hand it back to its half-size, lug it back into the garage, place it gently on its two red hooks.

Same garage, I tell myself. Same house. Same everything.

What I force myself to picture instead of the dead pigeon, probably crawling with who knows what out there, it's Tad and Kim Rogers in their lonely backyard. There's the silhouette of the swing set. There's the doghouse they got because it was a deal, and they were going to need it before too long, wink-wink.

Where they're looking mostly, it's straight up.

In one of the church stories, a dove brings back a twig or something, one that proves life.

Maybe that's what they're waiting for.

There's not that much difference in a pigeon and a dove, really. A pigeon's just a big dove that's learned to live a different way. A pigeon is to a dove as I am to Kara—I study for the SATs, yeah.

And I'm going to ace them. I'm going to blast off into the world and this Ben Rogers thing isn't going to stop me. He was just, literally, a speed bump, one I'll be the only one to ever know about.

Good-bye, Kara. I'm sorry. But you have to keep moving. If you don't, you end up living in this town forever.

I nod to myself about the honesty of this, and then it occurs to me that either Ben Rogers *or* the pigeon should have the leftover magic of that spell, right?

Then why is the pigeon dead out on the grass? I edge over to the foggy-cheap window, get a line on where the feet of the ladder were. Where I'm pretty sure there's a bird corpse. Some kind of black lump, anyway.

Which reminds me: *why* didn't the cops ever find Ben Rogers? Wouldn't there have been a giveaway tornado of flies out there? Don't any of the neighborhood third-graders play down there in the junk, just because they've been warned not to? Wouldn't a neighborhood dog have shown up with a left hand clamped between its happy teeth?

Except you ran over that dog, I tell myself.

Right after you ran over the boy.

I chuckle with the bad luck of it all, and the creaking I turn to before I even realize I'm turning, at first I think it's my dad standing in the door that goes to the kitchen.

But that door's still shut, exactly like I left it.

It's not the ladder creaking either, because I'm still touching the ladder, would *feel* it creaking, and the red hooks are dipped in plastic anyway.

My most sincere fear is that it's going to be Tad and Kim Rogers, their mouths just these grim lines, their eyes so disappointed. At least, before

I see the tiny hand guiding the lid of the washing machine up, I *think* they're my most sincere fear.

I did come back down the ladder into a different place.

I know that now.

I climbed down into a world of my own making, and now I have to live here, with Ben Rogers, who wants to crawl up my frontside, latch his mouth onto mine, and breathe into my throat whatever's rising in his.

Maybe his parents *will* find the doorway that opens up to us someday.

Or maybe Kara's shovel will.

I'll be waiting to feel that light on my face.

But hurry, please.

The Secret of Flight

A. C. WISE

THE SECRET OF FLIGHT
WRITTEN BY OWEN COVINGTON
DIRECTED BY RAYMOND BARROW

PROLOGUE
ACT 1
SCENE 1

SETTING: The stage is bare except for backdrop screen showing the distant manor house.

The lights should start at ⅛ and rising to ¾ luminance as the scene progresses.

AT RISE: The corpse of a man lies CENTER STAGE. POLICEMAN enters STAGE RIGHT, led by a YOUNG BOY carrying garden shears. The boy's cheek is smeared with dirt. The boy points with shears and tugs the policeman's hand. POLICEMAN crosses to CENTER STAGE and kneels beside the corpse. BOY exits STAGE RIGHT.

POLICEMAN puts his ear to the dead man's chest to listen for breath or a pulse. His expression grows puzzled. POLICEMAN straightens and unbuttons the dead man's shirt. He reaches into the corpse's chest cavity and withdraws his hands, holding a starling (Director's note: use C's, already trained). POLICEMAN holds starling out toward audience, as though asking for help. Starling appears dead but after a moment stirs and takes flight, passing over the audience before vanishing. (Director's note: C assures me this is possible. C concealed somewhere to collect the bird?). POLICEMAN startles and falls back. (BLACKOUT)

LEADING LADY VANISHES!
Herald Star
October 21, 1955
Betsy Trimingham, Arts & Culture

Last night's opening of *The Secret of Flight* at the Victory Theater will surely go down as one of the most memorable and most bizarre in history. Not for the play itself, but for the dramatic disappearance of leading lady Clara Hill during the play's final scene.

As regular readers of this column know, *The Secret of Flight* was already fraught with rumor before the curtain ever rose. Until last night, virtually nothing was known of *The Secret of Flight* save the title, the name of its director, Raymond Barrow, and of course, the name of its playwright, Owen Covington.

Raymond Barrow kept the play shrouded in mystery, refusing to release the names of the cast, their roles, or a hint of the story. He did not even allow the play to run in previews for the press. Speculation ran rampant. Was it a clever tactic to build interest, or was it a simple lack of confidence after the critical and financial failure of Barrow's last two plays?

Whatever Barrow's reasoning, it is now inconsequential. All that is on anyone's lips is the indisputable fact that at the culmination of the play, before the eyes of 743 witnesses, myself included, Clara Hill vanished into thin air.

For those not in attendance, allow me to set the scene. Clara Hill, in the role of Vivian Westwood, was alone on stage. The painted screen behind Hill was lit faintly, so as to suggest a window just before dawn. As the light rose slowly behind the false glass, Hill turned to face the audience. It appeared as though she might deliver a final soliloquy, but instead, she slowly raised her arms. As her arms neared their full extension above her head, she collapsed, folding in upon herself and disappearing.

Her heavy beaded dress was left on the stage. In her place, a column of birds—starlings, I believe—boiled upward. Their numbers seemed endless. They spread across the theater's painted ceiling, then all at once, they pulled together into a tight, black ribbon twisting over the heads of the theater patrons. You can well imagine the chaos that ensued. Women lifted their purses to protect their heads, men ineffectually swatted at the birds with their theater programs. There were screams. Then there was silence. The birds were gone. Vanished like Clara Hill.

Was it all a grand trick, a part of the show? The stage lights snapped off, the curtain fell abruptly, and we were ushered out of the theater, still dazed by what we had seen.

As of the writing of this column, neither Barrow nor any other member of the cast or crew has come forward to offer comment. Dear readers, as you know, I have been covering the theater scene for more years than I care to name. In that time, I have seen every trick in the book: Pepper's Ghost, hidden trap doors, smoke and mirrors, misdirection. I can assure you, none of those were in evidence last night. What we witnessed was a true, I hesitate to use the word miracle, so I will say phenomenon.

Prior to last night, no one save those directly involved with *The Secret of Flight* had ever heard the name Clara Hill. Last night, she vanished. Her name will remain, known for the mystery surrounding it, but I do not think the woman herself will ever be seen again.

Personal Correspondence
Raymond Barrow
December 18, 2012
Dear Will,

I know it's absurd, writing you a letter. But a man my age is allowed his eccentricities. 88 years old, Will. Can you imagine it? I certainly never intended to be this old. The young have a vague notion they will live forever, but have any of them thought about what that really means? To live this long, to outlive family and friends. Well, since I *have* lived this long, I will indulge myself and write to you, even though it's old fashioned, and there's no hope of a response. Forgive an old fool. Lord knows I feel in need of forgiveness sometimes.

It's been 57 years since Clara disappeared. Aside from you, she was my only friend. I wish you could have met her, Will. I think you would have got along—comrades in your infernal secrecy, your refusal to let anyone else in, but somehow always willing to listen to me go on about my problems.

I'm all alone now. The only one left besides the goddamn bird, the one Clara left me. It's still alive. Can you fucking believe it? Starlings are only supposed to live 15, 20 years at the most. I looked it up.

Rackham. That's what Clara called him. I didn't want to use him in the play, but Clara insisted, and now I'm stuck with the damn thing. He's not . . . natural. He's like Clara. I don't think he *can* die.

I'm ashamed to admit it, maybe you'll think less of me, but I've tried to kill him—more than once. He speaks to me in Clara's goddamned voice. Starlings are mimics, everyone knows that, but this is different. I tried to drown him in a glass of brandy. I tried to wring his neck and throw him into the fire. Do you know what he did? He flapped right back out into my face with his wings singed and still smoking.

To add insult to injury, he threw my own goddamn voice back at me, a perfect imitation. He said, "Leading ladies are a disease. You breathe them in without meaning to, and they lie dormant in your system. Years later, you realize you're infected, and there's absolutely nothing you can do about it. You spend the rest of your life dying slowly of them, and there's no such thing as a cure."

Do you remember? I said that to you, years ago. At least it sounds like the kind of pretentious thing I would say, doesn't it? I was probably trying to be clever or impress you. Did it work?

Pretentious or not, it is true. I'm infected, and Clara is my disease. She's here, under my skin, even though she's gone. Everyone's gone, Will. Even you.

Well, goddamn you all to hell then for leaving me here alone.

Yours, ever,

Raymond

Items Displayed in the Lobby of the
new Victory Theater

1. Playbill—*The Secret of Flight* (1955)—Good Condition (unsigned)

2. Playbill—*Onward to Victory!* (1950)—Fair Condition (signed—Raymond Barrow, Director; William Hunter, Marion Fairchild, Anna Hammond, cast)

3. Complete Script—*The Secret of Flight* (1955)—Good Condition (signed, Owen Covington)

4. Press Clipping—*Herald Star*—June 17, 1925

"Victory Theater Under New Ownership"

A staged publicity photo shows Richard Covington shaking hands with former theater owner Terrance Dent. Richard's brother, Arthur Covington, stands to the side. The article details plans for the theater's renovation and scheduled reopening. The article provides brief background on the brothers' recent immigration to America from England. A second photograph shows the family posed and preparing to board a ship to America. Arthur Covington stands toward the left of the frame. Richard stands next to his wife, Elizabeth, his arm at her waist. Elizabeth rests both hands on the shoulders of their three-year-old son, Owen, keeping him close. None of the family members are smiling. To the right of the frame, standing with the luggage, is an unidentified young woman with dark hair thought to be Owen Covington's nanny. A shadow near the woman's right shoulder vaguely suggests the shape of a bird.

5. Press Clipping—*Herald Star*—August 7, 1976

"Fire Destroys Historic Victory Theater"

A half-page image shows the burned and partially collapsed walls of the Victory Theater. Dark smudges above the ruins show a sky still heavy with smoke. Certain patches might be mistaken for a densely packed flock of birds. The article offers scant detail beyond that the fire started early in the morning of August 6, cause unknown. The blaze took several hours to bring under control. No casualties reported.

6. Press Clipping—*Herald Star*—December 1, 2012
    "A New Life for the Victory Theater"
    The image at the top of the page shows the exterior of the New Victory Theater. A brushed stainless-steel sign bears the theater's name, and below it, an LED marquee screen shows the word WELCOME. The article discusses the successful fund-raising campaign leading to the construction of the New Victory Theater at the site of the original building. Brief mention is made of the architects' intent to incorporate elements salvaged from the old theater into the new design, however all the historic pieces are held by an anonymous collector who was unwilling to donate or sell them. The majority of the page is given over to pictures of the gala opening. The article notes that Raymond Barrow was invited to serve as honorary chair of the event, but he declined.

**Incomplete Draft of *Murmuration* by Arthur Covington—
typed manuscript with handwritten notes**

(CLAIRE glances over her shoulder before hurrying to EDWARD's desk, rifling through the drawers.)

CLAIRE (to herself): Where is it? Where is he keeping it?

(As her search grows more frantic, she fails to notice EDWARD entering the room. EDWARD grabs CLAIRE by the arm.)

EDWARD: Are you trying to steal from me?

CLAIRE: You stole from me first. Where is it?

EDWARD: Stole from you? You live in my house. You eat my food. Everything you *own* is mine.

(CLAIRE tries to strike him. EDWARD catches her hand. He leans close, his jaw clenched in anger.)

EDWARD: Show me how it works, and I might forget about your attempted thievery.

(CLAIRE doesn't answer. EDWARD grips her harder, shaking her.)

EDWARD: There's some trick to it. Look at this.

(EDWARD rolls up his sleeve and shows CLAIRE a long gash on his arm.)

EDWARD: I shouldn't be able to bleed anymore. I shouldn't be able to die.

CLAIRE (her voice hard): It was never going to work for you, Edward. You can't steal a feather from a bird and expect to fly, or steal a scale from a fish and breathe underwater. You can't change the nature of a thing just by dressing it up as something else.

EDWARD: Then tell me. Tell me how it works, and I'll let you go.

(ANDREW enters STAGE RIGHT, freezing when he see CLAIRE and EDWARD. Unnoticed, ANDREW hangs back, watching. EDWARD strikes CLAIRE. CLAIRE doesn't react. He knocks her down, pinning her, and puts his hands around her throat.)

God, this is shit. The whole thing is shit. It isn't enough. It doesn't change what happened. It doesn't make up for the fact that "Andrew" just stood there and did nothing. I stood in the hall and listened to them yell, and then when I finally got up the courage to go into the room, I froze instead of helping Clara. Not that she seemed to need my help. Speaking of which, what about the birds? How the hell do I stage the birds? No one would believe it. I don't believe it, and I was there. The room filling up with beaks and feathers and wings. Hundreds of birds coming out of nowhere while Clara lay there, and Richard throttled her, and I did nothing.

What the hell am I doing, writing this thing? Shit.

SUICIDE ATTEMPT THWARTED AT THE VICTORY THEATER!
Herald Star—April 19, 1955
Betsy Trimingham, Arts & Culture

There is a hero in our midst, dear readers. One, it seems, who has been hiding in plain sight at the Victory Theater. For months now, the theater scene has been buzzing with speculation over the Victory's latest production, all of which is being kept strictly under wraps.

Last night, however, one cat escaped the bag. Owen Covington, son of late theater owner Richard Covington, prevented an unknown woman from leaping to her death from the theater's roof. As it so happens, not only is young Mr. Covington a hero, he is the author of Raymond Barrow's mysterious new play.

Although he declined to comment upon his heroic actions, I was able to unearth one piece of information at least. Owen Covington's play, scheduled to open at the Victory later this year, is titled *The Secret of Flight*.

As for the young woman whose life Mr. Covington saved, could she be a member of the cast? Has Raymond Barrow unearthed the next darling of the theater scene? Or is she merely some poor seamstress working behind the scenes? More scandalously, could she be Raymond Barrow's lover? The only clue Mr. Covington provided during my repeated requests for comment was an unwitting one. He said, and I quote: *Clara is none of your business.*

Who is Clara? Rest assured, dear readers, I intend to find out!

Personal Correspondence
Raymond Barrow
December 20, 2012
Dear Will,

Here I am, at it again. The old fool with his pen and paper. Did you know they reopened the Victory Theater earlier this month? Not *the* Victory Theater, of course, a new one with the same name where the old one burned. They wanted me to be on their godforsaken Board of Trustees or some bullshit. I almost wish I'd taken the meeting in person just to see the look on their bootlicking, obsequious little faces when I said no.

God, I'm an ass, Will. I was an ass back in the day, and I'm an ass now, just a donkey of a different color, as they say.

Maybe it's the new theater that has me dredging up all these memories. It's like poking an old wound, though there were some good times mixed in with the bad. There was Clara. And of course, there was you. If you could have seen . . . Well, it doesn't matter. I cocked it all up in the end.

I was so excited when Owen Covington brought me the script of his new play. He was a virtual unknown, this snot-nosed kid who couldn't hold his liquor, but God help me, I thought he would save my career. Old money and all that. I didn't know his family had fallen into ruin. His father murdered, his uncle a suicide. All their lovely money pissed away. I should have done my research, but live and learn.

The whole thing was a disaster from beginning to end. Even before Clara, before . . . The press was at my throat from the get-go, desperate to see me fail. Then goddamn Owen Covington goes and tries to kill himself. Like nephew like uncle, I suppose.

Clara saved his life. She stopped him from jumping off the Victory's roof, though the newspapers reported it the other way around. Made Covington out to be a hero. What was that horrid woman's name? Betty? Betsy Trimblesomething? She was the one who gave you that absolutely scathing review as my leading man in *Onward to Victory!* God I hated her.

But there I go, rambling. I was telling you about Owen and Clara. After she saved him, Clara told me how much she wanted to let Owen jump. She showed me her palms. They were all cut up where she dug her nails in trying to stop herself from grabbing him. But she couldn't. She told me she couldn't help saving Owen, no matter how much she hated his family.

That was the closest she ever came to telling me anything about herself. Of course, I knew bits and pieces from Owen, not that I believed half of it. But then here was Clara, someone I trusted, saying the same thing. She said she'd known Owen as a child, that she'd been his nanny, and he was the only good thing to come out of the Covington family.

I asked her what the hell she was talking about, she and Owen looked exactly the same age. I thought maybe she'd finally open up all the way, maybe I'd finally get the truth out of her. Hell, I'd have settled for knowing her real name because I'm sure as shit it wasn't *Clara Hill*.

Instead of answering, Clara pointed out a flock of starlings. We were up on the roof of the theater, smoking, the way you and I used to do after rehearsals. That was the first place you kissed me. Do you remember? I was certain my mouth would taste like ash and whatever rotgut we were drinking and you'd be disgusted, but you weren't.

Are you angry that I spent time with Clara up there? There wasn't anything between us. We were friends. Actually, we became friends because of the roof. We'd both been going up there separately to smoke, and then we banged into each other one day and started taking our cigarette breaks together. It's a lucky thing we never burned the goddamn theater down.

I suppose that's how she found Owen, snuck up for a quick drag on her own and ended up saving his life.

Anyway, the birds. The sun was just starting to rise, and the birds were winging back and forth across the sky like one giant creature instead of hundreds of little ones. Clara watched them for a while; then she said, "Can you imagine what it's like, Raymond? Being part of something larger than yourself, knowing exactly where you fit in the world, then having it all ripped away from you, and finding yourself utterly and completely alone?"

God, Will, it's been years, and I can still hear her asking it. Even when she asked it, it had been two years since you'd been gone. When you died, Will . . . Well, I knew exactly what Clara was talking about. You were everything, and I couldn't even be with you at the end. I couldn't tell anyone how my heart had been ripped out, or cry at your grave.

Things are different now, but there's no one I want to cry for the way I wanted to for you.

Maybe that's why Clara and I got along so well. We were alike in our loneliness. We both had things we couldn't tell anyone about ourselves. Not all ghosts are about guilt. That's something else Clara told me once, and I understand her now. Some ghosts are about sorrow, and loss. But God, Will, of all the ghosts to have haunt me, why did it have to be hers, and not yours?

Ray

Incomplete Draft of *Murmuration* by Arthur Covington— typed manuscript with handwritten notes

(EDWARD and CLAIRE face each other in EDWARD's office, the same setting as their earlier confrontation. Light flickers through a screen painted to look like a window, suggesting a storm. CLAIRE holds a gun pointed at EDWARD.)

EDWARD: Give me the gun, Claire. We both know you won't shoot me.

CLAIRE: You don't know the first thing about me. You have no idea what I'll do.

EDWARD: Elizabeth is upstairs. She'll hear the shot and call the police. There's nowhere for you to go. You'll be caught, and you'll hang.

CLAIRE (laughing bitterly): It doesn't matter. They can't kill me. It doesn't matter what you took from me, I still can't die. But you can.

(CLAIRE steadies the gun. EDWARD finally shows a hint of fear.)

EDWARD: Claire, be reasonable. I can—

CLAIRE: No, you can't. You can't do anything. You tried to steal from me, but my life can't be stolen, not that way. When you couldn't steal it, you broke it, and now I can't fly away either. I can't leave this place, not while you're alive.

(EDWARD reaches for CLAIRE. OWEN enters STAGE RIGHT, dressed for bed. He looks between CLAIRE and EDWARD, confused, and takes a step toward CLAIRE.)

OWEN: Will you tell my bedtime story?

(CLAIRE fires. EDWARD falls, and OWEN puts his hands over his ears and screams. CLAIRE stands still for a moment, then drops to her knees. Running footsteps can be heard from offstage.)

CLAIRE (barely audible): It didn't work. I'm still here. Oh, God, it didn't work.

This is still shit. That's how it happened, but no one will believe it. The truth is too strange.

Clara shot Richard while Owen watched, and she didn't run away. She let them arrest her. She confessed, but there was never a trial. She vanished out of the cell where they were holding her. The police were mystified.

Shit. I could write my play closer to the truth. No one would know the difference except Elizabeth. Then she'd start asking questions. What's the point? I can never produce this goddamn play, for her sake and for Owen's.

Clara shot Richard with Owen standing right there watching. He doesn't remember, at least not consciously. His young mind couldn't cope, so he shuttered the information away, but something like that doesn't go away completely. It changes a person. It leaves a stain.

I took Owen to see a hypnotist. Elizabeth doesn't know. Dr. Samson put Owen into a trance, and Owen recounted word for word the whole exchange between Clara and Richard. In real life, Owen didn't walk into the room the way I wrote it in the play. He was hiding under

Richard's desk, playing a game. He wanted to jump out and scare Clara. He saw the whole thing.

That's not the worst of it though. After describing his father's murder, Owen started laughing. Dr. Samson thought it might be some sort of defense mechanism, his mind, even hypnotized, trying to protect him. He asked Owen about it, and Owen said he was laughing because the bird-lady was making pictures in the sky. She was telling the starlings which way to fly, like she used to on the boat from England.

God help me, he was talking about Clara. I'm more sure now than ever—she isn't human.

TRAGEDY STRIKES THE VICTORY THEATER!
Herald Star—October 10, 1955
Betsy Trimingham, Arts & Culture

Owen Covington's life was cut tragically short yesterday when he was struck by a subway train. As regular readers of this column know, Mr. Covington was both a playwright, and a hero. I spoke with a police officer who was "unable to comment on an ongoing investigation." He declined to say whether foul play was suspected, but I do wonder how a young man in the prime of his life could simply slip from the subway platform in front of an oncoming train.

Keep your eyes on this column, dear readers. The truth will out eventually, and I will report on it.

Personal Correspondence
Raymond Barrow
December 22, 2012
Dearest Will,

Here I am again with my pen and paper. I've been thinking a lot about paper lately, the pages Owen had from his uncle when he first pitched me the idea of his play. He wouldn't let me read them for myself, he just sort of waved them around in front of me and said he was going to use them as the basis for his script. He only had fragments, Arthur Covington killed himself without ever finishing the play.

Of course I read those fragments eventually. It wasn't snooping, just protecting my investment. Besides, it was Owen's fault for passing out drunk on my couch with the damn pages still in his jacket pocket.

It was all there—Owen's father, Richard; his uncle, Arthur; and Clara. Of course in the play they were Edward, Andrew, and Claire, but it's obvious who they were supposed to be. Except it was fiction. Fantasy. Or maybe I was too stubborn to see what was right in front of my face.

This is what I think now: Owen's father did something terrible to Clara a long time ago. Clara murdered him, and Owen witnessed the whole thing. Of course, Owen didn't remember it happening, not consciously. Trauma and all that. But on some primal level he did remember. He was in love with Clara, or he thought he was. It was all tangled up in guilt and her killing his father, like some goddamned soap opera, but real.

Clara loved Owen too, in her own way. Not the way he wanted her to, but like a mother bird that hatches an egg and realizes a cuckoo has snuck its own egg into her nest. Her baby is gone and she's accidentally raised the cuckoo's child, but she defends it and she cares for it because that's her nature, and it's not the baby's fault after all.

It's why Owen tried to kill himself. He thought it would set her free. And it's why Clara couldn't let him.

At first I didn't believe it, any of it, but the more time I spent around them, the more time I spent with Clara . . . God, Will. You were gone, and I didn't have anyone else. I thought I could help Clara, do one good thing in my life and save her. I started thinking maybe Owen was right. Maybe if no one in his family was left alive, she could finally leave. I didn't . . . I just bumped him, really. He lost his balance. He was so utterly piss drunk, he probably didn't even feel it when the train hit him.

I never told Clara, but I think she knew. She was the one who insisted the play go on, in Owen's memory. I tried to convince her to leave. I'd just killed a man. I couldn't think straight. I was raving, shouting at her. I think I almost hit her. But Clara just looked at me with this incredible pity in her eyes. She put her hand on my arm, and said, "Grief can change the nature of a person, Ray, when nothing else can. Enough loss, and it weighs you down, you forget how to fly."

She told me everything I needed to know, Will, but I didn't know how to listen.

I didn't know how to listen when you told me you needed help all those years ago. The empty bottles, the needles; I refused to see it because I didn't want it to be true. I should have listened. I miss you, Will.

Yours, always,

Ray

Personal Correspondence
Raymond Barrow
October 20, 1955
Dear Ray,

This is it, our big night. *The Secret of Flight* opens, and I don't know what will happen after that. There's something I'm going to try, Ray, and if it doesn't work, I might not see you again. So I wanted to say thank you for everything you've done for me, and everything you tried to do. You're a good friend. I don't have many of those, so believe me when I say our time together meant a lot to me even though I couldn't tell you everything about me. Instead, I'm giving you this story. It's the best I can do, Ray. I hope you'll understand.

Love,

Clara

The Starling and the Fox

Once upon a time, there was a fox, and there was a starling. They weren't really a fox and a starling, they only looked that way from the outside, but for the purposes of this story, those names will do. This happened far away, in another country, many years ago.

The starling was flying, minding her own business, when she spotted a tree with lovely branches. She landed on one and discovered a fox lying across the tree's roots, crying piteously.

"Oh, they have killed me," the fox said. "I shall die if you don't aid me."

The starling couldn't see anything wrong with the fox, but she didn't see the harm in helping him either.

"What is it you need, sir fox?" she asked him.

"Only a feather from your beautiful wing, and I will be well again," the fox said.

The starling was doubtful. She looked again and she couldn't see any blood on the fox's fine fur, but he continued moaning as she looked him over, and it certainly sounded as if he might die.

The starling chose one of the small feathers near the top of her wing. She didn't think it would hurt to pull it out, and she didn't think she would miss it either. As she took hold of it in her beak, the fox cried out again.

"Not that feather! Only the long feather at the tip of your wing will do. The straight and glossy one that shines like a still pool at midnight, even when you think there is no light at all."

The starling thought the fox sounded a little foolish with his poetic language and the way he carried on, but the fox rolled on his back, weeping, and put a paw over his eyes. His tongue lolled from his mouth, and surely he would die at any moment if she did not help him.

The starling took hold of her longest and straightest feather with her beak and pulled. It hurt, worse than anything she had ever felt, like the stars and the moon and the sun going out all at once.

"Good. Now bring it down to me, quickly!" the fox said, jumping to all fours, even though he had been at death's door a moment ago.

Dazed with pain, the starling hopped down to him, half tumbling as she went. She presented the feather to the fox.

"Are you saved now?" she asked him.

"Very much so," the fox replied, and his eyes were bright.

"Then I will take my leave," the starling said.

She spread her wings, but when she tried to take flight, she found she could not. Without her longest, straightest feather, she couldn't fly. She leapt toward the sky again and again but crashed back to the ground every time.

The fox watched her impassively through all her attempts.

"Help me, sir fox," she said when she had finally exhausted herself.

"Surely I shall," he said, and stepped forward, snapped her up in his jaws, and swallowed her whole.

This is the moral of the story: You should never trust a wild animal. A fox cannot change its nature no matter how it dresses itself up, or what fine words it uses. It will always hunger. If you let your guard down, even for a moment, it will devour you whole.

iPhone Audio and Video Recording
Raymond Barrow

December 26, 2012

[The image swings, showing the floor, a man's feet, and a desk cluttered with papers. A starling perches on a corner of the desk, briefly visible before the camera turns to show the face of Raymond Barrow.]

BARROW: There, you see, Will? I've been dragged kicking and screaming into the twenty-first century after all. My great-niece, Sarah's daughter, gave me one of those infernal iPhone things. They were all over for Christmas yesterday, and spent most of the day showing me how to use it. Sarah suggested I might like to record some of my personal recollections of the good old days, something to preserve for generations to come. Ha! If the future is interested in a washed-up old has-been who failed at every important thing he ever turned his hand to, then I pity them. But there is something I want to show you, so maybe this thing will be good for something after all.

[The camera turns to face outward again, the image bouncing while Barrow holds the phone in front of him as he walks. The camera catches glimpses of an ornate entryway, a crystal chandelier, a sweeping staircase. Carvings, hangings, sketches, and paintings on the walls depict birds of all kinds. The camera approaches a massive grandfather clock standing next to a door set beneath the curving staircase. The wooden case is chased with mother of pearl, showing a heron standing placidly among a cluster of reeds.]

BARROW: You see, I did all right for myself in the end. Not that I deserved to, but life isn't fair, is it?

[Barrow reaches for the door, holding the phone steady in his other hand. A flight of stairs leads down. There's a rustle from behind the camera, and Rackham, the starling, flies past Barrow's shoulder, disappearing down the stairs. Barrow stumbles, catching himself against the wall, but doesn't fall.]

BARROW: Damn bird will be the death of me.

[The image is dark as Barrow gropes his way to the bottom of the stairs and flicks on a light. The camera shows rows of red velvet seats on a raked floor, facing a stage. The curtains are open, the set bare save for a painted screen backdrop, meant to look like a window.]

BARROW: It's the Victory Theater. I bought up everything they could salvage after the fire and had it all restored. What they couldn't restore, I had rebuilt, exact replicas.

[The image wavers again as Barrow moves to a row of seats halfway to the stage. He sits, steadying the camera against the back of the chair in front of him.]

BARROW: I salvaged too much, Will. I was right, all those years ago when I said leading ladies are a disease. I've been carrying Clara in my blood for fifty-seven years, and there isn't any cure. All I ever wanted to do was help her, Will, but I think I know why she chose me. It's what she said about ghosts, and loss, and sorrow. A man can't change his own nature, but the world can change it for him if he lets his guard down. I let my guard down. I fell in love with you. I left myself open, and where did it get me?

[Barrow doesn't move, but the house lights in the theater dim, and the lights begin to rise slowly on the stage. As the lights reach full, they reveal a woman with dark hair, wearing a beaded gown, standing center stage.]

BARROW: That's her, Will. It's Clara.

[There's a faint translucence to Clara's form, but the starling flies from behind the camera and lands on Clara's shoulder. She smiles.]

BARROW (softly): That's what all my love earned me, Will. A ghost, but the wrong one.

[Clara turns toward the camera, and the man behind it. Her expression is sad but fond. She smiles, but it's pained. Clara raises her arms. As they read their full extension, birds pour forth from the spot where she stands. Her dress falls, crumpled, to the floor. Dozens, hundreds of starlings boil up toward the ceiling like a cloud of smoke. When they reach the ceiling, they spread outward.

Barrow tilts the camera to show the birds as they pull together into a tight formation and fly toward him. He nearly drops the phone, and the view swings to show him in profile as the birds stream around him. Their wings brush his hair, his skin. His cheeks are wet.

The murmuration flows through the theater. The birds make no noise in their flight. Barrow steadies the phone, turning the camera to face him again. The birds are gone. He is alone.]

BARROW: It's the same thing every night. Every goddamn night for fifty-seven years. I tried to set her free, and she came back. She came back, Will, so why the hell didn't you?

[Barrow fumbles with the camera for a moment. The rustle of wings sounds and the starling lands on Barrow's shoulder. The recording ends.]

Isobel Avens Returns to Stepney in the Spring

M. JOHN HARRISON

The third of September this year I spent the evening watching TV in an upstairs flat in North London. Some story of love and transfiguration, cropped into all the wrong proportions for the small screen. The flat wasn't mine. It belonged to a friend I was staying with. There were French posters on the walls, dusty CDs stacked on the old-fashioned sideboard, piles of newspapers subsiding day by day into yellowing fans on the carpet. Outside, Tottenham stretched away, Greek driving schools, Turkish social clubs. Turn the TV off and you could hear nothing. Turn it back on and the film unrolled, passages of guilt with lost edges, photographed in white and blue light. At about half past eleven the phone rang. I picked it up. "Hello?"

It was Isobel Avens.

"Oh, China," she said. She burst into tears.

I said: "Can you drive?"

"No," she said.

I looked at my watch. "I'll come and fetch you."

"You can't," she said. "I'm here. You can't come here."

I said: "Be outside, love. Just try and get yourself downstairs. Be outside and I'll pick you up on the pavement there." There was a silence. "Can you do that?"

"Yes," she said. "Oh, China." The first two days she wouldn't get much further than that.

"Don't try to talk," I advised.

London was as quiet as a nursing home corridor. I turned up the car stereo. Tom Waits, Downtown Train. Music stuffed with sentiments you recognise but daren't admit to yourself. I let the BMW slip down Green Lanes, through Camden into the centre; then west. I was pushing the odd traffic light at orange, clipping the apex off a safe bend here and there. I told myself I wasn't going to get killed for her. What I meant was that if I did she would have no one left. I took the Embankment at eight thousand revs in fifth gear, nosing down heavily on the brakes at Chelsea Wharf to get round into Gunter Grove. No one was there to see. By half past twelve I was on Queensborough Road, where I found her standing very straight in the mercury light outside Alexander's building, the jacket of a Karl Lagerfeld suit thrown across her shoulders and one piece of expensive leather luggage at her feet. She bent into the car. Her face was white and exhausted and her breath stank. The way Alexander had dumped her was as cruel as everything else he did. She had flown back steerage from the Miami clinic reeling from jet lag, expecting to fall into his arms and be loved and comforted. He told her, "As a doctor I don't think I can do any more for you." The ground hadn't just shifted on her: it was out from under her feet. Suddenly she was only his patient again. In the metallic glare of the streetlamps, I noticed a stipple of ulceration across her collarbones. I switched on the courtesy light to look closer. Tiny hectic sores, closely spaced.

I said: "Christ, Isobel."

"It's just a virus," she said. "Just a side effect."

"Is anything worth this?"

She put her arms around me and sobbed. "Oh, China, China."

It isn't that she wants me; only that she has no one else. Yet every time I smell her body my heart lurches. The years I lived with her I slept so soundly. Then Alexander did this irreversible thing to her, the thing she had always wanted, and now everything is fucked up and eerie and it will be that way forever.

I said: "I'll take you home."

"Will you stay?"

"What else?"

My name is Mick Rose, which is why people have always called me "China." From the moment we met, Isobel Avens was fascinated by that. Later, she would hold my face between her hands in the night and whisper dreamily over and over—"Oh, China, China, China. China." But it was something else that attracted her to me. The year we met, she lived in Stratford-on-Avon. I walked into the café at the little toy aerodrome they have there and it was she who served me. She was twenty-five years old: slow, heavy-bodied, easily delighted by the world. Her hair was red. She wore a rusty pink blouse, a black ankle-length skirt with lace at the hem. Her feet were like boats in great brown Dr. Marten's shoes. When she saw me looking down at them in amusement, she said: "Oh, these aren't my real Docs, these are my cheap imitation ones." She showed me how the left one was coming apart at the seams. "Brilliant, eh?" She smelled of vanilla and sex. She radiated heat. I could always feel the heat of her a yard away.

"I'd love to be able to fly," she told me. She laughed and hugged herself. "You must feel so free."

She thought I was the pilot of the little private Cessna she could see out of the café window. In fact I had only come to deliver its cargo—an unadmitted load for an unadmitted destination—some commercial research centre in Zurich or Budapest. At the time I called myself Rose Medical Services, Plc. My fleet comprised a single Vauxhall Astra van into which I had dropped the engine, brakes, and suspension of a two-litre GTE insurance write-off. I specialised. If it was small, I guaranteed to move it anywhere in Britain within twelve hours; occasionally, if the price was right, to selected points in Europe. Recombinant DNA: viruses at controlled temperatures, sometimes in live hosts: cell cultures in heavily armoured flasks. What they were used for I had no idea. I didn't really want an idea until much later; and that turned out to be much too late.

I said: "It can't be so hard to learn."

"Flying?"

"It can't be so hard."

Before a week was out we were inventing one another hand over fist. It was an extraordinary summer. You have to imagine this—

Saturday afternoon. Stratford Waterside. The river has a lively look despite the breathless air and heated sky above it. Waterside is full of jugglers and fire-eaters, entertaining thick crowds of Americans and Japanese. There is hardly room to move. Despite this, on a patch of grass by the water, two lovers, trapped in the great circular argument, are making that futile attempt all lovers make to get inside one another and stay there for good. He can't stop touching her because she wants him so. She wants him so because he can't stop touching her. A feeding swan surfaces, caught up with some strands of very pale green weed. Rippling in the sudden warm breeze which blows across the river from the direction of the theatre, these seem for a moment like ribbons tied with a delicate knot—the gentle, deliberate artifice of a conscious world.

"Oh, look! Look!" she says.

He says: "Would you like to be a swan?"

"I'd have to leave the aerodrome."

He says: "Come and live with me and be a swan." Neither of them has the slightest idea what they are talking about.

Business was good. Within three months I had bought a second van. I persuaded Isobel Avens to leave Stratford and throw in with me. On the morning of her last day at the aerodrome, she woke up early and shook me until I was awake too.

"China!" she said.

"What?"

"China!"

I said: "What?"

"I flew!"

It was a dream of praxis. It was a hint of what she might have. It was her first step on the escalator up to Alexander's clinic.

"I was in a huge computer room. Everyone's work was displayed on one screen like a wall. I couldn't find my A-prompt!" People laughed at her, but nicely. "It was all good fun, and they were very helpful." Suddenly she had learned what she had to know, and she was floating up and flying into the screen, and through it, "out of the room, into the air above the world." The sky was crowded with other people, she said. "But I just went swooping past and around and between them." She let herself fall just for the fun of it: she soared, her whole body taut and trembling like the fabric of a kite. Her breath went out with a great laugh. Whenever she was tired, she could perch like a bird. "I loved it!" she told me. "Oh, I loved it!"

How can you be so jealous of a dream? I said: "It sounds as if you won't need me soon."

She clutched at me. "You help me to fly," she said. "Don't dare go away, China! Don't dare!"

She pulled my face close to hers and gave me little dabbing kisses on the mouth and eyes. I looked at my watch. Half past six. The bed was already damp and hot: I could see that we were going to make it worse. She pulled me on top of her, and at the height of things, sweating and inturned and breathless and on the edge, she whispered, "Oh, lovely, lovely, lovely," as if she had seen something I couldn't. "So lovely, so beautiful!" Her eyes moved as if she was watching something pass. I could only watch her, moving under me, marvellous and wet, solid and real, everything I ever wanted.

The worst thing you can do at the beginning of something fragile is to say what it is. The night I drove her back from Queensborough Road to her little house in the gentrified East End, things were very simple. For forty-eight hours all she would do was wail and sob and throw up on me. She refused to eat, she couldn't bear to sleep. If she dropped off for ten minutes, she would wake silent for the instant it took her to remember what had happened. Then this appalling dull asthmatic noise would come out of her—"zhhh, zhhh, zhhh," somewhere between retching and whining—as she tried to suppress the memory, and wake me up, and sob, all at the same time.

I was always awake anyway.

"Hush now, it will get better. I know." I knew because she had done the same thing to me.

"China, I'm so sorry."

"Hush. Don't be sorry. Get better."

"I'm so sorry to have made you feel like this."

I wiped her nose. "Hush."

That part was easy. I could dress her ulcers and take care of what was coming out of them, relieve the other effects of what they had done to her in Miami, and watch for whatever else might happen. I could hold her in my arms all night and tell lies and believe I was only there for her.

But soon she asked me, "Will you live here again, China?"

"You know it's all I want," I said.

She warned: "I'm not promising anything."

"I don't want you to," I said. I said: "I just want you to need me for something."

That whole September we were as awkward as children. We didn't quite know what to say. We didn't quite know what to do with one another. We could see it would take time and patience. We shared the bed rather shyly and showed one another quite ordinary things as gifts.

"Look!"

Sunshine fell across the breakfast table, onto lilies and pink napery. (I am not making this up.)

"Look!" A grey cat nosed out of a doorway in London E3.

"Did you have a nice weekend?"

"It was a lovely weekend. Lovely."

"Look." Canary Wharf, shining in the oblique evening light!

In our earliest days together, while she was still working at the aerodrome, I had watched with almost uncontainable delight as she moved about a room. I had stayed awake while she slept, so that I could prop myself up on one elbow and look at her and shiver with happiness. Now when I watched, it was with fear. For her. For both of us. She had come down off the tightrope for awhile. But things were still so precariously balanced. Her new body was all soft new colours in the bedside lamplight. She was thin now, and shaped quite differently: but as hot as ever, hot as a child with fever. When I fucked her she was like a bundle of hot wires. I was like a boy. I trembled and caught my breath when I felt with my fingertips the damp feathery lips of her cunt, but I was too aware of the dangers to be carried away. I didn't dare let her see how much this meant to me. Neither of us knew what to want of the other anymore. We had forgotten one another's rhythms. In addition she was remembering someone else's: it was Alexander who had constructed for me this bundle of hot, thin, hollow bones, wrapped round me in the night by desires and demands I didn't yet know how to fulfill. Before the Miami treatments she had loved me to watch her as she became aroused. Now she needed to hide, at least for a time. She would pull at my arms and shoulders, shy and desperate at the same time; then, as soon as I understood that she wanted to be fucked, push her face into the side of mine so I couldn't look at her. After awhile she would turn onto her side; encourage me to enter from behind; stare away into some distance implied by us, our failures, the dark room. I told myself I didn't care if she was thinking of him. Just so long as she had got this far, which was far enough to begin to be cured in her sex where he had wounded her as badly as anywhere else. I told myself I couldn't heal her there, only allow her to use me to heal herself.

At the start of something so fragile, the worst mistake you can make is to say what you hope. But inside your heart you can't help speaking, and by that speech you have already blown it.

After Isobel and I moved down to London from Stratford, business began to take up most of my time. Out of an instinctive caution, I dropped the word "medical" from the company description and called myself simply Rose Services. Rose Services soon became twenty quick vans, some low-cost storage space, and a licence to carry the products of new genetic research to and from Eastern Europe. If I was to take advantage of the expanding markets there, I decided, I would need an office.

"Let's go to Budapest," I said to Isobel.

She hugged my arm. "Will there be ice on the Danube?" she said.

"There will."

There was. "China, we came all the way to Hungary!" She had never been out of Britain. She had never flown in an aeroplane. She was delighted even by the hotel. I had booked us into a place called the Palace, on Rakoczi Street. Like the city itself, the Palace had once been something: now it was a dump. Bare flex hung out of the light switches on the fourth-floor corridors. The wallpaper had charred in elegant spirals above the corners of the radiators. Every morning in the famous Jugendstil restaurant, they served us watery orange squash. The rooms were too hot. Everything else—coffee, food, water from the cold tap—was lukewarm. It was never quiet, even very late at night. Ambulances and police cars warbled past. Drunks screamed suddenly or made noises like animals. But our room had French windows opening onto a balcony with wrought-iron railings. From there in the freezing air, we could look across a sort of high courtyard with one or two flakes of snow falling into it, at the other balconies and their lighted windows. That first evening, Isobel loved it.

"China, isn't it fantastic? Isn't it?"

Then something happened to her in her sleep. I wouldn't have known, but I woke up unbearably hot at three A.M., sweating and dry-mounthed beneath the peculiar fawn-fur blanket they give you to sleep under at the Palace. The bathroom was even hotter than the bedroom and smelled faintly of very old piss. When I turned the tap on to splash my face, nothing came out of it. I stood there in the dark for a moment, swaying, while I waited for it to run. I heard Isobel say reasonably: "It's a system fault."

After a moment she said, "Oh no. Oh no," in such a quiet, sad voice that I went back to the bed and touched her gently.

"Isobel. Wake up."

She began to whimper and throw herself about.

"The system's down," she tried to explain to someone.

"Isobel. Isobel."

"The system!"

"Isobel."

She woke up and clutched at me. She pushed her face blindly into my chest. She trembled.

"China!"

It was February, a year or two after we had met. I didn't know it, but things were already going wrong for her. Her dreams had begun to waste her from the inside.

She said indistinctly: "I want to go back home."

"Isobel, it was only a dream."

"I couldn't fly," she said. She stared up at me in astonishment. "China, I couldn't fly."

At breakfast she hardly spoke. All morning she was thoughtful and withdrawn. But when I suggested that we walk down to the Danube via the Basilica at St. Stephen's, cross over to Buda and eat lunch, she seemed delighted. The air was cold and clear. The trees were distinct and photo-graphic in the bright pale February light. We stared out across the New City from the Disney-white battlements of Fishermen's Bastion. "Those bridges!" Isobel said. "Look at them in the sun!" She had bought a new camera for the

trip, a Pentax with a motor-wind and zoom. "I'm going to take a panorama."
She eyed the distorted reflection of the Bastion in the mirror-glass windows of
the Hilton hotel. "Stand over there, China, I want one of you, too. No, there,
you idiot!" Snow began to fall, in flakes the size of five-forint pieces.

"China!"

For the rest of the day—for the rest of the holiday—she was as delighted by
things as ever. We visited the zoo. ("Look! Owls!") We caught a train to Szentendre. We photographed one another beneath the huge winged woman at the
top of the Gellert Hill. We translated the titles of the newsstand paperbacks.

"What does this mean, 'Nagy Secz'?"

"You know very well what it means, Isobel." I looked at my watch.

I said: "It's time to eat."

"Oh no. Must we?" Isobel hated Hungarian food. "China," she would
complain, "why has everything got cream on it?"

But she loved the red and grey buses. She loved the street signs, TOTO
LOTTO, HIRLAP, TRAFIK. She loved Old Buda, redeemed by the snow: white,
clean, properly picturesque.

And she couldn't get enough of the Danube. "Look. China, it's fucking
huge! Isn't it fucking huge?"

I said: "Look at the speed of it."

At midnight on our last day we stood in the exact centre of the Erzsebet
Bridge, gazing north. Szentendre and Danube Bend were out there
somewhere, locked in a Middle European night stretching all the way to
Czechoslovakia. Ice floes like huge lily pads raced toward us in the dark.
You could hear them turning and dipping under one another, piling up
briefly round the huge piers, jostling across the whole vast breadth of the
river as they rushed south. No river is ugly after dark. But the Danube
doesn't care for anyone: without warning the medieval cold came up off
the water and reached onto the bridge for us. It was as if we had seen
something move. We stepped back, straight into the traffic which grinds
all night across the bridge from Buda into Pest.

"China!"

"Be careful!" You have to imagine this—

Two naive and happy middle-class people embracing on a bridge.
Caught between the river and the road, they grin and shiver at one

another, unable to distinguish between identity and geography, love and the need to keep warm.

"Look at the speed of it."

"Oh, China, the Danube!"

Suddenly she turned away. She said: "I'm cold now." She thought for a moment. "I don't want to go on the aeroplane," she said. "They're not the real thing after all."

I took her hands between mine. "It will be okay when you get home," I promised.

But London didn't seem to help. For months I woke in the night to find she was awake too, staring emptily up at the ceiling in the darkness. Unable to comprehend her despair, I would consult my watch and ask her, "Do you want anything?" She would shake her head and advise patiently, "Go to sleep now, love," as if she was being kept awake by a bad period.

I bought the house in Stepney at about that time. It was in a prettily renovated terrace with reproduction Victorian streetlamps. There were wrought-iron security grids over every other front door, and someone had planted the extensive shared gardens at the back with ilex, ornamental rowan, even a fig. Isobel loved it. She decorated the rooms herself, then filled them with the sound of her favourite music—the Blue Aeroplanes' "Yr Own World"; Tom Petty, "Learning to Fly." For our bedroom she bought two big blanket chests and polished them to a deep buttery colour. "Come and look, China! Aren't they beautiful?" Inside, they smelled of new wood. The whole house smelled of new wood for days after we moved in: beeswax, new wood, dried roses.

I said: "I want it to be yours." It had to be in her name anyway, I admitted: for accounting purposes.

"But also in case anything happens."

She laughed. "China, what could happen?"

What happened was that one of my local drivers went sick, and I asked her to deliver something for me.

I said: "It's not far. Just across to Brook Green. Some clinic." I passed her the details. "A Dr. Alexander. You could make it in an hour, there and back."

She stared at me. "You could make it in an hour," she said.

She read the job sheet. "What do they do there?" she asked.

I said irritably: "How would I know? Cosmetic medicine. Fantasy factory stuff. Does it matter?"

She put her arms round me. "China, I was only trying to be interested."

"Never ask them what they do with the stuff," I warned her. "Will you do it?"

She said: "If you kiss me properly."

"How was it?" I asked when she got back.

She laughed. "At first they thought I was a patient!" Running upstairs to change, she called down: "I quite like West London."

Isobel's new body delighted her. But she seemed bemused too, as if it had been given to someone else. How much had Alexander promised her? How much had she expected from the Miami treatments? All I knew was that she had flown out obsessed and returned ill. When she talked, she would talk only about the flight home. "I could see a sunrise over the wing of the airliner, red and gold. I was trying hard to read a book, but I couldn't stop looking out at this cold wintery sunrise above the clouds. It seemed to last for hours." She stared at me as if she had just thought of something. "How could I see a sunrise, China? It was dark when we landed!"

Her dreams had always drawn her away from ordinary things. All that gentle, warm September she was trying to get back.

"Do you like me again?" she would ask shyly.

It was hard for her to say what she meant. Standing in front of the mirror in the morning in the soft grey slanting light from the bedroom window, dazed and sidetracked by her own narcissism, she could only repeat: "Do you like me this way?"

Or at night in bed: "Is it good this way? Is it good? What does it feel like?"

"Isobel—"

In the end it was always easier to let her evade the issue.

"I never stopped liking you," I would lie, and she would reply absently, as if I hadn't spoken:

"Because I want us to like each other again." And then add, presenting her back to the mirror and looking at herself over one shoulder: "I wish I'd had more done. My legs are still too fat."

If part of her was still trying to fly back from Miami and all Miami entailed, much of the rest was in Brook Green with Alexander. As September died into October, and then the first few cold days of November, I found that increasingly hard to bear. She cried in the night but no longer woke me up for comfort. Her gaze would come unfocussed in the afternoons. Unable to be near her while, thinking of him, she pretended to leaf through *Vogue* and *Harper's,* I walked out into the rainy unredeemed Whitechapel streets. Suddenly it was an hour later and I was watching the lights come on in a hardware shop window on Roman Road.

Other times, when it seemed to be going well, I couldn't contain my delight. I got up in the night and thrashed the BMW to Sheffield and back; parked outside the house and slept an hour in the rear seat; crossed the river in the morning to queue for croissants at Ayre's Bakery in Peckham, playing *Empire Burlesque* so loud that if I touched the windscreen gently I could feel it tremble, much as she used to do, beneath my fingertips.

I was trying to get back too.

"I'll take you to the theatre," I said. *"Waiting for Godot.* Do you want to see the fireworks?" I said: "I brought you a present—"

A Monsoon dress. Two small stone birds for the garden; anemones; and a cheap Boots nailbrush shaped like a pig.

"Don't try to get so close, China," she said. "Please."

I said: "I just want to be something to you."

She touched my arm. She said: "China, it's too soon. We're here together, after all: isn't that enough for now?"

She said: "And anyway, how could you ever be anything else?" She said: "I love you."

"But you're not in love with me."

"I told you I couldn't promise you that."

By Christmas we were shouting at one another again, late into the night, every night. I slept on the futon in the spare room. There I dreamed of Isobel and woke sweating.

You have to imagine this—

The Pavilion, quite a good Thai restaurant on Wardour Street. Isobel has just given me the most beautiful jacket, wrapped in birthday paper. She leans across the table. "French Connection, China. Very smart." The waitresses, who believe we are lovers, laugh delightedly as I try it on. But later, when I buy a red rose and offer it to Isobel, she says, "What use would I have for that?" in a voice of such contempt I begin to cry. In the dream, I am fifty years old that day. I wake thinking everything is finished.

Or this—

Budapest. Summer. Rakoczi Street. Each night Isobel waits for me to fall asleep before she leaves the hotel. Once outside, she walks restlessly up and down Rakoczi with all the other women. Beneath her beige linen suit she has on grey silk underwear. She cannot explain what is missing from her life but will later write in a letter: "When sex fails for you—when it ceases to be central in your life—you enter middle age, a zone of the most unclear exits from which some of us never escape." I wake and follow her. All night it feels like dawn. Next morning, in the half-abandoned Jugendstil dining room, a paper doily drifts to the floor like a leaf, while Isobel whispers urgently in someone else's voice:

"It was never what you thought it was."

Appalled by their directness, astonished to find myself so passive, I would struggle awake from dreams like this thinking: "What am I going to do? What am I going to do?" It was always early. It was always cold. Grey light silhouetted a vase of dried flowers on the dresser in front of the uncurtained window, but the room itself was still dark. I would look at my watch, turn over, and go back to sleep. One morning, in the week before Christmas, I got up and packed a bag instead. I made myself some coffee and drank it by the kitchen window, listening to the inbound city traffic build up half a mile away. When I switched the radio on it was playing Billy Joel's "She's Always a Woman." I turned it off quickly, and at 8:00 woke Isobel. She smiled up at me.

"Hello," she said. "I'm sorry about last night."

I said: "I'm sick of it all. I can't do it. I thought I could but I can't."

"China, what is this?"

I said: "You were so fucking sure he'd have you. Three months later it was you crying, not me."

"China—"

"It's time you helped," I said.

I said: "I helped you. And when you bought me things out of gratitude I never once said 'What use would I have for that?'"

She rubbed her hands over her eyes. "China, what are you talking about?"

I shouted: "What a fool you made of yourself!" Then I said: "I only want to be something to you again."

"I won't stand for this," Isobel whispered. "I can't stand this."

I said: "Neither can I. That's why I'm going."

"I still love him, China."

I was on my way to the door. I said: "You can have him then."

"China, I don't want you to go."

"Make up your mind."

"I won't say what you want me to."

"Fuck off, then."

"It's you who's fucking off, China."

It's easy to see now that when we stood on the Erzsebet Bridge the dream had already failed her. But at the time—and for some time afterward—I was still too close to her to see anything. It was still one long arc of delight for me, Stratford through Budapest, all the way to Stepney. So I could only watch puzzledly as she began to do pointless, increasingly spoiled things to herself. She caught the tube to Camden Lock and had her hair cut into the shape of a pigeon's wing. She had her ankles tattooed with feathers. She starved herself, as if her own body were holding her down. She was going to revenge herself on it. She lost twenty pounds in a month. Out went everything she owned, to be replaced by size 9 jeans, little black spandex skirts, expensively tailored jackets which hung from their own ludicrous shoulder pads like washing.

"You don't look like you anymore," I said.

"Good. I always hated myself anyway."

"I loved your bottom the way it was," I said. She laughed. "You'll look haggard if you lose anymore," I said.

"Piss off, China. I won't be a cow just so you can fuck a fat bottom."

I was hurt by that, so I said: "You'll look old. Anyway, I didn't think we fucked. I thought we made love." Something caused me to add, "I'm losing you." And then, even less reasonably: "Or you're losing me."

"China, don't be such a baby."

Then one afternoon in August she walked into the lounge and said, "China, I want to talk to you." The second I heard this, I knew exactly what she was going to say. I looked away from her quickly and down into the book I was pretending to read, but it was too late. There was a kind of soft thud inside me. It was something broken. It was something not there anymore. I felt it. It was a door closing, and I wanted to be safely on the other side of it before she spoke.

"What?" I said.

She looked at me uncertainly. "China, I—"

"What?"

"China, I haven't been happy. Not for some time. You must have realised. I've got a chance at an affair with someone and I want to take it."

I stared at her. "Christ," I said. "Who?"

"Just someone I know."

"Who?" I said. And then, bitterly, "Who do you know, Isobel?" I meant: "Who do you know that isn't me?"

"It's only an affair," she said. And: "You must have realised I wasn't happy."

I said dully: "Who is this fucker?"

"It's David Alexander."

"Who?"

"David Alexander. For God's sake, China, you make everything so hard! At the clinic. David Alexander."

I had no idea who she was talking about. Then I remembered.

"Christ," I said. "He's just some fucking customer."

She went out. I heard the bedroom door slam. I stared at the books on the bookshelves, the pictures on the walls, the carpet dusty gold in the pale afternoon light. I couldn't understand why it was all still there. I couldn't understand anything. Twenty minutes later, when Isobel came back in again carrying a soft leather overnight bag, I was standing in the same place, in the middle of the floor. She said: "Do you know what your trouble is, China?"

"What?" I said.

"People are always just some fucking this or that to you."

"Don't go."

She said: "He's going to help me to fly, China."

"You always said I helped you to fly."

She looked away. "It's not your fault it stopped working," she said. "It's me."

"Christ, you selfish bitch."

"He wants to help me to fly," she repeated dully. And then: "China, I am selfish."

She tried to touch my hand but I moved it away.

"I can't fucking believe this," I said. "You want me to forgive you just because you can admit it?"

"I don't want to lose you, China."

I said: "You already have."

"We don't know what we might want," she said. "Later on. Either of us."

I remembered how we had been at the beginning: Stratford Waterside, whispers and moans, You help me to fly, China. "If you could hear yourself," I said. "If you could just fucking hear yourself, Isobel." She shrugged miserably and picked up her bag. I didn't see her after that. I did have one letter from her. It was sad without being conciliatory, and ended: "You were the most amazing person I ever knew, China, and the fastest driver."

I tore it up. "Were!" I said. "Fucking were!"

By that time she had moved in with him, somewhere along the Network South East line from Waterloo: Chiswick, Kew, one of those old-fashioned suburbs on a bladder of land inflated into the picturesque curve of the river, with genteel deteriorating houseboats, an arts centre, and a wine bar on every corner. West London is full of places like that—"shabby," "comfortable," until you smell the money. Isobel kept the Stepney house. I would visit it once a month to collect my things, cry in the lounge, and take away some single pointless item—a compact disc I had bought her, a picture she had bought me. Every time I went back, the bedroom, with its wooden chests and paper birds, seemed to have filled up further with dust. Despite that, I could never quite tell if anything had changed. Had they been in there, the two of them? I stayed in the doorway, so as not to know. I had sold Rose Services and was living out in Tottenham, drinking Michelob beer and watching Channel 4 movies while I waited for my capital to run out. Some movies I liked better than others. I cried all the way through *Alice in the Cities*. I wasn't sure why. But I knew why I was cheering Anthony Hopkins as *The Good Father*.

"You were the most amazing person I ever knew, China, and the fastest driver. I'll always remember you."

What did I care? Two days after I got the letter I drove over to Queens-borough Road at about seven in the evening. I had just bought the BMW. I parked it at the kerb outside Alexander's clinic, which was in a large postmodern block not far down from Hammersmith Gyratory. Some light rain was falling. I sat there watching the front entrance. After about twenty minutes Alexander's receptionist came out, put her umbrella up, and went off toward the tube station. A bit later Alexander himself appeared at the security gate. I was disappointed by him.

He turned out to be a tall thin man, middle-aged, grey-haired, dressed in a light wool suit. He looked less like a doctor than a poet. He had that kind of fragile elegance some people maintain on the edge of panic, the energy of tensions unresolved, glassy, never very far from the surface. He would always seem worried. He looked along the street toward Shepherd's Bush, then down at his watch.

I opened the nearside passenger window. "David Alexander?" I called. I called: "Waiting for someone?" He bent down puzzledly and looked into the BMW. "Need a lift?" I offered.

"Do I know you?" he asked.

I thought: Say the wrong thing, you fucker. You're that close. I said: "Not exactly."

"Then—"

"Forget it."

He stood back from the car suddenly, and I drove off.

Christmas. Central London. Traffic locked solid every late afternoon. Light in the shop windows in the rain. Light in the puddles. Light splashing up round your feet. I couldn't keep still. Once I'd walked away from Isobel, I couldn't stop walking. Everywhere I went, "She's Always a Woman" was on the radio. Harrods, Habitat, Hamleys: Billy Joel drove me out onto the wet pavement with another armful of children's toys. I even wrapped some of them—a wooden penguin with rubber feet, two packs of cards, a miniature jigsaw puzzle in the shape of her name. Every time I saw something I liked, it went home with me.

"I bought you a present," I imagined myself saying, "this fucking little spider that really jumps—look!"

Quite suddenly I was exhausted. Christmas Day I spent with the things I'd bought. Boxing Day, and the day after that, I lay in a chair staring at the television. Between shows I picked up the phone and put it down again, picked it up and put it down. I was going to call Isobel, then I wasn't. I was going to call her, but I closed the connection carefully every time the phone began to ring at her end. Then I decided to go back to Stepney for my clothes.

Imagine this—

Two A.M. The house was quiet.

Or this—

I stood on the pavement. When I looked in through the uncurtained ground-floor window I could see the little display of lights on the front of Isobel's CD player.

Or this—

For a moment my key didn't seem to fit the door. Imagine this—

Late at night you enter a house in which you've been as happy as anywhere in your life: probably happier. You go into the front room, where streetlight falls unevenly across the rugs, the furniture, the mantelpiece and mirrors. On the sofa are strewn a dozen colourful, expensive shirts, blue and red and gold like macaws and money. Two or three of them have been slipped out of their cellophane, carefully refolded and partly wrapped in Christmas paper. "Dear China—" say the tags. "Dearest China." There are signs of a struggle but not necessarily with someone else. A curious stale smell fills the room, and a chair has been knocked over. It's really too dark to see.

Switch on the lights. Glasses and bottles. Food trodden into the best kilim. Half-empty plates, two days old.

"Isobel? Isobel!"

The bathroom was damp with condensation, the bath itself full of cold water smelling strongly of rose oil. Wet towels were underfoot, there and in the draughty bedroom, where the light was already on and Isobel's pink velvet curtains, half-drawn, let a faint yellow triangle of light into the garden below. The lower sash was open. When I pulled it down, a cat looked up from the empty flower bed: ran off. I shivered. Isobel had pulled all her favourite underclothes out onto the floor and trodden mascara into them. She had written in lipstick on the dressing table mirror, in perfect mirror writing: "Leave me alone."

I found her in one of the big blanket boxes.

When I opened the lid a strange smell—beeswax, dried roses, vomit, whiskey—filled the room. In there with her she had an empty bottle of Jameson: an old safety razor of mine and two or three blades. She had slit her wrists. But first she had tried to shave all the downy, half-grown feathers from her upper arms and breasts. When I reached into the box they whirled up round us both, soft blue and grey, the palest rose-pink. Miami! In some confused attempt to placate me, she had tried to get out of the dream the way you get out of a coat.

She was still alive.

"China," she said. Sleepily, she held her arms up to me. She whispered: "China."

Alexander had made her look like a bird. But underneath the cosmetic trick she was still Isobel Avens. Whatever he had promised her, she could never have flown. I picked her up and carried her carefully down the stairs. Then I was crossing the pavement toward the BMW, throwing the nearside front door open and trying to get her into the passenger seat. Her arms and legs were everywhere, pivoting loose and awkward from the hips and elbows. "Christ, Isobel, you'll have to help!" I didn't panic until then.

"China," whispered Isobel. Blood ran into my shirt where she had put her arms round my neck. I slammed the door. "China."

"What, love? What?"

"China." She could talk but she couldn't hear.

"Hold on," I said. I switched on the radio. Some station I didn't know was playing the first few bars of a Joe Satriani track, "Always with You, Always with Me." I felt as if I was outside myself. I thought: "Now's the time to drive, China, you fucker." The BMW seemed to fishtail out of the parking space of its own accord, into the empty arcade game of Whitechapel. The city loomed up then fell back from us at odd angles, as if it had achieved the topological values of a Vorticist painting. I could hear the engine distantly, making a curious harsh overdriven whine as I held the revs up against the red line. Revs and brakes, revs and brakes: if you want to go fast in the city you hold it all the time between the engine and the brakes. Taxis, hoardings, white faces of pedestrians on traffic islands splashed with halogen pink, rushed up and were snatched away.

"Isobel?"

I had too much to do to look directly at her. I kept catching glimpses of her in weird, neon shop-light from Wallis or Next or What She Wants, lolling against the seat belt with her mouth half open. She knew how bad she was. She kept trying to smile across at me. Then she would drift off, or cornering forces would roll her head to one side as if she had no control of the muscles in her neck and she would end up staring and smiling out of the side window whispering: "China. China China China."

"Isobel."

She passed out again and didn't wake up.

"Shit, Isobel," I said.

We were on Hammersmith Gyratory, deep in the shadow of the flyover. It was twenty minutes since I had found her. We were nearly there. I could almost see the clinic.

I said: "Shit, Isobel, I've lost it."

The piers of the flyover loomed above us, stained grey concrete plastered with anarchist graffiti and torn posters. Free and ballistic, the car waltzed sideways toward them, glad to be out of China Rose's hands at last.

"Fuck," I said. "Fuck fuck fuck."

We touched the kerb, tripped over our own feet, and began a long slow roll, like an airliner banking to starboard. We hit a postbox. The BMW jumped in a startled way and righted itself. Its offside rear suspension had collapsed. Uncomfortable with the new layout, still trying to get away from me, it spun twice and banged itself repeatedly into the opposite kerb with a sound exactly like some housewife's Metro running over the cat's-eyes on a cold Friday morning. Something snapped the window post on that side, and broken glass blew in all over Isobel Avens's peaceful face. She opened her mouth. Thin vomit came out, the colour of tea: but I don't think she was conscious. Hammersmith Broadway, ninety-five miles an hour. I dropped a gear, picked the car up between steering and accelerator, shot out into Queensborough Road on the wrong side of the road. The boot lid popped open and fell off. It was dragged along behind us for a moment, then it went backward quickly and disappeared.

"China."

Draped across my arms, Isobel was nothing but a lot of bones and heat. I carried her up the steps to Alexander's building and pressed for entry. The entryphone crackled but no one spoke. "Hello?" I said. After a moment the locks went back.

Look into the atrium of a West London building at night and everything is the same as it is in the day. Only the reception staff are missing, and that makes less difference than you would think. The contract furniture keeps working. The PX keeps working. The fax comes alive suddenly as you watch, with a query from Zurich, Singapore, LA. The air conditioning keeps on working. Someone has watered the plants, and they keep working too, making chlorophyll from the overhead lights. Paper curls out of the fax and stops. You can watch for as long as you like: nothing else will happen and no one will come. The air will be cool and warm at the same time, and you will be able to see your own reflection, very faintly in the treated glass.

"China."

Upstairs it was a floor of open-plan offices—health finance—and then a floor of consulting rooms. Up here the lights were off, and you could no longer hear the light traffic on Queensborough Road. It was two fifty in the morning. I got into the consulting rooms and then Alexander's office, and walked up and down with Isobel in my arms, calling:

"Alexander?" No one came. "Alexander?" Someone had let us in. "Alexander!"

Among the stuff on his desk was a brochure for the clinic. ". . . modern 'magic wand,'" I read. "Brand-new proteins." I swept everything off onto the floor and tried to make Isobel comfortable by folding my coat under her head.

"I'm sorry," she said quietly, but not to me. It was part of some conversation I couldn't hear. She kept rolling onto her side and retching over the edge of the desk, then laughing. I had picked up the phone and was working on an outside line when Alexander came in from the corridor. He had lost weight. He looked vague and empty, as if we had woken him out of a deep sleep. You can tear people like him apart like a piece of paper, but it doesn't change anything.

"Press nine," he advised me. "Then call an ambulance." He glanced down at Isobel. He said: "It would have been better to take her straight to a hospital."

I put the phone down. "I fucked up a perfectly good car to get here," I said.

He kept looking puzzledly at me and then out of the window at the BMW, half up on the pavement with smoke coming out of it.

I said: "That's a Hartge H27-24."

I said: "I could have afforded something in better taste, but I just haven't got any."

"I know you," he said. "You've done work for me."

I stared at him. He was right.

I had been moving things about for him since the old Astra van days; since before Stratford. And if I was just a contract to him, he was just some writing on a job sheet to me. He was the price of a Hartge BMW with racing suspension and 17-inch wheels.

"But you did this," I reminded him.

I got him by the back of the neck and made him look closely at Isobel. Then I pushed him against the wall and stood away from him. I told him evenly: "I'm fucking glad I didn't kill you when I wanted to." I said: "Put her back together."

He lifted his hands. "I can't," he said.

"Put her back together."

"This is only an office," he said. "She would have to go to Miami."

I pointed to the telephone. I said: "Arrange it. Get her there." He examined her briefly.

"She was dying anyway," he said. "The immune system work alone would have killed her. We did far more than we would normally do on a client. Most of it was illegal. It would be illegal to do most of it to a laboratory rat. Didn't she tell you that?"

I said: "Get her there and put her back together again."

"I can make her human again," he offered. "I can cure her."

I said: "She didn't fucking want to be human."

"I know," he said.

He looked down at his desk; his hands. He whispered: "'Help me to fly. Help me to fly!'"

"Fuck off," I said.

"I loved her too, you know. But I couldn't make her understand that she could never have what she wanted. In the end she was just too demanding: effectively, she asked us to kill her."

I didn't want to know why he had let me have her back. I didn't want to compare inadequacies with him. I said: "I don't want to hear this."

He shrugged. "She'll die if we try it again," he said emptily. "You've got no idea how these things work."

"Put her back together."

You tell me what else I could have said.

Here at the Alexander Clinic, we use the modern "magic wand" of molecular biology to insert avian chromosomes into human skin cells. Nurtured in the clinic's vats, the follicles of this new skin produce feathers instead of hair. It grafts beautifully. Brand-new proteins speed acceptance. But in case of difficulties, we remake the immune system: aim it at infections of opportunity; fire it like a laser.

Our client chooses any kind of feather, from pinion to down, in any combination. She is as free to look at the sparrow as the bower bird or macaw. Feathers of any size or colour! But the real triumph is elsewhere—

Designer hormones trigger the "brown fat" mechanism. Our client becomes as light and as hot to the touch as a female hawk. Then metabolically induced calcium shortages hollow the bones. She can be handled only with great care. And the dreams of flight! Engineered endorphins released during sexual arousal simulate the sidesweep, swoop, and mad fall of mating flight, the frantically beating heart, long sight. Sometimes the touch of her own feathers will be enough.

I lived in a hotel on the beach while it was done. Miami! TV prophecy, humidity like a wet sheet, an airport where they won't rent you a baggage trolley. You wouldn't think this listening to Bob Seger. Unless you are constantly approaching it from the sea, Miami is less a dream—less even a nightmare—than a place. All I remember is what British people always remember about Florida: the light in the afternoon storm, the extraordinary size and perfection of the food in the supermarkets. I never went near the clinic, though I telephoned Alexander's team every morning and evening. I was too scared. One day they were optimistic, the next they weren't. In the end I knew they had got involved again; they were excited by the possibilities. She was going to have what she wanted. They were going to do the best they could for her, if only because of the technical challenge.

She slipped in and out of the world until the next spring. But she didn't die, and in the end I was able to bring her home to the blackened, gentle East End in May, driving all the way from Heathrow down the inside lane of the motorway, as slowly and carefully as I knew how in my new off-the-peg 850i. I had adjusted the driving mirror so I could look into the back of the car. Isobel lay awkwardly across one corner of the rear seat. Her hands and face seemed tiny. In the soft wet English light, their adjusted bone structures looked more rather than less human. Lapped in her singular successes and failures, the sum of her life to that point, she was more rested than I had ever seen her.

About a mile away from the house, outside Whitechapel tube station, I let the car drift up to the kerb and stop. I switched the engine off and got out of the driving seat.

"It isn't far from here," I said. I put the keys in her hand. "I know you're tired," I said, "but I want you to drive yourself the rest of the way."

She said: "China, don't go. Get back in the car."

"It's not far from here," I said.

"China, please don't go."

"Drive yourself from now on."

If you're so clever, you tell me what else I could have done. All that time in Miami she had never let go, never once vacated the dream. The moment she closed her eyes, feathers were floating down past them. She knew what she wanted. Don't mistake me: I wanted her to have it. But imagining myself stretched out next to her on the bed night after night, I could hear the sound those feathers made, and I knew I would never sleep again for the touch of them on my face.

A Little Bird Told Me

PAT CADIGAN

Everybody in the flat is dead. Even the *plants* are dead. Welcome to Croydon.

I'm a big girl; this is nothing I haven't already seen like a thousand times, except for the plants—I mean, *jeez*. I want to turn around and go straight back to central London. Instead, I take the iPad out of my shoulder bag and make a walk-through video before I photograph individual faces. Getting full-face photos can be tricky because I'm not supposed to touch them. But if there's no other way, I have these things like oven mitts so I won't mark them or vice versa. Eight people in the room, six on the sofa or in chairs, two on the floor. One of the latter, man about forty, forty-five, trickle of blood drying on his upper lip, is staring right at me. I hate that. I leave him for last.

The iPad doesn't lessen his stare. Changing the angle a little doesn't help, either—he's like one of those creepy portraits where the eyes seem to follow you around the room. I try looking at a point past the edge of the iPad but his gaze keeps pulling at mine. This is partly because the soul is still in the body and partly because, like everyone else here, he's a cheater and all cheaters are tenacious bastards. This guy, however, seems to be especially bad and I think I know why.

Recognition software confirms it: Staring Guy was a double dipper. You don't find a lot of people who can cheat Death twice, but they aren't as rare as they used to be. This is the third one I've had in less than a year. Feh. Damfool didn't have a clue how much trouble he caused. Cheaters never do. They've got this idea they're badass rebels, striking a blow against the one thing no one's supposed to be able to beat. Like, Death be not proud, I kicked your ass.

Only they're wrong. Cheating isn't kicking ass and it isn't winning. It's more like dine-and-dash. I step over the double dipper and head down a short hallway, stopping at the first door on the left. It's the bathroom; occupied. Damn.

If people knew how often the average mortal dies while on the toilet, they'd all probably hold it till they exploded. I'm not grossed out—it ain't plutonium, just waste. What gets me is the total loss of dignity. Even when it's a cheater, it bothers me.

I do my job—video, then head-shot. Recog software IDs her as the owner of the flat and the facilitator for this little group of cheaters. She showed them how to slip by the Big One. Not for free, of course; judging by the size of the flat and the decor, she was doing better than okay and still managed to elude Death for an exceptionally long time, longer even than the double dipper.

Still, I feel sorry for her. I mean, isn't it enough she's freakin' *dead*? Why does she have to be found on the floor in her own waste with her pants down—to teach her a lesson? Like what—"Cheaters never prosper"? "Nobody lives forever"? "When you gotta go, you're *gonna* go"? Kinda late for that.

Additional notations are coming up on her photo. Before Death caught up with her, nothing was going the way she wanted despite her being so sure that all she needed was more time and she'd get everything right. That's the story of every cheater's stolen life. It never occurs to any of them, maybe things don't go right because they're cheating. She probably thought all she was doing was helping people live longer and even if she charged for it, that was a good deed and not a serious violation of the natural order.

Well, she didn't know better, but ignorance of the law is no excuse—any law, any place, any time. But I linger for a few seconds and think good thoughts over her while the soul is still in the body.

Back in the hallway, I'm just closing the door behind me when I hear a noise and I freeze. I shouldn't be hearing *anything*. The place is under wraps, complete insulation—nothing in, nothing out, other than me, not even sound waves. The movers don't come for the bodies till after I leave.

I don't know how long I stay there, listening to nothing. I mean, I really don't; time is all messed up in a place under wraps. It still passes, but it runs very slowly and not at the same rate from one moment to the next. Maybe, I think (hope), it was just some noise I made that got caught in one of those temporal inconsistencies.

Then I hear it again. It's a whispery whirring, the kind of sound that should actually be too soft to hear. I force myself to head down the hall toward an open door at the end. Maybe I'm imagining it, I think, but I know I'm not. I never imagine anything.

When I reach the doorway, I freeze again, unable to move. Whatever's still alive in there, I'm no match for. What if I can't even see it? I'm remembering that myth about the native people in North America unable to see Christopher Columbus's ships because they'd never encountered anything liked them before. It's bullshit—if it's visible and you have sight, you'll see it. I'm just scared to look.

I actually have to grab either side of the doorjamb and pull myself into the room. A weird little scratchy voice says, "What kept you?" and I jump right out of my skin.

Fortunately, safeguards pull me back in before my skin knows I'm gone. My eyes go every which way before they focus on a brightly coloured something moving around on top of the chest of drawers in the far corner.

A parrot. A freakin' *parrot*. It's a little smaller than a football, mostly blue and yellow with a small patch of green on top of its head; around its eyes are circles of white with thin black stripes. I gape at it while it picks a seed out of a silver bowl and cracks it with its big black beak. Jeez, who lets a parrot walk around on their furniture scratching it up with its claws?

Finally, I find my voice: "But even the freakin' *plants* are dead."

"I know, right? So excessive." The parrot helps itself to another seed. "Death is such an asshole."

No way I'm taking *that* bait. "What are you doing here? How are you here at all? Answer that first."

"Isn't it obvious?" says the parrot. "I'm a bird."

I wait for more but that's it. "And?" I prod.

The parrot turns its head to look at me sideways. "Don't you know *anything* about birds?"

"Not much about parrots. Except you guys talk a lot."

"Only when 'a lot' is appropriate, actually. Tsk, they really don't teach the service underclass anything these days, do they?" The parrot stretches upward, flapping its wings. "Never mind. Give Death a message from us."

"Who's 'us'?"

"Not your concern. Just tell that asshole mortality isn't what it used to be."

"Shouldn't I be hearing this from a raven?" I say. "Like, the 'never more' thing?"

"One more time, with feeling: Mor*tal*ity! *Isn't*! What it used to *be*! Got that?" Before I can tell it I don't ever come into contact with Death personally on the job or otherwise, the parrot turns and flies straight at the nearest window. It's closed, but the bird passes through the glass like it isn't there.

I run over to the window, open it, and lean out as far as I can. All I see are a few wood pigeons gliding in big, idle arcs above the street as if they're too bored to flap their wings.

As I pull my head back inside, I get a very bad feeling. I mean, *really* bad, the worst thing I've ever felt. *Maybe this time, I really* am *imagining it*, I think. Then I realise I said it out loud. "Or maybe I'm sick," I add, turning to look at the bureau.

The silver bowl is gone, seeds and all. Son of a bitch; now I have to go back to the living room to find out what I wish I didn't already know.

The bodies have begun to go bad, like they've never been anything but dead, soul-less meat. Staring Guy isn't staring any more; his eyes are clouded over and grey. The cheaters managed to cheat Death one more time. But . . . with a *parrot*?

Everybody has to be photographed again, and let me tell you, it's far more unpleasant with the souls gone, especially her in the bathroom. I send the photos to my supervisor and then hide out in the kitchen to wait for the movers because I'm not sure it's safe to leave. The concealment was formulated to include souls still present; now the only soul here is my own. If I leave, the encryption may not hold. I *don't* want to stay—the bodies are decomposing at an accelerated rate, which happens with cheaters—but it's the only thing I can think of that can't possibly make things worse.

When the movers come, my supervisor Madame Quill is with them. The movers are supposed to relocate the bodies to where they were originally supposed to die, or as close as possible. I doubt this crew's ever handled empties before. They're all suited up head to foot so only their eyes show, but I can tell all of them are feeling green around the gills. At least they don't have to move the one in the bathroom; she died right where she was supposed to.

While they're mopping up the remains and trying not to yack, Madame gives the bedroom a thorough inspection. After palpating the windows, tapping the walls, and stomping around the floor, she strips the bed, shaking out every sheet and blanket. Then she guts the mattress with a nasty-looking switchblade. I didn't know she had one but I'm not surprised either.

Madame is quite a character and not the lovable eccentric kind. You could mistake her for the kind of sweet little old lady who used to teach etiquette at an old-time finishing school but that could turn out to be your worst mistake if not your last. She's got more in common with a trained assassin, sans the whimsy. Even when she doesn't scare the shit out of me, she scares the shit out of me.

For a while, she surveys the mess she made. Then she turns to me and says, very gravely, "We should have been prepared. Birds are highly motivated little creatures. They don't want to die. What's more, they don't want to die *out*. Of course, that's a priority with all species, but it's more muted in humans; they think in terms of self-preservation rather than species preservation." She's staring at me so pointedly that I wonder what she's really looking at. But I do the safe thing and nod to show I'm paying attention. "Who would have imagined the bull-goose predator—no pun intended— would even consider an alliance with a class that includes species it *eats*?"

This time I don't so much nod as dip my head and shrug a little, like, *Yeah, people—who knows what they'll do?*

"Still, it does make sense," she continues. "Humans and birds have much to offer each other. Humans have the intellect and longer life span, birds have the freedom of flight, the wider range of vision, and a sense for magnetic fields. I guess opposable thumbs aren't everything."

Madame grabs my shoulders and, holding me at arm's length, gives me an intense once-over. Actually it's a thrice-over, like she's searching me with X-ray vision. Uncomfortable in excelsis deo—I don't know whether to make eye contact or squeeze my eyes shut and try to pass out till it's over. It could be two minutes or two lifetimes before she lets go. "You can do this," she says.

"I can do what?" I say before I can think better of it.

"There are feral parrots all over London," she says.

It's not just the non sequitur that throws me; something's happened to her face. It looks so weird. I've never seen it like that before—oh shit. She's *smiling*.

I am *so* doomed.

On the train back to central London, I look at the instructions Madame put on the iPad. They're embedded in an ebook called *Twitching: The Observant Lifestyle*, which I have to keep reading to find them. So far, I have learned 1) twitching is a kind of birdwatching where people concentrate more on just listing the birds they see rather than learning anything substantial about them, and 2) Madame threw me into the deep end. Well, I have only myself to blame.

Listen, if you ever start screwing around with necromancy and someone just happens to mention that it's maybe not the best idea you ever had, take it seriously and stop. Most of what passes for any kind of sorcery in the material world is completely harmless, rituals meant to blow off a little steam and dissipate the urge to act out in a more self-destructive way. That's *most*—not *all*. Every so often, some clueless civilian has the bad luck to hit on a live one and that never, ever, *ever* ends well. Trust me, I'm the voice of experience here.

Violating natural law in the material world is the Crime; do it and you'll find yourself answering to an authority called the Continuous Realm of All Things. Claiming you didn't know won't cut it, and there's no first offence thing or mitigating circumstances or pleading insanity because there's no trial. You did it, you're guilty, the end. And don't bother asking why live magicks are just lying around in the open where mere mortals can trip over them. You'll only get a long lecture about free will. I mean, a real lecture; you're stuck to a hard seat in an auditorium with hundreds of other people, most of whom seem to be grad students in philosophy for two hours. The q-and-a at the end, which you also have to stay for, goes almost that long and you're expected to take notes—lots of notes. If you don't, you have to sit through the whole thing again. And you'll still have to serve your sentence, which is for life, possibly longer, depending.

The Continuous Realm of All Things sentenced me to work as a census-taker of the recently deceased, both regular and cheaters, although lately I've had mostly cheaters. To the rest of the (natural) law-abiding world, I look like a meter-reader or a survey-taker or a door-to-door salesperson—if they even notice me, that is. The normal, un-enhanced, non-magical human gaze slides around me like oil in water and I blow past them like air. It's impossible to draw attention to myself. If I try, everything just gets very quiet and far away, like I'm straitjacketed in a soundproof room, staring down the wrong end of of a telescope

Anyway, I figured I'd be like a sort of coroner-cum-secretary, without any heavy lifting. I'd go to people who had just died, match faces with names, and check them off. Yep, they're dead all right; next case. I didn't know much about mortality.

I thought I did. I'd spent plenty of time with my mother when she'd been in hospice care. At the very end, she seemed to float away like a little boat on a receding tide. I talked to her for a good half hour after the nurses said she was gone; I had this very strong feeling that her little boat hadn't quite drifted completely away over the horizon.

Turns out I could have talked to her for another couple of days. Removing a soul from a body is done exclusively by Reapers, and that doesn't happen for at least twenty-four hours. The average time is somewhere between thirty-six and forty-eight hours, although it can be longer, even as much as a full week. It's got to do with the soul needing time to adjust and willingly accept release from the body, which makes reaping easier for all concerned. I can see how it might take a day for a soul to come to grips with such a drastic change. But leaving a soul in dead flesh longer than that seems pretty callous. And a week—! That's inexcusable; sadistic, even. And, as I've been told numerous times, not my concern.

When I'm not on the job, I wait for Madame to call me. I wait at bus stops, train stations, hospitals, clinics, government offices—anywhere there's space enough for me to blend in, most often with uncomfortable seating, crappy fluorescent lighting, and poor ventilation. Don't ask me what I do at night; I haven't seen a night since this started. The closest I get is dusk, and only now and then. Mostly one day slides into another. If I sleep, I don't know about it.

I don't know if my punishment is standard, or more severe than usual, or less. Like, maybe they've got someone on permanent night shift. I don't even know how many others are doing this kind of time, but I do have a theory about Reapers; I've never met any, but based on what I know from my own experience, it's not so farfetched to think Reapers are doing time for the Crime. Once I made the mistake of sharing this idea with Madame; only once. I ended up back in the auditorium listening to an incredibly esoteric lecture about ethics. I don't know why ethics. Maybe free will was full.

Back when I lived a regular material-world life, I would have thought all this, what I see, what I do, was magical in every sense of the word—astonishing, breathtaking, wondrous.

Now, I know what it really is: a lot of work. And it never ends.

When I get to King's Cross in London, *Twitching: The Observant Lifestyle* opens to a new chapter containing directions to something called the Macmillan Cancer Centre. That seems a little on-the-nose, I think. I find my way to the Underground. Easy journey, only two stops. For a moment, I'm seriously tempted to make a quick side-trip to Track 9 and ¾, just so I can say I've seen Harry Potter's luggage trolley sticking out of the wall. The only person I could ever say it to is myself but so what? It would just take a few minutes, what have I got to lose?

It occurs to me I was thinking something similar when I got into trouble. This is followed by the realisation that no, I certainly *don't* know what I've got to lose and the last thing I want to do is find out. Maybe on the way back.

While I'm on the tube, *Twitching* gives me basic information about the Macmillan Centre—cancer patients go there for chemotherapy and tests, and there's all kinds of support and information. There's also a lovely roof garden, which is where I'm supposed to go. I wonder if the seating will be uncomfortable—outdoor furniture leaves a lot to be desired. On the other hand, without crappy fluorescent lighting and poor ventilation it's probably as close to paradise as I can hope for.

No one gives me a glance when I walk in, not even the greeters, a couple of older guys stationed near the entrance to give people directions or help them check in. I take a minute to survey the lobby. From the ground floor, you can look straight up five stories and see the tiny little feet of people standing on the translucent floor of the roof garden. They're like cartoon footprints. Something about the sight sort of tickles me; I could stand there all day watching people's feet wander around.

The iPad chimes softly. I find a place to sit and check out the latest update to the observant lifestyle:

> *In the distant past, birds carried the souls of the dead to the afterlife. Unfortunately people caught on at some point, either because they somehow figured it out or (more likely) some self-important popinjay couldn't keep a secret. Residents of the natural world must by law know only natural-world phenomena; therefore new protocols had to be established. There have been many, many adjustments and refinements over the centuries; some were major improvements, some made little difference, and others were total snafus.*

I have to take a moment to appreciate that Madame Quill or someone like her used the word *snafu*.

> *Our current system has been in place in more or less the same form for longer than any other. It has been the cleanest, safest, and most organised method of postmortem processing. The average rate for errors, anomalies, and malfunctions combined comes to only 0.003% per calendar decade.*

Jeez, I think, who let the bean counters into heaven? (I *know* it's not really heaven—not Heaven-heaven—and this proves it. 0.003%; Jesus wept.) Then I reread the first part. "Clean"? What does *that* mean? "Safe" is an easy one—safe from humans. But make that *was* safe, past tense.

> *After careful study and consideration, it has been deter-*
> *mined the most likely explanation for recent episodes of birds*
> *taking custody of souls postmortem—*

Episodes, plural? This is news to me. Seriously, nobody tells me anything.

> *—is that a bargain has been struck between birds and*
> *humans. It seems unlikely that birds would initiate such*
> *a thing given their position with respect to humans in the*
> *food chain. It also seems unlikely that this could be a single*
> *overall bargain, as the resources required for such a thing*
> *are far beyond a single unit, even a unit containing thou-*
> *sands of members.*
> *After careful review of the situation, it has been decided*
> *there must be an investigation, conducted by agents indig-*
> *enous to the natural world but bound in service to the Con-*
> *tinuous Realm of All Things.*

So now I'm an agent. Am I working alone? I sneak a brief look around and spot a few people engrossed in something on their phones but that's nothing out of the ordinary. Still, I wonder if they're learning about the observant lifestyle or just checking email.

The next page comes up blank on the iPad screen. A faint circular animation twirls for a couple of seconds before the words fade in. Is Madame dictating this directly?

> *There's a high probability of people in this facility being*
> *favourably disposed towards making a deal: overt bargaining*
> *is associated with their particular physical pathology. The*

roof garden is accessible to birds. Remain alert and aware to the possibility of hearing, or overhearing, something pertinent. Chance always favours the prepared mind.

I feel sleazy before I even get on the elevator. So much for "clean."

For the next three days, I hang around the roof garden, moving casually from one seat to another. They aren't that uncomfortable, not until after the second day, anyway. People come and go, a lot of them dragging IV poles with long bags dangling above them, liquid dripping through long plastic tubing into a cannula or an unwieldy-looking plastic port stuck in a place that must make getting dressed awkward. Most of them wear hats or scarves; some leave their bald heads bare. Many have a friend or relative with them; some come back later by themselves, obviously wanting to be alone. Almost all of them have phones they check at least briefly, although most spend a fair amount of time engrossed in whatever is on the screen. None of them notice me, of course, even when I'm looking over their shoulders to see what's so fascinating. Usually it's a cat video or a game, nothing that suggests they're in the process of making a deal of any sort.

After a while, I can't help feeling like all I'm doing is killing time with busy work, hoping for a result while running the clock out to zero, either mine in particular or everyone's in general. I've been through the entire text of *Twitching* so many times that I can recite most of it from memory. (The term "twitcher" comes from the original guy who collected bird sightings, because he was twitchy; his name wasn't Twitcher or anything like it. You're welcome.) Of course, no other programs on the iPad will open because I can't get distracted. Madame Quill and her ilk want me alert, with a prepared mind that chance will favour. I'm pretty sure they're capable of embedding messages in any text or game or even video, but they won't. It's probably part of my punishment, just like the monotony of hanging around a roof garden on the off-chance that a bird looking to do some business might show up—excuse me, a *talking* bird.

If there really are feral parrots all over London, I think, they'll be in places with lots of trees, like parks or Kew Gardens. They'll be roosting in some big leafy oak, having a good laugh at the hapless drone stuck in a cancer clinic roof-garden. If jays have taught them to chuckle, they'll really sound snide.

Halfway through the third day, a green bird swoops down, circles the garden, then lands on the bench beside me. It stares at me for a couple of seconds before it hops onto my thigh, digging its claws in.

I yelp and swat at it reflexively, almost dropping the iPad. The bird launches itself out of the way, then lands on me again, this time without the claw action. It's pretty, like a feathered jewel, mostly bright green with a blue-grey head, orange beak, and pale yellow-green belly. On either wing is a patch of reddish brown that makes me think of military rank on epaulets.

"Sorry." I hold the iPad against my front to hide what's on the screen. Then I wonder if it can see a tablet screen at all. Its eyes are on either side of its head—not an arrangement for 3-D binocular vision. "That really hurt."

The bird looks at me, tilting its head from one side to the other. How *does* it see? I wonder. It's really bothering me now.

"So, what's the story—is my hanging around all day putting a crimp in business?"

The bird continues to look at me silently. There's nothing in its beady little eyes that indicates it understands what I'm saying. Maybe it doesn't speak English. If it speaks at all—maybe it doesn't. It's smaller than the bird in the Croydon flat, not so much parrot as a parakeet. Do parakeets talk? I have no idea.

"I'm wasting my breath, aren't I?" I say. "You are as you were made to be, a model denizen of the natural world. You'd never dream of flouting the protocols of human mortality. Would you?"

The bird cocks its head to one side. "That depends," it says in a scratchy little voice, "on whether you can make it worth my while. Which I doubt you can."

"Then you know who I am," I say, doing my best not to look surprised. I really thought it was just a bird.

"Well, not exactly who. But definitely what. And why you're here."

"And I know what you're here after." I've been waiting forever to say that.

"Good one," says the bird. "What are you going to do about it?"

"That's not up to me."

"Of course it isn't." Its voice is less scratchy now, more human-sounding. "What do your bosses in the Concomitant Rendition of All Tessitura—or whatever they're calling it now—think they can do about it?"

I get a weird sensation, like my brain went over a speed bump and everything in it was knocked all over the place. The concomitant *what*? Was that even the word? This is something I wasn't supposed to hear, I realise suddenly. Not because it's forbidden but because—because—

The only thing that comes to me is the image of tiny footprints the translucent roof-garden floor as seen from five stories below; bewildering. I surreptitiously turn on the iPad's record function—I hope it's surreptitious, anyway. The bird's face gives nothing away. I don't play poker, but if I did, I'd never play with a bird.

"You know," I say casually, shifting the iPad so the microphone is closer to the bird, "I ran into someone not too unlike yourself when I was on a job recently. Different colour scheme but same general idea. Got any friends in Croydon? Maybe even a relative, like a cousin?"

The movement the bird makes with its wings is an unmistakable shrug. "We get around. Can you narrow it down some more?"

"Sure," I say. "Bunch of cheaters, including a double-dipper, hiding out in a flat. Ringleader was quite the long-timer. Death was so pissed off the plants get caught in the blast."

"Oh, *that* Croydon." The bird makes a merry chirping noise and fluffs itself up. "They're all long gone, either migrating or getting ready to. Humans go all wackadoo over flight. You don't even have to say 'wings' and they're lining up for take-off."

"Not necessarily. I don't think most people would line up to be pigeons, aka rats with wings. Or carrion-eaters like vultures."

"Think again. There's a very, very long list of things people would rather be other than deceased, and neither 'pigeon' nor 'vulture' are anywhere near the bottom."

"Easy for you to say. You're not either—" I cut off as something occurs to me. "Okay, just between you, me, and the roof garden, who were you before you became a feathered biped?"

The bird stretches up tall and kind of rears back as it peers at me. I think I'm starting to learn some bird body language. "What would make you ask *that*?" it says, head tilting from one side to the other while I wish it weren't so damned cute.

"You sounded so certain, I thought you might be speaking from experience."

"Not human experience. I'm a professional like yourself, in a similar area. But without all the paperwork you're stuck with."

"There's no actual paper—"

"Files and forms are the sine qua non of clerical drudgery," the bird tells me loftily. "That's paperwork in any medium."

I do my best to keep my face neutral so it won't know how much we agree on that. "You sure have a big vocabulary for a—what are you, anyway, a parrot or a parakeet?"

"I'm an Alexandrine parakeet."

"What's the difference?"

"*Seriously?* Ever heard of Google? Or do they block web access?"

"I'll look it up later," I say, sneaking a glance at the iPad to make sure it's still recording.

Then a new voice says, "Hey, is that the new model?"

For the second time in under a week, I jump out of my skin; fortunately, the safeguards still hold.

"Sorry, I didn't mean to startle you." The woman standing in front of me with her IV tree is somewhere past fifty. She's got a blue scarf artfully tied around her head; it's the same shade of blue as her oversize T-shirt, which reads, SECRETLY HOPING CHEMO WILL GIVE ME SUPERPOWERS.

"I think your secret's out," I say, just so I know I haven't lost my voice.

"So everyone keeps telling me." She moves past me to sit down on my right. The wheels on the IV tree rattle loudly, as if they're about to come off. I'm trying to think of a way to phrase *Who the fuck are you and how the fuck can you see me?* so it sounds like small talk, not panic.

She offers her finger as a perch to the parakeet on my thigh. It promptly accepts. "Woo," she says, "you're heavier than you look. No offence, little buddy—you're not so much hefty as I'm just weak these days."

I manage to get out, "What. The fuck," before I'm mute again.

This woman doesn't hide her amusement. "I guess I gotta be the one to break it to you: you're not quite as invisible as you think. Take it easy;

it's not like everyone can see you. Most people still can't. Even a lot of the regulars here wouldn't notice you. At least, not right away. But I'd guess you've been here for a while. Two days ago, I was up here with a friend; she described you perfectly but I couldn't see you myself till I came back yesterday. But then, she's sicker than I am. She made her deal last week."

"Violating natural law is an extremely serious transgression." I'm cringing inside at how stilted and nerdy I sound. "The penalties are severe—"

The woman throws back her head and shouts laughter at the sky. "Bitch, please! What kind of severe are we talking about? Twenty years of hard labour? Or—" She draws her free hand across her throat and makes a grating noise. "News flash: I don't have twenty years. A couple of months, if that. You wanna kill me, stand in line. The Grim Reaper's got dibs, and as far as I know, dying is one of those things you can only do once."

Mixing up Death and Reapers is such a common mistake, I should be used to it, but it still gets me every time, even though there's no way any of them could know better while they live. But she knows *something*, I realise and I blurt it out before I can think to stop myself, "You're gonna cheat."

"Is that what you call it?" The woman raises a nonexistent eyebrow at me. "I bet that's another extremely serious transgression. If you want to hit me with one of those severe penalties, you'll have to catch me. Which might be hard." She smiles at the bird.

"Don't worry about her," the bird says, fluffing itself up on her finger. The woman has to rest her arm on one crossed leg and even then, I can see it's an effort. "She's working on an old business model she doesn't know is obsolete."

"Huh?" I say.

"It must kill you having to waste your wit on the dead," says the parakeet. "Oh, that was mean. I'm sorry. I know you don't have any say about any of this. You've probably been given the impression that mortality has always worked the way it does now, But it so happens—"

"Mortality isn't what it used to be," I say. "That message is actually for Death, but I figure I'm not telling you anything you don't already know."

"You got it," the bird says, and I could swear it sounds pleased. "At one time, *we* carried the souls of the dead to the afterlife—"

"Knew *that*." I can't help it being smug. The bird doesn't care.

"We alone could move at will from the world of the living to the realm of the dead. No other beings of any kind had that ability, not mortals, not gods, not spirits or demons, only us. A god that wanted to make such a journey had to petition us, then wait at our pleasure for an answer. Death was a nobody, a servant employed simply to quieten the flesh and keep it from flailing or struggling and allow souls to begin the journey with dignity.

Self-important popinjay, I think, but with no conviction. I have a growing feeling that I'm in the deceptively small presence of something very old that, after a long sleep, woke up displeased with the current order of things and decided to do something about it. And those responsible for the current order have no idea what's coming for them.

"Amazing," the woman marvels. "Who knew? Live and learn." Bird and woman laugh together.

"You can't do this," I say. "It's a violation—"

"Enough with the violation," the bird says.

"But the afterlife—"

"—is what comes after death," say the bird, stretching itself again. "We transport the souls of dead people. Therefore, wherever we take them, that's the afterlife."

"That's one hell of a loophole," I say. "But doesn't that mean you're no longer the only ones who can travel between the land of the living and the realm of the dead? I mean, if wherever you drop souls off is the afterlife—"

"Whatever happened to the classical education?" The bird looks at the woman, who shakes her head. "The realm of the dead isn't the afterlife. Dumbass."

"Yeah, well, nobody tells me anything," I say. Somehow I don't feel too stung by a parakeet calling me *dumbass*, although maybe I should.

Holding onto the IV tree with her free hand, the woman pulls herself to her feet. "Are we done here?" she says to the bird on her finger.

"All set. Just keep watching the skies," the bird says, and takes off, going up on a steep slant.

"Wait!" I jump to my feet. "What happened? What did you do?"

"Nothing that concerns *you*," the woman chuckles. She does something to her head scarf and I catch a flash of green. A feather?

"It *does* concern me, it's why I was sent here—"

As she walks away, I lunge for her. I haven't forgotten that I can have no contact with people, that I slip off and around and away from their awareness. *Most* people, all of them except this woman, who saw me even though it was impossible.

I don't even brush the back of her T-shirt. Suddenly she and everything around here look very small and I'm caught in hardening molasses. I know it's no good to keep trying but I can't help it. She *saw* me, she *heard* me, she *talked* to me. If I could just get to her, even though I can barely see her—

To my surprise, she turns around and for a moment I think she's looking at me. But all she sees is what anyone else would see: plants, a bench, translucent floor, more plants. There's no one here but her. Anyone looking up from the lobby will see only one pair of footprints and three dots made by the wheels on her IV tree.

She turns away and leaves. But it's another hour before I can move.

The Observant Lifestyle tells me to go back to King's Cross and get a train to Brighton. I'm grouchy but I don't feel like being stuck again so I do it. It's a really slow train; it seems to crawl from one stop to the next. I page through the ebook repeatedly but there's only the same blah text about making lists and ordering them by family or something.

It's very late in the afternoon when the train gets to Brighton. I've never waited in this train station before, but I can't imagine it'll be much different.

I look out the window and see Madame waiting for me on the platform. There's no way this can be good.

The first thing she does is take the iPad and give me a new one. It's bigger and apparently fancier on the inside. But instead of letting me try it out, she tells me to put it away and walks me toward the beach.

In the beginning, I was surprised they used iPads and smartphones and the like. I mean, they aren't bound by the strictures of the natural world so I thought maybe they'd have magic mirrors or something. But that's what an iPad is, except it operates within the law on the macro level. On the micro level—that's extreme micro—everything's loose and runny enough to allow things to pass between the Continuous Realm of All Things and the natural world. That may be true—I have no basis to doubt it—but personally, I think all it means is, everyone, regardless of race, creed, or cosmic origin, is wackadoo for gadgets.

Except for those who'd rather fly. Which might be a lot. I mean, I can see the appeal. Who couldn't? Well, besides Madame and everyone else in the Continuous Realm.

And who would that be, now that I'm thinking of it? Unbidden, the image of tiny footprints on a translucent floor blooms before my inner ear and I realise that's the state of my existence. In the natural world, in the Continuous Blah Blah of Blah Blah, and all points between and beyond, it's all just footprints, always out of reach.

I could have a breakdown but I know how that'll go.

We reach the Brighton Pier and stop. It's very late in the day now, almost dusk. I think I'm losing my sense of time, or maybe it's vice versa.

I'm waiting for Madame to tell me she's going to throw me into the water or something, but she doesn't say a thing. Finally, I can't stand it. "What now?" I blurt.

The way she looks at me, it's like she forgot I was there. "What else? You continue to do your job."

I'm not about to tell her that's not what I was asking. Things are freaky enough.

"There's no reason not to, just because a few birds have decided to muscle in," she says. "So they make a few deals with humans. They won't get all of them."

"Then why did I go to the roof garden? What was the point?"

Her expression says I'm the stupidest person in the world. "Information gathering. Now we know."

"But I only talked to one bird. No, two—"

"You weren't the only one." She sighs heavily. "Did you really think you were?"

"I have no idea," I say. "Nobody tells me anything and I'm out here all by myself."

"Fair enough." She sighs again. "My choice would be to do away with solitary. But it's not up to me."

I mean to ask who in the Continuous Realm of All Things is in charge of that area. But what I hear myself say is, "What's the Concomitant Rendition of All Tessitura?"

Several fleeting expressions pass over her face—shock, confusion, disbelief, horror, anger. I don't know whether she's going to hit me or hit me real hard. Then she laughs. "That's where you came in. That's you, as in the human race."

"Oh, right. I'm a human. Sometimes I forget." As soon as the words are out of my mouth, I want to bite my tongue off. I can't believe my nerve. If she doesn't call down a lightning bolt or something, I'll probably be stuck for a month.

But she's not mad, at least not yet. Madame's not mad and it's almost night now. I've fallen down the rabbit hole for sure. Suddenly she grabs my face and makes me look toward the light dying over the water.

Countless small, dark bodies swarm upwards and come together in a way I'd have thought was impossible in the natural world, performing an aerial dance. I watch as they make forms that flow into shapes, that become symbols flowing into creatures flowing into forces flowing into renditions—renditions of—

And then it's another day. I'm standing by the Brighton Pier with Madame, under a heavily overcast sky.

"I wanted you to see that," she says.

I look the question at her.

"For many reasons, all of them difficult to articulate at this angle. To show you that a few parrots don't know everything. Do you think humans could ever be capable of what you just saw—and still be human?"

"I bet a lot of them would like to try," I say.

Madame laughs again. "I bet they would. We'll just see. There are an infinite number of renditions, and not all of them desirable, no matter how attractive they might be." She pauses, gazing at me thoughtfully. "I really *don't* like solitary," she says. "But I have to admit that sometimes, it's the best bad choice there is."

She looks down and I follow her gaze to see a shiny black feather at my feet. Immediately, I stoop to grab it, but when I straighten up and open my hand, there's nothing. The feather is still on the ground.

"You need to give it another try or do you get the point?"

I turn away and walk back to the train station.

There's a new ebook on the iPad called *Symbols & Signifiers Throughout History*. It sounds like it should be a lot more interesting than *Twitchers* but it isn't.

I have a two-day wait in King's Cross before my next job, which gives me enough time to see half of Harry Potter's luggage trolley sticking out of a wall. Or maybe it's not his, just some nameless witch's or wizard's. I don't know and it doesn't matter.

Before, in my natural-world life, I'd have oohed and aahed anyway. *Magic—wow!* But it's nothing like that. Like I said, it's really just a lot of work. And it never ends, and there's no way out.

I guess that's why they call it eternity.

The Acid Test

LIVIA LLEWELLYN

*. . . the acid tests were much more than an excuse to
trip for hours and hear The Dead play for a buck. No,
there were people who passed and people who didn't
pass the test. We were trying to stop the coming end
of the world.*

—Timothy Leary

Someone calls on me or calls me or calls me out, I can't tell over the sitars and drumming, but then Suzanne gives me the little strip of paper, and I don't know, I really don't want to do it, but the music is wailing consent and I'm already high, and it just seems easier to stick out my tongue and let it dissolve in silence than shout *thank you no*. At that point, there's so much smoke in the room from all the grass and cloves and hashish that I'm already seeing dragons in the air, great snakes coiling and rippling against the beaded curtains and velvet curtains, horses with wings and beautiful birds with long hooked beaks whose wings brushed against the bookcases, knocking down textbooks and sending onionskin sheets of poetry floating through the air like large autumn leaves; or maybe that's just everyone turned on and dancing, or knocking up against the shelves as they gas on and on about Chomsky and Searle and Leary and Marcuse. And the theatre kids talk about Sartre and Godot and a group of the really weird kids argue at the edges of the room about Heinlein and Ellison, while the prettiest girls huddle on the bed and whisper about the Michigan Murders and how all those coeds who look like them are just gone just vanished into the wide American night, the same way the pretty young boys are disappearing in the desert cities of the southwest, the same way wide-eyed freshmen disappear on every campus here in the Northwest from down in Eugene all the way up to here in little old Victoria BC, and I can't care less about any of it to begin with because I'm an Ed major and no one wants to talk with me about Montessori education versus Waldorf, but I'd tried for the sake of beautiful Suzanne who'd been begging me to come to one of these stupid dorm mixers for a month now, and I didn't have anything better to do tonight. And anyway there was a guy I'd seen, a guy who always hangs out at the edges of the theatre actors groupies at plays and mixers, never talking but only watching like a beautiful predator, tall and thin with the grooviest clothes and these huge brown eyes and jet-black hair, and I figured maybe he was a grad student because he just seemed so cool and calm and above it all so he probably wouldn't show because this was a real amateur scene, but I thought he might be here anyway because this is a pretty big party and it's the end of fall semester and there isn't much else going on, and besides after this weekend everyone is going home for winter. But he isn't here, and no one here is that cute or mysterious, and so what the fuck, right? I wash my tongue with the last of my beer and let the empty can roll out of my hand onto the carpet and under a desk. No one notices. I wait to see, I don't know, dancing skeletons and far-out kaleidoscopes of universes and flowers and weird cartoon landscapes with purple penises trucking down candy cane roads, but everyone looks the same, just a bunch of college kids I don't know, grooving to the music and having a gas, and Suzanne gets bored of me like she always does and wanders away into a bunch of admirers who are already tripping over that long Malibu Beach–blond hair of hers and that perfect kewpie-doll model face and soft brown nipples that peek out of the holes of her crocheted sea foam green dress and I realize we aren't going back to the dorm together, not that we were supposed to because she always does her own thing even though we've been roommates three months now, and I stand up and the party seems to snap into focus as all the blood rushes back into my tingling legs, and I shakily push my way through the crowd and thumping bass and wailing sitars and suede fringe and Tibetan curtain beads hitting my face as people gyre like spinning tops, and then I'm spilling out into the hallway with the lovers and the fighters and the wanderers and the sick. All the people who can't fit, who can't find a way inside, and now, one again, I'm one of them too.

And so I curse those thoughts in me as I wander down the hall, discombobulated because it looks just like my dorm hallway and for one horrifyingly stretchy long moment I think it *is* my dorm or maybe there's just one long dorm we've all been trapped and wandering through this semester and I'm just walking and walking eternally with no way forward or back, but then I reach the end and push my way down the stairs past all the kids tripping on the graffiti or grinding in the corners, and then I'm outside, the air so peppermint crisp and cold it almost burns my lungs and skin, dark white from snow glistening all across the campus and the soft hiss of flakes against my hot face, flakes like stars, stars and universes whirling all around me in the low wind. I reach out and let the galaxies drift and settle across my skeleton fingers, and out of the gray night fingers touch mine, long and smooth and autumn brown, and I hear the words *hey girl* as his face floats up from out of the crystal-white mist of the stars and snow and my breath, and there he is like a statue, eagle-nosed and black-eyed and that cool sardonicus grin. The tips of his fingers are smooth and warm, little electric circus shocks running through them into my bones and up my arms and spiraling at the back of my neck, his breath melting the ice on my lashes as he sidles up in the dark against me in his tight cords, fabric crushing and catching between our bodies, as his words fall against my burning cheeks once again, *hey girl, this party is a drag, there's a private scene happening over in the grad dorms, let me take you there.* And now there is a Shift with a capital S that I feel in my feather-hollow body: I am above me and behind me and all around myself like snow like the prickling stars, watching in silence as he takes my hand, leads me down the walkway through the lawn and trees, deep into the campus, passing in and out of the pools of light under high sodium lamps, my long blond hair swaying back and forth against my aqua blue jacket, my long lean legs and round buttocks visible against the pale sea foam green of my crocheted dress, the dress that always looks so good on Suzanne, and a pale dim light flickers on inside my mind, deep in the foggy oceans of stars colliding throughout my brain as I realize that Suzanne had followed me outside, that the stone fox has been speaking to her, looking to her, he never saw me at all and when she speaks to him she speaks past through me, but I follow them anyway, stepping in her footprints and his, leaving no traces behind as I float and trip in their tracks, snatches of conversation and laughter wafting back with the midnight snow. *Where did you say we're going,* I hear her soft pretty voice say, and I imagine how his face looks as he replies *a secret spot in a basement of the dorms called the Purple Room, and oh how purple it is, ripe like grapes bursting on the killing floor of a distant sun,* those long brows arching under the black fringe of his silken hair, as he licks his marble teeth and grins his thin-lipped grin, and Suzanne laughing and saying *oh, see, everyone said you were such a square but I knew you always had it in you, languid stone fox, secret garden, murderer of possibilities,* and he replies, and his reply is lost in all my pyroclastic-cold and clammy dreams.

I think she wants to give me kicks I hear him say, as they wander through the campus in the queer quartz light of the snowy night storm, and behind them I flicker in and out of their icy tracks, shivering as warm ribbons of smoke and acid realities flake off my body in shimmering strips, trailing behind me in a patchouli-scented wake. My beautiful Suzanne and the man, the beautiful boy, the stone fox, the sly seductive raptor of my secret waking dreams, walk side by side through the white drifts, hands running up and down their backs, their arms, resting on curves and in hollows, sliding beneath unbuttoned fabric as snatches of laughter and secret mutterings fade in and out with the wind, rise up and catch in the thick boughs; and eventually as I knew it would their long graceful gaits slow as they move closer together, limbs crossing and colliding, stumbling off the wide campus path into the scattering of trees, where they come to rest at the wide round base of an evergreen, Suzanne against the bark like a sliver of ice and the man enveloping her as though the tree itself were closing around her pale dress and skin, but then he moves her around, his back against the tree and legs firm in the crisp stiff layers of snow as he unwinds his long scarf and lets it coil down between his feet for Suzanne's pretty knees, and her hands fluttering like white doves about his crotch and I hold my breath, let it build up in cold pillows behind my trembling lips and thickening tongue. The sodium lights are dull silver disks illuminating everything and nothing, and galaxies of bright snowflakes flock around Suzanne's hair like crowns of celestial roses as she pulls his thick cock from out behind the brass buttons and rows of stitching and neat seams, resting the plump dark head on her red, red tongue; and as his cool demeanor melts at her touch, she moves her glossy wet lips up and down the shaft, working the skin back and forth with one turquoise-ringed hand while the other burrows deep and furtive into the fabric, deep between his legs, somewhere deep I cannot see, and his large hands move over her head, enveloping it like a Venus flytrap. Tiny flowers blossom and explode all around them, bright small roses and tiger lilies and orchids, spurting clouds of yellow pollen into their hair and over their limbs as their bodies sway back and forth, and when he comes, she grows rigid and waves of purple lightning crackle all up and down her body, leaving behind trails of shining glitter, the same glitter that pours out of her mouth as his cock slides back, the same glitter that drips and coats the tip; and glitter in the air all around us and I can feel the winter storm sigh and silence, and fluttering warmth floods my limbs as I shudder and fall against the strong trunk of a bristling true cedar, the faint scent of pitch nipping at my lungs as I recede into then fly up through the shadows, pulling my hand out of my burgundy cabled tights as my dark wings spread against the celestial arms of the Milky Way, and it's all so beautiful and I can taste God at my fingertips, the tears of God that stream out from the primordial center of the world between my legs that is a perfect mirror of this sacred oval space of pure white snow and tall high trees and all the stars tangled up in the canopy of branches that bend down over Suzanne and the vulpine man bending over her, who pecks at her face like a mother kisses a child as his limbs part and divide into hundreds of feathery extensions that collide and wheel about his sharp bone white face, who raises his oil black unblinking eyes up past the branches to the starry airborne rivers of snow while his wings strike down again and again like a waterfall of black razors until she collapses at his feet in boneless folds of creamy skin, who bundles his now velveteen-soft cock back behind the thin folds of fabric and then bundles her gleaming ribs and femurs and fibulas and lovely smooth skull into a small jumbly barrow that catches the wind blowing through it and expels it like a lover's song, who cracks his scarf in the air like a whip and wraps it back around his neck as he lifts her lifeless form up and continues down along the snowy path, carrying her like a deboned winter fox in the relentless beaked embrace of a nocturnal predator. All about us and behind the trees loom the great halls and cathedrals of learning, gothic spires and carillon bell towers of the great university church, red brick and marble and gray granite arches, stained-glass eyes winking in the now quiet night, and there is only one set of steps to follow in, to place my own starry feet in, footfalls that are deeper now, deep and flecked with dark rubies like the shining strands of rubies dripping off her hair and skin and flecking the stiff wet fabric of her sea foam gown that drops in wet folds and melting crimson fans all about them in the snow as he turns in his slow path to fix his unblinking oil eyes on me even while he carefully with clever fingers crams and works the soft worm flesh of my boneless roommate past those rows of bright teeth into his ever-widening throat, and even as I run run run like a frightened winter mouse I can't help but listen carefully as I push my way through the drifts, can't help but hear the sonorous soothing lilt of his beautiful hushed voice that echoes back and forth against the barren trees, that tells the woman in his gullet of the great and mysterious beauty of the Purple Room that she'll never see now because she was a silly and impatient bitch who started too soon, but if Suzanne replies at all it's in a voice too deep inside of him to tell.

Gather tales of all your failings, the creature commands me from her circuit high above the student lounge in the main building, floating in languid arcs around the thick cedar beams and cream balloon-shaped lamps that sway over the main room of the student center like ossifying mushrooms. From far above it watches me drop against the burnt orange of pillows and cushions, letting the thin warmth of the air creep its way back through my indigo-veined legs still wet from the lash of the branches and the thigh-high drifts when I ran, ran after the beautiful stranger and the silent Suzanne, her hair and long hair spilling out from both sides of his body like wings of white and gold as he buried her within him and disappeared into the swirling dark, ran until I entered the heart of the campus and I was all alone again with the dregs of other parties who'd crawled and stumbled and meandered their way through the glass double doors, needle-fine torrents of pain rolling through all our muscles like the nighttime waves of thunder snow outside. But now I just ignore her like I ignore all the others that crowd around her on the beam, the Suzanne-shaped birds with the pecked-out eyes and boneless torso, and all the other chicks dripping down mascara and blood, because it's just the acid I say to myself, this is the bad part of the trip, the six-month visit to the underground part, the walk through the woods with the wolf to grandmother's house part, the place in the story where I'm going down like all the other women in history, sliding right past that three-headed dog straight into the prickly warmth of hell, and so I tell myself I'm not seeing what I'm seeing, just like I didn't really see out on the snowy paths to the dorms what I saw, that what happened is Suzanne is back at the party alive and dancing and running her hands up and down her California-tan body while all the boys and girls in the room nod and watch while in some other part of the campus the mysterious beautiful student falls asleep in the arms of a book or his woman, and there's no thick ribbons of crimson snow crisping cold under icicle bones and endless sky. Someone's brought a radio and they turn it on and now bottles of beer and whiskey are slipping out from underneath overcoats that plop onto the floor in damp heaps while dope and tobacco smoke begins to thread through the air, and the same conversations about philosophy and art and death and the universe begin again, only more muted and serious this time because we left all the parties behind and this isn't a party, this is life and we're students of life, I explain as I take a toke off whatever someone is holding to my lips, we're taking life and taking it apart and examining each bit, each shining gleaming moment of it that exists both in our timeline and outside of it, history and the future, we're astronauts riding in rockets of acid and mushrooms, traversing the vast cosmic expanse of our own uncharted unexplored selves, and I wonder out loud how far we're willing to travel within ourselves to find something new and astonishing event if it's terrible and not who we thought we were at all or who our parents tried to raise us to be, but maybe that dark place inside isn't a new discovery but the oldest truest part of ourselves finally set free, free of rules and morals and culture, the primal original ur-self let loose after a lifetime of false and flaccid chains to be one with a world in which all these traps and trappings around us this furniture these clothes these sentences are infestations that keep us from taking our place within the universal mother god node of creation and destruction and deconstruction and rebirth. And some people nod and others disagree and others just stare up at the beams that cross the ceiling like the ribs of a landlocked ship, and everyone's thoughts and words fill the air, sparking like the glowing embers of a contented and tired fire, and then someone asks the question, and I'm fairly certain that person is me, *hey, have you guys heard anything about a place in the dorms called the Purple Room?*

Even the most vague desire is a fire, and as soon as the words pour out of my mouth I hear the slight shift in the room, feel the hitch as if for a second everyone stopped talking, stopped breathing, a slight skip in the record that no one would notice unless they knew it was coming and even then they might miss it, but it's there just the same, and everyone around me keeps talking and most people haven't even heard the question, everyone's broken off into couples and triads and quartets of discussions and debate and manic musings, but the tone has slightly changed, as if my saying the words added a layer of sound, as if everyone's still getting their groove on without realizing that their needle's been bumped into another groove. And the guy next to me with the long sideburns and wispy moustache who keeps grabbing the knee of his wild-eyed girlfriend nods for a long time as if the motion is dredging up the information like an oil derrick, and finally he says, *yeah, man, I think I heard something about that my freshman year, I think, I think, yeah man, it's some old basement storage locker or laundry room that a couple of dudes on the basketball team turned into this wild sex pad, yeah, yeah man, with carpeting and mattresses everywhere and they painted the walls and ceiling with all this black light paint and shit and they replaced the fluorescents with black lighting and the whole room was like, whoa man, so when you were making it with your woman and you were coming it was like you were tripping into another dimension or something with all the purple lights flashing and glowing, yeah.* His girlfriend nods the entire time, mouthing the words *no way man* over and over again in between drags on her cigarette and pulls on a bottle of whiskey, and when her boyfriend is finished she stubs the cigarette out on the sofa arm and says *you are so way off you're not even on the planet anymore, man, not even in the fucking planetary system, I heard a bunch of religion students spent the summer in Tibet back in '64, and when they came back they made a meditation room in the basement of their dorm with purple walls and lotus flowers and lidless eyes everywhere, and when you're in the room and you start meditating and chanting, it helps you astral project right to the pyramids or wherever you want because it's built in the middle of a power line, man, this line that's part of a network of psychic rivers that run all over the planet and flow through time and space and all these dimensions, and you connect your pineal gland to the road, you just hit that astral road, man, you just chant your spirit straight to Stonehenge or some temple on the moon.* She pauses to catch her breath and take a long swig of the whiskey while her boyfriend shakes his shaggy head and mutters *no way man, no fucking way,* and I ask her if she's ever seen the room, does she know which dorm it's supposed to be in, but she's already deep in disagreement with the boy, and they're lost to me in the seductive reflections of their discord, so I turn to the woman sitting in the chair to my right, all limp brown suede and faded paisley cotton under a body-length cocoon of half-removed parka, a beaded fringe tied across her head weeping bright glass seed beads into her damp flat hair, who's been quietly listening to us the entire time with a growing furrow between her barely open eyes, and I ask her if she's ever heard of the room. She blinks slowly, several times, and says in a low monotone, *yeah, maybe, I think so, it's one of those things everyone hears about but no one's every met anyone who's been there, one of those campus stories everyone tells each other, and*

every time someone tells the story a little bit changes, like those round robin gossip games we used to play at summer camp, remember those? Yeah, but the story I was told was that it's a nest, a nest in the basement of one of the dorms, a room with purple walls all slick and wet and waxy-soft like a honey bee hive, with a door made out of twigs and branches and lost laundry and old books no one reads anymore and worn-down candles and incense sticks and glass sun catchers and the rib cages of lost chicks who stayed up too late and wandered through the halls past curfew, a jumble of things people threw away that block the door to protect the room, dead and lost things that warrior raptors who cry like sea gulls and fuck like wolves place against the door as protection for the void-queen that lays pulsing and birthing behind it . . . it's holy work . . . we have no choice . . .
Her voice trails off and her head rolls back against the chair, tiny seed beads scattering across her cheeks and shoulders as she passes out or trips into oblivion, and a delicate ribbon of stamps falls from her uncurling hand, and I realize as I reach over and slide the ribbon from her fingers and pop one square onto my tongue that I've come full circle and am right back where I started from. Just like two hours ago or three or four, the stamp melts against my hot saliva as I sit in the middle of a party watching people talk and laugh and drink and get it on while I stare at all of them, wondering where my place in all of it is or if there's a place at all for me or if I really even care, because the one thing I wanted that night was to make it with that beautiful grad student, the one with the ragged black hair like torn silk brushing against his snow white forehead and cheeks and wide thin mouth, the iridescent mysterian who shows up in all my trips and nightmares and dreams, the black-eyed raptor in burgundy velvet who's across the room opposite me right this moment, sitting on an olive green couch between a guy with one hand underneath the skirt of his wriggling girlfriend and an older woman with graying hair who's hunched over and weeping into her hands, and I know he wasn't there a moment ago, that the spot was empty, that he fizzled into life only when the acid disappeared on my tongue, as if he's just always there waiting behind the high.

Shall I let them see reality? he asks, sitting with his inviting thighs opened wide, arms spread out across the backs of the cushions as if he's ready to push off into flight, a long brown cigarillo as slender as an ancient rib in one raised hand as clean of blood as mine, the cherry flame tip coiling smoke into the air and around his head like a Catherine wheel, and my forehead grows warm and my vision blurs and the room washes away as we snap into each other's focus, as our consciousness threads across the space like the smoke, ectoplasmic cords that plug in and connect our meridians, and now we are tuned in, and I feel my body grow limp even as the thoughts and colors in our collective mind grow crystal sharp, speaking to each other the rush of blood, the flutter of lashes, the magnetic whispers of the night just beyond the cold glass doors. *Which story do you believe, little girl,* he says as he taps the ashes away, letting them flutter over the slender waist of a boy passed out at the side of the chair, *which story do you think is the closest to the truth, which version of the Purple Room do you want to see tonight?* He smiles as I mouth my answer with silent lips and tongue, my words and thoughts already traveling through the meridians of his limbs, *does Suzanne know which version is real,* and he smiles so wide and so bright I squint and flinch as I wonder in horror if I'll see her face pushing up from the back of his mouth, peeking out round-faced and wet from behind his joyful sharp incisors lining the edges of his predator grin, *maybe it's time the veil was torn from your glass-dark eyes* floating out from his mouth (or Suzanne's) in the cold quiet spaces between the music and the laughter and the soft murmurs of nothings he warbles sotto voce to the slender slip of the suede-clad chick that sidles into his lap as she whispers *and will you be the one to tear the veil away,* wrapping his arms around her shoulders like a cloak, and all the girl-shaped Suzanne birds hanging off the cedar rafters and their laughter echoing down at me as he ignores me, again, again, again, and again he burrows his black head in the perfect cream curves of the lithe sylph faded-paisley honey who is not me and I slide the bottle of whiskey out of the limp hands of the couple beside me, still locked in the barb-wired arms of their argument, let a long mouthful burn its pyroclastic way across my tongue and down my throat while the room grows warm and dark, and great mushroom shapes blossom and fester at the edges of the windows and glass-dark eyes, dropping to the ground in soft spore-puffing masses that burst apart like rotting whipped cream.

The girl slithers off his lap and onto her feet and he follows, pulling away from the bodies surrounding him like he's sloughing off all the disguises and guiles of previous lives, and they wend their way through the bodies and bobbing heads and nicotine conversations, the girl's hip-twitching gait so much like Suzanne's that I can't help but glance upward at the boneless ghost birds as if to confirm that they see it too, see how much they are alike, or used to be, but the rafters are barren and in that slip of a second he's already spirited her out of the room, the wake of their passage already fading and dissipating, fizzling like little bursts of psychic fireworks cobwebbing down to the ground, and once again I follow, earthbound and heavy this time, scattering purple dots like dying fireflies as I push through the trailing stream of their desire leading outside into the vast dark, through the leviathan's graveyard of black skull buildings, the hardened mid-breath frost of the quiet campus, the crunch and crush of my feet against the snow as I make my way through galaxies of seed beads she scatters behind like my hardened tears flung across the stars to the stairs of my old freshman dorm.

Memories and dreams, the stains, the dead remains, jumble together in the wash of warm air against my face, the fading scents of patchouli and perfume and the mildewing sweat of winter-wet, threadbare carpets mingling with the cloying and depressing animal funk particular to every dorm I've ever lingered in, every boy's room I ever crept in revulsion from late at night, every women's bathroom shower stall I sobbed in through the desperate early hours of dawn, every strange concrete hallway lined with indistinguishable wooden doors and corkboards blanketed in flyers and messages, graded papers crumpled into garbage cans alongside empty bottles and broken lipsticks and letters finished but never sent, letters and love bracelets and unused ticket stubs and damp tissues and postcards from relatives who can't understand why you won't come home or call, pleas and pleadings from parents, phone numbers you've torn up and wadded up into mealy balls of paper too minuscule to resurrect, and photos of a childhood you did everything you could to escape from and would do anything you could to return to, a decisionless moment in life when the waters were calm and the sky clear and the future as limitless and unwritten and perfect as Suzanne's lip gloss smile. And down linoleum-lined steps I pad, following whispering shadows that dance and pool out of cracks behind the crooked walls lining the abyssal basement hallway that skims the paralyzed skin of the planet, past rusting rows of washers and dryers hulking in pitch-black punctured with ribbons of light that dance and shimmer and curve up into bows only to untie themselves and start again, braiding themselves into an ouroboros that whips before the door of the janitor's room, a heavy metal slab that bulges outward slightly as deep purple light oozes from around its frame, spraying upward and out in thick slow jets that splash against the almond-colored machines that hum in deep sonorous tones, moaning and buzzing as they detach from their concrete moorings and drift toward the ceiling as if escaping what is to come as I reach out and touch the door handle, so long and hard in my hand, so unavoidable and infinite, all the mechanisms of the cosmos whirling and clicking as tumblers in some other room in some other universe sighs and opens its singular eye, and my eyes roll back as I feel all the weight of another world flow Nile-wide up through my bones and veins, all the weightlessness of something moving in the next room, rearranging her infinite limbs as she bears down and lets out a sound that shatters atoms and sends galaxies scattering apart like dust as the dazzling white round tip of something larger than this universe presses against the lips of her cloaca, so white, as white as the drifts of snow forming around the midden of Suzanne's bones, a void-white of un-creation contained only by the thinnest of egg shells, resting in steaming mountainous piles about the folds and feathers of her nesting flesh, waiting for the matter of this universe to stream in through the open door, eat away the delicate mottled prisons until . . . until . . . until . . . and his hand lightly touches mine, and I whimper only just a little as my broken fingers slide off the long handle, as I back away, trails of purple birthing matter clinging to my cheeks and throat, and the beautiful student with the jet-black hair and eyes like black pearls and raptor smile opens his mouth wide and first the paisley-clad girl slithers out in a wave of clear vomit, her long brown hair ribboning about her flat yet serene face like seaweed and her body hits the door in a slow wave, spreading across the cracks like jam, and then he convulses and barks out a second wet cough, and her hair looks so dark, her nipples so pale and tan skin shifting like beach dunes under a low tide as she flows apart and hits the door like dying glue, and deep in the back of my spine I feel the scream the plea the urgent cry for sight no more coalescing and pulling strands of all the shadows out of the room and up through the back of my head out through the center of my forehead and I grab the worm erupting from between my brows and twist it letting the blood of my thoughts run down my wrists and the world grows red at the edges, red dragons that shake their heads and flutter down like campfire ash over my bare limbs and he is over me now, dark and wide and wings spread about like a canopy of black tears, and that sharp stinging tap tap tapping all across my numbing face, and he is somewhere inside me, and from a great distance I hear his voice warbling like a love bird, *I knew you always had it in you, languid stone fox, secret garden, murderer of possibilities*, but if he hears my response, he's too deep inside the empty cup of my mind for me to tell.

And the sirens have long stopped wailing, but their red and blue lights flash all across the campus, hundreds it seems, a poisonous garden of light silently blossoming in the winter sun. Birds flock in the bare branches overhead, clouds of glossy black that rise and fall with the movement of the men as they transport the bones to the ambulances and vans. Everyone's story has been taken down, everyone who woke up in piles and heaps, running their dirty fingers across fuzzing teeth, adjusting torn clothes, creeping and shuddering their way from interrogations to their dorms and apartments, including my story of how I watched my roommate walk off into the snowy dark of night drunk and high and alone, never to be seen alive again. Outside in the hallway, the telephone rings over and over, crying out like a hungry abandoned bird, while beside me the radio on my headstand cackles with the news, and sometimes in the low afternoon light I think I see a faint movement behind its grooved surface, as if the machine is struggling to free itself from the invisible information pouring in and extruding out of the black plastic and metal of its captive brain. *You'll see things like that,* he mutters, touching his long nose to the cold glass as he stares down into the chaos of his own creation, *you'll see them all the time now, because you see the reality of all things, you see beyond the surface of all this,* and he presses his fingertips together, as if revolted at the touch of his own flesh, *the same way you see me as I walk through the campus and through this dimension but also the real me, the multiple being folded and clipped and hobbled in this pellet of a body that seems to set all your hearts racing so, the body that has to work so hard to keep this little egg of a world intact and separate from all the other eggs of our greedy mother void-queen,* and he moves from the window over to my bed, standing over me as I stare up into his face like a blade, and he leans down and grabs my breast with a grip so tight it makes me gasp as he whispers into my open mouth, *don't worry, I'll teach you how to rid yourself all of this, and then I'll teach you how much of them you can hold, and then I'll show you all the other purple rooms, all the other doors,* and when he kisses me with his acid tongue secreting little dribblings of his renderings of Suzanne and all the other chicks down my throat, I want to vomit in terror and disgust. But after a while the feeling passes and all that's left is sharp and sweet as a punch.

The Crow Palace

PRIYA SHARMA

Birds are tricksters. Being small necessitates all kinds of wiles to survive but Corvidae, in all their glory as the raven, rook, jay, magpie, jackdaw, and crow have greater ambitions than that.

They have a plan.

I used to go into the garden with Dad and Pippa every morning, rain or shine, even on school days.

We lived in a house called The Beeches. Its three-acre garden had been parcelled off and flogged to developers before I was born, so it became one of a cluster of houses on an unadopted cul de sac.

Mature rhododendrons that flowered purple and red in spring lined the drive. The house was sheltered from prying eyes by tall hedges and the eponymous beech trees. Dad refused to cut them back despite neighbours' pleas for more light and less leaf fall in the autumn. *Dense foliage is perfect for nesting*, he'd say.

Our garden was an avian haven. Elsa, who lived opposite, would bring over hanging feeders full of fat balls and teach us about the blue tits and cheeky sparrows who hung from them as they gorged. Stone nymphs held up bowls that Dad kept filled. Starlings splashed about in them. When they took flight they shed drops of water that shone like discarded diamonds. The green and gold on their wings caught the sun.

Pippa and I played while Dad dug over his vegetable patch at the weekends. The bloody chested robin followed him, seeking the soft bodied and spineless in the freshly turned earth.

Dad had built a bird table, of all things, to celebrate our birth. It was a complex construction with different tiers. Our job was to lay out daily offerings of nuts and meal worms. At eight I could reach its lower levels but Pippa, my twin, needed a footstool and for Dad to hold her steady so that she didn't fall.

Elsa taught me to recognise our visitors and all their peculiarities and folklore. Sometimes there were jackdaws, rooks, and ravens but it was monopolised by crows, which is why I dubbed it the crow palace. Though not the largest of the Corvidae, they were strong and stout. I watched them see off interlopers, such as squirrels, who hoped to dine.

After leaving our offerings we'd withdraw to the sun room to watch them gather.

"Birdies," Pippa would say and clap.

The patio doors bore the brunt of her excitement; fogged breath and palm prints. Snot, if she had a cold. She touched my arm when she wanted to get my attention, which came out as a clumsy thump.

"I can see."

Hearing my tone, Pippa inched away, looking chastised.

Dad closed in on the other side with a forced, jovial, "You're quiet, what's up?"

It was always the same. *How are you feeling? What can I get you? Are you hungry? Did you have a bad dream last night?*

"I'm fine." Not a child's answer. I sounded uptight. I didn't have the emotional vocabulary to say, *Go away. Your anxiety's stifling me.*

I put my forehead against the glass. In the far corner of the garden was the pond, which Dad had covered with safety mesh, unfortunately too late to stop Mum drowning herself in it. That's where I found her, a jay perched on her back. It looked like it had pushed her in. That day the crow palace had been covered with carrion crows; bruisers whose shiny eyes were full of plots.

I sit in a traffic queue, radio on, but all I hear is Elsa's voice.

"Julie, it's Elsa. From Fenby."

As if I could forget the woman who brought us birthday presents, collected us from school, and who told me about bras, periods, and contraception (albeit in the sketchiest terms) when Dad was too squeamish for the task.

"Julie, you need to come home. I don't know how to say this, so I'll just come out with it. Your dad's dead." She paused. "He collapsed in the garden this morning. I'll stay with Pippa until you get here."

"Thank you."

"You will come, won't you?"

"Yes."

Ten years and they jerk me back with one phone call.

The journey takes an hour longer than I expected. Oh, England, my sceptred and congested isle. I'm not sure if I'm glad of the delay or it's making my dread worse.

The lane is in dire need of resurfacing so I have to slow down to navigate the potholes. I turn into the drive. It's lined by overgrown bushes. I stop out of view of the house and walk the rest of the way. I'm not ready for Pip and Elsa yet.

The Beeches should be handsome. It's crying out for love. Someone should chip off the salmon-pink stucco and take it back to its original red brick. The garden wraps around it on three sides, widest at the rear. I head there first.

The crow palace is the altar of the childhood rituals that bound us. It looks like Dad's lavished more love on it than the house. New levels have been added and parts of it replaced.

I stoop to pick something up from the ground. I frown as I turn it over and read the label. It's an empty syringe wrapper. Evidence of the paramedics' labours. The grass, which needs mowing, is trampled down. I think I can see where Dad lay.

A crow lands on the palace at my eye level. It struts back and forth with a long, confident stride as it inspects me. Its back is all the colours of the night. It raises its head and opens its beak wide.

Caw caw caw.

It's only then that the patio doors open and Elsa runs out, arms outstretched.

Job done, the crow takes flight.

Elsa fusses and clucks over me, fetching sweet tea, "For shock."

"What happened to him?"

"They think it was a heart attack. The coroner's officer wants to speak to you. I've left the number by the phone."

"How can they be sure? Don't they need to do a post-mortem?"

"They think it's likely. He's had two in the last three years."

"I didn't know."

"He wouldn't let me phone you." I don't know if I'm annoyed that she didn't call or relieved that she doesn't say *Perhaps, if you'd bothered to call him he might have told you himself.* "Your dad was a terrible patient. They told him he should have an operation to clear his arteries but he refused."

Elsa opens one of the kitchen cupboards. "Look."

I take out some of the boxes, shake them, read the leaflets. There's twelve months of medication here. Dad never took any of it. Aspirin, statins, nitrates, ace-inhibitors. Wonder drugs to unblock his stodgy arteries and keep his blood flowing through them.

I slam the door shut, making Elsa jump. It's the gesture of a petulant teenager. I can't help it. Dad's self neglect is a good excuse to be angry at him for dying.

"We used to have terrible rows over it. I think it was his way of punishing himself." Elsa doesn't need to say *guilt over your mother.* She looks washed out. Her pale eyes, once arresting, look aged. "I don't think Pippa understands. Don't be hurt. She'll come out when she's ready."

Pippa had looked at me as I put my bag down in the hall and said, "Julieee," prolonging the last syllable as she always did when she was excited. Then she slid from the room, leaving me alone with Elsa.

Elsa's the one who doesn't understand, despite how long she's known Pippa.

Pip's cerebral palsy has damaged the parts of her brain that controls her speech. It's impaired her balance and muscle tone. It's robbed her of parts of her intellect but she's attuned to the world in other ways.

She understands what I feel. *She's* waiting for *me* to be ready, not the other way around.

Perhaps it's a twin thing.

Pippa stopped speaking for several years when she was a child. It was when she realised that she didn't sound like other children. That she couldn't find and shape the words as I did. Her development wasn't as arrested as everyone supposed. Dad, Elsa and her teachers all underestimated her.

I could've tried to help her. I could have acted as an interpreter as I've always understood her but I didn't. Instead, I watched her struggle.

And here she is, as if I've called out to her.

Pippa's small and twisted, muscle spasticity contorting her left side. That she's grey at the temples shocks me, despite the fact mine's the same but covered with dye. She's wearing leggings and a colourful sweatshirt; the sort of clothes Dad always bought for her. That she's unchanged yet older causes a pang in my chest, which I resent.

Pip looks at the world obliquely, as if scared to face it straight on. She stands in the doorway, weighing me up and then smiles, her pleasure at seeing me plain on her narrow face.

That's what makes me cry. For her. For myself. I've abandoned her again and again. As soon as I could walk, I walked away from her. As we grew older, my greatest unkindness towards her was my coldness. As a teenager, I never wanted to be seen with her. After our twenty-third birthday, I never came back.

"Julieee."

I put my arms around her. I've not asked Elsa if Pip was with Dad when he collapsed, if she sat beside him, if she saw the paramedics at work.

The onslaught of my tears and sudden embrace frighten her and I'm the one who feels abandoned when Pip pulls away.

Ten years since my last visit to The Beeches. Ten years since Dad and I argued. I drove home after spending the weekend here for our birthday. Elsa had made a cake, a sugary creation piled up with candles that was more suitable for children.

Dad rang me when I got back to my flat in London.

"I'm disappointed, Julie."

"What?" I wasn't used to him speaking to me like that.

"You come down once in a blue moon and spend the whole time on the phone."

"I have to work." I was setting up my own recruitment agency. I was angry at Dad for not understanding that. I was angry that he thought I owed him an explanation. "I'm still getting thing off the ground."

"Yes, I know your work's more important than we are."

"It's how I make a living. You sound like you want me to fail."

"Don't be preposterous. All I'm saying that it would be nice for you to be *here* when you're actually here."

"I drove all the way to be there. It's my birthday too."

"You act like coming home is a chore. Pippa's your sister. You have a responsibility towards her."

"Yes, I'm her *sister*, not her mother. Aren't I allowed a life of my own? I thought you'd be happier that you've only got *one* dependent now."

"Don't talk about Pip like that."

"Like what?"

"Like you're angry at her. It's not her fault that your mother killed herself."

"No? Whose was it then? Yours?"

Those were my final words to him. I don't know why I said them now.

The following morning's a quiet relief. I wake long before Pippa. The house is familiar. The cups are where they've always lived. The spoons in the same drawer, the coffee kept in a red enamel canister as it always had been when I lived here. It's like returning to another country after years away. Even though I recognise its geography, customs, and language, I'll never again be intrinsic to its rhythms.

My mobile rings.

"Ju, it's me." Christopher.

"Hi."

I'm never sure what to call him. Boyfriend sounds childish, partner businesslike and lover illicit.

"The new Moroccan place has opened. I wondered if you fancied coming with me tonight."

Not: Shall *we* go? There's *him* and *me* with all the freedom between *us* that I need.

"I can't. Take Cassie." There's no jealousy in that remark. Over the two years I've been seeing Chris, seeing other people too has worked well for us. It's precisely why I picked a man with form. A player won't want to cage me but Chris keeps coming back to me, just when I expect him to drift off with someone new.

"I stopped seeing her months ago. I told you."

I don't care. It makes no difference to me.

"My dad's dead," I say, just to try and change the subject.

"Oh God, Julie I'm so sorry. I'd just presumed he was already dead from the way you talked about him. What happened?"

"Heart attack."

"Where are you? I'll come and help."

"No need."

"I want to."

"And I don't want you to,"

"I'm not trying to crowd you, but may I call you? Just to see if you're okay."

"Sure. Of course." He can call. I may not answer.

I hang up.

"Julie."

Pippa sidles up to me. We're both still in our pyjamas. It's an effort but I manage a smile for her.

"Do you want breakfast, Pippa? Cereal?"

I'm not sure what she eats now. It used to be raspberry jam spread thickly on toast. She tugs on my sleeve and pulls me up.

A trio of swallows hang from her bedroom ceiling. It was sent one Christmas, like all my presents to her for the last ten years, chosen for being flat packed and easy to post. Pippa reaches up and sets the birds in motion as she passes.

It's the bedroom of a child. No, it's the bedroom of an innocent. It needs repainting. The realisation makes me wonder what I feel. Our future's a knife.

"Look." Pippa beams.

Her childhood collection has grown to dominate the room. It's housed in plastic craft drawers that are stacked on shelves to a height that Pippa can reach. Her models are lined up above the drawers, on higher shelves.

She used to make them in plasticine. They were crude lumps at first. Now she's graduated to clay. They must fire them at the day centre. Her years of practice are in the suggestive details. A square tail. The shape of the head with a pinched beak.

They're crows, over and over again.

Pippa opens one of the drawers and picks out buttons, one at a time, and drops them into my open hand. Each one's unique, only their colour in common. They're white plastic, mother of pearl, enamel, stained fabric, and horn. She laughs as they spill through my fingers. The rest of that block of drawers contains buttons, each separated by compartment for the rainbow.

"Pippa, are all these from the crow palace?"

"Yes, birdies." She mangles some of the syllables but she's definite.

She shows me more. Her collection is sorted by type of object, or by shape where Pippa was unsure. Coins and bottle tops. Odd earrings. Screws. Watch parts. The tiny bones of rodents, picked clean and bleached by time.

I used to have a collection of my own, the crows left us treasures on the crow palace in return for food. They came with presents every day. I threw mine out when I started high school.

I regret it now, as I sit here with Pippa.

"Here." She thrusts one of the drawers into my hands.

Something lonely rattles around inside. I tip it out. I hold it up between my forefinger and thumb. A ring designed as a feather that wraps around the finger. Despite the tarnish, it's lovely—the hard line of the shaft, the movement of the hundreds of vanes and downy barbs.

It's impossible that it's here because I'm sure Mum was buried with it. I watched Dad lay out the things for the undertaker: a silk blue dress, tights, a pair of leather heels, a lipstick, and this ring. He put her wedding band and diamond engagement ring in a box and placed it in his bedside drawer. *For you, when you get married*, as if this was given.

The feather ring was kept to go with her into the grave. *We were on holiday when she realised she was expecting. She chose this from an antiques shop in France the same day that she told me. I was thrilled. I think she'd want to wear this.*

I close my eyes. Had I imagined that? As I do, the ring finds its way onto the ring finger of my left hand, which goes cold. I can feel the blood in my wrist freezing. I yank it off before ice reaches my heart.

"Where did you get this?" My voice is shrill. "Pippa?"

"Crows," she says.

I force myself to go into Dad's room. It's stifling. Being north facing and a dull day, the poor quality light brings out the green undertones in the patterned gold wallpaper. The dark, heavy furniture makes the room crowded and drab.

Everything's an effort. There's something about being back here that's put me in a stupor. I'm procrastinating about everything.

Looking through Dad's things should hurt but it doesn't. It's like rifling through a stranger's personal effects for clues. He was an unknown entity to me because I didn't care enough to want to find out who he was. Shouldn't blood call out to blood? Mine didn't. I felt more for Pip, my dead mother, and for Elsa. Dad's love was smothering and distant all at once as if I was something to be feared and guarded closely.

I pile his clothes in bin bags to take to the charity shop. I pause when I find box files full of football programmes. I never knew he was a fan. It looks like he went regularly before we were born. It crosses my mind that they might be worth something, but then I chuck them on the pile to get rid of.

It's only when I'm clearing out the second wardrobe that I find something that piques my interest. There's a steel box at the back with his initials on it, under a pile of moth-eaten scarves. It's locked. I spend the next hour gathering together every key I can find, searching drawers and cupboards for them. Nothing fits.

I carry the box downstairs and put it on the kitchen table. It's too late in the day to take it to a locksmith. I'll go tomorrow.

Who knew that death is so bureaucratic? I'm relieved there won't be a post-mortem but there's still the registering of Dad's death and meetings with the undertaker, bank and solicitors. Elsa's a brick, taking Pip to the day centre or over to her place if I have things to arrange.

The future leaves me in a stupor of indecision. I stare out of the kitchen window at where the pond used to be. Now it's a rockery in the same kidney shape.

What sort of people would have a pond with young children in the house?

The pond was where I found Mum's body, looking boneless as it slumped over the stones at the water's edge. I was four. I thought she'd just fallen over. I ran out to help her get up. A jay sat on her back. The bird is the shyest of all Corvids, flamboyant by comparison to its family, in pink, brown, and striped blue. It normally confines itself to the shelter of the woods.

I paused as the wind blew up her skirt, revealing the back of her thighs. Her head was turned to one side. The jay hopped down to look at her face, then pecked at one of her open, staring eyes.

The jay turned as I approached and let out a screech, blood on its beak. Or maybe I was the one screaming. I'd put my hands over my ears.

A shriek comes from the sun-room, next door. I drop my coffee cup, imagining Pippa has conjured the same image. She'd followed me out that day and seen Mum too. By the time my cup smashes on the floor and sends hot coffee up my legs and the cabinets I realise something's actually wrong.

Pippa's pressed against the window, shouting and banging with her fists.

"What is it?"

I grab her shoulders but she twists around to look outside again. From here we have an interrupted view of the back garden.

A magpie deposits something on the crow palace, then starts to make a racket. Its blue-black-white colouring reveals its affinities for the living and the dead.

Only then does the sudden whirring motion draw my gaze down to the lawn. The cat's bright pink collar contrasts with its grey fur. A second magpie is pinned by the cat's paw on its spread wing. Its other wing is a blur as it struggles. The magpie's mate flies down and the cat breaks its gaze with its prey and hisses.

I know it's the natural order of things but I'm sickened and trembling. I open the patio door and clap my hands as if such a banal gesture can end this life-and-death struggle. Pippa's more decisive, stumbling out and I hold her back for fear she'll be scratched.

Flat black shapes with ragged wings darken the sky. Ravens. One swoops, catching the cat's ear with its bill as fierce as pruning shears as it passes over. The cat contorts, blood on its fur, releasing the magpie which makes an attempt at broken flight.

The cat crouches, a growl in its throat. Its ears are flat to its head, its fur on end, doubling its size. The birds are coming down in black jets, from all directions. The cat raises a paw, claws unsheathed, to swipe at its assailants. The ravens take it by surprise with a group attack. One lands, talons clutching the nape of the cat's neck. It writhes and screams. The sound cuts through me. The birds are like streaks of rain. I can't see the cat anymore. It's been mobbed by darkness.

Pippa and I clutch each other. The cat's silent now. The ravens lift together into the sky and all that remains on the grass are steaks of blood and tufts of fur.

I remember later that the magpies left us a gift, a task that made them careless of their long collective memory of their past persecutions by gamekeepers and farmers.

The key they left on the crow palace shines as if calling to me. The metal's so cold that it hurts to hold it, as if it's just come out of a freezer.

I have the queasy feeling that I know what it's for. It slides into the padlock on the steel box with ease and I feel its teeth catch as I turn it.

Everything I know about Mum is distilled from scant memories. I'm shaking at the prospect of something concrete. I open the lid. Here's where Dad buried her significant remains.

It contains a random assortment. A lady's dress watch. A pair of pearl earrings. A silk patterned scarf. An empty perfume bottle. I open it and the stale fragrance brings Mum back to me on a drift of bluebells. I wipe my eyes. I'd forgotten she always wore that. There's a birthday card signed *With more than love, Karen.*

What is there that's more than love?

We weren't a photographed family. There aren't any happy snaps that feature Pip and me. This pile of photographs are of Mum and Dad when they were young, before we were born. I shuffle through them. Mum and Dad at the beach, on bicycles, another in formal dress. Their happiness grates. Why couldn't they saved some of it for us?

The last thing out of the box is a handkerchief. Whatever's knotted within clinks as I lift it out. It's a pair of eggs. They're unnaturally heavy, as if made of stone. And they're warm.

I can't resist the impulse to crack one of them open. Fluid runs over my fingers. I sniff it. Fresh egg white.

A baby's curled up within, foetal like, her tender soles and toes, her genitals displayed. She's perfect. I don't know what she's made of. Something between rubber and wax that's the colour of putty.

I break open the second one. Another girl. This one's different. She has massive, dark eyes that are too wide set to be normal. There are sparse, matted feathers on her back. Faint scale cover her feet.

I carefully rewrap the pair, trying not to touch them, and put them back in the box.

My phone rings. Then stops. Starts again. There's nothing for it. I answer it.

"Chris." I try not to sound irritated.

"How are you?"

"Busy. You know."

"No, I don't. Tell me."

"Stuff to sort out. Dad and for my sister."

"You have a sister? What's her name?"

"Phillipa. We call her Pippa."

"What's she like?"

Pippa? She likes birds, me, the colour turquoise, chocolate, having a routine, crow gifts, sunshine. She gets frustrated when she can't make herself understood. Her eyes are hazel brown and she has eczema.

"She has cerebral palsy. My dad took care of her."

"Will I meet her at the funeral?"

I'm about to say *Of course she'll be at the funeral* but then I realise that Chris is assuming he's invited.

"Why do you want to come? You never met him."

"Not for him, for you. Tell me your address."

"I don't need you here."

I don't understand. It feels like an argument, full of unspoken baggage that I didn't even know we were carrying.

"Julie, what are we doing?"

His tone sets off an alarm bell in my head.

"You must know that I—" Don't say it. Don't say *I love you*. He falters, "You must know how much I care about you."

I feel sick. I thought we were alike. Just my luck to find a man who falls in love with the one woman who's not chasing him.

"I'm not talking about marriage or children."

Children. For all the carelessness of my affections there's never been a child.

"I told you at the start that I'm not like other people. You promised me that you understood completely."

"There's more to us than just sex."

I can't believe he's doing this.

"Don't you get it?" I should be angry but a column of coldness is solidifying inside me. "There *is* no more. I'm not broken, so you can't fix me. I don't love you because I can't love anyone."

"Julie, please . . ."

I hang up and bar his number.

There's never been so many people in the house. I don't like it. I wanted it to be just us, but Elsa went on so much that I relented. I wish I hadn't now.

I forgot to pack a black dress so I had to buy one in a hurry. I took Pippa with me, there being nothing suitable in her wardrobe either. The shop assistant stared at her while she touched the expensive silks. The woman's tune changed when it was clear that I didn't have to look at the price tags.

I picked out a neat black dress myself and a black tunic, leggings and ankle boots for Pippa. On impulse, I took her to a salon to get her hair dyed and styled. She was more patient than I expected. She liked being somewhere new. My favourite part was Pippa's smile when the shampoo was massaged into her scalp.

It was a nice day.

Today isn't. When we went out to the funeral car, Elsa said, "Look at the two of you. Pippa, you look so grown up. And Julie, wonderful. Black suits you more than any other colour. You should wear it more."

Grief fucks people up.

The mourners come in, folding up their umbrellas like wings, dripping rain on the parquet floor.

"Elsa, are any of the neighbour's coming?"

"God, no. All the one's you'd know are dead or moved away."

I don't know the people here. Some used to work with Dad, apparently, others knew him from Pippa's day centre or through Elsa. They all greet her like she's long lost family.

It's unnerving that they line up to speak to me, something more suited to a wedding than a funeral.

The first is a tall, broad man, dressed in a shiny tight suit and winkle pickers. Spiv's clothes but he's gentle, paternal even. He takes my hand and looks right into my eyes, searching for something.

"My name's Charlie."

"Thank you for coming."

"I'm so very pleased to meet you, my dear. You're as lovely as I thought you'd be. I understand you're a smart lady too." Then as if he's just recalled why we're here, "I'm sorry for your loss."

A pair of elderly ladies are next. They're twins. Both have the same bob, cut into a bowl shape at the front, hooked noses and dowager's humps that marks their identically crumbling spines.

"Do you have children?" says the first one, which isn't the opener I expected.

The second one tuts and pushes her sister along. They're followed by a couple who call themselves Arthur and Megan. A first I think they're brother and sister as they're so alike, but the way he hovers around her suggests their relationship is more than familial. Her arm's in plaster.

"How did you know Dad?"

"Through my father." The man waves his hand in a vague gesture that he seems to think explains everything.

Young men, a few years younger than I am, come next. They're all in designer suits. Each is striking in his own way. They stand close to me as they introduce themselves. One even kisses my hand. The last one interests me the most. He's not the tallest or best looking but I like his quiet confidence and lively face. There's a yearning in his voice when he says my name that tugs at me. To smile at him seems weak, so I nod.

"My name is Ash."

"Ash." The word coats my tongue with want.

A woman edges him along.

"I'm Rosalie."

She has the manner of entitlement that only certain hard, beautiful women have. Her fingernails are painted black. The lacquer's like glass. She looks me up and down as she passes.

I sip my drink as more people introduce themselves, then go off to decimate the buffet and the wine boxes. I try not to look at Ash's every movement. It's a lovely agony. I close my eyes, the tannin in the red wine shrinking the inside of my mouth.

"How is Julie settling back in here?" It's Charlie.

"Well, she's here for now." I don't like Elsa's tone. She must be drunk too.

I open my eyes. Charlie's suit can't settle on a single shade of black.

"I'm sorry Elsa. You must be missing Michael."

I turn away a fraction, not wanting them to know I'm listening. From the periphery of my vision I see him embrace Elsa.

The young men congregate by the hearth. Rosalie's berating them for something. I catch her final words: "I don't see what's so special about her anyway."

I know she's talking about me because Ash looks over and keeps on looking even though he's caught me eavesdropping. "Don't you?" he replies with a smirk.

"I'm Stephanie." A woman gets in the way, just when I think he's going to walk over and join me. "You're Julie, yes?"

"Hello."

There's a long pause. I sigh inwardly. I'm going to have to try to make conversation with her. She's in her fifties. She's lost one of her earrings and most of her hair's escaped from her bun.

"Where are you from?"

"From?" she says.

"Your accent . . ." Her pronunciation's off kilter, her phrasing odd.

"I've lived in lots of different places." She glances around the room. "I think Elsa would rather I hadn't come."

She reaches out and swipes a sandwich from a plate, gobbling it down in two mouthfuls. "These are delicious."

The volume of the chattering around us bothers me. I've drunk too much on an empty stomach.

"This place hasn't changed since your mother's funeral."

"You met her?"

"Tennis club."

Tennis. How little I knew about her.

"Such a gracious, joyous woman," Stephanie twitters on. "Want and need. How they undo us."

"Pardon?"

Stephanie blinks.

"There are so many crows in Fenby now. They've quite pushed out the cuckoos." She speaks in a comedy whisper, getting louder with each word. "Your mother guessed that they'd double-crossed her."

The chatter's dying. Everyone's watching us now.

"You know how it works, don't you? They laid one of their own in your mother's nest . . ."

Charlie comes over and puts an arm around her.

"Stephanie, what are you taking about? Julie doesn't want to hear this rubbish." He pulls a face at me. "It's time for you to go home."

"You can't push me around. I have a right to be here. We had a deal." She breaks away from him and seizes me in a hug.

"I'm sorry. For all of it," she whispers in my ear. "It's true. Look under the crow palace."

I want to ask her how she knows that's what we call the bird table but Ash comes and takes her arm.

"Aunt Steph, I'll see you home."

"I'm not your aunt."

"No, Ash, you should stay." Elsa joins us.

"It's fine." Ash kisses my cheek. My flesh ignites. "May I come and see you again? Tomorrow?"

"Yes." It's as easy at that.

"Until then." He steers Stephanie towards the door.

The noise starts up again in increments. Ash's departure has soured my mood.

Pippa can't settle. As the mourners gathered around Dad's grave she cringed and started to wail as if finally understanding that he's gone. Now she's wandering about, refusing to go to her room but flinching when any of our guests come near her. She stands, shifting her weight from foot to foot, in front of the twins who are perched in her favourite armchair.

"Oh for God's sake, just sit somewhere will you?" I snap.

Pippa's chin trembles. The room's silent again.

Elsa rushes over to her but Pippa shoves her away. Elsa grabs her wrist.

"Look at me, Pippa. It's just me. Just Elsa." She persists until Pippa stops, shaking. "Better? See? Let's go outside for a little walk."

Pippa's face is screwed up but she lets Elsa take her out onto the patio.

I lock myself in the bathroom and cry, staying there until everyone leaves. I've no idea what I'm crying for.

I wish this humidity would break. It's sticky, despite yesterday's rain. I feel hungover. Lack of sleep doesn't help.

I wave goodbye to Elsa and Pippa as they go out. Elsa's keen to be helpful. *I'll drop Pippa off, I'll be going that way to the shops. Why don't you go and get some fresh air on the lawn? You'll feel better.*

I can't face sorting out the last of Dad's clothes. The thought of the hideous green-gold wallpaper in there makes me want to heave. Instead, I take boxes of papers out to a blanket I've laid out on the lawn. It's prevarication. I'm pretending that I'm doing something useful when I should be sorting out our future.

All the ridiculous talk of swapped babies and symbolic eggs seems stupid now that I'm out in the fresh air.

I imagined it would be cut and dried when Dad died. Sell the house. Find somewhere residential for Pippa or pay Elsa to take care of her. Now I hate myself. I have all along, and have taken it out on Pip. She's the purest soul I know. There's such sweetness in her. How can I leave her to the mercy of others?

How can I love her so much yet can't bear to be near her sometimes? I fought everyone who tried to bully her at school. I became a terror, sniffing out weakness and reducing other children to tears. I started doing it just because I could. They hated me and in return and I felt nothing for them, not anger, not contempt. That's how damaged I am.

I'm afraid that everything people think of me is true, but I'm not afraid enough to change. I *am* selfish. I like my own silence and space. I hated Dad for saying, "You will look after Pippa won't you? The world's a terrible place."

Need. Nothing scares me more.

Then I look at Pippa, who is far more complete a human being than I am. She's no trouble, not really. I could work from here and go to London for meetings. All I need to run my business is a phone. It would only need a bit of will to make it work.

I pull papers from the box. It's an accumulation of crap. Receipts from electrical appliances, their warranties long outdated, bills, invitations and old business diaries.

It's so quiet. I lie back. There's not even the slightest breath of a breeze. I shield my eyes as I look up. The trees are full of Corvidae.

Birds don't roost at eleven in the morning, yet the rookeries are full. Sunlight reveals them as oil on water creatures with amethyst green on their foreheads and purple garnets on their cheeks.

Rooks, weather diviners with voices full of grit who sat on Odin's shoulders whispering of mind and memory in his ears.

How Elsa's lessons come back to me.

She taught me long ago to distinguish rooks from crows by their diamond shaped tails and the bushy feathers on their legs. I find these the strangest of all Corvidae, with their clumsy waddles and the warty, great patch around the base of their beaks. It's reptilian, Jurassic, even. A reminder that birds are flying dinosaurs, miniaturised and left to feed on insects and carrion.

I turn my head. Crows have gathered too, on the patio furniture, the bird baths, the roof and, of course, the crow palace. The washing line sags under their weight.

I daren't move for fear of scaring them. Perhaps *I'm* scared.

Ash walks through their silence. They're not unsettled by his presence. He's still wearing the same suit. His stride is long and unhurried.

He doesn't pay attention to social niceties. He falls to his knees. I lean up, but I'm not sure if it's in protest or welcome. It's as if he's summed me up with a single glance when I'm not sure what I want myself. He presses his mouth against mine.

He pushes my hair out of the way so he can kiss the spot beneath my ear and then my throat. The directness of his desire is exhilarating, unlike Chris' tentative, questioning gestures.

He pulls open my dress. I unbutton his shirt. He pulls down my knickers with an intensity that borders on reverence.

His body on mine feels lighter than I expect, as if he's hollow boned.

When he's about to enter me he says, "Yes?"

I nod.

"Say it. I need to hear you say it. You have to agree."

"Yes, please, yes."

I'll die if he stops now. The friction of our flesh is delicious. It's as necessary as breathing.

When Ash shudders to a climax, he opens his mouth and *Caw, caw, caw* comes out.

I wake, fully dressed, lying on a heaped-up blanket beneath the crow palace. There's a dampness between my legs. I feel unsteady when I get up. The shadows have crept around to this side of the house. It must be late afternoon.

When I go in, Elsa's in the kitchen. She's cleaned up after yesterday.

"I'm sorry. I was going to do that . . ."

"It's okay." She doesn't turn to greet me.

"Where's Pippa?"

"Having a nap. We're all quite done in, aren't we?"

She turns to wipe down the worktops. She looks so at ease, here in Dad's kitchen.

"What happened to my mother?"

I have to take the damp cloth from her hand to make her stop and look at me.

"It's all on record."

"I want to hear what's not on record."

"Then why didn't you ask Michael while he was still alive?"

I've been expecting this but the anger and resentment in Elsa's voice still surprises me. I take a deep breath. Retaliation won't help my cause.

"Because he hated talking about her."

"Then it's not my place to tell you, is it?"

"Of course it's your place. You're the closest thing to a mother that either of us have ever had." I should've said it long ago, without strings. The tendons at Elsa's neck are taut. She's trying not to cry. I didn't just leave Dad and Pip. I left her too.

"You were born in this house. The midwife didn't come in time. Your father smoked cigarettes in the garden. Men didn't get involved in those days. I helped bring you both into the world. I love you both so much. Children fly away, it's expected. I just didn't realise it would take you so long to come back."

"I know you loved Dad too. Did he love you back?"

"He never loved me like he loved your mother." Poor Elsa. Always at hand when he needed her.

"You sacrificed a lot to be with him." Marriage. A family of her own.

"You've no idea." Her voice is thick with anger. "It's utterly changed me."

Then she bows her head. The right thing to do would be to comfort her. To hold her and let her weep on my shoulder. I don't though. It's a crucial moment when Elsa's emotions are wide open.

"The papers said Mum had postnatal depression and psychosis."

An illness that follows childbirth. A depression so deep that it produces bizarre beliefs.

"They were desperate for children. They would've done anything."

"Anything?"

"Fertility treatments weren't up to much back then."

"So what happened?"

"Well, you happened. A surprise, they told everyone. I remember holding you in my arms. It was such a precious moment."

"When did she get ill?"

"When it became clear that Pip wasn't doing so well. You were a thriving, healthy baby but Pippa was in and out of hospital because she was struggling to feed. She slept all the time. She never cried. You were smiling, then rolling over, then walking and she was falling further and further behind."

"And Mum couldn't cope?"

"The doctors became worried as she had all these strange ideas. And you were a real handful."

"Me?"

"I'm sorry, maybe I shouldn't say this."

"Tell me."

"You were just a little girl, trying to get their attention. You'd bite Pippa, steal her food. When you were big enough, you'd try to tip her from her high chair."

"And what exactly was it that Mum believed?"

"She insisted she'd been tricked by the birds. They'd helped her to conceive and then they went and swapped one of you for one of their own."

I wake in the hours when the night turns from black to grey to something pale and cold. My mind's full. It's been working while I sleep.

Mum's insistence that she'd been tricked by birds. That they'd helped her to conceive.

They laid one of their own in your mother's nest . . .

Cuckoo tactics. Mimic the host's eggs and push out one of their own. Equip your chick for warfare. Once hatched, the hooks on its legs will help it to heave its rivals from the nest.

Look under the crow palace.

I pull on jeans and a sweatshirt. Dad kept his tools in his shed. I pull the shovel from the rack, fork and a trowel for more delicate work.

It's chilly. I leave footprints on the damp lawn. It takes a while because I go slowly. First I take up turf around the crow palace. Then I dig around the base. The post goes deep into the rich, dark soil. My arms ache.

I lean on the post, then pull it back and forth, trying to loosen it. It topples with a crash. I expect the neighbours to come running out but nobody does.

I have to be more careful with the next part of my excavation. I use the trowel, working slowly until I feel it scrape something. Then I use my hands.

I uncover a hard, white dome. Soil's stuck in the zigzag sutures and packed into the fontanelle. The skull eyes me with black orbits full of dirt that crawl with worms.

I clean off the skeleton, bit by bit. Its arms are folded over the delicate ribcage. Such tiny hands and feet. It's small. She's smaller than a newborn, pushed out into the cold far too early.

Mum and Stephanie were right. Here is my real sister, not the creature called Pippa.

Oh my God, you poor baby girl. What did they do to you?

"Are you okay?" Elsa ushers me into the kitchen. It's eight in the morning. She has her own key.

I can't bring myself to ask whether Pippa, my crow sister, is awake. How was the exchange made? Was it monstrous Pippa who heaved my real sister from my mother's womb? Was she strangled with her own umbilical cord? And who buried my blood sister? Was it Mum and Dad? No wonder they were undone.

"What happened to you?"

Elsa opens a cupboard and pulls out a bag of seed mix, rips it open and tips out a handful. When she eats, some of it spills down her front. She doesn't bother to brush it off. When she offers me some I'm hit by a wave of nausea that sends me across the room on rubbery legs to vomit in the bin.

"You've got yourself in a right old state." Elsa holds back my hair.

I take a deep breath and wipe my nose.

"Elsa, there's a baby buried in the garden."

She goes very still.

"You knew about it, didn't you?" I sit down.

She pulls a chair alongside mine, its legs scraping on the tiles. She grasps my hands.

"I didn't want you to know about it yet. I wish that cuckoo-brained Stephanie hadn't come to the funeral. And Arthur and Megan hadn't interfered with that damn key. You found the eggs, didn't you?"

I think I'm going to faint so I put my head on the table until it passes. Elsa rubs my back and carries on talking. When I sit up, Elsa's smiling, her head tilted at an odd angle. A gesture I don't recognise. "I'm actually relieved. It's easier that you know now you're staying."

"Elsa, I can't stay here."

"It's best for everyone. You've others to consider now."

I press my fists to my closed eyes. I can't consider anything. My mind's full of tiny bones.

"Mum knew that Pippa wasn't hers, didn't she?" I'm thinking of the human-bird-baby in its shell.

"Pippa?" Elsa's eyes are yellow in this light. "No, she knew that it was you that wasn't hers. She had to watch you like a hawk around Pip."

I vomit again. Clumps of semi-digested food gets caught in my hair. Elsa dabs at my mouth with a tea towel. Her colours are the jay's—brown, pink and blue. Was it her, stood at Mum's back and pecking at her eye?

Pippa stands in the doorway looking from my face to Elsa's and back again. I've never seen Pip's gaze so direct.

Now I know why my heart's loveless. Pip's not the aberration; I am. I'm the daughter of crows, smuggled into the nest. Pippa is how she is because of my failed murder attempt. I affected her development when I tried to foist her from the womb.

It's all my fault.

Pippa edges around the room, giving the woman who raised her a wide berth. She tucks herself under my arm and puts a hand low down on my abdomen. She peers into my face, concerned, and says, "Birdies."

Permissions

About the Contributors

RICHARD BOWES has published six novels, four story collections, and eighty short stories. He has won World Fantasy, Lambda, Million Writer, and IHG Awards.

His 9/11 story "There's a Hole in the City" recently got a fine review in *The New Yorker*. It's online now at *Nightmare* Magazine. Recent appearances include *Queers Destroy Fantasy* and *The Doll Collection*.

A new edition of his 2005 Nebula Short list novel *From The Files of the Time Rangers* is forthcoming. Bowes is currently writing stories for a fix-up novel about a gay kid in 1950s Boston.

PAT CADIGAN has won the Locus Award three times, the Arthur C. Clarke Award twice, and most recently a Hugo and a Seiun. The author of fifteen books, she emigrated from Kansas City to gritty, urban North London, where she lives with her husband, the Original Chris Fowler, and Gentleman Jynx, the coolest black cat in town. She can be found on Facebook and tweets as @cadigan. Her books are available electronically via SF Gateway, the ambitious electronic publishing program from Gollancz.

JEFFREY FORD is the author of the novels *Vanitas, The Physiognomy, Memoranda, The Beyond, The Portrait of Mrs. Charbuque, The Girl in the Glass, The Cosmology of the Wider World,* and *The Shadow Year*. His story collections are *The Fantasy Writer's Assistant, The Empire of Ice Cream, The Drowned Life, Crackpot Palace,* and *A Natural History of*

Hell. His short fiction has appeared in a wide variety of magazines and anthologies in the US and abroad, and his books and stories have garnered many awards, both national and international. He's been a professor of literature and writing for thirty years and has been a guest lecturer at Clarion Science Fiction and Fantasy Writers' Workshop, the Stonecoast MFA program, the Richard Hugo House in Seattle, and the Antioch University Summer Writers' Workshop. He lives in Ohio.

M. JOHN HARRISON was born in 1945. His novels include *Climbers* and *Empty Space.* He reviews fiction for the *Guardian* and the *Times Literary Supplement.* He is a winner of the Boardman Tasker Prize and the Arthur C. Clarke Award and recently received an honorary DLitt from Warwick University. He lives in Shropshire.

STEPHEN GRAHAM JONES is the author of sixteen novels and six story collections. Most recent is *Mongrels,* from William Morrow. Stephen lives in Boulder, Colorado.

SANDRA KASTURI is the author of two poetry collections: *The Animal Bridegroom* (with an introduction by Neil Gaiman) and *Come Late to the Love of Birds.* She is also co-publisher of ChiZine Publications. Sandra's work has appeared in various venues, including *Prairie Fire, Evolve, Chilling Tales, ARC Magazine, Taddle Creek,* and *Abyss & Apex.*

ALISON LITTLEWOOD is the author of *A Cold Season.* The novel was selected for the Richard and Judy Book Club, where it was described as "perfect reading for a dark winter's night." Her sequel, *A Cold Silence,* has recently been published, along with a *Zombie Apocalypse!* novel, *Acapulcalypse Now.*

Littlewood's short stories have been picked for *Best British Horror 2015, The Best Horror of the Year,* and *The Mammoth Book of Best New Horror* anthologies, as well as *The Best British Fantasy 2013* and *The Mammoth Book of Best British Crime 10.* She also won the 2014 Shirley Jackson Award for Short Fiction with her story "The Dog's Home," published in *The Spectral Book of Horror Stories.*

Littlewood lives with her partner, Fergus, in Yorkshire, England, in a house of creaking doors and crooked walls. You can talk to her on twitter @Ali__L and visit her at www.alisonlittlewood.co.uk.

LIVIA LLEWELLYN is a writer of horror, dark fantasy, and erotica whose fiction has appeared in *ChiZine, Subterranean, Apex Magazine, Post-scripts, Nightmare Magazine*, as well as numerous anthologies.

Her first collection, *Engines of Desire: Tales of Love & Other Horrors*, was published in 2011 and received two Shirley Jackson Award nominations, for Best Collection and Best Novelette. Her story "Furnace" received a 2013 SJA nomination for Best Short Fiction. Her second collection, titled *Furnace*, was recently published by Word Horde. You can find her online at liviallewellyn.com.

USMAN MALIK is a Pakistani writer of strange stories. His work has won the Bram Stoker Award and the British Fantasy Award, been nominated for the Nebula and World Fantasy Award, and has been reprinted in several *Year's Best* anthologies. He resides in two worlds.

SEANAN MCGUIRE is a firm believer in counting crows, both the rhyme and the band, and can often be found performing corvid divination. Australia, which has a lot of corvids, was a revelation. When not looking at birds, she writes, and publishes an average of four books a year under both her own name and the name Mira Grant. When not writing or bothering the local wildlife, she travels, visits haunted corn mazes and Disney Parks, and hangs out on the Internet. Seanan is rumored not to sleep. The rumors are probably true.

MIKE O'DRISCOLL lives and writes in Swansea. When not writing he works with adults with mental health problems. His fiction has been published in *Black Static*, as well as in *Interzone, Fantasy & Science Fiction, Crimewave*, and *Albedo One*. He's also had stories in numerous anthologies, including *Inferno, The Dark, Lethal Kisses, Gathering the Bones, Darklands, Subtle Edens, The Year's Best Fantasy & Horror*, and two volumes of *Mammoth Book of Best New Horror*.

His story "Sounds Like" was adapted by Brad Anderson for the *Masters of Horror* TV series. He wrote a regular column on aspects of horror in popular culture as well as on genre television for *Black Static*. His novella *Eyepennies* was published in 2012.

JOYCE CAROL OATES is one of the most prolific and respected writers in the United States today. Oates has written fiction in almost every genre and medium. Her keen interest in the Gothic and psychological horror has spurred her to write dark suspense novels under the names Rosamond Smith and Lauren Kelly, as well as several collections of dark fiction including *The Doll-Master and Other Tales of Terror, Give Me Your Heart: Tales of Mystery and Suspense, The Corn Maiden and Other Nightmares, Black Dahlia and White Rose*, and *Evil Eye: Four Novellas of Love Gone Wrong*. Among her Gothic novels are *The Accursed, Bellefleur*, and *Mysteries of Winterthurn*. She has edited *American Gothic Tales*.

Oates has won the Bram Stoker Award, the National Book Award, the O'Henry Award, the PEN/Malamud Award, the Rea Award for the Short Story, and has been honored with a Life Achievement Award by the Horror Writers Association as well as the President's Medal in the Humanities. She has been a member of the American Academy of Arts and Letters since 1978.

Oates's most recent novels are *Carthage* and *The Man Without a Shadow*. She teaches creative writing at Princeton and New York University.

NICHOLAS ROYLE is the author of *First Novel*, as well as six earlier novels, including *The Director's Cut* and *Antwerp*, and a short story collection, *Mortality*. In addition, he has published more than a hundred short stories. He has edited nineteen anthologies and was series editor of *Best British Short Stories*. A senior lecturer in creative writing at MMU, he also runs Nightjar Press, which publishes new short stories as signed, limited-edition chapbooks, and is an editor at Salt Publishing.

PRIYA SHARMA is a doctor who works in the UK. Her short stories have appeared in various places, including *Black Static* and *Interzone*, and on Tor.com. Her novelette "Fabulous Beasts" won the British Fantasy

Award and was nominated for the Shirley Jackson Award. She's been reprinted in many *Best of* anthologies. She is a Shirley Jackson Award finalist and a British Fantasy Award winner. More about her writing can be found at www.priyasharmafiction.wordpress.com

PAUL TREMBLAY is the author of the novels *A Head Full of Ghosts, Disappearance at Devil's Rock, The Little Sleep,* and *No Sleep Till Wonderland. A Head Full of Ghosts* won the Bram Stoker Award. He is a member of the board of directors for the Shirley Jackson Awards, and his essays and short fiction have appeared in the *Los Angeles Times* and numerous *Year's Best* anthologies. He has a master's degree in mathematics and lives in Massachusetts with other beings who tolerate him.

A. C. WISE's fiction has appeared in *Clarkesworld, Apex, Shimmer, The Best Horror of the Year,* and *The Year's Best Dark Fantasy and Horror,* among other places. Her debut collection, *The Ultra Fabulous Glitter Squadron Saves the World Again,* was published in 2015. In addition to her fiction, she co-edits *Unlikely Story,* and contributes a monthly review column, *Words for Thought,* to *Apex Magazine.* Visit her online at www.acwise.net.

About the Editor

Ellen Datlow has been editing science fiction, fantasy, and horror short fiction for more than thirty-five years. She currently acquires short fiction for Tor.com. In addition, she has edited more than ninety science fiction, fantasy, and horror anthologies, including the series *The Best Horror of the Year, Lovecraft's Monsters, Fearful Symmetries, Nightmare Carnival, The Doll Collection, The Monstrous,* and *Children of Lovecraft.*

She's won multiple World Fantasy Awards, Locus Awards, Hugo Awards, Stoker Awards, International Horror Guild Awards, Shirley Jackson Awards, and the 2012 Il Posto Nero Black Spot Award for Excellence as Best Foreign Editor. Datlow was named recipient of the 2007 Karl Edward Wagner Award, given at the British Fantasy Convention for "outstanding contribution to the genre," was honored with the Life Achievement Award given by the Horror Writers Association, in acknowledgment of superior achievement over an entire career, and the Life Achievement Award by the World Fantasy Convention.

She lives in New York and co-hosts the monthly Fantastic Fiction Reading Series at KGB Bar. More information can be found at www.datlow.com, on Facebook, and on Twitter as @EllenDatlow.